T0279225

Inevitable Fate

LINDSAY K. BANDY

CamCat
Books

CamCat Publishing, LLC
Fort Collins, Colorado 80524
camcatpublishing.com

Hardcover ISBN 9780744310849
Paperback ISBN 9780744310863
Large-Print Paperback ISBN 9780744310924
eBook ISBN 9780744310917
Audiobook ISBN 9780744310931

Library of Congress Control Number: 2024933260

Book and cover design by Maryann Appel
Interior artwork by AnastasiiaM, Cattallina, Chihiro Sawane, Grace Maina, Lazarev, Seamartini

5   3   1   2   4

FOR MY SISTER,
WHO REMEMBERED.

AND MY GRANDFATHER,
WHO FORGOT.

CHAPTER ONE

I F LIFE WAS a highway, Evan Kiernan's consisted of riding
shotgun while his mother inched along in the right lane of I-95
looking for an exit so his little sister could pee.

This time, they were headed to Manhattan. It should have been
only a two-and-a-half-hour drive from Lancaster, Pennsylvania, but in
Evan's experience, what *should be* rarely translated to reality. For example, kids *should* know who their fathers are. Diamond rings (plural)
should lead to weddings (preferably singular), instead of pawn shops
and moving trucks (plural). Five-year-olds *should* have a greater blad-
der capacity, and seventeen-year-olds *should* still be in high school—
not riding shotgun while their mothers drive them to move-in day
at NYU.

But maybe, for once, Evan Kiernan was about to be exactly where
he should be. According to his mother, the Promising Young Artist
program was his destiny, as if the sparkle-winged gods of the arts had
arranged for his early college acceptance. Really, it was her, conspiring
with his art teacher, Mr. Burns, to fill out the application behind his

back. Evan had been sure he had no shot in hell at getting into the elite program, which accepted one upcoming senior. *One.* But somehow, against all odds, they'd chosen him. He was still convinced it was some sort of mistake, due to his mother's exaggerated belief that her son was exceptional and Mr. Burns's glowing recommendation letter.

But the written application wasn't the main criteria. His portfolio had gotten him into the program, and he couldn't deny being proud of that, even if he wasn't sure he was really Greenwich Village material. And as Hailey kicked the back of his seat in time with "Look What You Made Me Do" on the radio and wailed about needing to pee for the thousandth time, he couldn't deny his that it would be amazing to have a little time to himself for once.

"Rest stop ahead!" his mom exclaimed, removing her hands from the steering wheel to applaud as she read the sign. "One more mile, okay, Hails? Envision the desert. *Be* the camel, baby." She brought her thumbs and forefingers together as if meditating before taking hold of the wheel again.

Evan glanced at the speedometer. They were crawling along at six miles per hour. He ran a hand through the dark curls flopping into his eyes, then pressed his palm against the freshly trimmed sides, trying to ignore the small feet pounding his back. The song switched to "Flowers," and when his mother started singing along with Miley Cyrus, he cringed and tried to go somewhere else—anywhere else—in his mind. He could have envisioned the desert, or been the camel, but instead, he went back to Advanced Drawing class.

To the day he drew *her.*

The drawing that changed everything.

It was his first day at Pennwood High School. They'd just moved out of their mother's ex-fiancé Dave's house and into a little Cape Cod with peeling white paint and a picket fence missing a few teeth.

That morning, he'd pulled rumpled jeans and a black-and-red flannel shirt from the box at the foot of his bed, wishing for another ten years of sleep. Hailey had woken him multiple times through the night, scared and disoriented in her new room. His mom was downstairs already, in her bathrobe and slippers, cooking the traditional fresh-start breakfast/peace offering. He wondered, sometimes, if she'd become a realtor just to have the inside scoop on immediately available rental properties.

"You want me to iron your shirt?" she'd asked over her shoulder while flipping a pancake.

"Nah." He gave her a sideways hug with one arm and reached for the coffee pot with the other.

She rubbed her cheek where his had brushed against it. "You should shave."

"I can't find the razors," he said, even though he hadn't really looked. "It's fine."

"Come on." She cracked an egg into sizzling butter. "Don't you want to make a good first impression?" She said it a little too brightly, and even without his contacts in he could see from the puffiness of her eyes that she'd been crying already this morning. He wanted to throttle Dave.

First impressions had lost their charm years ago, but transferring to Pennwood had been easy enough. After reviewing his portfolio the previous week, the head of the art department had agreed to place him in Advanced Drawing, Ceramics, and Advanced Painting Techniques.

"Honestly," Mr. Burns had said during Evan's registration appointment, glancing between his sketchbook and his mother. "He's probably more advanced than the staff here. Have you considered art school?"

"He's always been exceptional," his mom had gushed while Evan looked at his shoes. She'd insisted he be tested for the gifted program in kindergarten, and ever since, she'd been using that word. *Exceptional.* She might as well have called him an alien. Exceptional was just another word for different. He'd read somewhere that all great artists and writers feel that they experience the world fundamentally differently from everyone else, and he assumed that's why so many of them became alcoholics and vagrants and mental patients. But Mr. Burns made Evan feel like maybe it was possible to be both *different* and *normal* at the same time—that unconventional didn't have to mean unhealthy. And best of all, he kept a framed photo of his husband on his desk, which meant his mom wouldn't be trying to line up any dates with another one of his art teachers.

His first assignment in Advanced Drawing class was to draw a face entirely from memory, so Evan closed his eyes and tried to picture Hailey. He couldn't believe how hard it was to conjure up a detailed image of his own sister's face. She had brown eyes like his, but how far apart were they in relation to the corners of her mouth? Her nose was . . . kid-sized, but what was the exact shape? Glancing around at his classmates' work, they seemed to be having the same problem, laughing at each other's attempts to draw friends or teachers from other classes. People they recognized, but who were all strangers to him.

Mr. Burns went behind his desk to pop a CD into an ancient-looking stereo system, and suddenly the deep thrum of electronic trance music transformed the atmosphere of the room. The rhythm became hypnotic as the beats per minute steadily increased and the notes blurred, like a dream. Evan stared at the backs of his eyelids, feeling like he was lost in some sort of European dance club. He tipped his chin toward the ceiling, and flashes of red flared through the darkness. Splotchy afterimages danced like flames, like the time they went camping with Dave and Hailey wouldn't quit shining a flashlight in his face and gave him a migraine.

But then slowly, like a Polaroid picture, a pair of eyes began to develop.

Not brown and familiar. Not his mom's or his sister's or anyone's from his old school. These eyes were a startling jade green, peering at him around a huge, heavy black door.

A girl.

Her nose and the apples of her cheeks were sprinkled with freckles, and her mouth was open in a tiny gasp of surprise, revealing a small space between her two front teeth. She was frozen in this expression, as if he'd knocked on her door and snapped a photograph as she opened it, shocked to find a stranger there.

He was afraid that if he opened his eyes, he'd lose the image, so he fumbled for a pencil and began drawing furiously without looking at the paper. Who was she? Why was she opening the door? Would she invite him in?

He didn't want to be a stranger to this girl.

But as soon as he finished the last wavy strand of her soft, black hair, it was as if the door closed.

The sound of murmuring and stools scraping the floor brought him back. When he opened his eyes, the whole class was gathered around his table, staring in silence.

It was only pencil, but the luminosity of the eyes was apparent even without color. He'd captured the girl's surprise, and there was something so perfectly adorable about it.

"Who is she?" someone whispered.

Evan opened his mouth, then closed it again. He couldn't tell an entire classroom full of seniors that he had no idea who she was. Not on his first day at a new school. Probably not ever.

"Just . . . a girl I used to know," he said with a shrug, and looked into her pencil-drawn eyes again, overcome with a sense of wonder.

She was beautiful, but not in a magazine cover way.

She was beautiful because she was so . . . so . . . real.

And that, he knew, was ridiculous because she was absolutely not real. He was sure he'd never seen that girl before in his life.

He would have remembered.

Ten months later, here he was, pulling into a rest stop in New Jersey with his mom and sister on his way to NYU because of her. *The*

Green-Eyed Girl, painted life-sized in oil, became the centerpiece of his portfolio. The piece that earned the attention of his program mentor, Dr. Vanessa Mortakis.

Absolutely luminous, she'd called it in the acceptance letter. *Intensely realistic and gorgeously sensitive. I can't wait to work with you in New York.*

<hr/>

WHEN DR. MORTAKIS strode into the admissions office later that afternoon, Evan exchanged a surprised glance with his mom at Dr. Mortakis's hourglass figure in a tight black dress, glossy ebony hair to her waist, and blood-red heels that defined her calves beyond professional levels. None of that had shown up in her headshot.

"Evan Kiernan!" she exclaimed warmly, as if greeting an old friend. "Welcome to NYU!"

"Thank you so much." He shook her cool, slender hand, and her delicate bracelets jangled. "This is my mom, Melissa. And my sister, Hailey."

"You must be so proud," Dr. Mortakis said, clasping hands with Evan's mother, then bending down to shake with Hailey, too. "And you must be really proud of your big brother."

Hailey bounced up on her toes and nodded, and Evan felt a twinge in his chest. Ever since the acceptance letter arrived, his mom had been waving off his concerns about the cost of after-school care for Hailey and who would drive her to ballet or tuck her in when their mom had to work late. *You're her brother, not her dad*, she kept insisting. *It's your job to grow up and live your life. It's my job to take care of the two of you. Okay?*

"You are cute as a button!" Dr. Mortakis exclaimed, booping Hailey's nose, and she giggled. Clearly, the professor hadn't been along for the car ride.

"He's so good with her," his mom bragged as they took their seats in the admissions office. "He even illustrates little stories for her."

Dr. Mortakis's eyes brightened. "Really? Well, we have an excellent illustration department. That could be a great option for you."

Evan smiled politely but kicked his mom under the table, hoping she wouldn't pull out any doodled-on receipts or grocery lists from her purse to display *The Adventures of Kitty-Corn*. Whenever they were sitting in the waiting room at the doctor's office or waiting for their food at a restaurant, Kitty-Corn embarked upon another zany adventure. It kept Hailey occupied, but it wasn't exactly Promising Young Artist material.

"Let's take a look at your course load for this semester," Dr. Mortakis continued, and Melissa Kiernan's purse remained mercifully on the floor. "I'll answer any questions you have, give you a little tour, and then let you settle in before classes start up on Monday. Okay?"

She donned a pair of red reading glasses and opened his welcome packet on the desk. Evan's heart raced with anticipation, making his face tingle a little.

He was really here. Really going to college early. Really a promising young artist.

"So, all our first-year students take English Composition and World History in their fall semester. You'll get a science gen ed out of the way with Bio, and then Fundamentals of 2-D is a prerequisite for upper-level studio art classes. However, I thought I'd sign off on one upper-level art history class, so you're enrolled in Mythology in Modern Art, as well. I teach that one, and I'm here any time you need me, okay? If you're ever feeling concerned or overwhelmed or even just homesick, I'm only a text, email, or two-block walk away. Melissa," she said, covering his mom's hand with hers. "I'm going to take great care of your son."

"I know you will," his mom said, smiling, but Evan could see the tears in her eyes already.

A few hours later, his clothes were unpacked and his desk was set up, and she and Hailey were all-out weeping in the doorway.

"This was your idea, remember?" he said, trying to make her laugh, and it worked. "If you don't want me to stay, I can just tell Dr. Mortakis what a forger you really are—"

"You'll do no such thing." She laughed, and kissed his cheek. "And I'm not repentant."

After they left, he sat alone on the twin XL mattress, waiting for his roommate to arrive. Waiting for his new life to begin. He was used to fresh starts and new schools, but this was different. As long as he kept his scholarship, New York would be his home for the next four years. He'd never lived anywhere for four whole years. And after graduation, if he liked it here, he could stay.

For seventeen years, his life had felt like painting by someone else's numbers, waiting for grown-ups to tell him where to color next.

Watching the sun go down over New York City, he let it sink in. He wasn't someone else's canvas anymore. Now, he was the hand, holding the brush.

CHAPTER TWO

E VAN ANGLED HIS flea-market chrome desk fan toward his face and closed his eyes. It was too hot to draw. The sweat on his palms kept smudging the pencil lines, and he was beginning to panic. He had to turn this smudgy mess in by two o'clock.

His son-of-a-billionaire roommate, Henri, was out, but his socks remained, stinking up the room. Evan got stuck with the Czech student who spoke no English but was somehow passing all his classes. Rich dads work wonders—not that he would know.

His first assignment for Mythology in Modern Art was to choose an ancient culture, then explain and illustrate three symbols of their mythology in a contemporary and relevant style.

Evan chose Egypt and decided to render the symbols as tattoo designs. He began with the scarab beetle. The ancient Egyptians believed that every morning the sun was pushed into the sky by a scarab beetle—a symbol of power and determination. He stylized it heavily in black and white—the sun and each section of the insect's body and outstretched wings containing a different line pattern.

Next, the wedjat eye. Horus, the falcon god, supposedly had an eye that could heal and protect humans against evil. He sketched the almond-shaped eye with thick lines, the half-lidded pupil, the hooked J-line and then the straight one coming down from the bottom lid. It needed something—a hint of stippling on the inner lids for dimension. But of course, as soon as he got it perfect, he smudged it.

Damn it.

Holding his sticky palms up to the fan, he closed his eyes and of course he thought of *her*. That wedjat eye would look incredible peering out from her inner forearm. Or maybe—

Stop it, he told himself, and opened his eyes. *She's not even a real person. This is pathetic.*

He cleaned up the smudges with a putty eraser, determined to complete his work on time. The final symbol he'd chosen was the phoenix. Sacred firebird. Symbol of immortality, rebirth, and life after death. Though he'd been too nervous to draw the beetle and the eye without the option of an eraser, he went straight to ink for the fiery bird. Flames had to be drawn without thinking, so he let his subconscious do the work. Zero to permanent in less than ten minutes. Perfection.

Evan smiled, sure Dr. Mortakis would be impressed.

His first full week of independence was coming to a close, and he'd decided he could get used to it. Afternoon classes meant sleeping in, and there were no bells telling him when he was allowed to eat. He didn't have to rush home to get Hailey off the bus. He'd sketched out a few frames of *Kitty-Corn Explores New York*, but he'd spent most of his free time drawing for fun. His thoughts, his time, and his paper were all gloriously his own.

Blowing on the page then tapping a phoenix feather with his index finger, he declared it dry and slipped it into a plastic, waterproof sleeve. It was definitely going to rain—he could smell it. It only takes one ruined masterpiece to learn your lesson: always use protection.

Stomach growling, Evan slung on his backpack and hooked his lucky golf umbrella over his arm. It was one o'clock, which left an hour to grab something to eat and hopefully dodge the storm before class. He knew he should go to the cafeteria or one of the restaurants around campus that accepted his meal plan, but he was in the mood to splurge a little. The stairwell was oppressive. Even the painted cement was sweating. The second clap of thunder shook Manhattan just as Evan hit street level. Scanning the sky between the scrapers, he saw a definite black cloud line.

The air itself seemed excited by the promise of a downpour as he passed through the gates of Washington Square. The wind kicked up, swirling little tornadoes of trash in the street as people hurried their dogs along and pedaled their bicycles faster. Evan walked faster, too, until a girl's voice stopped him short.

"Oh, shit!"

In a sudden gust of wind, a long slip of paper somersaulted across the sidewalk in front of him, then flew into a cluster of evergreen bushes, followed by a frantic girl.

"Shit, shit, shit!" She dove down into the mulch, thrusting her arm into the thick greenery. Evan stepped closer, unsure of whether he should try to help retrieve the paper or guard her bag, which she'd abandoned beside a stack of books on the wrought-iron bench to his right.

The wind made the decision for him. Like a wild bird, the girl's paper took flight, and she continued the chase. He moved protectively toward the bench, eyeing her belongings with curiosity. A worn unzipped backpack lay on its side, advertising a wallet, a hoodie, and a pair of drumsticks to the pickpockets of New York. On the other side of the bench, she'd left a stack of library books: a splashy biography of The Who's drummer, Keith Moon, sat on top of a poetry collection and a thick self-help volume entitled *Freeing Yourself From the Narcissist You Know*.

The first, fat raindrop fell on Evan's nose, and immediately, umbrellas popped up all around him, like fast-motion blooming flowers. People scrambled indoors and under awnings, holding their belongings a little closer as they ran. Evan glanced around the park for the girl while struggling to open his umbrella, finally turning around so the wind could help instead of strong-arming it closed. But as soon as the rusted metal button loosened the carriage, he lost control. Metal-spiked nylon careened inside-out, directly toward a cluster of pedestrians.

"Sorry!" Evan shouted, trying to grab the rim and right the umbrella without poking anyone in the eye. He heard a yelp, and then someone was grabbing onto the other side and helping him pull it down and right side out again.

As soon as the umbrella popped back into shape, Evan blinked in surprise at the girl suddenly standing under it with him, close enough to touch.

Green eyes.

Freckles.

Wisps of dark hair escaping a long, damp braid.

And a soggy slip of paper clutched triumphantly between her thumb and forefinger.

"Sorry," he repeated, feeling as if he'd been struck by lightning.

"It's okay," she said with a breathless laugh, brushing the windblown hair from her face as she looked up at Evan, then paused. Instead of ducking back out like any stranger would, she blinked as if trying to place him.

The city rushed around them in a wave—rain pelting their legs, people scrambling past in annoyance—but her eyes were like pieces of sea glass, shining like something broken and lost and beautiful. He was afraid to look away, sure she'd melt like sugar in the rain, but she just stood as if the same electricity was running through her, rooting her to the ground—

Until tires squealed and a cab driver laid on the horn and the girl blinked as if waking up from a dream.

"Oh, my books!" she exclaimed, scrambling toward the bench.

He followed, holding the umbrella over her as she shook the books in an attempt to dry them.

"Can you hold this a sec?" she asked with a grimace, handing him the slip of paper before yanking the hoodie from her backpack.

She'd handed him a receipt from the New York Public Library, but as it fluttered in his grasp, he noticed the handwritten stanzas scribbled in purple ink all over the back.

"Thanks," she said, snatching it back. "Sorry. That was weird, wasn't it? I mean, *I'm* weird, showing up under your umbrella and asking you to hold my stuff when I don't even know you."

"It's okay," he said with a smile, nodding toward the paper. "Glad you found it."

Her wet cheeks flushed pink and she pressed her lips together. "Oh. You witnessed that?"

"It must be a really good poem," he said. "To leave your wallet for it."

"Actually, it's a song lyric," she said, slinging her backpack over one shoulder. "But yeah. Thanks for not robbing me blind."

"Your eyes are much too pretty for that," he blurted, then shook his head as heat rushed to his face. "Sorry, that was . . . that was weird."

"Well, now we're even." Her smile bloomed, revealing a slight gap between her front teeth, and he felt like one of those stunned cartoon characters with little birdies circling his head, ringing bells.

Her phone buzzed in her palm, and when she checked the screen, she let out a groan. "Shit, I'm late again!"

With an apologetic wave, she stepped back out into the storm, attempting to cover her head with the hoodie. Her long, black braid swung like the pendulum of a clock, and in a flash of panic, Evan realized she was walking away.

"Wait!" he called, just as she reached the Washington archway.

Her head whipped around, and his heart stopped.

This is impossible.

"Here." He extended the umbrella, motioning for her to come under it.

She hesitated, cocking her head and squinting, droplets falling from her eyelashes, but the sky roared again, and she quickly ducked under, grimacing at the clouds.

"Are you headed to class? I can walk you. I have time." His stomach was growling, and another sizzle of lightning made him think about Benjamin Franklin and kites and keys and sudden death by electrified lucky golf umbrella. But lucky golf umbrellas don't get you killed. They help you meet your dream girl in the rain.

"No, I'm not in school," she said, tucking a strand of hair behind her ear. "I'm headed to work."

"Where do you work?"

Her phone buzzed again, and she let out a frustrated sigh. "The Black Cat Café. It's just off the square. I was supposed to be there at one."

"Me, too."

She arched a suspicious eyebrow, and he felt his face go hot.

"Well, I don't work there, I eat there. I mean, I was on my way to buy food there. Assuming there is food there?"

She nodded, suppressing a smile. "Drinks, too."

"Great. That's great. Because clearly, my brain stops working when I'm hungry."

"This way," she laughed, pointing to the left, and they started walking, trying to avoid puddles as the downpour slowed to a steady purr. Following her lead, Evan found himself exiting the park, staring at the blinking yellow light of the crosswalk when he only wanted to look at her. It was easier to convince himself that they weren't really identical when he was looking straight ahead instead of into her eyes. The light changed, and her arm bumped his as they huddled close to stay dry while crossing the street. He thought he'd spontaneously combust.

He shot her a sideways glance. Were there really deep purple undertones in her black hair? It was the perfect color to complement her green eyes, striking as Georgia O'Keeffe's black violets.

They ducked under the awning of the Black Cat Café, and Evan collapsed his umbrella. A pair of window boxes overflowing with red geraniums framed either side of the heavy black door inset with a sleek line painting of a sitting cat, its tail curled into a backward S on the glass.

Opening the door, she shivered in the blast of cool air on her wet skin, and he wished he had a jacket to wrap around her shoulders.

As soon as they stepped inside, a girl with unnaturally red hair started laughing from behind the counter. "Oops. Forgot we only have one umbrella."

"Yeah, it's mine on the way home," the girl with the black hair replied with a pointed look, then unzipped her backpack and tented the wet books on a table by the window to dry. She hung her sweatshirt over the back of a chair, checked her phone, then looked down and sighed at her soaked shoes. "I need to go stand under the hand dryer or something." She turned to Evan apologetically. "I'll be right back."

Evan's chest throbbed when she turned away, and he thought of the time Hailey's father, Bill, took him fishing. The tug on the line. The resistance. The way his reel spun as the fish swam away from the shore with a hook in its lip while he fumbled for a hold to pull it back.

He had painted that for the spring Fine Arts Festival, too. *The One That Got Away* hung right beside *Green-Eyed Girl*.

Who is she? Everyone asked the question when they passed the larger-than-life girl peeking out from behind a heavy, black door. "Come on," his mother had whispered slyly. "You can tell me." But how could he? There was no model, no *girl he used to know*. He didn't even copy some girl from the internet. "I just . . . I had this dream . . ."

he began, but his mother threw up her hands and started laughing. "Okay, TMI!"

"It wasn't that kind of dream," he'd insisted, but she just offered a patronizing, "Sure, honey, whatever you say," and went downstairs to take dinner out of the oven. It hadn't even been a dream, exactly, and certainly not the kind she was insinuating.

Suddenly, he became aware of the redhead's stare and turned away to inspect the menu printed on a large wall-mounted chalkboard. His face was hot as he struggled to focus. He was in a New York City café, where people were expected to order and eat food.

Looking over the prices, his empty stomach sank. If he was going to eat anywhere other than the cafeteria this semester, he needed to find a job. He had already stopped by the university library, food services, and the custodial offices, but nobody had an opening for the seventeen-year-old kid spending his senior year of high school at NYU. Evan didn't want to ask his mother to Venmo him more money. Maybe if she closed a deal on another property, she would send more, but he didn't want her to have to do that. She needed that money for Hailey's after-school daycare now.

He tried to ground himself to reality and study the daily specials. Lots of girls had green eyes and black hair and a gap between their front teeth. So, he had a type. So what? It was his empty stomach making him lightheaded, muddling his thoughts. How could he have seen clearly in that downpour, anyway?

But the way she looked at him.

There was *recognition* in her eyes.

Wasn't there?

"So, you're a friend of Mara's?" the red-haired girl asked.

"Yeah, kind of," he said, shrugging, but all ten pints of his blood rushed to his head. *Mara.* The name clicked as if he'd been trying to remember it. It fit perfectly. It should have been the title of the painting—except he hadn't known her name when he painted her.

It wasn't her, he reminded himself.

"I mean, we just met on the way here."

Evan looked toward the register, where someone had decorated the display cups with black marker and arranged them in ascending order: a twelve-ounce undersea small with studded octopus tentacles gripping the cup; a sixteen-ounce *Día de los Muertos* medium covered in blooming skulls; and a twenty-ounce Empire State large with the geometric skyline of Manhattan.

"Yeah, those are Mara's, too." The redhead sighed. Evan read her name tag, scrawled in loopy handwriting, *Samantha*. "It's sickening, the way she's good at everything, isn't it?"

He laughed uncomfortably. He hadn't even known her name until thirty seconds ago, let alone what she was good at. She was a living, breathing stranger—not the girl whose portrait had gotten him into NYU.

Still, try telling that to his heart when she returned, smoothing her still-damp braid. "Okay, so, what can I get for you?"

"Um . . . How about this?" He pointed to the Empire State large display cup.

"A large? Sure. Large what?"

"Surprise me. As long as I can keep the cup."

"This cup?" She picked it up, eyebrows scrunched in confusion.

"Yeah. I'm kind of like a collector of disposable art," he blurted, immediately wishing he hadn't.

She pressed her lips together, and Evan could hear Samantha stifle a snort from the back room.

"Disposable art?"

"Yeah. It's a thing. And you know, whoever designed those cups is a really good artist. So, I thought maybe I could buy one."

"Well, I guess I could sell it to you. But then I'm going to have to make a replacement."

"Wait, *you* made these?" he said, feigning surprise.

"I draw when I'm bored," she said, shrugging and trying to push the smile off her lips. She grabbed the cup. "So, what do you want in it?"

"Umm, coffee I guess?"

"Hot or cold?"

"Uh, hot I guess?"

She picked up a marker but paused. "Are you sure? You want to think about it for a minute?"

"No, I'm sure. Hot coffee. That's my final answer."

She laughed. "Name?"

"It's Evan. I mean, I'm Evan."

"I'm Mara." She smiled, holding his gaze for an extra beat. "You want something to eat, too? You said you were hungry."

"Right . . . um . . ." He leaned back, looked in the case, and blurted out the first thing he saw. "I'll take one of those bear claws."

"Oh-kay, coffee and a bear claw coming right up."

He thanked her as the door opened and a pair of girls walked in, relieving them both from his painfully awkward ordering process. Pretending to read something on his phone, he took a seat by the front window and considered that, on the hottest day of summer, he had ordered steaming coffee and a bear claw for lunch. She must think he was a real idiot. She was probably right.

Evan dropped his hand below the table to open his gallery. Swiping back to April, he scrolled through the photos of the Spring Fine Arts Festival.

He stared at *The Green-Eyed Girl* for a long minute, then hit delete. The only thing weirder than meeting a disposable art collector would be meeting a complete stranger who painted you last year.

He jumped when a phone buzzed from the empty table beside him, and he realized Mara had left it behind with her library books. He tried to catch her eye, but she was busy steaming milk for the girls at the counter. When Samantha brought his coffee and bear claw to the table a few minutes later, he pointed toward the phone, which was buzzing again.

Samantha took one look at the screen and rolled her eyes. "She *so* needs to block her."

Without further explanation, she picked up Mara's phone to decline the call, and Evan could see that the screen was lit up by a caller simply labeled "X."

Shaking her head, Samantha carried the phone behind the counter, where she shoved it into Mara's back pocket and whispered something into her ear. The steamer went silent, and Mara's hands went to her face in before shaking her head. Samantha raised her palms in surrender before going into the back room.

Evan looked from Mara's sagging shoulders to the library books on the table.

Freeing Yourself From the Narcissist You Know.

If the caller was Mara's ex, that at least meant she was single—but from the way her posture changed after finding out about the call, maybe not quite free?

The bell above the door jangled as a sudden rush of dripping, laughing students poured through the front door of the café, forming a line that would keep Mara and Samantha busy for the foreseeable future. Tables began filling up, so Evan rose to throw his dirty napkins away and set the crumby pastry plate in the dish tub. Feet anchored beside the garbage can, he wanted to say *it was nice to meet you*, or *that was a really tasty bear claw*, but Mara was occupied with the blender. With a sigh of resignation, he turned for the door. But just as he reached for the handle, he heard his name.

"Evan?"

His heart jumped.

"Thanks for the umbrella!" she called.

"Sure," he said, trying to swallow his heart so he could speak. "Yeah. Any time."

"See you later?" Across the crowded café, she held his gaze, unmistakably inviting. As if whoever "X" was, they were completely irrelevant now.

He nodded, feeling a smile consume his entire body. "Absolutely."

⚜

WHEN DR. MORTAKIS asked if anyone would like to come up to the front to share their three symbols of an ancient culture's mythology, Evan slid a little lower in his seat. A few students displayed cartoonish Greek and Nordic symbols that were clearly not as skillful as Evan's Egyptian ones, but he wasn't ready to share in an upper-level art history class quite yet. He was also too distracted by his empty cup and the girl who'd written his name on it.

Mara.

She wanted to see him later—but how much later? After class was too soon. Was tonight too soon? He could go back tomorrow and ask her to dinner, or to a movie. He didn't have to babysit, didn't have to ask his mom if he could borrow the car. He was in the driver's seat of his own life now. He could go wherever he wanted, whenever he wanted, with whoever he wanted—

But then Evan remembered he was really just a high school senior. He was only seventeen—and she was out of school. Did that mean she was twenty-two? Twenty-three?

"Your next assignment," Dr. Mortakis said from the podium, clearing her throat and jolting Evan back to the present. "Is to visit an art exhibit here in the city. It can be anything that intrigues you—a museum such as the Met or MoMA, or a small gallery in the Village. Your job is to search for the past in the present. You'll need to find three pieces of artwork that are considered *modern*—remember, nothing before 1860—that incorporate an ancient or mythological subject. To ensure that you've put your time in, I'm requiring both a photograph and a sketch. I have some flyers here at the podium if you would like some ideas, but let's take a look at a few examples up on the screen so you know what to look for."

Evan tried to pay attention to the flurry of slides depicting a Cubist Virgin Mary, a Dada collage of Greek heroes, and an Impressionist version of Icarus plummeting into the sea, but he wasn't sure how much to write down. Would she test them on these slides if they weren't in the book, or were they only examples? He wrote furiously, but even as his pen flew across the page, his mind drifted to Mara. What kind of song was she writing on the back of that receipt? Did she sing or play the drums, or both? Who was this narcissist she was trying to free herself from—and just how persistent were they? Was she in actual danger? Should he check in sooner rather than later, just to be safe?

"Many people believe that modernism was about leaving the past behind," Dr. Mortakis said, as the screen went dark and the lights came up. "But that's not only incorrect, it's impossible. Modernists left tradition behind in favor of experimentation. Rather than strict realism, these artists began incorporating their own interpretations of reality into their visual art. But they were not attempting to erase the past. They simply interpreted it through a new, more interesting lens. As King Solomon said so eloquently in the Book of Ecclesiastes, 'What has been, will be again. What has been done, will be done again. There is nothing new under the sun.'"

Finally, the hour was up. Slinging his book bag over one shoulder and hooking the soggy umbrella over his elbow, he picked up his empty skyline cup and headed for the door.

"Evan?"

Dr. Mortakis smiled warmly at him, fanning a stack of papers.

"I thought you might really enjoy this exhibit," she said, handing him a glossy postcard advertising Coney Island: A History in Pictures, at the Neptune Gallery. "It's only open for a few more days, though, so you'd better hurry."

"Thanks." He nodded, scanning the info. "Oh, hey, I wanted to ask you—do you know of any place I could get a job on campus? Something flexible with my class schedule?"

"Hmm." She tapped her lips with a crimson-tipped finger. "I'll see what I can do. And let's make that first mentor appointment, okay? How about Monday for lunch? With Labor Day, I don't have any classes, so we'll have plenty of time to chat."

"Sure. Um, where's your office again?"

"Actually, there's a little place I like off Washington Square—the Black Cat Café. How does that sound? Twelve thirty?"

"Perfect," he said, attempting to appear nonchalant, as if she weren't some sort of fairy godmother making all his wishes come true. "I'll be there."

CHAPTER THREE

THE FOLLOWING MORNING, Evan attempted to untangle the New York subway map, seeking the best route to the Neptune Gallery, but his eyes keep crossing. Should he take the Q to the F line? D line then B? Or walk a quarter mile then get the bus?

Coffee.

He'd figure out how to get to the gallery once he'd had some caffeine. Glancing at the cardboard cup he'd carefully rinsed out and placed on top of his dresser, he shoved the postcard advertisement into his pocket and headed for the stairwell.

Inside Washington Square Park, the grass and flowers were still wet from last night's rain. A squirrel shook fat water droplets down from the trees, and Evan had to step around puddles and stranded earthworms on the cement. He smiled, thinking about how Hailey would stop and rescue them all, one by one. It was impossible to get anywhere quickly with a five-year-old. And then the rush of guilt washed over him. Was the new babysitter taking good care of her? Was she helping Hailey keep her *b*'s and *d*'s straight?

Pausing near the fountains, Evan scooped up a worm from the curved pathway, snapped a picture, and texted it to his mom's phone. *Look! I made a new friend at the park today!*

Turning his palm upside down near a bush blooming with white flowers, he watched the worm fall to the soft, soaked earth and burrow to safety. "It's your lucky day. I've changed your fate, buddy."

He glanced around quickly to make sure no one had overheard him speaking to an earthworm after photographing it. That was odd behavior, even for Greenwich Village, and especially considering the irony of what he'd just said. If he had "saved" that worm, he was just playing the part written out for him long, long ago. And if it shriveled up and died? Well, then that was the Plan all along.

It made him think of his mom standing on Dave's front step last year, pressing her palm to the door one last time before they left. From the driveway, he'd seen her lips moving, and he knew she was saying it again: *when God closes a door, you have to trust that what was behind it just wasn't meant for you.*

"Bullshit," he'd muttered, under his breath so Hailey wouldn't hear. God hadn't closed that door. Melissa Kiernan had, after realizing how foolish she'd been to think a guy like Dave would embrace monogamy. If Evan had learned anything from the revolving door of temporary dads in his life, it was that attraction doesn't mean forever. Meet-cutes only led to happily-ever-afters in the movies.

But when Mara had been under his umbrella, New York hadn't felt so huge. When she'd smiled at him, he hadn't felt so alone. And looking into her eyes, he hadn't felt tragic. He'd felt . . . *alive.*

Facing the scalloped awning and red flowers at the Black Cat Café, Evan took a deep breath. He had to open that door one more time.

"Hey there. Back for another bear claw?" Samantha winked from behind the counter, amused as ever, while Evan scanned the café.

"Actually, I was kind of hoping to catch Mara. Is she here?"

"Nope. Sorry."

"It's okay. I'll just um, I'll take a large iced coffee to go. I need some caffeine."

"Coming right up."

When Samantha turned her back, Evan took a step closer to the display cups and grinned. To replace the Empire State large, Mara had drawn King Kong terrorizing the Big Apple.

"Here you go." Samantha offered a clear plastic cup filled with milky brown liquid and ice. "Coffee with a shot of espresso. Caffeine jackpot."

"Oh, um . . . I hope it's not too much trouble, but . . . I actually wanted that cup." Evan gestured toward the gorilla.

"Oh my god. You weren't actually serious about that disposable art collection, were you?"

"I'll make a replacement." The words were out of his mouth before he could catch them. His hands were itching to draw, always a step ahead of him. "Just give me a plain white one, and a marker. It's okay—I'm an art major."

"Oh-kay." She shrugged, grabbing a marker out of the pen cup. "Here ya go."

The Caffeine Jackpot waited patiently on the counter as Evan Kiernan draw a large, stylized umbrella and two bodies from the waist down, one wearing short shorts and combat boots, the other wearing cargo shorts and skate shoes. Without thinking, he sketched little broken circles around their feet for puddles, then unleashed the sideways rain. Spinning the cup around, he drew the awning of the Black Cat and, in one smooth stroke, the cat silhouette. With manic speed, he spread the sidewalk beneath their feet, added a few sprigs of grass, some flowers, and a few simple lined trees.

But it needed something.

The raindrops were too flat. Too boring. Too . . . *ordinary*. So he made the ones closest to the shared umbrella sparkle a little.

"Acceptable?" he asked, offering it to Samantha.

She examined it under the caged Edison bulb dangling over her head. "You don't mess around, do you?"

Evan opened his mouth, but nothing came out. He hadn't really thought about it.

He just picked up the marker.

"My boyfriend never does stuff like this." Samantha dumped ice and coffee into King Kong with a slosh. "Unless he's been an ass. And even then, it's only flowers. Like carnations—the cheap ones. No creativity."

"Sounds like you need to find a better boyfriend." Evan made a face and took the cup but was flooded with relief. She thought it was cute. Unless she was being sarcastic. Was she being sarcastic?

"Yeah, well, he's the front man for our band. So we make it work."

"Cool. Well, um, tell her I said hi."

The entertained grin returned as Samantha wiggled the cup in his face. "I'm pretty sure *this* will say hi all by itself. See you around, Umbrella Boy."

He coughed on his first sip of coffee. "It's Evan."

"Oh, I know."

⚜

THE TRAIN RIDE to Coney Island was longer than he expected. Why did he think it would be quick and easy to get around in New York? Square mile for square mile, everything was so much closer than in suburban Pennsylvania, but he could have crossed two county lines in his mom's Honda in the time it took to ride the train from Manhattan to lower Brooklyn.

It allowed him plenty of time to imagine the employees of the Black Cat Café being highly entertained by the star-crossed little art major who drew sparkling rain on a cardboard cup, thinking he had a shot with Mara. She was already out of school, presumably the drummer and songwriter of her own band, probably twenty-two or three. He assumed he was the laughingstock of Instagram by now.

Umbrella Boy.

Shit.

He couldn't even imagine what nickname he'd earn if they saw the painting.

When Evan finally wrapped his fingers around the loose crystal doorknob of the Neptune Gallery, he determined to pull his thoughts away from Mara. So what if she laughed at him? So what if it didn't work out? It wasn't like he was *in love* with her, because love at first sight was just a myth.

The question crept up the back of his neck on little spider legs: *Was yesterday* really *the first time you saw her?*

Yes, he answered himself. *Yes it was.*

Just because two people looked similar didn't mean they were the same person. And right now, he had work to do. Mythological subjects to find. A scholarship to keep. Retrieving his sketchbook from his backpack, he took a deep breath and steeled his resolve.

It was slow going. The gallery was deserted and in disrepair, with uneven floorboards creaking under thinning Persian carpet, and much smaller than he had expected. Like everything on Coney Island, it seemed to be falling apart, trying to recall better days. The yellow wallpaper was water stained with brown-ringed blotches, the photographs arranged in a halfhearted attempt to hide them. The place was more flea market than gallery, but Evan had spent his share of hours rummaging through thrift shops, so he didn't mind. Sometimes you had to dig through junky bargain bins to find your prize, like the time he found a pristine collection of 1950s horror movie posters under a mildewed suitcase at the Goodwill.

The photographs on display were interesting, but hardly of mythological proportions. He beheld a panoramic, six-foot-long framed roller coaster, then a three-foot tall, life-sized image of a little person dressed up like a cowboy, slinging a pair of guns. Evan finished perusing the first room of the gallery and ducked under a low doorway into another room with deep-red velvet-tufted wallpaper and dusty cherry floorboards. Here, he viewed baseball players in baggy, dirty pants, cheeks fat with chew, and gangsters grinning in dark pressed suits. A rearing carousel horse was mounted to the floor, its eyes blank, its teeth broken, the saddle paint worn away to white.

Why had Dr. Mortakis suggested he visit a photography exhibit to search for mythological subjects, anyway? Photography was the most immediate form of artwork, capturing only a flickering instant in time.

When he came to a photograph of Luna Park, he was finally on to something. A quick search on his phone confirmed that Luna was the Roman personification of the moon, a goddess worshipped twice a month, and the entrance to the park was decorated in large, crescent moons.

He snapped a photo, planning to sketch it later, and moved on to the Cyclone, the iconic roller coaster at Luna. Wondering if perhaps Cyclone, too, was a god, he typed it into his search bar but was disappointed to find only Cyclopes, the giant who lost an eye to Odysseus. The next hour was spent in frustration, finding only a blurry photo of the entrance to El Dorado at Steeplechase Park featuring statues of possibly-Trojan-style warriors. He snapped a photo, just in case he didn't find anything else.

Evan pressed on into the final room of the gallery, the darkest and smallest of all. The paneled walls were painted black, and wrought-iron sconces cast light on framed sepia-toned photos of circus freaks:

A pair of female conjoined twins with one body and two beautiful faces.

A man with scales for skin, his nails grown to resemble claws, his teeth sharpened to points.

A 689-pound woman nicknamed Jolly Irene posing for the camera in a short satin dress, a sly grin on her painted lips.

An empty-eyed girl with thick hair covering her arms and face, hunching in a cage crudely labeled *Monkey Girl.*

And then, beside a woman with two extra-tiny legs dangling between her regular-sized ones was a boy covered in tattoos, his photo framed in cheap black plastic. His dark eyes were focused directly on the lens, giving him the unnerving effect of staring directly into the viewer's eyes. Directly out of the past and into the future.

Goosebumps prickled Evan's neck.

It was like looking into a black-and-white mirror labeled *Circa 1911, on loan from Taffy's on Surf.*

That was it. No name or title. No explanation. No credit to the photographer. Just *Circa 1911.*

Evan stared at the shirtless boy—his lean arms and chest, the dark hair combed slick to the left. He touched his own scalp; his hair parted naturally on the left, too. The only difference between them was the tattoos.

So many tattoos.

Some were traditional images—eagles, anchors, mermaids. But some were extraordinary. Intricate butterflies and exotic birds in flight. Flowering vines and words he could only read part of. The Great Sphinx with its nose broken off, and a leopard stalking its prey through tall grass. A curling, crested wave rolling in to the shore.

Evan's eyes returned to the boy's face. He'd heard of people finding their doppelgängers before, but this was ridiculous. They had to be related. It was the only possible explanation.

Pulling his phone out of his pocket, he texted his mom.

Hey. Would I have any relatives in New York?

Not that I know of. Why?

Maybe on my dad's side?

What?

You know . . . my biological father. I want to know if he has any family in NYC.

Oh honey I don't know.

Even via text, Evan could hear her usual impatience, her usual emphasis on *don't*, implying *don't* ask me any more questions, *don't* go looking for him, *don't* make me think about all the stupid mistakes I've made.

Check this out.

He snapped a photo of the portrait and texted it to her.

One week on your own, and you're covered in tattoos, huh?

What's next, jail?

Funny story . . . I don't even remember getting them. Must have been all that meth.

Ha ha. Did you photoshop your face on there or what?

No, it's hanging in a gallery on Coney Island with a bunch of circus freaks.

Seriously. What kind of filter are you using?

I'm on Coney Island. At an art gallery. And this is hanging on the wall. Not a joke.

Weird. I still think you're pranking me.

He frowned at his phone. No filter would make tattoos that intricate, but his mom never used the features on her phone to know the difference. She might as well have gone to the kiosk for senior citizens at the mall instead of the Apple store.

I swear, it's real. So we have to be related, right?

What does it say under the photo? On loan from someplace?

Taffy's on Surf.

I guess you could ask for more information.

But you don't want me to, right?

The pasta is behind you for a reason

***past**

And God closes doors and opens windows and all that jazz. I know.

Exactly. Call me this weekend, okay? You know I hate to type on this phone.

Okay. Love you.

Love you, too.

In middle school, Evan had become obsessed with finding out what happened to his dad. His mom finally explained that in college, she was not very well-behaved. During her junior year, she went to New Orleans with some friends for Mardi Gras and met a guy named Matt. They exchanged numbers and, apparently, didn't stop there. The trip was more alcohol than memory, but a month later, she realized she was pregnant. He never called back, and she still didn't know his last name, so she gave Evan hers. That was it. End of story. Water under the bridge.

But now, he felt all the questions bubbling again, like someone had poured vinegar on the baking soda of his DNA. Nobody looks that similar unless they're blood.

We have to be related.

KINGS PARK ASYLUM

1 9 1 1

I, KIERAN FLYNN, attest that I am of sound mind as I write this letter.

I am not a lunatic, contrary to my brother's written statement of committal to this dismal institution; only a lunatic believes he's lived a life before this one and will live yet another to come.

"Only a person of compromised sanity would write a letter to himself," said Dr. James, when I begged him for paper and ink. I am, however, persistent.

"I will give you ink," he bargained, "if you use it to write your confession."

"I'll write the truth, sir," I promised, for that was always my intention. "I'll write what happened, as it happened. And when I finish, I'll return it to you on one condition."

"I hardly think you're in a position to make demands, Flynn." He cleared his throat, annoyed that I dared up the ante of his bargain.

In his moment of pause, a scraping shuffle approached from the hall.

And then, the wailing began.

Some wail, some growl and bare their teeth, others converse with the voices in their minds. But all of them stare at my skin, just like everyone did on the boardwalk—though nobody pays a penny for a look around here.

"You trusted me once," I reminded the doctor.

"I was intrigued by you. There is a difference." True. All those months ago before Dreamland Park burned to the ground, he paid me nickels and dimes to examine the picture-stories on my skin. He paid for a tale that would raise the hairs on his neck—not for friendship.

Not trust.

"I am aware of the difference," I said, but if my father taught me one thing, it's this: discovering your opponent's greatest desire is key to victory. So I remained quiet, waiting for his curiosity to get the better of him.

The doctor sighed and petted his mustache as the wailing went on in earnest in the hall. He glanced at the door, for he was needed by someone truly unwell.

"What's your condition?"

"You must file it. In your library. Keep it in the Psychical Center's catalog for as long as there is such an establishment."

He looked at me long and hard, his eyes reviewing the visible portions of my tattooed skin. There, on my right arm, he could see the train—so unlike any locomotive he'd ever seen. And the face of the black cat, its eyes knowing and wild, staring at him from the back of my left hand.

"All right," he said finally, his curiosity inevitably overpowering reason. "Get writing."

I thanked him with all my heart because this paper and ink is our only hope.

Reader, if you are who I think you are, you love a girl.

A doomed girl.

And you desire, more than life itself, to change her fate.

How do I know this? Because, Reader, I felt her last breath. I drew it into my lungs and held it there, knowing she would breathe again. For you. And I've seen how you will lose her if you cannot outsmart our unseen opponent.

So read on, for time is but a trick, and little remains.

CHAPTER FOUR

S THE UPTOWN train carried him back to Manhattan, Evan stared out the window and the city became a blur. His thoughts came so fast, he couldn't catch them.

The past is behind you for a reason.

Maybe for once, his mom was right.

He didn't want anything to do with a guy who knocked a girl up on Bourbon Street then disappeared. She told him she was pregnant, and he didn't call back. He didn't want to be a father. Didn't want to have a son.

Regardless of his DNA, Evan Kiernan would never be like Matt-with-no-last-name, or Bill, or Dave, or any of his mom's other hit-and-run boyfriends. Maybe he had "one of those faces," or maybe the tattooed boy really was a relative, but it didn't matter. He wasn't the kind of guy to decorate a cup for a girl and never call again.

As he neared Washington Square, his phone buzzed with a text notification. His mom had sent him a *Kung Fu Panda* GIF, with a quote from Master Oogway.

Yesterday is history, tomorrow is a mystery, but today is a gift. That's why it's called the present.

He rolled his eyes and sent her a thumbs-up, then got off the train and headed straight to the Black Cat. The café was uncharacteristically empty, and his stomach did a loop as he opened the door and met her eyes over the counter.

"Hi," she said, her gaze darting to the Rainy Day large and back to his. "They say the thief always returns to the scene of his crime."

"Thief?"

"Um, King Kong?"

"I thought of it as more of a trade," he said, blushing and relieved that Samantha seemed to have clocked out for the day. "But I swear, my collection is complete now."

She looked between him and the cup again. "It's . . . adorable," she said, motioning toward the display. "And so are you, but—"

Her phone pinged in her apron pocket, and his stomach dropped as she bit her lip, instinctively checking the notification.

"But . . . you're seeing someone?"

"No," she said quickly, pocketing the phone and taking a deep breath. "No, I'm just kind of . . . going through some stuff right now."

"Well, if you ever need a friend, you know, somebody to talk to . . ."

"Thanks." She smiled, brushing a strand of hair behind her ear. "But I'm sure you've got way better things to do than listen to my drama."

"Actually, I really don't," he said, puffing a small laugh. "I know exactly one person in New York City, and she only talks to me because it's her job."

"Let me guess . . ." She glanced back at the cup, biting back a smile. "Your parole officer?"

"Worse. My program mentor."

Mara studied him curiously. "What kind of program?"

He sighed, then hung his head. "Full disclosure, I should still be a senior in high school. But here I am, the youngest person in the art department at NYU. So I get a mentor."

"Oh my god, are you serious?" She laughed. "I thought you were like twenty-one or something!"

He grimaced. "Is seventeen better than twenty-one? Or worse?"

"Better," she said, resting her elbows on the counter, and he let out a dramatic sigh of relief. "This should be my senior year, too, actually. I just turned eighteen in June. So, how'd you get into NYU early?"

"My art teacher nominated me for this scholarship program, and I got lucky," he said, flushing again at the thought of the contents of his portfolio. "What about you?"

"Oh. I kind of dropped out. To do music." Her smile evaporated as her phone pinged three times in quick succession. "And because I was having some . . . issues at home."

"I get that," he promised, as her eyes dropped to the screen. "And if you need to answer it, go ahead. I don't mind."

She shook her head, then held the power button in with controlled ferocity until the screen went dark. "I'm not even supposed to have this at work," she said, dropping the phone into her apron pocket with a sigh. "I'm supposed to be working. So. What can I get you to drink?"

"Something cold? I don't know . . . What do you recommend?"

She thought for a second, tilting her head from side to side. "Caramel frappé?"

"Yasss," he agreed, pumping his fist enthusiastically. "I'm in."

She smiled. "Coming right up."

Mara went to work pouring the coffee and running the blender and swirling whipped cream. After presenting the finished product with a flourish, she drummed both thumbs on the counter. "So, how do you like the city?"

"Um . . . it's a little overwhelming. I don't know if I'm cool enough for Greenwich Village."

Mara laughed out loud. "Greenwich Village isn't cool enough for itself. Everybody's always trying so hard, you know? It's just . . . it's exhausting."

"I literally saw a person with stacks of encyclopedias duct-taped to their feet for shoes last night." Evan slid off his stool to mimic the clomping, heavy steps. "All the way around Washington Square, like this. I mean, the guy must have thighs of steel."

"Just another day in the Village," she laughed.

"Coney Island's a different vibe, though," he said. "I had to go out there for an assignment today. Really wasn't what I expected."

"What kind of class sends you to Coney Island?"

"Mythology in Modern Art."

She pushed out her bottom lip, amused.

"Go figure, right? My professor sent me to this dumpy little photo gallery out there, looking for symbolism."

"Steal anything?"

He laughed. "Nah. Nothing worth stealing there. But I did see this. Check it out."

He opened his phone gallery, mentally patting himself on the back for deleting *The Green-Eyed Girl* in advance. With trembling hands, he enlarged the photo of the tattooed boy.

Her eyebrows flew up. "Did you go into one of those old-timey photography studios?"

"No. It's not me."

"Shut up."

"It's not me! I'm serious. It was hanging in the Neptune Gallery."

She leaned on her elbows on the counter, studying the photo and then Evan's face. He wondered if the heat creeping into his cheeks showed.

"That's weird," she decided, then shrugged. "Maybe you should get some tattoos, though. It's a good look on you."

"You think so?"

She nodded, the spaces between her freckles turning pink.

"So, what kind of music do you play?" he asked, wanting to turn the conversation back to her and away from uncanny look-alikes or anything that might short-circuit his brain and ruin this new momentum.

"Indie rock, mostly," she said, then paused, chewing on her lip. "We're playing a show Tuesday night. You could come—if you want to, I mean."

"That would be cool. Where is it?"

"A couple blocks from here at Blossom & Spies."

Evan started typing the name of the club into his phone, but stopped when Mara grabbed a new white cup and a marker. He thought she was going to write the address, but she wrote seven numbers in a boxy 3D font instead. Offering it to him with a shy smile that short-circuited his brain, she said, "Think you have room for one more in your collection?"

"I could probably move some things around."

He typed the numbers into his phone. "There. Now you'll have mine, too."

"I'll text you the info." She pulled her phone out of her apron pocket, and as soon as it powered on, it started to ring. Confused, she looked up, but Evan shook his head.

"Oh, it's Sam," she said, giving him an apologetic look before answering the call.

While she talked to Samantha about that night's practice and the cost of printing up color flyers, the back door opened and a midforty-ish woman entered carrying a stack of pastry boxes. She started talking to hair-netted employees in the kitchen, her tone clipped with authority, and Mara glanced toward the kitchen anxiously.

"Shit, I've gotta go. We'll figure it out tonight," she whispered into the phone, and quickly hung up. *My manager,* she mouthed to Evan, as the woman made her way to the counter Mara was suddenly wiping.

Simultaneously, the front door opened for a group of students, and Evan took his cue to leave.

"Thank you," he said, in earshot of the manager, who looked up and smiled as he threw crumpled napkins in the trash can. "Everything was great."

Really, really, really great.

꘏꘏꘏

IT WAS HIS first Friday night in New York City, and Evan had absolutely nothing to do. His roommate had made no efforts to include him in his weekend plans, or even say goodbye. Henri was always speaking Czech on the phone, but when his lacrosse buddies stopped by, Evan discovered his English was good enough to have a conversation if he wanted to. Henri just didn't want to.

Glancing around his empty room, his gaze settled on the cup decorated with digits. He let his thumb hover over Mara's number in his contacts.

It was too soon to call. Wasn't it? He started to type a text, just to play around with what he'd say. But then he was too afraid of bumping send prematurely, so he just sat on his bed, staring into his phone, waiting for seven o'clock.

At 7:01, he called his mom's cell, knowing Hailey would pick up because their mother would be driving her home from dance class. She picked up on the first ring.

"Evan!"

"Hey, Hails, how you doing?"

"I miss you," she wailed, flooding him with guilt.

"Miss you, too, buddy. Did Mommy get you to dance okay?"

"Mm-hmm," Hailey said, and Evan breathed a sigh of relief. "We weren't even late this time. How's school? Did you meet any more friends or just worms?"

"I met some humans, too," Evan said, and his face burst into a dopey grin. "I met a girl in a rock band. She's pretty cool. And her hair's your favorite color."

"Purple?"

"Yup."

"I colored Barbie's hair purple with your markers but Mommy said . . ." Hailey trailed off, and Evan could hear their mother's voice in the background. He heard a muffled argument, then Hailey's pint-sized sigh.

"Mommy wants to talk to you. Here she is. Love you, bye."

Evan answered his mother's questions like a distracted caveman, then zoned out while she updated him on her most recent property listings.

He read the numbers on the cup over and over again until he could see them with his eyes shut.

"Hey, Mom?" he interrupted, and she made a startled noise, as if just now remembering he was there. "I met a girl."

"What?" Evan's mother squealed so loudly, he had to pull the phone away from his ear. "Spill the tea, mister!"

"Okay, so here's the thing—don't laugh."

"I'm not laughing."

"You're going to laugh."

"I swear, I won't."

"It's just that she . . . um . . ." He sucked in a deep breath, squeezing his eyes shut before forcing the next words out in a rush. "She looks just like my painting."

His mother laughed.

"Mom!"

"I'm sorry, I'm sorry. So. You met the *girl of your dreams*. Tell me more."

"I don't really know that much about her. Just that she works at this café close to campus."

"And she's cute."

"Well, yeah."

"Did you tell her you painted her?"

His voice cracked, as if he were twelve again. "No!"

"Good," she said, and snorted. "Not even Bill would use a pickup line that bad. So did you talk to her or just look at her?"

"We talked. Her band is playing a show on Tuesday and she invited me. I'm going to go."

"So *she* asked *you* out. Okay."

"Well? Aren't you going to say it?" he asked, irritated with himself that he wanted her to say it.

"Say what?"

"That it's *fate* or *destiny* or whatever?"

"Hmm," she hummed teasingly. "I don't know. It's probably just a coincidence. And aren't *you* going to say it?"

"Say what?"

"Looks aren't everything, Mom," she said, in an exaggerated imitation of Evan's voice.

"Ha ha. Touché. I'll get to know her better before going to Jared. But don't you think that's weird? I mean, wouldn't she think it was weird if she knew? Which, she doesn't. But if she did, she'd think I was some kind of creep!"

"So, you're saying you want me to destroy all your paintings on the off chance she's as awesome as you hope she is and you can bring her home to meet your mother?"

He laughed at how stupid it sounded.

"You're an excellent judge of character, so consider it done. Okay, we're pulling in the driveway now and I've got to cook dinner for your cranky sister."

"Guess I should go eat something, too."

"Veggies, okay?"

"Goodbye, Mom."

Half an hour later, while eating gristly chicken strips and canned peas at a sticky cafeteria table, he wondered if time had actually started moving more slowly or if it was just playing a trick on him. The girls behind him were talking loudly about costuming for *Hairspray*, swearing and squealing as if he were invisible. He was the only person sitting alone, and it suddenly felt like every group of laughing students was laughing at him.

It got so loud, he didn't even hear his phone ping.

He didn't see the message till he started to pack up and checked the time.

OMG I just saw the encyclopedia shoes.

The message was ten minutes old. How had he missed it? He sank back into his seat with a smile, dropping his backpack on the table.

LOL . . . what statement do you think he's making?

Knowledge is directing his steps?

Or he's stomping on the past?

Did you know the park used to be a cemetery?

Used to be? Where are the bodies?

Still there . . . he's stepping on thousands of dead people with his encyclopedias . . . Wait, I just realized he's wearing a Fuck Trump T-shirt under his jacket

Now it all makes sense?

Lol people are weird

Are you still in the park?

His heart was pounding so hard, he could see his shirt moving. Hoisting his backpack up over his shoulders, he stood without taking his eyes off his phone. Heading toward the exit, he nearly tripped on a pair of feet, but hardly looked up to mumble an apology before continuing on. He dangerously crossed two streets and the misty white spray topping the fountains came into view before she answered.

Nope. I'm getting on the train for band practice. Because I have no life.

I'm pretty sure the definition of having no life is eating Grade F chicken alone in a cafeteria.

I'm working again Monday if you want another bear claw?

That would be an improvement over my current food situation

Hot tip: the cheese Danish is superior. Gotta go . . . my stop. See you Monday!

CHAPTER FIVE

D R. MORTAKIS MET Evan at the counter of the Black Cat with a warm smile. "So glad you could make it."

"Thanks for making the time," he said, shaking the professor's hand but looking toward the back room.

"Of course. I've got us a table back here." She led the way to a small, round table with three chairs, one of which was already occupied by an elderly woman knitting and wearing a nubby beige shawl. "This is my grandmother," Dr. Mortakis said, touching the woman's shoulder. "Everyone calls her Nona. She can't be left alone for long because of her health. I hope you don't mind."

"No worries. Hi, Nona," Evan said, taking the third seat and smiling at the old woman. Briefly, her eyes rose from the deep, purple yarn to glare at Evan before returning to her work.

"Nona, did you hear Evan? He said hello to you," Dr. Mortakis said loudly, nudging her grandmother's arm and looking uncomfortable.

Again, the old woman lifted her eyes and squinted at him. "I heard."

She sucked her teeth, then went back to knitting. Evan shot Dr. Mortakis a questioning look.

"She's getting very old," Dr. Mortakis mouthed, tapping her head to indicate senility before raising her voice to normal. "Nona lives with me upstairs. We look after each other, don't we, dear?"

Nona didn't look up.

"That's nice," Evan said, averting his eyes from the grouchy old woman's chin, which sprouted several hairs. He would have much rather looked at Mara, but the only person working counter was a pimple-faced boy sporting a jet-black mullet.

"How are you feeling after your first week at NYU?" Dr. Mortakis asked.

"I'm feeling great," he said, forcing his gaze away from the Mara-less counter and back to the professor's kind eyes. "Everything's going really well."

"Is your workload manageable?"

"So far, so good." Evan nodded and stole another glance past the mullet, toward the back room. Was she on break? Or just not scheduled for the lunch shift?

They had texted a little over the weekend, but the lag in reply time made conversation difficult.

"So," Dr. Mortakis continued, clearing her throat and shuffling a stack of papers until the edges were perfectly aligned. "Have you found an on-campus job yet?"

"Nope. But I've been looking."

"I was hoping you'd say that." She rubbed her hands together and smiled conspiratorially. "I'm drowning in paperwork, and I need someone I can trust to do some grading and data entry. Ordinarily, office assistant jobs are reserved for grad students, but I've discussed it with the department chair and we're prepared to make an exception. If you're interested."

"Seriously? An exception for me?"

She nodded, quirking her lips and leaning her elbows on the table "Ten hours a week, fifteen dollars an hour. Resume-building material. Whaddya think?"

He thought manna just fell from heaven.

The professor laughed softly, and he realized his mouth was hanging open. "Is that a yes?"

He pressed his lips together and gathered up what dignity he had left. "Yes. Thank you. That's a great opportunity. Thank you."

"I'll show you my office after lunch. What do you say we order? My treat."

They walked up to the counter together, and just then, the back door opened. Heat rushed over him like an open oven door even though he was standing right under the air conditioning vent. Mara's hair was down in soft waves framing her face, and her cheeks were pink from the sun.

"Hey, Vanessa!" she said with a wave, then glanced past Dr. Mortakis to see Evan. Her eyes widened in surprised, but then she smiled, and he was sure the pink on her cheeks deepened.

"Ah, there's my girl!" Nona interrupted before Evan could even say hello. She dropped her knitting on the table. With a grunt, she started to push herself up, but Mara hurried to her.

"Don't get up," Mara said, and extended her arms for a hug. "I'll come to you."

Evan watched, mystified, as Nona's surly glare transformed into a doting grandmother's smile. She patted Mara's cheek.

"Look at this hair," Nona said, affectionately stroking a curl. "Extra pretty today."

"And you finished the shawl," Mara returned, tugging gently at the tasseled edge in approval. "It's beautiful."

The old woman's smile widened. "I'll have yours finished before the first frost. The dye is almost ready, but you simply cannot rush purple. It's the color of love."

Mara glanced at Evan. "She's a fiber artist," she explained, before turning back to Nona. "The usual?"

"No rush," Nona said, nodding, and returned to her work. "I have time."

"The usual for you, too, Vanessa?" Mara asked, taking her place behind the counter again.

"You know what I like," Dr. Mortakis said, winking. "Evan, what will you have?"

Mara's eyebrows shot up, connecting the dots. "Wait, you two know each other?"

Dr. Mortakis gave a firm nod and touched Evan's shoulder. "He's my mentee in the Promising Young Artists Program. But I didn't realize *you* two knew each other."

"Yeah, we got stuck in that storm the other day. Evan let me borrow his umbrella."

"That was a heck of a storm," Dr. Mortakis said, her eyes suddenly lighting on the Rainy Day cup.

"Caramel frappé?" Mara asked Evan, her lower lip slipping into the gap between her top teeth.

He nodded, feeling his own face redden. "And a BLT. Extra bacon. Please."

"Coming right up."

Dr. Mortakis paid for their meals and they returned to the table, where Nona was busy knitting and acting like Evan didn't exist. He tried to return the favor as the professor asked him about his family and hometown.

She was particularly amused by his stories of passing Amish buggies on back roads in Lancaster County, and eager to question him about the hex signs that decorated their barns. Were the ones for sale at tourist shops real or just gimmicks? Evan had to admit he didn't know but was able to give firsthand testimony that the Amish really did not believe in wearing deodorant.

"Order for Vanessa!" Samantha called from behind the counter, and Dr. Mortakis quickly rose to retrieve their tray. She passed out the food—a cup of tea and a muffin for Nona, a vanilla Chai latte and strawberry-spinach salad for herself, and the BLT for Evan.

"Oh," she said, lifting the final plate, confused. "Who ordered a cheese Danish?"

"I think that's me," Evan said, glancing toward the counter before taking the plate and stifling a twitterpated grin.

Between bites, Dr. Mortakis suggested student organizations and clubs, study groups and theaters, but Evan retained none of it. His senses were consumed with cheese Danish.

Finally, Mara stopped by to see how they liked their food, and Nona put her knitting down.

"Perfect," she said, and patted Mara's hand. "Just perfect."

"Life-changing," Evan added.

"I know, right?" Mara said.

Dr. Mortakis shot him a funny look, then turned to Mara. "Do you have those flyers?"

"Oh my god, I almost forgot!" Mara smacked herself in the forehead before disappearing into the back room. A minute later, she returned with a large manila envelope. "Thank you so much."

"I promised to hang some up for her around campus to advertise the show," explained Dr. Mortakis, tucking the envelope into her briefcase. "Speaking of which, you should go! Get out and have a little fun tomorrow night."

"He's too busy with his studies," Nona announced, without looking up.

Dr. Mortakis rolled her eyes for Evan's benefit and stood to dispose of their trash.

"I'll be there," he mouthed to Mara, and winked.

Brushing crumbs from her hands, Dr. Mortakis returned. "Back upstairs we go, Nona."

"I am comfortable here," Nona answered, deftly looping deep purple yarn. "Mara will walk me up later, won't you, love?"

"Of course."

"Are you sure?" Dr. Mortakis asked Mara softly. "You don't have to do that."

"I really don't mind. We'll have some tea together, right, Nona?"

Nona grinned. "Extra sugar for you."

Dr. Mortakis raised her hands in surrender. "Whatever," she said, brushing a stray crumb from her black skirt. "Ready?"

Evan wasn't, but he followed her anyway.

As they stepped out into the sultry, early September afternoon, Dr. Mortakis lowered her voice. "You know," she said, glancing over her shoulder toward the café. "I hadn't thought about it before, but Mara really resembles the girl in your painting. The big one. Don't you think?"

"I guess so." The sun seemed to be boring holes into his black T-shirt. "Funny, huh?"

"Who was your model?"

"Umm . . . just this girl I used to know," he lied, staring at the Do Not Walk sign and shifting from foot to foot.

"You should show Mara a picture of the painting. Who knows, maybe it's her long-lost twin or something."

"No!" he blurted, then laughed nervously. "I don't want her to think . . . I mean, she'd think that was really weird, right? Like, creepy?"

Dr. Mortakis shrugged, shielding her eyes from the sun as they crossed the street. "Or she'd call it fate."

Stepping into the park, Evan felt ten degrees cooler in the shade of the enormous elms. As they passed the fountains, Evan chose his words carefully. "Do you believe in fate, Dr. Mortakis?"

She turned. "Don't you?"

"Um . . . no. Not really."

"Hmm," the professor said, and began walking again, her heels clacking on the paved pathway. "You know, the ancient Greeks believed that the Fates were untouchable. Not even the greatest of the male gods could change their plans. And I've always thought they were onto something there."

Evan didn't know how to respond. The heat was making him feel lightheaded, and he wondered how she could walk so fast in such high heels, let alone in this heat, without even breaking a sweat.

"Why would they have made something like that up?" Dr. Mortakis mused. "I mean, in a patriarchal society like that, why would they have invented three women who were more powerful than any man, unless there was a little bit of truth in it?"

"So, you think God is female?" Evan asked, trying to follow her logic.

Dr. Mortakis laughed. "*God* is a tricky word. So's female, for that matter."

He nodded as they approached the Steinhardt building, and Dr. Mortakis opened the door for him. She led him through the air-conditioned lobby and into the elevator.

"But speaking of females," she said, pushing the button for the third floor. "Mara likes you. She lit up like a Christmas tree when she saw you, even without the whole *fate* bit. So if you're as smart as I think you are, you'll go to that show tomorrow night."

"I will," he promised, as the elevator carriage pushed upward. "But please don't say anything to her about the painting?"

Dr. Mortakis gave him a sly smile and mimed zipping her lips as the elevator made a little *ding* and the doors opened.

He followed her to the end of a godforsaken hallway. Just as he was giving up hope that he'd ever find his way out again, he saw the rectangular, oak-veneered plaque engraved in gold, Dr. Vanessa Mortakis.

"Voilà," she said, lifting her hands like a magician who'd just pulled a trick. The key took some finagling, but finally the unstained wooden door squeaked like it hadn't been opened since the eighties.

"Welcome to the pretenure offices," she said drily, her scarlet lips quirked. Evan prepped himself for ugly and stale-smelling, but when the door opened the rest of the way, his jaw dropped. She'd done wonders with the wood-paneled box of an office—it had her written all over it. A gleaming, ebony desk with a red leather chair. A chrome lamp topped with a sleek, black shade. Impeccably level, evenly spaced black frames lined one wall, each containing a distinct, yet somehow uniform, inked parchment. Egyptian hieroglyphs? Nordic or Celtic symbols? Mandarin characters? Cave drawings?

He had no idea what most of them even were, but they all looked like they meant something. They were carefully selected and hung with precision, like the words of a mind-blowing sentence only she understood.

Directly above her desk hung the picture of a man wrestling a lion. It looked like it was taken from Roman pottery, Evan thought, as he considered the textured terra-cotta browns painted with black figures. A muscular man struggling with a ferocious lion. White lines against black. Black against brown. Man against nature—or was he a god?

"Like it?" she asked, clearing her throat.

"Yeah. Where did you get it?" he asked, pointing at the lion.

"A gift from the artist," she said, then laughed at her own joke. "Actually, it was a gift from my mother. You wouldn't even believe how Greek my family is. Like, have you seen *My Big Fat Greek Wedding*? That was my childhood. The myths were my bedtime stories. And we broke a hell of a lot of plates every time one of my cousins got married."

"It's cool to have a connection to your family's history," he said, with a twinge of jealousy. "And your office is great."

"I'm glad you think so, since this is going to be your office, too." With a warm smile, she offered him the employment contract, her chair, and her pen. Evan scanned the conditions mindlessly and signed his name.

He started entering grades electronically right away—including his own. He was given the answer keys for multiple choice exams and rubrics for essays and projects. He could handle it, she said. She was confident in his abilities and honesty. She even gave him a little silver key to the office before heading out to check on Nona.

"Oh." She paused in the doorway. "Did you get a chance to visit that gallery?"

"I did," he replied, hoping she wouldn't ask him too many questions about it. Mara wasn't the only one with a long-lost twin, but he wasn't about to bring up his trashy family history to Dr. Mortakis. And then it dawned on him—he hadn't found three mythological symbols at the Neptune Gallery. He'd been so distracted, he'd stopped at two.

"Can't wait to see what you come up with." She tapped the doorframe twice and grinned before turning for the hall.

Alone in the office, he racked his brain, trying to remember what else he'd seen at the gallery in addition to Luna Park and the possibly Trojan soldiers at El Dorado. Baseball players, circus freaks, animals. Just portraits of an era gone by. But even if he could remember a third image, remembering wasn't enough. He was supposed to turn in a sketch *and* a photograph.

His gaze strayed from the spreadsheet of grades as anxiety buzzed through his limbs. How had he managed to mess up already? This was only his second assignment, and he was already falling behind. He couldn't think around the rush of blood in his ears. His heartbeat was everywhere.

No, no, no.

He couldn't fail.

He wouldn't.

He'd complete the assignment, even if it meant going back to the gallery a second time. His time was his own. He didn't have to rush home to get Hailey off the bus or drive her to ballet. All he had to do was keep up with his class work.

He made copies and entered grades steadily until the alarm he'd set on his phone went off, alerting him that his work hours were up. After scanning the office for orderliness, he locked the door and leaned his back against it. Closing his eyes and taking a deep breath, he promised himself he had time to finish the assignment.

On his way to the elevator, he passed a crumbling old cork board wearing a brand-new flyer: Switched Flip, Live at Blossom & Spies Tuesday @ 9:00 p.m.

Mara's band was staged in some purposefully decrepit building, with peeling wallpaper and chunks of plaster missing from the walls, knocked out windowpanes, and exposed wooden beams. Five people squeezed onto a yellow-green vintage couch beneath a dangling Edison lightbulb. Dust motes were suspended in the air around their heads.

The lead singer was the only one looking into the camera, centered on the couch, resting his elbows on his knees, hands folded. The photographer had played with the filter to make his eyes an eerily intense blue and Samantha's hair cherry red. She sat on his right, her legs crossed, the tip of her thumb seductively between her teeth. Beside her, a pale, reptilian-looking guy wearing a fedora smiled at something on the ceiling. On the front man's other side, a girl with deep-brown skin hung upside down, one leg sticking up above the back of the couch, the other bent. One side of her head was shaved, and the long black braids cascading from the other side skirted the floor.

Mara sat on the far left, wearing white. Her bottom lip caught between her teeth, she held a leather notebook and a calligraphy-nibbed pen. Leaning against the arm of the old couch, she was turned away from the rest of them, writing. In her own little beautiful world.

He had to find a way into that world.

And that meant he couldn't fall behind and lose his scholarship. He'd find another mythological symbol, even if he had to start from scratch at the Met.

The air felt like soup as he trudged back to his dorm, heavy with exhaustion, to look at the only thing he'd brought back from the Neptune Gallery, the photo of the tattooed boy.

There were so many images on the boy's skin, it was hard to make out the details on a small phone screen. Evan zoomed in. Between his fingers, an eagle eye stared intensely from the boy's forearm. Evan figured an eagle had to symbolize something in somebody's mythology—at least Americana, but he wasn't sure if that was quite ancient enough for Dr. Mortakis's tastes. So he slid his fingers around the zoomed-in image, making a list of pictures the guy had permanently marked himself with:

Eagle, twin mermaids, anchor, black cat, train.

Snake feeding off its own tail, triple swirl.

And was that a phoenix wrapping around his side?

Surely, it was his imagination that the tattooed firebird looked just like his drawing from ancient Egypt. Wasn't it? He couldn't compare the two because Dr. Mortakis hadn't returned his assignment. But all phoenixes looked similar, didn't they? He zoomed out and looked at the face one more time. *Not that similar.*

Evan told himself there had to be a logical explanation for this set of coincidences. DNA sequences repeated themselves, creating doppelgängers even outside of immediate families. The very existence of a habitable world, and intelligent life, was a rare and fortuitous sequence of coincidences. Likely? No. Possible? Sure.

Logic said the hairs on the back of his neck should lie down already.

But that firebird stared back at him, like a dare.

KINGS PARK ASYLUM

1 9 1 1

DR. JAMES ASKED *me to write my confession. He says that if I admit my guilt, I'll be able to go to a proper jail with sane criminals instead of this place of constant noise and wailing, of filth and needles and despair. All I must do, he says, is admit that I set fire to Dreamland.*

Reader, there are times when the only person a man can trust is himself. This is why I am writing this letter to you. Just as you know in your own heart that you would never do such a thing, you know that I am innocent. And I know that you, too, are innocent, of whatever lunacy they will accuse you of.

The doctor says my motive was to prove my predictions correct. Yes, I saw flames. I told him the flames were coming, all those months ago, when I showed him the sacred firebird on my side. I told him this story because I thought he would help me. But the doctor only wanted to satisfy his curiosity. I wanted to save Mary's life.

My father never told me what sort of work he expected to find when he arrived in America, but while detained in port, watching sailors in shirtsleeves loading and unloading their cargo, the work found him.

Restless as always, my father paced the perimeter of our confines, try-ing to figure out how to fit himself into this new framework. And that's when he saw the firebird. It was 1891, and Samuel O'Reilly had just patented his electric tattoo machine.

On the loading dock, a barrel of oil had spilled, soiling the clothes of some of the dockhands. A certain man removed his shirt to wipe his face, and in that moment, my father's artistic eye was drawn to the man's skin, to the magnificent orange and yellow phoenix engulfing his back. He hurried for a closer look and marveled at the details. The precision. The man directed my father to the tattooist responsible, and my father convinced him to teach him the art.

His work was surprisingly good, and soon in high demand, though my mother didn't live to see his success. I was too little to remember her at all, but my brother, Donnie, says I cried inconsolably for days and days. Somehow, Dad managed to raise two boys on his own—me always by his side, watching the way he worked magic with ink, Donnie always at the rat pits with older boys.

My father knew the tale of the phoenix, but as he tattooed navy and merchant sailors from all over the world, he learned it was not one tale, but many. Around the world, people told stories of a sacred firebird that rises from its ashes and remakes itself—gifted with immortality by whatever god or gods the storyteller believed in.

Dad told me this tale when I turned sixteen and he tattooed the bird on my side, promising in a soothing voice that if I listened to the stories he told, I wouldn't feel a thing.

My father kept talking, his careful, fine needle crafting winged flames. The machine buzzed and pulsed, interrupted in even intervals by my father's gentle touch, wiping away excess ink and blood. As the hours wore on, I grew numb to the sensation and slowly drifted off to sleep.

It was during this hypnotic sleep, lying on a table, being tattooed by my father at the age of sixteen, that I first saw Mary, engulfed in flames.

CHAPTER SIX

THE SIGN FOR Blossom & Spies was small and easy to miss—just a little painted placard of orange blossoms with eyeball centers. Curving branches with arrow-tipped leaves pointed Evan down concrete stairs. Tentatively, he went below street level, not quite sure he was at the right place until he saw the door and walls papered with posters for upcoming shows. There they were, in color: *Switched Flip*.

He was embarrassingly early.

He peered in through the door glass, trying to figure out the best way to enter a place like this. Would they card him? He wasn't even eighteen yet. But he did have a student ID, which the sign said would get him a discount. He'd have to just act like he belonged in a dark and smoky bar, where red lights illuminated bottles of whiskey and bourbon and hopefully a Dr Pepper on tap.

He walked in unnoticed and took a seat in the back where the shadows could make him look older. He ordered cheese fries and ate them one at a time, watching the minutes tick by until nine. The club was getting crowded and noisy, and he seemed to be the only person who had come alone. But then, he felt a hand on his shoulder.

"You came!"

He still couldn't believe how green her eyes were. Or that she'd touched his shoulder.

"Do you . . . want a cheese fry?" he asked, immediately feeling like an idiot.

"I can't eat before shows," she said, scrunching her nose and taking the empty seat across from him. Her hair was up in a high, wavy ponytail, a black lace top accentuating her neckline. "I get too nervous."

"Well, you don't look nervous."

She laughed. "Thanks. We're all going to get pizza after the show, so, maybe you'd like to come with?"

"Sure," he said, forcing himself to sound casual. "That would be cool."

Her phone vibrated on the table, and, glancing at the time, she frowned. "I've got to go warm up. See you after the show?"

"I'll be here," he said, suddenly too nervous to finish his own cheese fries as the lights went down and Switched Flip took the stage.

He'd never watched a girl drum before. It was miraculous.

Her hair was all over the place, while the spotlights shone in her eyes and glinted off her rings. Through the black lace of her top, he could see a deep purple bra, and all that softness-in-motion made his mouth dry. Between sets, he went up to the bar and ordered another soda. Sipping Dr Pepper through a straw, he watched the bearded bartender mix vodka with strawberries for a couple of girls who were commenting on just how badass the girl drummer was.

Their cover of the Killers' "Glamorous Indie Rock & Roll" ended, and seamlessly, Mara's rhythm changed. Samantha flipped a switch with her foot, and the sound of her guitar transformed into something haunting and beautiful, peppered with a piano melody that was catchy

and new. When the lead singer started in, Evan smiled. It was obvious
he hadn't written these lyrics.

When I was scared I climbed into your bed
And then you told me stories to mess with my head
Oh, you told me that you loved me
That I was your girl.

As the melody progressed, the chords became more aggressive and
he watched Mara's face. The beat intensified, but didn't speed up, and
a single tear slid down her cheek.

She ignored it, but Evan didn't.

This was her song.

And it wasn't fiction.

After Samantha's guitar wailed one last, mournful chord, the club
went wild with applause. Each of the band members turned to nod or
wink at Mara, but she just rubbed her cheek with her sleeve and headed right into the next song.

The lyrics stayed with Evan as the band moved on through a mix
of unique cover arrangements and originals. She'd said she was going through some stuff, but this sounded pretty intense. He wanted to
throttle X.

At eleven o'clock, the front man thanked everyone for coming out
to hear them play, and the next thing Evan knew, he was sitting next
to Mara at a sticky table crowded with musicians. She introduced him
to Ben, the lead singer whose arm was slung around Samantha's shoulders. Gwen, the bassist with the piercings and long black box braids on
one side of her head saluted him, and Darren, the keyboardist, tipped
his fedora.

"So, Vanessa's your mentor huh?" Samantha said, picking up a
sweating, brown beer bottle and taking a swig. "I always thought she
must be *such* a cool professor."

"She's great," Evan agreed, suddenly feeling very young. Were they all twenty-one?

"Have you met her grandma yet?" Gwen asked with a smirk.

Evan grimaced. "Yeah, but I don't think she likes me very much."

They all burst out laughing, and Samantha said, "She doesn't like *anyone* very much. Except Mara."

Mara waved dismissively. "Oh, come on. She's sweet."

"To you!" Samantha protested, then turned to Evan. "You should see how it goes down when she's not at work. If I have to bring that woman her tea, it's always *too hot, too cold, I didn't want that cup, there's a crumb on my spoon, the saucer doesn't match, and where's Mara?*"

Mara shrugged innocently. "I can't help it if she likes me best."

Samantha pinched Mara's cheek. "You're just so wuv-able. Mara's the baby of the band," she explained to Evan.

"Ugh." Mara rolled her eyes. "Here we go again."

"Since we talked her into quitting school to drum for us, we keep an eye on her. Make sure she's eating her vegetables and not staying up past her bedtime."

"I'm eighteen!" Mara argued.

"Come on," Gwen chimed in. "We're the best parents you ever had. Aren't we?"

A shadow flickered across Mara's eyes. "Yeah," she agreed, but her smile was tight. "You're the best."

A few seconds of uncomfortable silence settled over the table before Ben turned the conversation toward their next show, which was scheduled as a running Tuesday night gig at Blossom & Spies. If they kept drawing crowds like tonight, he said, they'd get the coveted Friday night slot.

"Which means we *need* some real cover art," Ben said. "And not just that stupid photo of us in the Bronx."

"You're like, an art major, right?" Samantha said, suddenly pointing at Evan. "Maybe you could do some cover art for our album?"

"We could use some on our website, too," Gwen agreed. "We really need to be consistent with branding across our socials."

"No pressure, though," Mara piped up, biting her lip. "I mean, you're probably really super busy with school."

"No, I could totally do that," Evan said. "What would be, like, your ideal cover?"

They all started talking at once, laughing and fighting over the hottest covers of all time. *Fame Monster. Tragic Kingdom. Sticky Fingers. Pearl. Bitches Brew. London Calling. She's So Unusual.* The designs had absolutely nothing in common, which probably explained why they didn't have consistent branding across their socials. Evan wondered how hard it would be to come up with a design that would please all five of them, but he really only cared about making the drummer happy.

At one o'clock in the morning, the restaurant staff began flipping chairs upside down on the tables, shooting the six remaining customers *hurry up* looks. They gathered their things, but as her friends headed toward the door, Mara hung back.

"I'm really glad you came tonight." It was surreal, looking into her eyes, hearing her say that.

"Me, too."

"We're going to miss our train!" Samantha shouted across the now-empty restaurant, motioning for Mara to get moving.

"I guess I have to go," she said, glancing over her shoulder, before giving him one last smile and wave. "But I'll see you around, Umbrella Boy."

CHAPTER SEVEN

EVAN OPENED HIS eyes to the sun slicing through the venetian blinds. He considered stopping by the Black Cat for a cheese Danish, but knew it was too soon. He should wait at least a few more hours before texting or showing up at her workplace. Shouldn't he?

He grabbed breakfast at the dining hall and finished his assigned chapter of *Circe*, which detailed the gruesome punishment of Prometheus. Because he had defied Zeus by stealing fire from Mount Olympus and giving it to humanity, Prometheus was brutally whipped, then chained to a rock for eternity, sentenced to have his liver eaten daily by a bird of prey. Each night, his liver would grow back again so he could be torn open by the bird the next day. And yet, even after such intense suffering, he refused to repent and showed no remorse.

He must have loved one of those mortals, Evan thought. Prometheus must have found someone worth suffering for.

By two o'clock, he was caught up on all his work except for the third mythological image, which was due the next day. There was no way around it. He had to go back to the Neptune Gallery because he couldn't hand in a photo of "himself" with tattoos. Dr. Mortakis would probably accuse him of academic dishonesty, strip him of his scholarship, and send him back to Pennsylvania. Or at the very least, have some questions.

As the train carried him back to Coney Island, he replayed Mara's song in his head and tried to envision artwork to go along with it. Closing his eyes, he tried to empty his mind and let his subconscious kick in the way Mr. Burns had taught him, but all he could see was Mara, her lower lip caught between her teeth. Those eyes. She'd be the perfect album cover. The perfect everything.

The train squealed and lurched to a stop, and Evan opened his eyes to Eighth and Surf Avenue. He looked up at the station walls, decorated with colorful fish and marked *New York Aquarium*. New York Aquarium? That wasn't along his route. He'd gone too far.

How had he missed Neptune Avenue?

Checking the map on his phone, he realized he'd only gone one stop too far, and hurried to the platform. It would be no problem to walk an extra mile or so. After nearly an hour of sitting, it felt good to stand up and stretch. Without being forced to take phys ed this year, he could use the exercise.

Reaching street level and blinking in the steamy Coney Island sunlight, he waited for his phone to recalculate directions to the Neptune Gallery. Attempting to orient himself, he looked left and right, noting four rutted lanes of traffic, where cars sped by bumping and dipping like ships on the sea. Newspapers, candy wrappers, and smashed plastic water bottles lay at his feet. Across the street, he saw rattlesnaking roller coasters, a Ferris wheel, and big lollipop lights blinking *Luna Park*.

His signal was failing, continually recalculating, so he crossed Surf Avenue to get a better look at the park. It reminded him of the time Bill had loaded them up in his work truck for a vacation to Atlantic

City. The park and the surrounding area shared the same dilapidated, past-its-prime feel—loud and trashy with whooshes and screams and carnival music. Laughter and the creaking of metal on metal. The smell of buttered popcorn and grilling meat. Vinegar and the sea.

Evan hated it.

Turning back toward the aquarium, he took in the gaudy, candy-colored paintings of fish and undersea vegetation adorning the outer walls and shook his head.

This is all wrong.

He'd gotten off at the wrong stop, he wasn't supposed to be here, but that wasn't it.

Not quite.

Something was off—like it wasn't him in the wrong place, but the aquarium itself.

It was like visiting Grandma's house but finding a big blister of a Walmart on the corner where Rachel's greenhouse had always been. The aquarium, the fish, the walled-in water—none of it was supposed to be there, and the most unsettling part of it was, he knew what was supposed to be there.

An angel.

As the word formed soundlessly in his mind, the syllables beat like wings. The air stirred—or was it his imagination that everything was moving but him? Grabbing at the blue fencing that walled in the parking lot, Evan's knuckles went white and the world spun like a carousel.

The aquarium flickered and blurred behind the metal posts, and everything changed in a whoosh—trees shrank, buildings vanished, people walked backward, clouds zipped across the sky. It was like reverse time-lapse photography, the sun rising and setting, rising and setting in a series of flashes until—

Stop.

Vertigo knocked him off-balance and he lost his grip on the fence. Ears ringing, Evan clutched his rolling stomach, struggling to focus his vision. The fence he had just been holding was gone, and an angel towered before him, carved from white stone.

Her outstretched, downturned wings formed a double-arched entryway off Surf Avenue. A skein of cloth covered her hips, but bare granite breasts stood out above her belly. People were lined up, waiting to get inside—a few brazen enough to stare at the larger-than-life nudity above them.

They weren't dressed like tourists. The men wore dark suits and the ladies donned long dresses, all of them in hats like they were attending the Kentucky Derby.

It was an entrance, but the people were not going inside an aquarium. They were going inside—what? What was this place?

Shifting his eyes downward, he could see that behind the angel, beneath her wings, was a sign. *Dreamland.*

And then, an automated voice broke in. "Head North on Eighth Street toward Neptune Avenue."

His vision cleared instantly, like flipping the channel. It was just the entrance to the aquarium again, crawling with people in short shorts and strappy sundresses and baby strollers. Just like the satellite connected to his phone said.

His nerves buzzed, overwhelming him with an electric, tingly sensation. He should get the hell out of there, head north on Eighth Street toward Neptune Avenue, but he kept walking along Surf Avenue, along the perimeter of the aquarium, still feeling tingly and strange.

"Make a U-turn now . . . Recalculating . . ."

As Evan circled the aquarium complex, the sea breeze lifted his hair. Listening to splashing, clapping and squealing children, and the amplified voice of an emcee narrating a sea lion show, he assured himself this was just an aquarium along a boardwalk with rides and arcades.

But he felt suspended in time, weirdly weightless and slow, as if he were under water, himself. The breeze picked up, and then, like an incoming wave, a spinning surge blurred his vision. The sun went up then down, faster and faster, as the waves rolled backward.

Flash—

Flash—

Stop.

He stumbled into a bench and stared at another entrance.

This one looked like a castle, with white stairs leading up to a huge, pitch-black archway. Not a fairy-tale castle. And leaning on top, arms crossed, elbows hanging over the stone walls, leered the devil. His veiny bat wings stretched possessively across the top, and little capital letters dangled down into the blackness. Hell Gate.

"It's not real," he whispered under his breath. "It's not real."

But then what was it?

He quickly pulled out his phone to take a picture. Photographs showed reality. Cameras couldn't hallucinate. The sun flared on the screen, making it impossible to see whether or not he was getting a good shot, but he stretched his arms out and aimed at the devil.

The shutter clicked.

A shudder ran through him as the devil dissipated, like a million little bubbles popping.

Evan rubbed his eyes and gripped the metal armrest of the bench. It was just an aquarium again. Just a rickety old boardwalk, a loose board squeaking beneath his nervously bouncing foot.

He stood up, turning away from the sun, and pulled the picture back up on his phone. Shielding the screen from the glare with a cupped hand, Evan stared into the image. No devil. No stairs. Nothing but children skipping up to the door and mothers pushing strollers and fathers pulling out their wallets so their families could admire marine animals.

He looked away from the screen and back at real life.

The scenes matched.

Of course they matched.

He smacked his palms against his cheeks and ran shaky fingers through his sweaty hair. He was losing his mind.

A passing woman pulled her toddler a little closer, so Evan tried to smile like a normal person. *Normal people don't see things that aren't there.*

But it had been so clear. So . . . real. Down to the sign. How could he have made that up, too?

Dreamland.

It did sound like the kind of place his subconscious would cook up while going haywire, but he needed to be sure. He Googled *Dreamland, New York Aquarium.*

Wikipedia was the first result: *Dreamland (1904 Amusement Park).*

He couldn't breathe as he clicked on the article. An amusement park used to be there, on the site of the New York Aquarium, but it burned to the ground in 1911.

Scrolling down, Evan's heart stopped, then throbbed against his ribs.

It was the angel.

The same angel he saw welcoming people wearing dark suits and dresses into the park. The caption labeled it as an exhibit portraying the biblical account of the first six days of creation, which opened onto Surf Avenue—exactly where he'd seen her. On the right side of the photo was a sign for Zeller's Coney Island Pharmacy and a banner advertising cigars at city prices. A sign for ice cream. Five cent sodas. A couple of parked bikes and crisscrossing electrical wires attached to poles.

She was real.

Not now, not anymore.

But over a hundred years ago, she was real.

He scanned the other photographs of Dreamland, skimming the captions.

Dreamland's Trained Wild Animal Arena.

Roltaire's Arabian Nights Theater.

The remains of the Balloon Swing.

And then at the bottom, *Hell Gate.*

That same devil's elbows draped over the top of the wall, bat wings outstretched. The same dangling letters spelled out *Hell Gate* beside a sign that read, *10 cents to ride.*

Evan read the caption: *Hell Gate, a boat ride through the caverns of hell, was the start of the Dreamland Fire in 1911. During late-night preparations for opening day, an electrical malfunction caused a black-out. A worker knocked over a bucket of tar in the dark, which immediately caught fire . . .*

He needed to sit down.

Crossing the boardwalk, which was still surprisingly crowded with late tourists, Evan found a bench and decided to take off his shoes. It had been a long time since he'd felt sand between his toes. Not since Atlantic City, when he'd spent hours on an intricate sand-castle while his mom and Bill fought over losing two thousand dollars at the casinos.

He walked down the seawall steps, holding the rail for balance. Staring out at the circling gulls, he let the cool tide wash up to his ankles, then rush back to the sea.

In, out. In, out.

This is real. This is now.

Reaching down, he cupped a little cool water in his hands, then splashed it onto his face. He just stood there for several minutes, listening to the rhythmic crash of waves on the shore. It reminded him of the background noise in his mother's yoga videos, the ones she did religiously after Bill left.

Breathe in.

Let the universe embrace you with its calm . . .

It wasn't working.

He had to get away from here.

When he finally reached the Neptune Gallery, he found a Closed sign hanging from the crystal doorknob. A poster on the display window announced that the exhibit had ended yesterday, and a new wave of panic crashed over his brain.

How was he going to finish his assignment? Did he have time to go to the Met, take three photos, and make three sketches before tomorrow? How was he going to pass Dr. Mortakis's class? Would she fire him as her office assistant if he couldn't complete his work? Would NYU send him home, back to high school? Would he ever see Mara again?

But as he glanced up at the gallery sign once more, he found exactly what he needed—Neptune's trident.

Relief chased the panic, leaving his knees weak. As he snapped a photo, he could hear his mom as clearly as if she were standing beside him. *The universe provides.* For once he didn't mutter *bullshit.*

Feeling like a wrung-out rag, Evan followed signs to the nearest station. The elevated train rocked in a comforting rhythm as it carried him uptown, and he used his backpack as a pillow and tried to even out his heartbeat.

Clearly, something was wrong with him.

Staring out the window at the tarry rooftops, spindly fire escapes, and sloppy graffiti of Brooklyn, he considered visiting the university's health clinic, but a rolling wave of dread washed over him.

This wasn't some run-of-the-mill hallucination he could blame on misfiring neurons or imbalanced chemicals or eating Grade F chicken.

He'd hallucinated history.

There was no scientific explanation for that.

No campus doctor would believe that he'd really seen the past. They'd refer him to a psychiatrist, who wouldn't believe him, either. And then there was the matter of filling out yet another family health history form. Did his father have high blood pressure or skin cancer? Obesity or psychosis? He hated that, for the rest of his life, he'd have to leave half the questions blank, letting death sneak up on him from behind.

He got off the train and walked slowly toward Washington Square. He wanted a cup of coffee, but he was afraid he looked as freaked out as he felt, so he wandered toward the fountains, where little kids splashed and played in the sun. He stood just close enough to feel a little of the spray, trying to slow his breathing.

The sun soaked into his black T-shirt as he started walking again, not sure where he was headed. He poked around in a few thrift shops in the Village but didn't buy anything. Thirsty and overheated, he decided to head back to his room, but found himself taking the long way, skirting around the Black Cat.

He rounded the corner and saw her hair.

Mara was sitting on a bench beside the dumpster, face in her hands, hair flopped forward. As she lifted her head, he saw that she was crying at the same instant she saw that he was looking.

"Hey," he said, closing the space between them as she hastily wiped her cheeks. "You okay?"

"Yeah," she said, running her index finger along the rim of her lower eyelid, checking for running mascara. "I'm fine. Sorry."

"What's wrong?"

"I just . . . I got this stupid voice mail from my mom. I mean, my ex-mom."

"Your . . . what?"

She huffed a sigh. "I was adopted, but she lied to me about it, and she keeps lying to me because that's just what she does, and it shouldn't even upset me anymore, you know? But she's . . . I'm sorry. This isn't your problem. It's just really embarrassing."

"It's okay," he said, as the true identity of X clicked into place. "Everybody has problems, you know?"

She sighed and ran her hands through her hair. "Here's the thing," she said, her eyes darting to his and then to her sneakers. "You're going to college early. You're a *promising young artist*. And you know what I am? I'm a high school dropout, sitting on a bench beside a dumpster, crying because my life is imploding."

"You want to go somewhere and talk?" he asked, tilting his head and trying to catch her eye again. She thought *she* wasn't good enough for *him*? That was a turn he wasn't expecting.

"I have to be back to work in about three minutes," she said, sniffing and rubbing at the corner of her eye again. "And anyway, you're probably thinking I need a therapist, not a date right now, huh?"

He sat down beside her.

"I'm *thinking*," he said, then paused, waiting for her eyes. "That I'd like to sit on this bench with you for about three minutes. Is that okay?"

She nodded and pressed her shoulder into his.

"What time is your shift over?"

"Nine."

"You want to hang out after?"

"I won't cry again," she said, laughing at herself as she nodded. "I promise."

"Despite my lumberjack appearance," he joked, pounding a fist on his chest like a caveman. "I'm a pretty good listener. And in touch with my sensitive side."

She laughed, and he felt a door opening. He didn't know why he'd painted her last year, or why he'd seen an extinct amusement park that afternoon, or what it all meant for the future or his mental health. But he did know that Mara wasn't crying anymore.

He couldn't go back and change the past, and he couldn't guarantee the future. But he could make Mara Cassidy smile for at least three minutes.

And that was something.

KINGS PARK ASYLUM

1911

IT WAS A hot and cloudless Sunday.

I was standing on the boardwalk, turning to show a group of knicker-wearing kids the ship on my back, when I looked up and saw Mary for the first time.

She was draped in golden cloth—a shimmering, rose-gold robe over a matching sequined leotard. Her dark hair was slicked into little ringlets and pinned up like a crown. She held her head high, walking the boardwalk like a goddess, as if Dreamland, and all the world, belonged to her.

She stopped for an apple fritter at the vendor across from me, and I felt a hot jab in the chest, like a poker fresh from the fire. It's her.

When she turned to walk away, I abruptly looked at the kids and said, "Sorry, show's over." I ignored the boy who said he wanted his penny back. It was her—the girl who kept dying in my dreams. I didn't know she was real. I didn't know she was alive. Though of course, I had hoped. Perhaps is full of hope. And foolishness. And wisdom, too. All of life is, perhaps.

Being a summer Sunday, the boardwalk was crowded enough that she didn't notice me. I followed her nearly to the park gates, where she stopped and looked up at a newly strung high wire. It stretched across the walk, above the heads of everyone entering Dreamland. She removed the golden robe and tossed it to a boy who held a rusted turquoise ladder.

I felt a moment's shame. She had no tattoos. There was not a single picture on her skin, nothing but freckles on her muscular shoulders. I couldn't bear the thought of her staring at me the way those boys had— like the spectacle I was.

The sequins of her leotard shining in the afternoon sun, she began to climb. The way her toes curled around the wire was miraculous. She put one foot in front of the other, easily walking over the heads of the crowd. I watched with my mouth open—she floated like a feather. Upon reaching the little platform on other side, she twirled and bowed to great applause. Then, on her return trip, she drew gasps—cartwheeling across the wire without loosening a single curl on her perfect head. I watched, mesmerized, as she stood on her hands, then slowly curved her back around until her toes were hooked around the wire and she was twisted like an upside-down pretzel. She smiled artificially at the applause, and then, suddenly, her eyes found mine.

Strikingly green—just like I'd dreamed them. I'd seen them through the window of a dirty little shack, and wide with surprise on the other side of a forbidden Door. I'd dreamed them in the rain, lined dark with made-up lashes. And here they were, lingering on mine, as if she thought perhaps she knew me from somewhere.

As if, perhaps, she wanted me to come closer.

She climbed down that turquoise ladder, and the crowd swallowed her up. I tried to catch her eye again, but a man came and whisked her away before I could push through the clot of tourists to follow her.

So I waited.

As the sky went from pink to indigo, framed by the gigantic white towers that marked the entrance to Dreamland Park, thousands of electric lights buzzed to life. Soon, the park would close and I would have no choice but to go home. But she must be here somewhere, I thought, so I wandered along Surf Avenue in hopes of meeting her gaze once more.

I edged along the Lilliputian Village, waving to the little people who lived there. Tom Thumb was parking his miniature firetruck, having put out at least ten pretend fires that day. Visitors to the park loved the miniature neighborhood, built to scale for the little people, and gawked at them as if they were animated dolls who existed for their amusement. But once the sun went down, they went about the ordinary business of cooking and sleeping, washing and loving. Tom offered me a wave as he hopped down from his truck, but I nodded and kept walking. I was running out of time, and besides, his wife would be wanting him home.

Farther along Surf, I stopped at a familiar building that rose above the boardwalk like a pop of pink sugar. The sign blinked on and off: "All the World Loves a Baby! The Hall of Life."

For twenty-five cents, anyone could go inside to see the rows of new-fangled incubators filled with infants born too soon. For twenty-five cents, even a boy covered in tattoos could visit the babies. It was the most expensive exhibit in the park—part spectacle, part medical facility. It bordered the Dreamland Freak Show and was funded by gawkers because the hospitals couldn't afford to care for babies so likely to die.

That night, I wandered through the Hall of Life, happy to see several of the little ones proving the hospital doctors wrong—and hoping to catch sight of Mary before going to buy a hot dog. At closing time, they were half price. Everyone who worked in the park could be found at the hot dog vendor after dark.

But not her. Not Mary.

Heavy with disappointment, I ate my hot dog slowly, savoring each bite as I walked toward the tattoo shop. Toward home.

And that's when I saw her again. She was walking the opposite direction, a sweater pulled round her lovely, proud shoulders. Instantly, I turned on my heel.

It was late. The lights buzzed with dying electricity and my skin tingled with anxiety. I was just a boy covered in tattoos; she was the goddess who walked in the sky.

But the shadows emboldened me. Clinging to the darkness, I followed her all the way to the animal arena. She walked past the horses and elephants, past the monkey cages, finally stopping before Captain Jack's great cats.

She was close enough to Black Prince's cage that he could have licked her fingers. She was close enough to smell the blood on his breath, and the lion looked at her, his amber eyes sad and wise and silent.

"You poor boy," she said, wiggling her fingers in front of his nose. I thought I heard him purr. "You don't belong here, bowing down to Captain Jack. You don't belong locked in a cage, jumping through hoops for stupid people who pay a nickel to watch. How'd you end up here? Hmm?"

In reply, he lowered his head. I watched her long fingers stroke his nose and forehead, envious.

"You know what I told myself when I left Seattle? I said, where other people break, I bend. Where other people fall, I fly." Here, she laughed ruefully. "But it never ends up the way we planned, does it? The truth of it is, we're both captives."

At her shaky exhale, I ventured forward. I cleared my throat, and she whipped her head in my direction. A low noise escaped from the throat of the lion, but she shushed him.

"What do you want?" she demanded.

I simply raised my hands and shook my head.

"Who sent you?"

"Nobody sent me," I assured her. "I'm Kieran Flynn, and I was just taking a walk, that's all."

She cocked her head and smiled sarcastically. "In the animal arena? After dark?"

"Same as you."

"Sure," she said, and a joyless laugh escaped her lips. "That's what they all say. Look, you're going to have to go through Mulligan like everyone else. If he catches you here—"

A key turned in the rusty lock of my memory . . .

A lock within a lock.

A door within a door . . .

Fitz Mulligan.

I knew that name.

I knew what he made her do.

She didn't just walk the tightrope. She didn't just wear pretty clothes to do gymnastics. There were men who wanted to know just how far she could bend. All kinds of men who would pay Fitz Mulligan for half an hour alone with her in the Tin Elephant hotel to find out.

Fitz Mulligan. I remembered his face: watery-white skin, like strips of paper dipped in paste for papier-mâché. Cigar-rotten mouth. Opium-dazed eyes. I'd seen him in my dreams, against a backdrop of flames.

"I have no business with Mulligan—or you," I said, and my head tingled as her gaze went sharp with suspicion. "Listen, miss, I don't want to hurt you. I want to help you."

"I can take care of myself, thank you very much." She moved to leave, adjusting her golden robe, then paused anxiously, as if expecting me to chase after her.

But I didn't move. I simply nodded and said, "Well, then, goodnight."

"Goodnight . . . Kieran Flynn," she said, and walked off into the darkness.

Alone with the great cat, I revisited the way she'd said my name. The way the ferocity left her voice after goodnight.

CHAPTER EIGHT

S HORTLY AFTER EVAN returned to his dorm room, it began
to drizzle. Tentatively, he read a little more about Dreamland
Park, looking at pictures on the internet and waiting for something weird to happen, but none of the images triggered him into hallucinating. *Hallucinating.* Was that even the right term for what had
happened to him? He looked up the medical definition of the word, trying to diagnose himself with something. Preferably something treatable.

According to HealthLine Online: *Hallucinations are sensory experiences that appear real but are created by your mind. They can affect
all five of your senses. For example, you might hear a voice that no one
else in the room can hear or see an image that isn't real.*

Okay. So, it was a hallucination. He saw something not real, not
there, that affected all his senses—

Except that what he saw really *was* there. It really *had* been real. It
just wasn't there anymore.

So, how would the internet diagnose a realistic sensory experience
of something that actually happened? Evan drummed his fingers on

his desk. That was basically just the description of a vivid memory, which was ridiculous because he wasn't alive to see it the first time around. Still, the concept intrigued him.

He searched: *Are vivid memories actually hallucinations?*

The first search hit was a scholarly articled entitled "Hallucinations as Trauma-Based Memory," and the abstract stated that Sigmund Freud argued hallucinations were actually a product of forgotten or repressed traumatic memories entering the conscious mind. Intense flashbacks, especially those associated with PTSD, were actually hallucinatory memories affecting all five senses.

Freud's theory would have made perfect sense if Evan had actually been alive in 1911 to witness the fire that started in Hell and destroyed Dreamland . . . but he was born approximately nine decades too late.

If this was a memory, it wasn't his.

And then, his skin prickled with goosebumps.

On loan from Taffy's on Surf. Circa 1911.

The boy in the photograph would have remembered what Dreamland looked like. He would have seen it the way Evan did.

The way Evan *remembered.*

Holding his breath, he typed another question into his search bar. *Can memories be passed down through DNA?*

The internet didn't provide a clear-cut answer, but he did find a few related scientific studies. He read an article explaining one study of lab rats who inherited phobias from their electroshock-conditioned grandparents. The first generation of rats were exposed to the scent of cherry blossoms every time they were zapped, but two generations and no shocks later, the baby rats were terrified of cherry blossoms.

Evan decided this was not only cruel and unusual, but also all the evidence he needed. If phobias could be passed down genetically, so could the memories of angels and demons and flames. It was a logical conclusion with supporting evidence.

It was weird, but it made sense.

A researcher might want to study him like a lab rat, and Freud certainly would have been intrigued, but at least he wouldn't call him crazy. Maybe just . . . interesting. Exceptional, like his mother had always insisted.

It was weird, but maybe it was also kind of awesome to be given an actual window into the past.

He felt connected to the tattooed boy in a way he didn't feel connected to his father. Like they shared something deep and important enough to transcend space and time. Like maybe he was trying to tell him something, trying to find him. It was comforting. And creepy.

The past is behind you for a reason.

He chose to focus on the comforting part.

Evan sat at his desk, staring out at the drizzle, wondering if the past was just an illusion. Tonight's rain would evaporate in tomorrow's sun, but it wouldn't really go away. It would just come back in a different form. If sixty percent of the human body consisted of water, maybe souls were made of water, too. Maybe the past was alive in everyone and everything, just waiting to go from gas to liquid. To become visible again.

<hr>

BY EIGHT THIRTY, when he opened his lucky umbrella to walk toward the Black Cat, it was pouring. The park was quiet, hushed by the steady rain. The sun went down imperceptibly behind a screen of clouds as Evan took his time, noticing the movement in the water. Spilling from leaves. Rushing through gutters. Slipping down windowpanes like beaded strings of liquid light.

Rounding the corner, he saw Mara through the glass of the Black Cat, and the light spread to his chest. She was wiping down tables in the glow of dangling Edison bulbs, and when she looked up, she smiled and motioned for him to come in.

"Almost finished," she said over her shoulder as he opened the door, jingling the little bell. And then he saw Nona, knitting at a table in the corner. The last customer.

"Hi Nona," he said, slowly walking toward her. "What are you working on there?"

"Gifts," she replied, without looking up. "For the babies."

Her knitting needles clicked faster. Her speed was incredible. Evan glanced to the floor at a wicker basket filled with tiny hats in every color of the rainbow.

"Do you have a lot of great-grandkids?" he asked.

"All babies are my grandchildren," she said, and he tried not to look at the hairs sprouting from her chin. He studied the basket, instead, and estimated there were at least thirty-five baby beanies.

"She's making hats for the preemies," Mara interjected, wiping down the table beside them. "We're going to deliver them to the NICU at Mount Sinai, right?"

Nona beamed at her, nodding, and dropped a completed pink hat on the top of her stack.

"That's nice," Evan said. "You know, I was a preemie. Six weeks early."

"It suits you." Nona scowled, picking up a skein of baby blue. *Click, click, click.* "Always arriving too soon."

Evan and Mara exchanged a look, stifling laughter.

"It's closing time," Mara said, resting a hand on Nona's shoulder. "I'll walk you up to your apartment, okay?"

Nona sighed and began gathering her knitting supplies. Mara hooked the basket handle around her right elbow, then offered her left to Nona.

"I'll just be a minute," she promised Evan, but he was sure Nona walked extra slow to spite him.

Fifteen minutes later, Mara reappeared. "Sorry. She was chatty."

"She sure likes you," he said. "Not that I can blame her."

"She's lonely." Mara waved the compliment off. "And I guess I kind of am, too."

She wiped Nona's table and flipped her chair upside down, then disappeared into the back room, where Evan could hear her saying goodnight to her manager.

She hung her apron on a peg behind the counter, then looked toward the window, scrunching her nose. "Sam took the umbrella. Again."

"Good thing I came prepared," he teased. "Again."

Together, they stepped into the muggy rectangle beneath the striped awning. He opened his umbrella, and she moved closer.

"So, where do you want to go?"

She shrugged, and her shoulder brushed his. "Are you in the mood for pizza?"

"I'm always in the mood for pizza."

"I know a good place about a block from here. Pie in the Sky," she said, and took an awkward step as her forehead bumped the metal prong of his umbrella. "Ouch."

"Here," he said, offering the handle to her, and she wrapped her fingers around it just below his so that her left index finger rested against his right pinkie. Together, they stepped into the downpour. She led him across Sullivan Street and to the left, skirting the saturated square and taking a right into a block Evan had not yet explored.

Warm, yellow light spilled from the window and was mirrored on the wet sidewalk as they approached Pie in the Sky. The smell of baking dough mingled with the sweetness of the rain, and he realized he was starving.

"You want pepperoni?" he asked, shaking the excess water from his umbrella before propping it against the red-and-white striped wall.

"How did you know?"

"Artists pay attention to details."

"Well, so do musicians, so make it half mushroom."

They walked up to the counter and gave their order to a large Italian man with two gold teeth. Pie in the Sky was a narrow, grease-shined restaurant with sticky floors and crumbs on the tables, like a hallway with mirrored walls offering an illusion of space. A few metal tables with wobbly chairs were arranged on the floor, but Evan and Mara headed for a pair of stools at the high-top counter affixed to the long wall.

"So," Evan said, "Do you think it's better to make eye contact in the mirror? Or to turn to the side when talking? What's the etiquette here?"

She held his eyes in the mirror, cocking her head thoughtfully, then spun on her stool to face him. "I like this better."

"Me, too." He grinned. "So, you ready for next week's show?"

She puffed her cheeks out and exhaled. "I think so. We've practiced these songs to death. We're as ready as we can be."

"How long have you guys been playing together?"

"Well, the band has a lot of history before me," she explained. "But until this summer, they were just a cover band. I mean, they were a great cover band with lots of gigs lined up, but no original songs."

"So they hired you to write?"

"Well, they hired me to drum, but then I started writing. Sam and I went to high school together in Florida—she was a senior when I was in ninth grade. She graduated and came up here, met Ben, and they formed the band. They had all these shows lined up and then their drummer quit last spring, so she called me, wanting to know if I'd come to the city for the summer to fill in. It was good timing because things were pretty bad at home, so I said yes. And then I just kind of . . . stayed." She fidgeted with the amethyst ring on her thumb. "School was supposed to start last week, but I didn't go back."

"Is that why your . . . ex-mom was calling?"

"Yes and no. It's a long story."

"I've got time," he said, swiveling a little on his stool so that his knee bumped hers.

She gave him a *you-might-regret-this* look before saying, "Okay, so last year, my appendix ruptured. My parents thought I was out on the anesthesia when the nurse asked about my family medical history, and my mom said, 'Her *birth mother* didn't leave any information.'"

"Oh, wow," Evan said. "What did you do?"

"Kept my eyes closed and listened while she made the nurse promise not to tell anyone—especially not me—that I was left in a Safe Haven in Tampa when I was just a few hours old. And that's when I opened my eyes and tried to sit up. I told them I heard everything, but my *mom*"—she paused to insert dramatic finger quotes—"played dumb. She said she didn't know what I was talking about, I must have had a bad dream, I was confused, I was sick, blah, blah, blah. The nurse just kind of slipped out, but my dad stood there nodding like her minion. It was ridiculous."

"He was in on it, too?"

She nodded. "But unlike him, that nurse wouldn't lie for her. Later that night, after they went home, she told me I'd heard everything correctly."

"That's wild," he said, as a tall server in a grease-stained apron unfolded a pizza stand behind them, followed by a short, sweaty guy carrying the tray.

"Mushroom or pepperoni?" the server asked Mara.

"Pepperoni for me. Oh, this smells amazing." She took a deep inhale, closing her eyes. "I haven't eaten since breakfast."

Evan quirked an eyebrow. "You work at a restaurant . . .?"

"It's way overpriced," she said, accepting a plated slice. She dabbed at the pepperoni grease with a napkin. "And you can only eat so many bagels. But pizza, on the other hand," she said, rolling her eyes back as she took a large bite.

"Never gets old," he agreed, serving himself a slice of mushroom. Every time he took a bite, he had to remind himself that this was really happening.

He was eating incredibly delicious pizza with the girl of his dreams, and as far as he could tell, he was both awake and alive.

"You have to try a bite of this," she said, offering him the point of her second slice of pepperoni. She held it while he took an awkward bite, then watched his face in anticipation while he chewed.

"That's good pepperoni," he said, keeping an eye on his teeth in the mirror in case they were full of oregano. He swallowed, then reached for a new slice of mushroom, which he held out to her. "But nothing compares to the fungus."

She gave him a doubtful look, then leaned in for a bite, her eyes meeting his while sinking in her teeth mock-seductively. As she pulled back, a long string of mozzarella came stretched between them, then broke and smacked her in the chin.

"I am so smooth," she said, turning red as he handed her a napkin.

"As smooth as the fungus itself," he said, tapping his own chin to show her where she'd missed a speck of sauce.

"Do you always compare your dates to pizza toppings?" she asked, snatching up the pizza from his plate and taking another bite.

"Only when I'm hoping for a second date."

She snorted, then covered her mouth with her hand while she finished chewing. "Okay, that is really good though."

Together, they polished off the entire pie, intermittently stealing toppings from each other's plates. When she returned from the soda fountain with a refill, he said, "So you never finished your story. What happened when you got home from the hospital? Did your parents finally fess up?"

Mara laughed ironically and shook her head. "Jill Cassidy is one of those people who are physically unable to admit they were wrong. She's like a fucking Donald Trump or something, and my dad turns off his brain and votes her for her every time. Honestly, it was a relief to find out I'm not related to her, but my dad? I still can't believe he lied to me all those years. Or that he chose her over me."

"You guys were close?"

"Yeah." Her eyes suddenly rimmed red and she swallowed hard. "He was like, my best friend. Took me to my first concert, bought me my first bra, made time whenever I needed to talk. But as soon as I started questioning her, he shut me down. It's like he's been controlled by her for so long, he actually believes her lies. She's made him forget he even *has* a choice."

"I went through something like that with my mom a while back," he said. "She had this fiancé who was a pathological liar. I tried to tell her, but she didn't want to believe me until she caught him red-hand-ed, stealing from us."

"Bet even then the son of a bitch denied it to the bitter end," she said with a snort.

"Yeah, actually," he laughed. "He did."

"Textbook narcissist," she said, shaking her head. "And trust me, I've read a lot of textbooks. The library's cheaper than therapy—especially when you don't have health insurance."

"I was just reading some interesting psychology articles this afternoon," he said, and he wanted to tell her. He wanted to look her in the eye—not just in the mirror, but face-to-face—and tell her he was exceptional. He could see the past, and wasn't that sexy?

He immediately panicked at the realization he'd even considered telling her that. A first date at a pizza shop in Greenwich Village was not the place to start talking about electro-shocked lab rats. He told himself to keep his mouth shut and his ears open.

"I was actually thinking about going to college to study psychology," Mara continued with a sigh, stacking their plates and gathering dirty napkins. "Or maybe writing."

"You're a great songwriter already," he said. "Even without college."

"Thanks." She picked up a half circle of pepperoni left on the pizza tray and popped it into her mouth, then started picking at some hardened cheese. "I guess I don't want you think that just because I dropped out of school I'm not . . . I don't know. That I'm not *smart*. I've been in honors classes since junior high, which is partly why my mom called this afternoon to inform me that I'm throwing my future away."

"I didn't think that," he said, lifting his palms. "Honest."

"Thanks. But the thing is, it's not even about *my* future. It's about *her* image," she continued, violently picking at the last burnt piece of cheese. "Which I don't give a shit about anymore."

"Hey, last I checked, college isn't the only path in the Game of Life," he said. "I mean, Richard Branson dropped out of school at sixteen to start Virgin Records, right?"

She finally looked up from the scratched-up pizza tray. "How did you know that?"

"I happen to have a vast amount of useless knowledge stored in my head."

"I will keep that in mind if we ever do a game night," she said with a smirk, and stacked the plates on top of the tray. "Well. Enough of my drama. Want to take a walk?"

He glanced toward the window, spattered with the still-steady rain. "Outside?"

"As long as you don't mind sharing your umbrella?"

He pulled a face of exaggerated annoyance, making her laugh as they strolled toward the park, pressed shoulder to shoulder, each with a hand wrapped around the umbrella handle. If not for the moisture in the air, his fingers would have caught fire.

"Just so you know . . ." He could feel her eyes on him, but he kept looking toward the Washington Arch, lit golden and shining with water. "I think you're very smart."

They stepped around a pedestrian walking a corgi wearing a miniature raincoat, and he shot her a sideways glance. She smiled.

They dodged a few more umbrellas, and then they were under the arch. It wasn't wide enough to keep them completely dry, especially since the wind was blowing sideways, but it was quiet. And they were alone.

"So I've never been to Pennsylvania," she said, leaning her back against the marble. "What's it like?"

"Depends on the town."

"*Your* town," she said, kicking at his sneaker with hers. "Duh."

"We actually moved a lot," he said, and leaned against the curve of the arch beside her. "For a little while, we lived in downtown Lancaster, but then we rented a farmhouse and I went to this little Mennonite preschool. Then Strasburg, then Lampeter, then Manheim Township. Every time my mom had a breakup, we moved again. If I stay at NYU till I graduate, four years in the same place will be a record for me."

"That really sucks."

He shrugged. "It led to my sister's existence, I guess. And mine. So it hasn't been all bad."

"How old's your sister?"

"Five. Here, I'll show you."

He handed her the umbrella, then reached into his back pocket for his phone. Quickly, he scrolled past the tattooed boy and was again pleased with himself for having the foresight to delete *The Green-Eyed Girl*.

When he showed Mara a picture of Hailey, all pigtails and summer freckles, she melted. "Oh my god, she's so cute! Do you guys have the same dad?"

"Nope. I'm a byproduct of Mardi Gras. He never returned her calls."

"Wow. What an asshole."

"Yeah. Hailey's dad stuck around a little longer, but she doesn't remember him like I do. Which is probably for the best, really. But it sucks, not knowing anything about half my DNA, you know?"

She nodded. "I've been thinking about trying to find my birth parents. I want to know, but I'm scared they're in prison or something."

"Remember that photo I showed you? From Coney Island?"

She nodded.

"I keep thinking he must be related to me—somebody on my dad's side."

"Are you going to look into it?"

"I don't know." He ran his hand through his hair, and his eyes followed the trunk of a towering elm all the way to the sky. Had the tattooed boy seen that tree? It would have been thinner and shorter in 1911, but it had to be well over hundred years old. Some of the trees in this park were pushing four hundred.

"I don't really need another asshole in my life," he said, sighing and watching the wet-black leaves dance and shimmer in the street-light. "But then sometimes I think, you know, people can change. And besides, your dad's side of the family isn't just your dad. It's a whole group of people. People who are part of you. So maybe knowing who they are would help me to know who I am."

"If you do it," she said, lifting her pinkie finger. "I'll do it."

"Deal," he agreed, hooking his smallest finger around hers.

They started walking again, headed nowhere in particular, com-paring the climates of New York and Pennsylvania and Florida. Their sneakers were soaked and their legs were gritty, but they walked and talked until Mara spotted an empty bench beneath the awning of a closed halal restaurant.

She sat closer than she had to, and the wrought-iron lamps spilled light worthy of an Edward Hopper painting. She reached into her purse to check her phone, and when the screen lit up, he thought she looked like the girl in *Automat*, holding a phone instead of a cup of coffee. All she needed was a green coat to go with those eyes.

"Sam's been texting me," she said, frowning. "Hang on."

"Everything okay?"

"Yeah. She was just worried because I didn't come home after work."

"Understandable."

She looked up from the screen and rolled her eyes. "It gets a little annoying sometimes. I wish they'd drop the whole 'band baby' thing."

"It's pretty adorable, really," he said, nudging his shoulder into hers as her thumbs moved swiftly over the screen.

"Well." She dropped her phone back into her purse. "It *is* getting late. I guess the park closes soon."

"Want me to walk you home?"

"I have to take the train. Our apartment's downtown a few stops."

"Yours and Samantha's?"

"And Ben's and Darren's and Gwen's. We all split rent on this two bedroom basement hole-in-the-sidewalk in Brooklyn. For two hundred a month, I get the couch."

"Is it a nice couch?"

"Nope."

"Well, I'd invite you to hang out at my place, but I have a roommate who likes to pretend he can't understand anything I'm saying."

"Ooh. Awkward."

"Yeah. But this has been really nice."

She smiled and stifled a yawn with the back of her hand. "Sorry . . . I've been up since, like, four."

"That's almost twenty-four hours."

He stood, pulling her up beside him, then shook the excess water from his umbrella before opening it again. They headed for the nearest metro station a few blocks away, and in the dim, brick shelter at the top of stairs leading underground, they hesitated.

"Thanks," she said. "For the pizza. And the umbrella. And the listening."

"Any time."

The lamplight glittered in her eyes, and he wanted to kiss her. The station was deserted, and the street was quiet except for occasional cab tires swooshing through puddles. She let go of his umbrella, but he didn't want her to leave.

"Take it with you," he offered.

"You'll get soaked!"

"No more than you."

"But I'm the dumbass who didn't check the weather. I deserve it."

"Did you ever consider," he said, leaning close to her ear. "That maybe I just want an excuse to see you again?"

She caught his free hand in hers, and he wanted to kiss her there, beneath his umbrella in the middle of New York City like some sort of modern day Gene Kelly, but he didn't want to close his eyes. People only looked at each other like that in the movies and perfume commercials—not real life. Not for long.

Slowly, she slid her fingers away from his until only the tips were touching, then paused.

"I'm going to miss my train," she whispered, tugging at his fingertips with hers.

He tugged back. "Okay."

She let go, but then, on impulse, she went up on her toes and gently brushed her lips against his. She pulled back a few tentative inches, asking the question with her eyes. *Is this okay?*

Yes, he answered, pulling her close with his free arm, balancing the umbrella precariously above them. *Absolutely.*

She hurried to catch her train then, and Evan stood on the sidewalk in the rain, still dizzy from that kiss as he watched her go.

KINGS PARK ASYLUM

1 9 1 1

NIGHT AFTER NIGHT, I watched the men come and go. It took me some time to gather the courage to intrude on the cat's lair again.

"What do you want?" she asked, looking around the animal arena while the great cat eyed me. "Why do you keep following me?"

"Because . . . I can listen as well as a lion?" I ventured, and she laughed. "Maybe even better?"

She reached out to pet Black Prince's nose. "I doubt that very much. Look, I told you, you're going to have to go through Mulligan—"

"That's not why I'm here."

She rolled her eyes, then turned back to the cat.

"You're left-handed," I said.

"So?"

"So. That's unusual."

"Out of all the strange things in this place, Kieran Flynn, you call that unusual?"

She was trying not to laugh, and I was trying to keep up with the images flooding into my mind. They were sad and familiar, blurred by time, and all I really wanted to do was bring that laugh to the surface. To hear it bloom.

I began pacing around, kicking at clumps of loose straw on the floor. "Once upon a time," I began slowly, "women were hung as witches for being left-handed."

She gave me the strangest look, her fingers trembling on the cat's nose. "How do you know that?"

I shrugged. "My mind overflows with useless knowledge."

"Well, I've endured enough slaps on my left wrist to believe it," she said, and snorted. "When I was a little girl, my teachers said I couldn't write with my left hand because I'd smudge the ink all over the page and turn my hand black, and nobody would be able to read the words. They said the world was made for right-handed people, so I'd better learn my place in it."

"So did you learn to use your right?"

"No," she said, eyes glittering with mischief. "I ran away from school. I sat up in my favorite tree with paper and pencils and wrote whatever I wanted."

I laughed at the thought of her, pencil in hand, legs dangling down from the boughs of an elm. "And your parents let you skip school and write stories up in the trees?"

A dark cloud floated over the green sea of her eyes. "Do you think I'd be here if they had?"

"Well, my father is a wonderful storyteller, and he isn't afraid of a little ink," I said with a gentle laugh, then stretched out my own, tattooed, left hand. "It was him who made me what I am."

"And your mother?" she asked, rubbing the great cat's flank and making him purr. "What does she think of . . . what you are?"

"I couldn't rightly say, as she died bringing me into this world."

"I'm sorry," she said sadly. "I never knew my mother, either. But my father always said she was strange. Like me."

"I don't think you're strange."

"*Do you need glasses?*" *She laughed, suddenly twisting her body into a truly unnatural pose that made me laugh, too. She straightened her spine, then sat down a little closer to me than she'd been before. "People come here to look at us because it makes them feel good about themselves. They might be too fat or have a boring job or a nasty landlord, but at least they have the correct number of legs, you know? At least God loved them enough to make them full-sized and right-handed."*

"*Looking at you doesn't make me feel good about myself at all,*" *I admitted.*

"*Oh?*" *she laughed, taken aback. "And why is that?"*

"*Because surely someone as lovely as you could never care for someone as strange-looking as me.*"

She leaned a little closer to examine the pictures on my arms. My breathing stopped. My skin blazed.

"*These are quite beautiful, actually,*" *she said, pointing toward the delicate wings of my blue butterfly. "Can you tell me what they mean?"*

One by one, I explained the images my father had wrought upon my skin, telling her the stories he'd told me. And night after night, little by little, she explained to me how she'd found herself in the employ of the notorious Fitz Mulligan.

Once upon a time, she said, when the circus left town, a baby girl was left for dead on the steps of the mortician, who took her as his own and discovered she was no easy pet to tame.

The town was called Seattle, and the girl was called many things, but the mortician called her Mary and gave her the task of replacing pints of cold blood with formaldehyde and applying rouge powder to dead-white faces.

He told her never, ever to show her strength, for this was unbecoming of a lady. But at night, when she thought nobody was looking, she climbed and twirled in the moonlight. She wrote smudgy stories in the trees, then flipped down to cartwheel over the lawn. But in the morning, peeking children called her monkey, monster, ghost. Selfish people smacked her hands and broke her heart, so, she ran from this town, this false father, to join the circus in hopes of finding the strange, strong woman who'd left her to die.

But she did not find her mother.

She found trouble, instead.

Yes.

Mary met a man who made promises—promises he never planned to keep. Fitz Mulligan said he would help her find her mother, but she found herself as one of his small collection of traveling oddities, instead:

Ingrid, whose chin sprouted thick, reddish hair.

Natsuko and Noyuri, twins joined at the skull.

The Alligator Man, whose skin was diseased with scales and whose teeth had been sharpened to points.

Nephi, the Mermaid Girl, who wore a prosthetic fin and splashed passersby with her webbed fingers.

And then there was Taffy, the Incredible Stretching Girl.

I just listened. I did not touch her. Not even when tears shone in her eyes, because I'd promised I wouldn't.

Not unless she asked.

And she didn't ask.

Not yet, anyway.

I didn't tell her what I saw or what I knew. I didn't tell her that the park was going to burn one day, that there'd be a gun and a scream and a stiff sea breeze blowing sparks and ash. I didn't tell her because I wasn't going to let it happen.

Perhaps now you are thinking these are the words of a lunatic, after all. So let me tell you something. I saw you just this morning while I was milking a cow. Yes, here at Kings Park they put us to work. We're self-sufficient, growing our own food, weaving our own cloth, producing our own electricity. The doctors have made it so that we never have to leave—

As if we had a choice.

At dawn this morning, I was milking the cow because the doctors say that repetitive work like squeezing milk from udders grounds the senses in reality. However, repetitive work is also quite boring, so I fell asleep. I began to dream. And I'll tell you what I saw: your reality.

Both the girl and the city had changed from my time to yours. She wore black lace and had deep purple in her hair, making her eyes all the more green, and you walked through Manhattan—through a lush park lit with cast-iron lanterns that glittered in the pouring rain.

I know the place. They call it Washington Square. First a burial ground for the poor of the city. Then a Tammany parade ground, and finally a park crafted to celebrate the patriotism of George Washington. I saw you walk beneath the marble archway that I know so well, and I could almost feel the sparks flying between you.

The university had grown, laying claim to the old Triangle Shirt-waist Factory. A placard labeled it the Brown Building now—a place to train young scientists, yes? You walked right past this building, but you only had eyes for her.

Sometimes I wonder, why didn't I know this factory would burn? Why did I only foresee Dreamland burning, not the poor girls leaping out of the flaming windows to their deaths? Could I have prevented it, had I known?

These are the thoughts that torment me here: what might have been.

The dreams and visions, as you have surely come to know, are a curse. When our eyes are open, the world changes before us to show us the past. In sleep, we see terrible things to come.

We are being punished.

But by whom?

And for what?

This, Reader, I do not know. For if there was a heaven above, and a good god in it, Mary's heart would be beating still.

CHAPTER NINE

WHEN HIS PHONE rang, Evan was sitting at the counter at the Black Cat, explaining RBG color theory to Mara. Instead of finishing his essay for English Composition, he'd spent the morning working up a simple, recognizable logo for Switched Flip—a single lightbulb encapsulating a photograph of meadow and sky—and then inverted the colors.

Just as he'd hoped, she both loved it and had questions. Had he taken the photo himself? What made him decide to turn the grass purple and the sky yellow? Excitement buzzed under his skin as he pulled up a color wheel to explain the science behind photographic negatives, why you can stare at a red dot then close your eyes and see a green afterimage, and why Mara's hair dye was scientifically optimal for bringing out the green in her eyes.

"The meadow is pinkish purple because when you invert the colors in an image, all the greens turn shades of magenta," he was explaining as his phone began vibrating on the counter beside his laptop. "And reds invert to cyan. Hang on—it's my mom."

"Hey," he said, squeezing the phone between his ear and his left shoulder so he could keep his right index finger on the touch pad, continuing to adjust the saturation. "What's up, Mom?"

"Where *are* you?"

"Umm, I'm at the Black Cat Café. Why?"

"I've got a surprise for you!" There was something weirdly enthusiastic in her voice. His stomach plummeted and his jaw tightened. He knew that tone.

"What's his name?"

"Goddard," she said, and he blinked at the deepening yellows of the sky on his screen as she started laughing. "Goddard *Hall*."

"Okay, you're making no sense."

"Hailey and I are in Goddard Hall, knocking on your door, and you're not answering."

"You're here? In New York? Right now?"

"Surprise!"

Evan caught Mara's eye over the counter, and she raised her eyebrows in concern. He gave her a thumbs-up, then closed his eyes and exhaled slowly.

"Hello-o?" his mom said, singsong, and he could hear Hailey whining in the background. "Are you there?"

"Yeah," he said. "Yeah, I just . . . why didn't you call ahead?"

"Because surprises are fun!"

For you.

"Okay, okay. Give me a couple minutes. I have to gather up my stuff and walk back."

He hung up and clicked to save the design before flipping his laptop closed.

"Everything okay?" Mara asked, glancing up from the bakery case.

He nodded, shifting his book bag onto his shoulder. "My mom and sister decided to visit unannounced."

"They're here now?"

He rolled his eyes. "I've got to go."

As soon as he climbed the landing and rounded his corner of Goddard Hall, Hailey spotted him. She squealed and ran full speed ahead. Evan squatted down and opened his arms, scooping her up. She smelled like Sour Patch Kids and baby shampoo, and when she squeezed his neck into a mini choke hold, he really was happy to see her.

Their mom hung back, smiling adoringly at them until he put Hailey's feet back on the floor.

"You look good," she said, pulling him into a hug and rocking him side to side. "You smell good, too. Were you at *her* café? Hmm?"

"Uh, yeah," he answered, patting her back before pulling free of her arms. He reached into his pocket for his keyring, then pushed it into the knob. "So, are you guys here for the day?"

"I found a great weekend deal at the Best Western on Coney Island."

Flinching, he swung the door of his room open. "Coney Island?"

"You were talking about it the other day, and I realized I'd never been there," his mom said, stepping into the room and taking in the boy mess. "And then once Hailey found out there was an aquarium? Well. You know how much she likes fish."

Not good.

"There are sea lions!" Hailey exclaimed, suddenly bouncing on Henri's bed. "They let you feed the sea lions!"

"You can't jump on there, Hails," Evan said, gritting his teeth and pointing to the pile of blankets and books on his bed. "That one's mine, remember?"

Hailey obediently climbed down and walked across the room to Evan's bed, where she stood and started jumping on his pillow, still wearing her worn purple Velcro sneakers.

He cringed, knowing those shoes had just been in the gutters of New York.

"I already bought the tickets," his mom continued, fishing in her purse for the printouts. "The Aquatheater show is at two, so we thought we could grab an early lunch with you and then hop on the train. Okay?"

Evan stared at the tickets in her hand. *Three.* There were three. Instead of finishing the logo for Switched Flip and asking Mara if she wanted to hang out after her shift, he was going to have to ride the subway with a five-year-old and attend a sea lion show.

"Did it occur to you that I might already have plans?" he said, flaring his eyes at his mother.

She lifted an eyebrow. "Do you?"

He sighed and began picking up dirty laundry from the floor. "Not exactly."

"Do you want to invite a friend?" she asked, as if he were the five-year-old. "I'll buy another ticket."

He opened his mouth to say *no* just as Hailey bounced from her feet to her bottom, knocking a stack of books onto the floor and screaming in alarm.

"Okay, enough!" his mom exclaimed, marching over to Hailey and lifting her from the bed to the floor. "Did you hurt yourself?"

Hailey shook her head and pouted.

"I know you had to sit in the car for a long time, but you're driving me crazy!"

Hailey started to cry. She always cried if someone yelled at her, and Evan felt another pang of guilt for leaving them alone together.

"You will settle down and behave like a big girl at lunch, do you understand me?"

She wailed.

"Let's make a new Kitty-Corn adventure at the restaurant, okay?" Evan shouted over them, rummaging through his desk drawers for some scrap paper and a Sharpie. Hailey quieted. "There's a good pizza place about two blocks from here."

"We're going to lunch," his mom said sternly, then gave Evan a *this-is-final* look over her shoulder before turning back to Hailey. "At your brother's girlfriend's café."

❊❊❊

HE SENT MARA a warning text, knowing she probably wouldn't see it. Saturdays were crazy busy, and her phone was technically supposed to be in her bag, anyway. His mom had threatened Hailey with no dessert for life if she said a word about Evan's paintings, but he sweated the entire way to the Black Cat. All it would take was one honest sentence, one look at his mom's photo gallery, and Mara would be history.

"This place is so cute," his mom kept repeating as they waited in line to order. Evan could see her checking out every girl in the place, trying to find one with green eyes, but Mara wasn't there. Maybe she'd gotten his warning text, after all, and run for the hills.

Hailey reached her arms up, asking to be held, so Evan hoisted her onto his hip. "What do you want to eat?" he asked. "They have pretty good mac and cheese."

"That," Hailey said, pointing at the bakery case. "The purple one."

Evan smiled at the cake pop. "Okay, but you've got to eat real food first."

She hugged him around the neck, squishing her cheek against his, and the customers in front of them paid and stepped out of the way.

"What can I get for you?" the jet-black mullet guy working the register asked, and Evan's mom began rattling off their order. All the while, he could see her scanning the back room.

Nona was in her usual spot, knitting furiously beside a half-drained cup of tea, so Evan led his mother and sister to a table at the opposite side of the café. Glancing toward the basket beside Nona's feet, he saw twice as many tiny hats and remembered that today was the day Mara was helping her deliver them to the NICU.

Evan pulled a few sheets of paper out of his bag and began sketching Kitty-Corn for Hailey. He could feel his mother's eyes boring into his forehead, and even though he tried to ignore her, he felt his own irritation rising.

"What?" he said finally.

"Where is she?" she whispered.

He shrugged and bugged his eyes. "Probably out on break. I don't know. I don't have her microchipped."

She pursed her lips.

"Maybe if you had let me know you were coming, we could have made actual plans." He broke eye contact with her and went back to the cartoon cat.

And then, he heard his sister gasp.

"She's real!" Hailey exclaimed, pointing a finger toward the back door, where Mara was coming in from the sunshine.

"Well," his mother said. "So she is."

Evan grabbed Hailey's hand and pulled it down below the table. With a warning look, he whispered, "Cake pop."

She clapped her hand over her mouth.

Mara caught his eye across the café and waved before picking up a tray loaded with macaroni and cheese, a BLT, and whatever premium sandwich his mom had ordered.

She added a cheese Danish and the cake pop, then brought it to their table.

"Hi," she said. "Order for Melissa?"

Evan stood. "That's us. I mean, that's her," he gestured awkwardly toward his mother. "Mom, this is Mara. Mara, this is my mom. Melissa."

Mara met Melissa Kiernan's eyes and smiled with perfect composure. "It's nice to meet you," she said, then set the dish of the macaroni and cheese in front of Hailey. "And you must be Hailey."

Hailey beamed and nodded enthusiastically.

"I've heard a lot about you," Mara added, offering the purple cake pop on a tiny white plate. Hailey shoved it into her mouth before Evan could stop her.

"Purple's my favorite color!" she said, with her mouth full.

"Mine, too," Mara whispered with a wink, then passed out the rest of their food. "Let me know if you need anything, okay?"

Evan tried to thank Mara with his eyes for not running away.

Once she was safely out of earshot, taking orders behind the counter, his mom said, "Well, you weren't exaggerating."

"You didn't believe me?"

She nodded and took a bite of her asiago, basil, and cucumber sandwich. "Of course. Just . . . wow. You really weren't kidding. She seems very sweet, honey. Very nice."

"I'm a good judge of character, remember?" he said, then clenched his jaw. Had she really shown up unannounced just to steal a look at Mara? To try to decide whether or not she was good enough for him?

He glanced toward the counter and sighed. He just had to get through a sea lion show without losing his temper with his mom or seeing the gates of hell.

⤞❧⤝

ON THE TRAIN, Hailey bounced from her mother's lap to her brother's. Evan wrapped his arms around her belly and rested his chin between her high pigtails, looking out the window as the city rushed by.

The train slipped underground and went dark, and Hailey clung to his neck. She shoved her thumb into her mouth and whimpered, curling up and making herself small. He hugged her close and it took him back to when she was even smaller.

He remembered trying to rock Hailey back to sleep while their mother and Bill yelled at each other in the kitchen of Bill's double-wide trailer. She was just six months old, then, and Evan was only twelve, but he remembered the way she watched him—those baby blue eyes searching his for comfort. For answers. So he held her against his chest and hummed, his changing voice cracking every few notes. The vibration was enough to calm her, though, because she didn't understand the words her parents were saying to each other, or that they'd soon need to find a new place to live, or that she'd probably never see her father again. But Evan had seen this coming. He'd anticipated it long before hearing the rev of Bill's truck engine and squinting against the flash of headlights through the bedroom window as he drove away, before Hailey wailed at the clatter of breaking glass as their mom threw dishes at the cabinets and swore.

Finally, Melissa had stopped throwing things and started crying, too. Evan changed Hailey's diaper, snuggled her close, and hummed some more, rubbing her back as her eyes drifted closed. And after he laid her in the crib with her tiny thumb in her mouth, he tiptoed out to the kitchen and swept broken glass into the dustpan. He brought his mom a box of tissues and let her cry.

He'd cleaned up mess after mess for her. Loaded truck after truck and moved furniture upstairs and down. He'd taken Hailey to dance class every Friday night for the last two years without a complaint. And now, she had the nerve to spy on him? To invite herself to the Black Cat and buy aquarium tickets with the assumption he'd just do as he was told? And then, his anger turned toward himself. He'd done just that. He'd walked them through Washington Square. He'd gotten on this train. He hadn't even put up a fight.

"You don't need to be scared of the dark," his mom was saying to Hailey, pulling up candy-colored cartoons on her phone. "You're a big girl now. Come on. Sit up."

But Hailey buried her face deeper against Evan's neck and shook her head.

"It's okay, buddy," he whispered to her. "We're almost out of the tunnel, and then we're going to have lots of fun. Promise."

When she nodded, her pigtails tickled his nose.

As the train rose to daylight in Brooklyn, her small body relaxed, but every muscle in Evan's body clenched. Adrenaline readied him for a fight or a flight, but he wasn't sure which one would come first. He wasn't going to let his mom run his life anymore, and he'd find the right moment to tell her so, even if she got mad. But soon, their train would stop at West Eighth Street, New York Aquarium. In a few minutes, he would be entering a tunnel of his own, and he wasn't sure what would be on the other side.

They got off the elevated train at West Eighth Street, pausing on the skywalk to gaze out over Luna Park and Riegelmann Boardwalk. From that height, they could see all the way to the ocean.

"Look at the roller coaster!" Hailey exclaimed, pointing toward the whooshing wooden Cyclone across the street. "Can we ride it?"

"You're not tall enough for roller coasters yet, Hailey-Boo," their mom said, reaching for her hand. "Sorry, baby."

"There's a carousel at Luna Park," Evan whispered, taking Hailey's other hand. "Maybe we could ride it later."

He instantly regretted offering to spend more time on the boardwalk. What if reality washed away before his eyes all over again? Would he be able to act normal enough to hide it from his mom? On a different day, under different circumstances, he might have tried to explain it to her. *You always said I was special . . .*

She would believe him.

She always believed him.

He felt a stab of guilt for being so angry with her. If she hadn't believed in his talent so strongly, he'd still be living in her house. He'd still be going to high school, still feeling like *this* every day of his life. He hadn't realized just how different he felt here, in such a short time. He owed this new beginning, and the freedom and possibilities that came with it, to his mother. And yet, she was the whole reason he needed a new beginning in the first place.

He wanted this city—and Mara—to be his alone.

Evan kept his eyes on his feet, playing jump-over-the-cracks with Hailey along Surf Avenue past the smooth, white facade of the Terazo Lounge, smelling the coffee wafting from the open door of a Starbucks as they approached the crosswalk.

"Surf Avenue," his mom said, tipping her chin toward the street sign as they waited for the signal to walk. "Isn't this where you saw that photograph?"

"No," Evan answered, his chest constricting. "It was on Neptune."

The light changed, and they hurried between the cars paused in the intersection.

"We should stop by after the sea lion show," his mom said, stepping up onto the curb.

"Stop by where?"

"The art gallery. I'd like to see the photo."

He stopped walking and pinned her with his eyes. "Why?"

She shrugged oddly and turned, tugging both of her children behind her on the uneven sidewalk, past a row of parked box trucks and industrial dumpsters toward the aquarium. Threading between rows of cars in the parking lot, his ears burned. What was she up to? First, Mara, now the gallery? He wasn't in the mood to play her games. If she were visiting him, she should have to play by his rules here.

Running his fingers along the rungs of blue fencing like guitar strings, he followed a few paces back. His mom had told him that the past was behind him for a reason and to let the whole thing drop, but he was more certain than ever that he couldn't do that.

And he was sure, now, that he didn't want to.

Staring up at the aquarium's entrance, he found himself willing the angel to appear. Every time he blinked, he was ready to open his eyes to a different scene entirely. He wanted to learn something—something he could keep from his mother, because she wasn't the only one holding the keys to his family history anymore. All kinds of information could be encoded in his DNA, and now, all he needed to do was lean into the connections and remember for himself.

He was ready . . .

But nothing happened.

They passed beneath what used to be angel's wings, showed their prepaid tickets, and strolled into an enormous room made of water and glass. Sea creatures surrounded them on all sides, so close and plentiful it was like scuba diving without an air tank. Hailey pressed her palms against the thick glass, but Evan said, "Look up."

Even the curved ceiling was made of glass. Above their heads, a school of black-and-white striped fish with electric-blue tails darted in synchronization, flying like water birds. He lifted her onto his shoulders, then held fast to her hands so she wouldn't topple backward. The entire watery chamber glowed blue, punctuated all around with pops of yellow, orange, and pink coral and flickering with snatches of scales in every color of the rainbow.

"Oh, God, it's one thirty, already!" his mom said, checking her phone. "We'd better head toward the Aquatheater."

She hurried them through the hands-on coral reef and past the glowing jellyfish tanks. Room after room, tank after tank was filled with captives. Evan thought about the people who used to live and work here—the people whose portraits he'd seen at the Neptune Gallery. Was this how they felt as people hurried past them, stealing glances at their unusual shapes and colors?

He thought about the "monkey girl," her skin completely covered in thick hair, and tried to imagine how she got here. Had she chosen to be on display, to use her condition to her own financial advantage, or was this her last resort?

Had someone seen her as an opportunity to make money and brought her here against her will? That's the only reason any of these creatures were here today—the jellyfish, the otters, the penguins, the sea lions. They were all part of someone else's plan. Here for someone else's enjoyment, with no idea that the freedom of the Atlantic was only a block away.

The thought made him claustrophobic.

They arrived at the open-air Aquatheater twenty minutes early and were lucky to find an empty bench in the splash zone. Evan went in first, followed by his mom, who instructed Hailey to sit on the end for the best view. Evan rested his elbows on his knees, face in his hands, and took a deep breath.

"You okay?" his mom asked.

He didn't open his eyes. "Not especially."

"I'm sorry," she said softly. "I should have called."

"Mm-hmm."

"You're mad."

Evan sighed and sat up straight. He rubbed his face, then turned to her. "What are you really doing here, Mom?"

Now it was her turn to sigh. She drummed her fingers on her crossed legs and frowned. Hailey was fully absorbed in watching the trainers set up for the show, but his mother lowered her voice anyway. "I haven't been completely honest with you," she said, uncrossing and recrossing her legs. "About your father."

"Okay." A tingle spread from his neck to his shoulders. "I'm listening."

She looked away, toward the animal trainers carrying pails of fish. "He did call."

"What? When?"

"While I was pregnant with you. And after you were born. He called a lot, actually."

"Why didn't you tell me?"

She exhaled, long and slow. "Because he called from the hospital. The *psychiatric* hospital."

Suddenly, carnival music blared through the speakers. Evan's hands flew to his ears reflexively, but he quickly lowered them, his face hot.

"Psychiatric hospital?" he repeated, but his voice was drowned out in the music and applause as the trainers took their places at the edge of the pool.

"Ladies and gentlemen, welcome to the New York Aquarium's Aquatheater!" a wet-suited woman said into her headset, and her voice reverberated through the speakers. She raised her hands, and two sea lions popped up out of the water. Hailey clapped and laughed.

Evan's mom leaned closer. "He was a paranoid schizophrenic," she said, and he could smell the mint in her gum. "I didn't know it at first."

"Did you really meet him at Mardi Gras? Or was that a lie, too?"

Out of the corner of his eye, he could see that the words stung.

"We *went* together," she said, staring straight ahead and blinking too fast.

"So it was a lie."

Clenching on her gum, his mother's jaw flickered. She cocked her head, agreeing halfway. "It's not that simple."

"We're going to need three volunteers from the audience!" the lead trainer announced from the diving board, and game-show music started playing through the speakers as hands shot up all over the Aquatheater. Hailey wiggled in her seat, practically falling into the aisle as she waved her hand in the air. Evan glared at his mom.

"Why didn't you tell me?" he hissed.

"I just . . ."

"She picked me!" Hailey suddenly squealed. "Mommy! She picked me!"

"Go on up, honey," their mom said tensely, nudging Hailey to her feet. "I'll, um, I'll take a video."

"I'm scared," she said, reaching her hands toward Evan. "I don't want to go by myself."

"Your brother will go with you. I'll take the video."

"Why don't you go," he said through clenched teeth. "I'll just hang on to your phone for you. In case somebody calls."

His mom pressed her lips into a thin line. "All right. Let's go, Hailey."

"I want Evan!" She wiggled her fingers toward him, pleading. "Please? Please? Please?"

He relented.

"Come on," he said, gritting his teeth and shooting his mom a look. He stood and led his sister poolside, then took a few steps back to let her take center stage. As the trainers demonstrated hand motions and offered her the bucket of fish, Evan's gaze remained fixed on his mother. Her phone was out at arm's length, taking a video he knew Hailey would show her whole kindergarten class. All eyes were on them, so he tried to look pleasant. Every time Hailey turned around to gauge his reaction, he gave her a thumbs-up.

But he felt like he was drowning.

As the syllables of *paranoid schizophrenic* crashed like choppy waves over his head, he thought of Mara in her hospital bed, hearing the words *birth mother* for the first time. The afternoon sun was intense, and he wished he hadn't worn black. He wished someone would turn the music down. He wished the trainer hadn't picked his sister. That he hadn't come here at all.

Finally returning Hailey to her seat, Evan told his mother, "I'll meet you outside."

"Where are you going?"

"I need a minute."

"*Evan—*"

"No, Mom. You had seventeen years. You're going to give me a minute."

Weaving through the bleachers toward the exit, his face was burning. He didn't know where he was going, but he found himself out on the boardwalk, where he'd seen Hell Gate. He turned his back on the aquarium, eyes stinging, and crossed to the sand. He didn't want to see Hell Gate, now.

With a huff, he sat on the seawall and kicked off his shoes, letting his feet dangle and his head fall into his hands.

Paranoid schizophrenic.

His father saw things and heard things that weren't there.

Like father, like son.

His heart was in his throat, but he *knew* he hadn't made it up. What he had seen here wasn't just some commonplace hallucination. It was history.

Another thought struck him. What if his dad had seen real things, too, but nobody had believed him? What if he'd seen the very same angel and demon, but instead of being labeled *exceptional*, he was labeled *crazy*?

As his phone buzzed with texts from his mom, he felt as if the air itself was closing in on him. Why the hell had she decided to tell him now? Why hadn't she just told him in eighth grade when he'd started that pathetic internet search and wrote letters to the newspaper? After all the messes he'd cleaned up for her, all the nights he'd put Hailey to bed, all the mac and cheese dinners he'd cooked while she worked late, how could she tell him at a fucking sea lion show?

His phone buzzed again, and he groaned before glancing at the screen.

But this time, it wasn't his mom.

It was a picture of Mara and Nona on the subway, holding the basket of rainbow baby hats, with the caption *Chillin' on our way to the NICU.* Nona's face was stretched into such a wide grin, her nose hooked down over her bristly top lip. Her head rested against Mara's, and Mara was smiling, too, leaning her head against Nona's as if they really were family. As if Nona didn't scowl at everyone in the world but her. He felt the hint of a smile creeping in as he typed.

You are the chosen one.

She sent an angel emoji wearing a halo, just as another text buzzed in from his mom. *Taking H to the coral reef. Meet us there?*

He ignored it, toggling back to Mara's window, which was blinking with an incoming text.

How's the aquarium?

Not great.

You okay?

Not really.

He watched the three little dots blink, showing that Mara was typing, then stop, then blink, then stop.

Please tell me your family is okay?

Yeah. Everybody's okay. But my dad's in a mental hospital.

What?

My mom lied. He didn't disappear. He has paranoid schizophrenia.

WTF? She knows where he is?

She did, anyway. I don't know all the details bc I walked out . . . she told me in the Aquatheater and I was mad and I just needed to breathe.

She told you in the Aquatheater?!?!

At a sea lion show.

That's lame.

Yeah. Sorry. I shouldn't be telling you all this now.

You're busy with Nona and the baby hats.

You know I understand.

I know. Still. Sorry.

Don't be. Call me tonight when you're free?

Okay.

You're more than your DNA, okay?

Okay.

But also, genetically speaking, you've got some great assets.

You think so?

I like your eyes.

I like your eyes, too.

And you've got a great smile.

You're stealing all my lines.

I like your elbows.

LOL.

And I've been fantasizing about your ankles.

Well, I like the space between your front teeth.

We should really make plans to discuss this further. In person. ASAP.

Idk how long this will take with my mom.

But plans will be made.

I'll be thinking about your elbows.

He smiled and closed his eyes, wishing everything else in the world would go away.

And then, it did.

His eyes flew open as the sensation of rushing backward overwhelmed him.

Flash—

Flash—

Stop.

The sun was gone.

He was gagging on a cloud of smoke. Flames shot into the night sky like rockets. People were running frantically toward the sea as the sound of frightened animals jumbled with anguished voices.

And then, the lion roared.

In confusion and terror, the crowd parted, everyone running backward to get out of the way. Through the smoke, the beast came running toward the water tossing his head and crying out in pain. His mane was on fire, and the faster he ran, the brighter it burned. His sides were lacerated, shining with fresh blood, and as the lion cried out again, Evan's heart broke.

Black Prince.

The name dropped into place like a puzzle piece.

KINGS PARK ASYLUM

1 9 1 1

"DID IT HURT?" Mary asked, jutting her chin toward my arm. I was sitting on the floor across from her in the animal arena, wearing a button-down shirt with the sleeves rolled up. She was staring at my skin.

"You get used to it." I shrugged, remembering those hours my father spent telling me stories. *"Some areas are easier than others."*

"What does it feel like?" Her eyes were wide in the dim light; Black Prince nuzzled her fingers through his bars.

"Like a cat scratch," I said, and she laughed.

"A cat like Prince?"

"On the ribs, yes," I said, touching my firebird unconsciously. *"But most other places, just like a little kitty scraping a claw against your skin."*

"Like this?" she asked, lifting an eyebrow and dragging her fingernail from my cuffed shirtsleeve down to the back of my hand. It was the first time she'd ever touched me, and my skin prickled with goosebumps.

"No. That didn't hurt a bit."

Her eyes held mine, and she flattened her pointer finger on my hand. The rest of her fingers followed suit. *"I want one,"* she said.

"A tattoo?"

She nodded.

"Please?"

I knew she was asking for more than a tattoo. She said please, so I turned my hand over beneath hers. Palm to palm, I let her decide if she wanted to hold on.

When her fingers wrapped round the black cat on my hand, she smiled.

⁂

THE NEXT AFTERNOON, she came to the tattoo shop. It would steam Mulligan, she said, which suited her fine. My father was there when she arrived, and he took to her right away. When he took her coat, he loudly announced that I should tattoo her with the prettiest things imaginable. He made up the bed with pillows and called her Princess. Dad always got funny around pretty girls, but Mary laughed along. It was Dad's idea to call the place Taffy's—but that wasn't till later. I'm getting ahead of myself.

Mary sat on the edge of the bed, and my dad winked at me before busying himself upstairs. Her eyes roamed our strange place—the sketches on the walls, the jars of ink—and then returned to mine. "Well?" she asked. "What's the prettiest thing you can imagine?"

"You."

She looked at her hands. "I meant for a tattoo," she said, but I could see the smile playing on her lips.

"Oh, I don't know. Some flowers, perhaps? A butterfly? A bird?"

"A bird," she said, with a definitive nod. "If I die, I'd like to come back as a bird."

I smiled and stroked my chin. "Why's that?"

"Because they can sing," she exclaimed. "And fly. They're absolutely free—and made of music. What could be better than that?"

"A bird it is, then." I flushed, knowing the question I must ask her next. "Where would you like it?"

"Somewhere discreet," she whispered. "And not too painful. I was thinking . . ." She began to unbutton her blouse. I could barely breathe as she pointed to the lower section of her right breast. "Here?"

"How large?" I must have stuttered. I was only seventeen, and no woman had ever unbuttoned her blouse for me.

She lay down on the pillows, arching her back. "You decide."

I reached for a pen at my workstation, then sat on the nearby stool to draw the design. But she caught my hand before it even touched her skin. She took the pen and flattened my palm against her breast, then brought her lips to mine.

"You're different from the boys I know," she whispered to me, still holding my pen. "You have a good heart."

CHAPTER TEN

BLACK PRINCE.

As soon as Evan remembered the cat's name, the vision cleared. The smoke evaporated, and the sun shone white-hot on the sand again. The people around him wore bikinis and swim shorts and walked dogs and tossed Frisbees and laughed with their kids. The lion was gone. Long gone. There was nothing Evan could do for the poor cat now. He flexed his fingers and clenched his fists a few times until his hands were steady enough to type *Black Prince Dreamland Park* into the search bar.

He knew what he would find, but it still took his breath away. There it was, on multiple websites chronicling the history of Dreamland Park. A three-year-old Nubian lion named Black Prince had, indeed, run through the streets ablaze the night the park burned, until he was shot dead by police. Evan's throat thickened and his eyes burned.

That lion meant something to him.

No. That lion meant something to someone else, someone whose grief had been transferred as clearly as the scent of smoke.

His phone vibrated in his sweaty palm and he jumped, dropping it in the sand. Cursing under his breath, he picked it up and flipped it over.

He exhaled and accepted his mom's call. He couldn't keep ignoring her. It had been well over an hour already.

"Hi."

"Hi. We're done. Are you . . . still here?"

"Yeah. I'm sitting on the beach. Just go straight out from the aquarium and you'll see me."

"Okay. Be there in a minute."

She hung up, and he waited for his mother and sister to find him. Breathing deeply and slowly, he let the wave of adrenaline from the memory recede.

He needed to look normal when they arrived. He dug his toes into the sand and rubbed granules between his fingers, grounding himself to reality. Mara had told him he was more than his DNA, but what if his DNA was more than him?

Somehow, he was carrying someone else's memories inside his brain, but he couldn't tell anyone that yet. Not until he knew more about the tattooed boy. Not until he had hard proof that they were actually family.

"You missed the penguins!" Hailey exclaimed from behind, and Evan turned his head to see her running through the sand so fast she tumbled onto her knees. "They were so, so, so cute. I took a picture for you, see?"

"They *are* so cute," he agreed, shielding the screen of his mom's phone from the sun so he could see his sister's slightly blurry photograph. "Good composition, buddy."

"Do you feel better?" she asked, resting her hand on his forehead as if taking his temperature.

"Yeah," he lied. "Yeah. Sorry I missed the penguins. Thanks for taking pictures for me."

"I was telling her how, when you were five, you were obsessed with penguins," his mom said, digging her big toe into the sand. She shot him a sideways glance. "You drew entire flocks of penguins for me back then. With bowties and glasses and baseball hats and electric guitars and harmonicas. Remember?"

He smiled against his will. "Yeah. I remember."

"I still have them, you know. Anyway, I promised Hailey some ice cream. You want a cone?"

He pushed himself up off the sand, suddenly aware of just how hot he was from sitting in the sun for so long.

They walked the boardwalk and Hailey scrolled through all the pictures she took while Evan had been outside, but he felt disconnected from his body. He wanted to feel angry again. He tried to summon all the accusations and questions he'd been ready to sling at his mother, but his thoughts were rushing by too fast to focus on any one of them.

They inched forward in line at the ice cream shop, and finally, Evan ordered a cone of vanilla-chocolate swirl. He helped Hailey turn her cone to keep up with the avalanche of vanilla goop and sprinkles, feeling like he was like living in the Dalí painting where all the clocks were melting.

The image gave him pause as yet another name clicked into place. Dalí had titled that painting *The Persistence of Memory*.

AT A SOUVENIR shop on the boardwalk, Evan's mom bought toys for Hailey to play with in the sand: a bucket, a shovel, star-shaped molds, and a bag of mermaid princess figurines. She grabbed three oversized beach towels with end-of-season clearance stickers and a bottle of nearly outdated sunscreen before heading to the checkout counter.

"Now," she said to Evan, replacing her credit card in her wallet and taking the overstuffed bag from the cashier. "We need to talk."

They spread the towels on the sand and watched Hailey run down to the shoreline to fill her bucket with salt water. Evan rubbed coconut-scented sunscreen on his already burned face and waited for his mother to start talking.

"I should have told you sooner," she finally said, taking the bottle from him and squirting a pool of lotion into her palm. "I should have done a lot of things differently. But here we are."

"Here we are," he echoed, as a pair of seagulls swooped down a few feet away.

"I don't know where to start."

"How about his last name."

"Smith. Your father's name is Matthew Smith."

"Okay."

The gulls called to each other, cocking their heads from side to side in search of food, then flew away, disappointed.

"He could be very sweet," his mom continued. "Very charming. It wasn't his fault that he had . . . problems. But he could be very manipulative. Messed with my head. He was a good liar, and I didn't want him to lie to you."

Evan raised his eyebrows. "So you lied to me instead."

"Yes," she snapped, closing the bottle of sunscreen and forcefully wiping her hands on the towel. "Yes, I did, because I wasn't going to let him hurt you. I needed to protect you, so I did what I had to do. God knows I've made my share of mistakes, but babies don't come with instruction manuals and neither do men. I just . . . sometimes I just look at you and wonder how on earth such a smart, levelheaded, talented person could have come from *me*. When you were in the NICU, I remember looking into your eyes through the glass and wondering how the hell I was going to keep you alive. I was twenty-two and all alone, but you stared back at me like, *I've got this,*

Mom. Even in your incubator, you looked so wise. Like a little old man." She laughed.

He feigned offense. "Like an old man?"

"Newborns are weird looking," she said. "But you grew into your cuteness pretty quickly," she cooed, pinching his cheek. "And you haven't grown out of it yet."

He swatted her hand away but smiled.

"You're nothing like your father," his mom continued, serious again. "You've always been steady and reliable. But two look-alikes in one day? First the boy and then the girl? I just had to make sure."

"Make sure . . . of what?"

"That what you were seeing was *real.*"

It all fell into place with a sickening thud in his stomach. She wasn't there to decide whether Mara was good enough for him. She was here to make sure he hadn't lost his grip on reality.

"Well, I'm sorry I can't take you to the Neptune Gallery," he said bitterly. "But if you want to walk by and look in the windows, be my guest."

"No," she said, resting a hand on his shoulder. "I believe you. Just please try to understand why I had to make sure you were okay."

"I'm okay," he said flatly, looking out toward the shoreline where his sister sat on her knees, slopping wet sand into her bucket.

"I'm sorry," she said. "I'm sorry for showing up like this. And I'm sorry if I did the wrong thing, not telling you."

He just nodded and scooped up a fistful of sand, letting it slip through his fingers.

He didn't know what to say.

"Next time we visit, I'll call."

He nodded and plunged his hand into the sand again.

"And next month, you'll be eighteen. So if you still want to try to find your dad then, I'll help you."

He froze. "Really?"

"I haven't talked to him since you were in diapers, so I have no idea how he's doing. But if that's what you really want, I'll respect that as your adult decision and do what I can to help you," she said, reaching for his hand and giving it a squeeze. "Okay?"

"Okay," he agreed.

She bit her lip. "What are you thinking right now?"

"I don't even know," he said. "It's a lot to take in all at once."

"I'll tell you anything you want to know," his mom promised, just as Hailey came running up to ask them to play.

Together, the three of them built a sandcastle for the plastic mermaids, but every time Hailey was distracted, Evan asked his mother another question about his father. She met his gaze and answered softly, explaining their long custody battle, which ended before Evan's childhood memories began. She described the two sides of Matt Smith—the sweet, sensitive history education major who took his medication, and the jealously erratic, angry boyfriend who didn't. And slowly, as the sky turned pink, Evan began to understand why his mother had kept it from him for so long. He wasn't sure he forgave her for it, but he didn't hate her for it, either. He needed time to process, and he wanted more than anything to talk to someone who understood.

As dusk settled on the beach, their mother took Hailey back to the hotel to get ready for bed, and Evan walked to the Surf Avenue station alone. Waiting for the uptown train, he texted Mara.

Finally heading back to Manhattan.

How did it go?

Better, I guess. Can I see you?

I'm at the Battery doing some writing. Meet me here?

On my way.

He took the Q line to Sheepshead Bay, transferred to the B line, then finally rode the 5 to Bowling Green, wondering how anyone navigated New York Public Transit before smartphones. He wound along the quiet, lamppost-studded pathways of Battery Park to the waterfront until he saw her. Bent over a notebook, she sat cross-legged on a bench overlooking the Hudson, tapping a pen and nodding in rhythm. The black water glittered with the reflection of the skyline, mirroring the glow that rippled in Evan's chest as he slid onto the bench beside her.

She dropped her bare feet to the ground beside a pair of black flip-flops. "Hi."

"Hi." He glanced at her open notebook, covered in smudged scribbles and chord progressions. "What are you working on?"

"A new song. About her." Mara pointed her chin out toward the water, where Liberty Island glowed, bright and small, in the distance.

He lifted his eyebrows. "The Statue of Liberty?"

She nodded. "I come out here sometimes when I need a break from the chaos of our apartment. And today I was thinking about how she's this icon of independence, but it's kind of ironic that an international symbol of freedom isn't free at all, you know? She's stuck on that island because men put her there, and then hordes of people come and walk all over her, and she can't do anything about it."

"Huh," he said, squinting toward the island. "Never thought about it that way."

"I think she's having an existential crisis, actually. Everyone recognizes her, but nobody really knows her. Nobody stays. So she wonders, is independence really just loneliness in disguise?"

He watched her face, her eyes drifting out to the island and the statue, obscured by darkness. "Is that how you feel?"

Slowly, she turned to meet his gaze and smiled. "Not with you."

"So . . . can I hear the song?"

"No way!" She snapped her notebook closed. "It's not done yet."

He laughed and raised his hands. "Okay."

Dropping the pen into her purse, she rubbed the ink-smudged edge of her left hand on her denim shorts.

"You're a lefty?"

"It's inconvenient sometimes," she said, showing him the blackened side of her hand before rubbing it against her shorts again.

"I've heard lefties are more creative," Evan offered.

"Well," she began, excitement dancing in her eyes at the opportunity to discuss psychology. "It has to do with brain lateralization. Right-handed people have more neatly categorized brains, which means less work. But lefties store information differently, which makes us go back and forth between hemispheres to search for information, and then sometimes, along the way, we find new solutions to problems. But overall, the world is made for right-handed people. Do you have any idea how expensive a left-handed guitar is?"

"Nope," he said, shaking his head. "But I heard that back in the day, left-handed women were hung as witches."

She sat very still, blinking slowly. "Where did you hear that?"

He really couldn't remember where he'd heard it. How he knew it. And suddenly, he wished he hadn't said it aloud.

"Just another one of the random, useless facts I store in the attic," he said, tapping his temple. "It might not even be true, really."

"Hmm," she sighed, then brought her feet up onto the bench again, resting her arms on her knees. "How'd it go with your mom?"

"Okay." He shrugged. "She said she'd help me get in touch with my dad if I want."

"Is that what you want?"

"I don't know yet."

He sighed, looking down at her toes wiggling off the edge of the bench. The soft lilac polish was half worn away, like she hadn't painted them in weeks because she was too busy reading psychology books and crafting existential metaphors to set to music—and he found it infinitely more attractive than fresh polish and full makeup. She was a girl who spent her time on things that mattered to her, and she was spending some of that time on him. She listened intently as he explained what he'd learned about his father, nodding to affirm his mixed feelings of resentment and gratefulness toward his mother, and smiling at his exasperation with how hard it was to stay mad at her even though she drove him crazy.

"Sartre says that freedom is what you do with what's been done to you," Mara said, her voice gentle as the stars, quiet and soft and glittering, filling him with wonder. She listened so beautifully, he thought, he could tell her anything.

Everything.

And then, he stopped short.

She wasn't some faraway dream anymore. She wasn't the girl in his painting. That girl had been safe only because she wasn't real. But this girl—this girl could break his heart.

And he could break hers.

The thought terrified him.

He could hurt her, even without trying. He could end up like his father. She could end up like his mother.

"Look, I understand if you don't want to see me anymore," he blurted.

Her toes stopped tapping. "Um, what?"

"I mean, it might happen to me, right? What if I start seeing things that aren't there, or hearing voices or something, you know?"

Her eyebrows pulled together. "Then you'll take meds and do therapy and be fine."

If he were brave, he would have told her. He would have said, *I saw a lion on fire today. I smelled the smoke and heard the roar and knew his name, even though he died over a hundred years ago.* But he wasn't feeling particularly brave, so he settled for, "I just don't ever want to hurt you."

It was the truth.

She nodded, quiet for a few beats, while his breath came shallow and fast. He waited for her to back away. To tell him he wasn't worth the risk. She pressed her lips together, and he could see her working up the right way to thank him for the easy out. She set her notebook on the grass and stood up.

Her face was serious when she asked, "Have you ever played a string instrument?"

Evan's tension burst into a bubble of laughter. "What?"

"I *said*, have you ever played a string instrument? You know, like a guitar or violin or ukulele?"

"Um, no?"

"Okay," she said, taking a few steps toward the metal railing separating them from the Hudson. "When we get ready to play a show, this is what Gwen and Sam do. First, they tune up individually, but then they do this test. Gwen will sit on one side of the room and play an E on her bass, and if Sam's guitar is perfectly in tune, her E string will vibrate from the other side of the room without even being touched."

"That's . . . interesting," he said, as a whoosh of a breeze came off the river and swept her hair away from her face. She motioned for him to come closer, so he rose and leaned against the rail beside her, utterly confused as she continued.

"Okay, I feel like . . . god, this sounds corny the more I have to spell it out," she laughed. "But that's how you make me feel, okay? Like, I'm the guitar string and you're the bass string, and we're connected by something invisible and powerful and . . . and beautiful. So I don't care who your parents are, or what might happen someday, just so we stay in tune with each other, okay? No secrets, no lies. Just you and me."

As she reached for his hand, slipping her cool fingers between his, he felt every brick in the wall he'd built around his heart crumble.

"I don't think I can follow that metaphor up," he admitted. "But I feel the same way. Really."

She squeezed his hand.

"Also, I wore low-cut socks just for you."

She laughed, craning her neck to check out his ankles. "I swoon," she said, like a Southern belle.

"You want a better look at the elbows, too?" He bent his arms and waved his elbows around, pouting and posing like Derek Zoolander.

"Oh my god, stop it," she laughed, grabbing his arms.

"You have fantastic freckles." He brushed away the hair that had blown across her cheek, then trailed his fingers along the length of a curl. She bit her lip and closed her eyes, and when he kissed her, her body melted against his, warm and soft, and he surrendered.

He was completely in the moment, and for the first time in his life, he wasn't afraid. He'd rebuild that wall around their two hearts together, and no force on earth would be able to knock it down. He didn't think about what might go wrong, or if he would look for his father, or why he'd seen Black Prince.

He'd never let himself kiss a girl like that, never taken such a risk, but already, he could feel the colors of his world changing, becoming brighter and warmer beside hers.

CHAPTER ELEVEN

"TODAY, WE WILL begin to really dig into our textbook," Dr. Mortakis said, displaying a slide that enlarged the cover of *Flying Too Close to the Sun: Myths in Art from Classical to Contemporary.* "You're responsible for memorizing the artist, title, and date of any slide we discuss in class. It's all fair game for the exam. Also please remember that there are rich, valuable, and interesting mythologies that we simply will not be able to cover in this class due to time constraints. My expertise lies in Greek and Roman mythology, but I hope you will take other classes that broaden your understanding beyond western culture and art. Here at NYU we offer magnificent classes in Native American, Asian, and African mythologies and artistic traditions, and I encourage you to sign up for these in future semesters.

"So, let's begin at the beginning. The short story is this. From Chaos, Earth developed and birthed Sky. Sky and Earth had sex and made some Titan babies. For reasons unknown, Mother Earth told her son Kronos to castrate Father Sky and toss his massive genitals into the sea. Kronos then became ruler of the Titans, but, worried his own children would follow his example and chop off their father's precious parts, Kronos decided to eat them instead. And this was the inspiration for Goya's disturbing masterpiece of 1820, *Saturn Devouring His Children.*"

Dr. Mortakis displayed the painting on the screen behind her, and though Evan had seen the painting before, he'd never seen it so enlarged. He stared at the frenzied, paranoid eyes of Saturn as Dr. Mortakis continued.

"Saturn, a.k.a. Kronos, is shown here devouring an infant headfirst, dripping with blood, and looking absolutely wild with the desire to keep his genitals intact. This begs the question, why did Goya choose to paint this hideous, ancient scene in the year 1820?"

Dr. Mortakis scanned the room, waiting for someone to raise a hand, but no one did. Like Evan, they were all transfixed on the enormous, gory scene behind her.

"Kronos," Dr. Mortakis said after a lengthy pause. She began pacing across the front of the room, speaking slowly and deliberately. "Chronology. Kronos. *Time.* Saturn was the god of Time. And doesn't Time devour us all?"

Evan frowned. He'd always just thought Goya was a disturbed and morbid man, but suddenly, the dark cavern of Saturn's mouth looked deeper and darker and a little more . . . real.

Dr. Mortakis moved from the origins of the gods to the origins of mankind.

"Prometheus created mortal men and gave them fire, but Zeus ordered Hephaestus to create the first woman, Pandora."

Dr. Mortakis switched the slides again, this time to a beautiful, curly-haired woman with intense blue eyes dressed in flowing tangerine robes. She was opening a box, allowing an ominous orange smoke to escape.

"Today, Pandora is associated with streaming music and kitschy jewelry, but in ancient times, she was the Greek equivalent of Eve.

Pandora was beautiful, clever, and oh-so-curious, so when the gods gave her a box with strict instructions not to open it, she couldn't help herself. And so, evil came into the world through a beautiful woman. Dante Gabriel Rossetti portrayed her here, in 1871, as the ultimate femme fatale, and doesn't that fit with the mindset of the Victorian age? That evil and chaos enter the world the instant a woman disobeys?"

Evan knew memorizing the artists, titles, and dates of so many slides would be a grind, but the class itself was strangely entertaining, like listening to Dr. Mortakis tell messed-up bedtime stories with high-quality pictures.

She closed out her slideshow and flicked on the lights. "All right, that's all for today. Be sure to read the first chapter on creation myths for Tuesday, and have a nice weekend, folks."

Weekend. Evan was still getting used to the fact that his weekends were his own—as long as his mother didn't show up unannounced with tickets to a sea lion show. But he believed her when she promised to call first from now on. He believed her when she said she would help him find his dad.

Before he could think about finding his dad, though, he needed to tell Mara everything.

Her voice was like an echo bouncing off the walls of his heart:

We're in this together . . .

No secrets . . .

No lies . . .

Still, coming to terms with the fact that your new boyfriend has vivid visions of history was a tall order. And so, instead of reading for Mythology in Modern Art or doing his post-lab analysis for Biology, Evan spent Friday night rehearsing how he might tell her everything without sounding absolutely nuts.

He couldn't start with the painting. Yes, he'd show it to her eventually, but it definitely was *not* the place to start. Besides, *The Green-Eyed Girl* had nothing to do with his visions of the past.

The only logical starting place was the tattooed boy. Mara had already seen the photo, already knew he suspected it might be a long-lost relative. Maybe if he could just learn a little more about the person whose memories he had relived, and exactly how they were connected to one another, it would be easier to explain. Staring at the picture on his phone, he read the placard one more time. *On loan from Taffy's on Surf.*

A quick Google search told him that Taffy's on Surf was a tattoo shop on Coney Island. He wasn't sure what he had expected—a museum or historical society, maybe, but not a tattoo shop. Still, it made sense. And that was a good omen.

Soon, Evan promised himself sleepily, *this whole thing is going to make sense.* He finally dozed off to the lullaby of a plan: he'd call Taffy's when they opened at noon, and then, he'd tell Mara everything.

No secrets.

No lies.

⊹⊱✦⊰⊹

AT 12:01 P.M. the next day, Evan tapped the green call button, and as soon as it started to ring, his stomach churned.

"Taffy's," a male voice answered, thick with Brooklyn. "This is Tony. What can I do for ya?"

"Hi, I was wondering about a photo I saw on display a few weeks ago at the Neptune Gallery. It said it was on loan from Taffy's on Surf?"

"For that, you hafta talk to Lillian," he said. "But she's not here right now."

"Should I . . . call back later?"

"She doesn't hear too good on the phone, but if you stop by the shop around four, she should be here to talk."

"Four? Sure, I'll be there," Evan said quickly, shot through with a current of anxious excitement. "See you at four."

This time, he made sure to get off the train at the right stop. Taffy's was west of the aquarium, but he walked briskly, trying not to look around too much until his phone said *your destination is on the left*.

Elevated train tracks ran directly over top of the dilapidated two-story building marked Taffy's, and the approach of a train set the neon sign rattling. It didn't light up anymore, or maybe they kept it dark until dusk. Thick curtains blocked the windows, and the door glass was cola-bottle black. Evan stood on the sidewalk waiting for the roar of the train to subside, and the whole building seemed to shudder at its passing. In its quiet wake, he took a deep breath and reached for the door handle.

It took his eyes a few seconds to adjust. The walls were painted a deep shade of purple, nearly black. Behind the counter, a shelf lined with kewpie dolls framed a massively-armed man in a white tank top. He looked up from his phone and lifted an inked hand in greeting.

"Hey, man."

"Uh, hi," Evan said, suddenly feeling self-consciously nerdy.

The big man came out from behind the counter and extended his hand. "I'm Tony. You know what you want, or you wanna check out some samples?"

"Oh, um, I'm not actually here to get a tattoo," Evan said, returning the handshake. "I called earlier. About the photograph?"

"Yeah, yeah. Right." Tony picked up a vintage turquois-enamel telephone receiver that Evan would have loved to hook up to his dorm jack. "Hang on a sec. She just got in about fifteen minutes ago."

Evan watched the skulls on Tony's knuckles as he spun the rotary dial and listened as he asked someone named Lillian to come downstairs to talk to a kid about a photograph. Tony told Evan to wait on the red velvet high-backed sofa because it was going to take her a couple minutes to come down from her upstairs apartment.

The whole place felt like an abandoned movie set. One wall was collaged with old electric guitars, some with a few strings, others looking like they'd been dug out of a dumpster. Framed sketches, some signed by Tony, hung at irregular intervals around the three workstations. Each tattoo artist had their own beat-up, chipped wooden vanity table with its own, personalized decor. Tony's vibe was death—skulls and monsters, snakes and blood.

Another vanity mirror was marked "Angel," and she specialized in botanicals and beautiful women. The third was marked "Lillian," but looked like it hadn't been used in years. The stool was pushed in all the way, and instead of drawings, the wall around her vanity table was covered in yellowing family photographs.

Tapping his fingers anxiously, he heard the descending buzz of an electric stair lift, feet on the floor, and a raspy female voice saying, "Hey, Tony, where's the kid?"

"Right behind you, Lil," the big guy said, and Evan stood to greet Lillian.

She was impossibly old, with badly dyed hair and crinkling tattoos, wearing a frilly purple skirt and crocs with socks. She smiled, her blue eyes bright.

"What can I do for you, hon?"

"Um, I was wondering about a photograph I saw at the Neptune Gallery."

She reached into a small purse for a pair of cat-eye glasses, and her orange-penciled eyebrows immediately tightened. Evan slowly took another step toward her, trying to look nonthreatening, but she stiffened.

"I'm Evan Kiernan," he continued, extending his hand to shake. "I was just wondering who—"

"Jesus Christ," Lillian whispered, her right hand frozen midshake, her left adjusting her glasses "You look . . . just like him."

Evan nodded. "That's what I wanted to talk to you about."

She just stood there, staring at him. He shifted his weight uncomfortably, allowing her to process what she was seeing.

"What . . . did you say your name was?" Lillian finally asked, taking Tony's colossal arm and letting him lead her over to the red couch. She said she felt a little faint and didn't trust her own legs.

"Um, Evan. Evan Kiernan."

"Am I on *Candid Camera*?" she asked, squinting at Tony, who shook his head. "April Fool's Day?"

"Uh, no," Evan said, and his scalp tingled. "It's September. I'm sorry if I—"

"That boy you saw," she interrupted, waving off his apology. "He was my uncle, Kieran Flynn."

"Kieran? Like, my last name without the *n*?"

"That's right."

"Wow. Okay."

"Are you recording this for the internet or something?"

"No," Evan promised. "No. I just saw the photo and wanted to know more. So I came to ask you if you think we might be related? If he was your uncle, you know, maybe we're in the same family."

The old woman shook her head slowly. "I doubt that very much. All those kids over there—they're my family. My brother's and mine. I still send them all a card at Christmas—never miss a single one."

"She designs them herself," Tony added, and Evan realized he must get a card, too.

"But what about your uncle?" Evan pressed, because he wasn't here to talk about Christmas cards. "Did he have any kids?"

"Well, maybe." Lillian began picking at a loose button on the velvet couch, and Evan looked to Tony, who shrugged. She was quiet for a long moment, stroking the velvet like a cat. "Families are funny things," she said finally, without looking up. "People can live together, eat together, sleep in the same room for years, and then one day—poof."

"*Poof*?"

Lillian's filmy, blue eyes held Evan's. A tremor twitched at the skin around her eyes and mouth. "Kieran Flynn disappeared."

"Disappeared?" he whispered, his heart in his throat. "What do you mean?"

"It was before I was even born," she said with a wave of her loose-skinned hand. "I only know what I've been told. My uncle used to tell stories on the boardwalk for pennies, one of the freaks, as they called them. But he had a sweetheart—another freak. She was bendy. One of those, oh, what do you call them? Contusionists?"

"Contortionist?" Evan suggested gently, trying to keep his breathing even.

"Yeah, that's it. They met at Dreamland, before it burned. But here's the strange thing," Lillian whispered, her blue eyes huge as she leaned forward. "He predicted it. He knew it was going to burn. But nobody believed him till it was too late."

Evan's mouth opened silently.

"He was a strange fella, my uncle, and didn't get on so well with my dad. A freak in more ways than one, Dad used to say. Here, let me show you something," she said, pushing herself up off the couch. Tony offered his arm, but she shooed him away. Lillian was steady on her feet again, though Evan didn't trust his own. She opened a drawer at her tattoo vanity and removed a stack of photo albums.

"Here we go. This is the one," Lillian said, selecting a flimsy brown scrapbook. "Mind if I smoke?"

Evan shook his head, even though he hated the smell, and Lillian asked Tony for a light. Her tobacco-stained nails were so long, they hooked downward, and she had to lick her fingers repeatedly to turn the laminated scrapbook pages.

"There," she said, lifting the plastic and removing an old newspaper clipping, fragile as a pressed flower. "That was her. His sweetheart, Mary Thompson. My granddad and Uncle Kieran renamed this place for her—see? Her stage name was Taffy—stretchy, you know. She was the first lady to ever work with the ink in a place like this. Paved the way for girls like Angel and me."

As soon as Evan saw the black-and-white image, his heart punched him in the lungs. It was a young woman on a highwire, balanced on one foot. She wore a leotard without sleeves or straps, boldly displaying the tattoos covering her body—arms, legs, and chest. The caption read, *Tattooed Taffy*.

Evan's skin tingled, and he grabbed the back of the velvet couch.

The gap between her front teeth.

That smile—he'd know it anywhere.

And the eyes—even in newsprint black and white, he could tell they belonged to the *Green-Eyed Girl*.

To Mara.

"Did your uncle, um, do her tattoos?"

Lillian nodded. "They loved each other, once upon a time."

"And her name was . . . Mary?"

"Mm-hmm."

Extending his trembling pointer finger, he dared to touch the fragile paper.

They loved each other, once upon a time . . .

It was absurd. This whole thing was absurd.

"What's the matter, hon?" Lillian asked, and Evan snapped his attention back to her face. Was she curious? Suspicious? Ready to call Bellevue? "You look like you saw a ghost."

"Sorry," he mumbled, but his eyes were drawn into the artwork on Mary's skin. The picture was too small to see the intricate details, but he could see basic designs—the flowers winding around her arms, the majestic black lion staring out from her left shoulder, the birds taking flight from her right.

"Can I take a picture of this?" he asked, suddenly remembering why he was here. Lillian nodded, so he snapped a picture of Mary with his phone.

"You said Kieran Flynn disappeared, but what about her?" Evan asked, pointing at the photo. "What happened to Mary?"

"She died the night Dreamland burned."

"But the internet said nobody died in the fire. I read that on Wikipedia. A few animals died, but no people were killed."

Lillian began drumming her fingers on the album, nodding slowly. "That's what the papers said."

She rubbed her sagging cheeks thoughtfully, as if weighing her words. Evan waited, glancing at Tony, who shrugged again and went back to playing on his phone.

"They throw this phrase around all the time now on CNN," Lillian finally said, jutting her chin toward a dark wall-mounted TV screen. "*Fake News.* You've heard it, haven't you?"

Evan nodded.

"Newspapers don't outright lie—they're too clever for that. They just don't tell you the whole story. See what I mean?"

Evan nodded again, panic gripping his chest because he really didn't know what she meant. "Do you know the whole story?"

Lillian laughed out loud, a crackling, wheezy smoker's laugh. "Lord, no. But I know Mary Thompson died the night Dreamland burned. And I know it wasn't the flames that killed her."

"How do you know that?" he whispered.

"Because somebody took a picture of her in the casket," she said, and started flipping ahead in the album, licking her fingers furiously again. "Not a burn mark on her. Look at that."

Nausea rose from Evan's stomach to his throat.

It was Mara.

And she was dead.

Cold sweat prickled his face, and he forced himself to swallow. *It's not her*, he told himself. *It's Mary, not Mara.*

"Did your uncle leave anything else? Anything at all that would tell . . . what happened?"

Lillian sucked her teeth, then flipped to the back of the album, where a yellowed business card was sandwiched between the cover and the pages. She handed it to Evan, then asked Tony for another cigarette.

The letters *ASPR* were printed vertically on the left in a rectangular logo. Some sort of acronym. The horizontal text read, *Dr. William James, Professor of Psychology and Philosophy, Researcher of the Paranormal and Unusual.*

"Did you know Dr. James?" he asked.

Lillian pursed her crinkled lips and exhaled a long stream of smoke toward a shelf stocked with decorative false teeth. "No. My father wouldn't tell me who he was. I found that card a long, long time ago, along with these pictures. But my dad didn't want to get on the subject of his little brother. He said to let bygones be bygones."

"Did you? Let bygones be bygones, I mean."

"I looked them up in the phone book a few times," she said, taking a long drag and shaking her head. "Any idea how many people there are in this city named William James? At least a hundred, and none of them were doctors. Not a single soul by the name of Kieran Flynn, either. I started looking too late."

Evan studied the card, turning it over in his hand. "What's the point of a business card without a phone number?"

Lillian's laugh crackled into a cough. "That was back in the days of the hello girls," she said. "You'd tell the operator the city and the name of the person, and they'd connect you. Didn't need a number yet, hon."

"So, what does *ASPR* stand for?"

"Beats me." Lillian shrugged, opening the drawer of her tattoo vanity and closing the album.

"Do you have the portrait in there? The one from the Neptune?"

Lillian paused. "It's up on my dresser. Be a doll, Tony?"

Tony jogged up the steps, and Lillian pointed at the business card in Evan's hand. "You can keep that card. Maybe you can figure it out now, with that goddamn internet."

"I'll give it a try."

She nodded in approval as Tony's heavy footsteps clattered back down the steps. Slowly, Tony's head swiveled between the photo and Evan's face.

"Holy shit," Tony said, handing the framed photograph to Lillian, but she raised her palm.

"I think he'd want this boy to have it."

Evan hesitated. "Are you sure?"

She took it from Tony and thrust it toward Evan. "What the hell am I going to do with it? Take it."

Evan took the photograph gently, feeling like Indiana Jones. "Thank you."

She put the cigarette in her mouth and took his hand, but she didn't shake it. She just held it in hers for a long minute, staring into his eyes.

"You let me know if you find anything, okay kiddo?"

Evan promised that he would, but he quickly realized that Lillian had overestimated the powers of the internet.

On the uptown train, he typed the letters into his search bar: ASPR. But all the results were for the office of the Assistant Secretary for Preparedness and Response, a government division of the Health and Human Services department. All the related web pages were for the Center for Disease Control and government medical offices— nothing to do with a tattooed boy who disappeared after his girlfriend died. Dr. James was probably just the man who pronounced her dead.

Evan rubbed his eyes, blinking away the image of Mara in a casket. *That was Mary, not Mara*, he reminded himself, but the resemblance was much too close for comfort. Coming across his own lookalike had been weird enough—why did she have to be part of this?

And yet, without admitting it to himself, he'd known all along they were in this together. How else would he have painted her before even meeting her?

But at least in his painting, she was alive.

Staring out the window of the train at tar-sticky rooftop gardens and graffiti splattered fire escapes, he rested his forehead against the glass in exhaustion. Time was playing some sort of trick on him, he thought as the train slipped underground and went dark.

Evan closed his eyes against the flashing lights studding the subway tunnel. The past few weeks were the closest thing to a religious experience he'd ever had, but unlike his mom's mystical *feelings*, he had evidence. He opened his backpack and stared at the portrait of Kieran Flynn. He had photographic evidence that proved . . . what? That he had a doppelgänger in the past? He'd snapped a picture of the news clipping of Mary on the tightrope, which meant he had evidence that Mara had a doppelgänger, too. The tattooed boy's true love, who died the night Dreamland burned.

He could show Mara the photos. If she didn't believe him, they could take the paper to a lab and have it dated. The paper was old and fragile. He could prove it wasn't a photoshop trick. He could also prove that he'd painted Mara almost a year ago, which meant he could prove that he'd remembered history—

Except Mara was here, in the present.

If she was just his ancestor's memory, how had she arrived in New York City in the present day? How had they found each other? And how had they felt so instantly connected unless . . .

Unless he wasn't just remembering history.

He was repeating it.

KINGS PARK ASYLUM

1 9 1 1

IT WAS THE Fourth of July, and the park was decked out in red, white, and blue. An oom-pah band played as vendors sold tiny flags, and people flocked to the center of Dreamland to watch Mary walk in the sky. She was dressed as the Statue of Liberty, a spiked crown atop her head and a flaming torch in her hand.

Silvery sequins glinted in the afternoon light as she climbed the turquoise ladder one-handed, then paused on the platform to raise the flame above Dreamland to great applause. When her eyes found mine in the crowd, we relished our secret.

No one had seen the bird but us.

As "The Star-Spangled Banner" began to play on the ground, Mary began her tricks.

And then, a rough shoulder shoved into mine. Mulligan.

"She's not for you," he said, his chin jutting up toward the girl in the sky.

"She's not for anybody," I answered. "That girl belongs to herself."

"No," Mulligan said, biting a cigar between his molars. "She doesn't."

"She's Lady Liberty." I pointed out as she twirled the flaming torch from hand to hand above our heads.

"Do you know who bought her that costume? Do you know who paid for that crown?"

I turned and looked him in the eye, lifting my chin. "Yeah. And I know where that dirty money came from, too."

"You're playing your cards wrong," Mulligan said, his dark eyes cruel and level with mine. "The aces are all mine, see? You can't have that girl. I'd sooner see her dead."

And just like that, he disappeared into the crowd.

The music stopped, and Mary raised her torch and smiled, just for me. She hadn't seen him. He'd made sure of that.

And I realized with a rush of sickening anger, that he, too, had seen the bird.

❦

SUMMER BURNED HOT, and people flocked to our little edge of sea. My days were long, waiting for sundown, waiting for Mary beneath the pier. We never had much time. Never enough.

"I want to get away from here," she said to me one night as the night-black water rushed over our ankles. "I want to be yours."

"Mine?"

She nodded.

"I heard what you said to Prince that night," I said slowly, thinking of Mulligan's words without mentioning the encounter. "About being a captive. A prisoner. I thought you wanted to be free."

She took my hand and placed it over the bird. "Free to choose."

Weak in the knees, I said, "Where do you want to go? What do you want me to do?"

"Teach me to use your machine?"

"The tattoo machine?"

She nodded. "Then I won't need to work for Mulligan anymore. Then I can be yours."

"On one condition," I said to her, as the softness of her body pressed against mine beneath the pier. She lifted her eyebrows, waiting for my condition. "That I can be yours."

❦

WE WORKED BY firelight when the electricity of Dreamland was turned off. She came to me from the Tin Elephant, when her work was done and Mulligan slept. With every passing night, she said, he became more irritable. He paid the other women to watch her, promising to kill her if she tried to leave. It was her friend, the bearded girl, who lied for her so she could come to me and learn a new trade—one that no woman had ever taken on. My father promised her a job as soon as she was skilled enough.

There were still a few areas of my skin left untouched by my father's ink. Her hand was steady and her lines were crisp as, little by little, she tattooed my thigh with an angel of her own design.

"Mulligan says he's taking us to Florida at the end of the season," she told me, gently wiping ink and blood from my skin. "In September."

"So, let him leave without you. You'll have a job here by then."

"How will I get him to leave without me?"

"I'll sneak you off the train," I said, winking.

She brushed hair from her face and smudged ink on her nose. Her smile was bright. "Mulligan's away for the night."

"Tonight?"

She nodded. "Can I stay?"

There was sweetness that night, beyond anything I had ever known. We fell asleep as the sun came up, in no hurry to get to the park. My stories, her tightrope—they could wait.

But the future, Reader, does not wait.

It comes to us in dreams so vivid, so terrifying, we cannot ignore it.

I slept with Mary by my side, her hair spread on my pillow like a dark sunburst, and I dreamed. I dreamed of the flames that would soon consume Dreamland Park, leaping like skyscrapers licking at the heavens. I could hear the splintering wood of collapsing structures. I could smell the smoke and taste the ash. Everyone screamed and wept, and the animals brayed and howled.

I found myself on the boardwalk, staring up at a towering, winged devil with blank eyes. Like a statue, it stood in the midst of the flames unmoving. I looked from sea to shore, water to smoke. I couldn't find her. I couldn't find Mary. I began to run.

I ran through flames and did not feel their heat. I swam through the sea and still breathed air. My arms spread like wings and I soared above the sand like a gull until I found her. I swooped to her side and took her in my arms. She was bleeding—not burned—and covered in sand. Her eyes rolled back, and the green was gone. My girl, my Mary, was gone.

I woke with a cry and frightened her awake.

"What were you dreaming about?" she asked. When I told her, she laughed softly, touched that I had been so frightened at the thought of losing her. She kissed my lips and promised it was only a dream.

But of course, Reader, it was not.

She fell asleep again but I lay awake, realizing it was not enough to get her away from Mulligan, to plot a great caper of sneaking her off a train. I had to get her away from Dreamland, too.

"What do you think about opening a shop of our own?" I asked her in the morning. "Someplace warm, maybe? So you could wear sundresses all year round."

She gave me a look. "Not Florida."

"Of course not Florida. But somewhere . . . else?"

She shrugged. "We'd need a lot more money."

I began to calculate the costs and quickly realized it was impossible with my meager savings. I needed a second job, but who would hire an

Irish boy covered in tattoos? Who would hire a freak? Not a restaurant, not a factory, not anyone but my father or a circus.

Desperate, I gathered my nickels and dimes and followed my brother to his beloved rat pits. I soothed my conscience with the notion that, whether I was there or not, there would be blood. My presence would not change the poor rats' fates, but it might change Mary's.

The place was underground, dark and illegal. The doors were flanked by gangsters, their eyes dazed with opium but their pistols sharp enough. Thick with smoke and the smell of unwashed bodies and stale beer, the air was sickening to breathe. It wasn't only the smell that sickened me. It was the eagerness for suffering. The eagerness to profit from it.

My brother was a ratcatcher. He was paid handsomely for trapping hundreds of rats, caging them, and bringing them here for the dogs to shake to death in their teeth. Donnie had been catching rats for the big bosses since childhood, and I'd never hidden my disgust for it. So when he looked up to see his little brother set foot on his territory, he had to look twice.

"You here to turn me in to the cops?" he asked, leaning with his elbow on the waist-high wall that enclosed the little sawdust arena. "Or is Pop dead?"

"I need money," I said, motioning him to sit with me on the wooden bleachers. I explained my situation, the dreams, the visions, the girl. I asked him to tell me which dog to bet on, so that I could win.

"You actually think you can see the future?" Donnie asked over the growls of the dogs. It was soon time to release the rats, and they were nearly as anxious as the men in the thickening crowd. He puffed at his cigar, then stamped it out with his foot. "Then shouldn't you be telling me which dog will be the winner?"

I tried to explain it to him that it didn't work that way. I had no control over what I could or couldn't see. But as the rats squealed in their cages and the dogs strained at their leashes, waiting to taste blood, my brother laughed at me.

"You belong in the looney bin," he said, and turned away to tend to his rats.

I bet on a Jack Russell named Queenie that night and lost every coin in my hand.

The next day, I met Dr. James.

CHAPTER TWELVE

HEN EVAN OPENED the door to the Black Cat, he found Mara sitting at a small table with Nona.

She stood up and hugged him, and over her shoulder, he caught the old woman's scowl.

"I just clocked out for break," Mara said. "You wanna step out back with me?"

Evan dropped his book bag on a chair at Nona's table and followed Mara through the kitchen to the back door, which led to a tiny walled-in courtyard with a bench and climbing crimson roses. As soon as the door thudded closed, she went up on tiptoe to kiss him.

"What are you up to today?"

He shrugged, attempting to appear casual. "I have some studying to do. Like three million slides to memorize for Mortakis and a sketch for 2D. But remember Taffy's on Surf?"

She nodded, and his heart began beating in his throat.

"It's a tattoo shop," he said, determined to keep his voice from going up an octave. "I went there this afternoon."

Her eyes widened. "You got a tattoo? Let me see!"

"I didn't get a tattoo," he said, shaking his head. "But I found something."

She clasped her hands together excitedly and did a little run-in-place. "Tell me!"

"I'll show you." Reaching into his pocket for his phone, his hands were unsteady and slick. But his phone wasn't there. He patted his other pockets and frowned. "Huh. Guess I left it in my bag."

Mara waved her keycard in front of the door sensor, leading him back through the kitchen and into the café.

"Back already?" her coworker with the mullet asked, glancing over his shoulder from the sink.

"Forgot something," Mara explained as Evan unzipped his bag, panicking at the thought of having lost his phone. Had it been stolen in the park? Finally, he found it at the bottom, below his sweatshirt, wedged between his Fundamentals of 2D textbook and his colored pencil case. Strange. He didn't remember putting it there.

"You want me to refill your tea, Nona?" Mara asked as Evan opened his gallery and swiped through pictures and panicked all over again.

Nona looked up from her knitting to smile at Mara. "I am just fine, love. But thank you."

"Sure." Mara patted the old woman's arm before resting her chin on Evan's shoulder to look at his phone. "So . . . what did you want to show me?"

It wasn't there.

He swiped left and right, but it wasn't there.

He checked his download folder, his camera roll, and recently deleted items.

"Where did it go?" he said slowly, realizing his mouth was moving and words were coming out. He couldn't feel his face.

Left.

Right.

"Where did what go?" Mara asked. "Come on, you're keeping me in suspense!"

Left.

Right.

"The picture I was going to show you. It's . . . it's gone. Where would it have gone?"

Mara shrugged. "What was it?"

"Well I . . . it's hard to describe. You'd kind of have to see it for yourself. I just don't understand this."

"I guess you'll just have to take me to Coney Island so I can see it in person," she said with a conspiratorial smile.

"Yeah, um, maybe sometime. It's pretty . . . fun . . . there," Evan mumbled. He didn't want to go anywhere near that beach or show up on Lillian's doorstep with another living dead person. He just wanted the picture to show up on his damn phone.

"Hey, I wanted to show you something, too," she said, taking his hand and leading him back outside to the bench. Crossing her legs and resting her phone on her knee, she pointed to the screen. "You inspired me. I joined this site called Connections that helps adopted kids find their birth parents. I made a profile, see?"

She handed him the phone, and he skimmed her profile information. Birthday, location, circumstances.

"That's a really pretty picture of you," he said, scrolling back up to the top. *Better than the picture I was going to show you*, he thought. How could it have disappeared? It had been real, though. He knew it had been. He hadn't imagined it.

"Isn't it weird to think there might be somebody out there who looks just like me? Somebody could be searching this site right now . . . and boom! They basically find a picture of themselves like twenty years ago."

"Yeah," Evan said, trying to keep his voice steady. "That would be pretty unreal."

Unreal.

The word made him nauseous. Kieran Flynn was real. The original portrait was sitting on his desk, and Lillian had seen the resemblance as soon as she walked into the room. Tony had seen it, too.

"I think about her all the time," Mara was saying, opening her notification page. It was empty, so she started scrolling profiles of birth mothers seeking their babies. "She could have been younger than I am now, you know? I read all these women's stories, and it's incredible, the stuff they've been through. I read this one last night . . . look." Mara pointed to the profile picture of a beautiful, olive-skinned woman with haunted eyes and a deep scar on her left cheek. "She was an Afghani refugee who gave birth thirteen years ago, and she doesn't even know her son's name. She's hoping his adoptive parents might reach out to her and get them in touch."

"Are there any dads on there?"

"A few," Mara said, going back to the profile directory. She tapped a picture of a smiling guy wearing his college graduation cap and gown. "This one says his ex-girlfriend put their baby up for adoption without telling him. He didn't even know he was a father until later, when a mutual friend told him, and by then it was too late. He's trying to find his three-year-old daughter."

"Hope he finds her." Evan's stomach twisted, feeling foolish all over again for writing those letters to the newspaper. What if his dad really had read it, but couldn't respond due to the restraining order? Or what if he'd read it from a psychiatric hospital?

Mara squeezed his hand. "Hey," she said. "Look at me. Whatever we find, we're still *us*, okay?"

He looked at her—this girl he'd known for less than a month. He was afraid that if he tried to say something, he'd cry, so he wrapped his arms around her. He hugged her close enough to feel her heart beating, and it was a beautiful heartbeat, rhythmic and perfect and synced with his. She wasn't making excuses, or looking for the next big thing, or telling him some yoga instructor was going to be a better father than his could have ever been.

"We're still us," he repeated softly, his cheek pressed against hers. He closed his eyes as she swirled her fingers on the back of his neck, savoring the sensation as her chest rose and fell against his. He wanted to stay in this moment and never think about his dad or Kieran Flynn or Mary Thompson in a casket again. He didn't want to have to tell Mara that he might be a genetic freak or maybe just a kid following in his father's footsteps.

All he wanted was to be close to her.

This time, it couldn't be temporary.

The realization didn't scare him like he thought it would. He loved Mara Cassidy. And he knew, in that moment, that he would love her forever.

CHAPTER THIRTEEN

Evan sat at his desk, erasing furiously. He couldn't draw. Couldn't think. Couldn't read or sit still. He crushed the sketch into a ball of trash, swiped eraser dust all over the floor, and got up to pace.

Mara was right. He must have bumped delete.

Except he knew he hadn't.

Deleting photos was a two-step process. He never would have hit confirm.

So maybe he'd moved it while in gallery view, accidentally trading places with something else. He swiped left and right, left and right, then all the way right. He went backward through two years' worth of photos. Luna Park and the possibly Trojan soldiers and the tattooed boy and Neptune's trident. Mr. Burns with a proud arm around his shoulder at his going-to-college party. The celebratory cake his mom had baked the night he received his acceptance letter. Their first Christmas in the new house. Hailey's fourth birthday. The two of them on the couch at Dave's house, snuggled up with his cat.

Mary Thompson really wasn't there, but Lillian still had the original, along with the newspaper clippings. Maybe he should take Mara to visit Taffy's, after all. Maybe it would be easier that way, with an impartial, third person in the room. He could introduce Mara to Lillian. She was good with old ladies—Nona loved her. It would all be okay.

Taking a deep breath, he dialed the number.

"Taffy's."

"Hi, is this Tony?"

"Yeah, who's this?"

"It's Evan. Evan Kiernan. I was in yesterday to talk to Lillian, and I wondered if I could ask her a couple of questions?"

Tony let out a long, heavy sigh. "She's in the hospital right now, actually."

Evan's stomach dropped. "Is she okay?"

"Not really, man," Tony said. "One of my aunts from upstate was in this morning gathering up photos and stuff. They don't think she's gonna make it through the night."

"They took her photos? Why?" he repeated, reeling. They couldn't be gone.

"She said they're going to need them for services. It's not looking good at all."

"That's . . . I mean, what happened?"

"It was last night." Tony's voice was tight with emotion, and he took a long, loud breath. "Couple hours after you left. I sat with her till the paramedics came, but I don't know if she even knew I was there. They said she had a massive heart attack, and now she's in a coma."

Evan could hardly breathe. *The pictures.* It was wrong for him to be thinking of the pictures at a time like this, when Lillian was on her deathbed, in a coma.

"Could you let me know what happens?" Evan asked, grasping at a shrinking ember of hope. "I'd like to see her again if I can. She's a great lady."

"Yeah. She sure is," Tony said, and sniffed. "I'll let you know."

He ended the call and stared at the framed photograph Lillian had given him. He picked it up and turned it over, lifting the little metal clasps that held the backing tight. Maybe there were more photographs tucked behind the portrait, he thought, loosening the thick, black rectangle of cardboard.

Lifting it away, Evan found nothing but words written in pencil on the back of the photograph, *The American Society for Psychical Research. East Seventy-third Street, New York New York.*

American Society for Psychical Research?

ASPR.

He typed it into his web browser, shivering when the home page popped up. It still existed, with a main office on East Seventy-third Street. Just a train ride away. He clicked on the About tab.

The American Society for Psychical Research is the oldest psychical research organization in the United States. For more than a century, its mission has been to explore extraordinary or as yet unexplained phenomena that have been called psychic or paranormal and their implications for our understanding of consciousness, the universe, and the nature of existence. How is mind related to matter, energy, space, and time? In what unexplained ways do we interconnect with the universe and each other? The ASPR addresses these profoundly important and far-reaching questions with scientific research and related educational activities including lectures, conferences, and other informational services.

The ASPR was founded in 1885 by a distinguished group of scholars and scientists who shared the courage and vision to explore the uncharted realms of human consciousness, among them renowned Harvard psychologist and Professor of Philosophy, William James.

William James was a Harvard psychologist. And he'd been to Taffy's to research paranormal activity? Evan read on to find that prominent members included dream researchers, philosophers, quantum physicists, and astronomers. The Society's studies continued through the decades, but there didn't seem to be any Harvard alumni working on the website, which looked like it hadn't been updated in twenty years. There were online surveys to fill out about your near-death experience or your 9/11 premonitions. Links to articles about ESP and their scientific journal, in which the newest publication was listed as 1976. Black-and-white photos of researchers in plaid suits in the credits of articles on Exceptional Human Experiences (EHE).

Evan clicked on the virtual tour of the libraries, but it was hardly a tour. Just a simple image of shelves lined with ragged-spined books and drawers of archived articles available to "qualified researchers"—just no explanation as to what qualified you.

Hope—and fear—surged in Evan's chest. Those archives must hold information about Dr. James's work, and Kieran Flynn, too. He'd been to Taffy's. He'd left his card. Evan held his breath and clicked on the contact page. There was a phone number. Shakily, he exhaled and dialed it before he could chicken out.

He expected the ring to sound eerie, like his mom's gag Halloween phone from Target, but the line rang like any other. He assumed a place like the American Society for Psychical Research was used to dealing with weirdos, but he didn't want to sound like one of them. He wanted to sound like a serious researcher, a student working on a project for classes at NYU. The woman who answered sounded as standard as the ring. He guessed sixtyish, nonsmoker, in bed by nine every night of the week.

"Hello, thank you for calling the American Society for Psychical Research, this is Dr. Weaver. How may I help you?"

"Hi, um . . . my name is Evan Kiernan and I'm a student at NYU. I'm working on a research project, and I was wondering if I might be able to make an appointment to come in and take a look at some of the archives?"

"Have you purchased a student membership?"

"Um . . . no?"

"With your student identification card, you may purchase a yearly membership for sixty dollars. You may make this purchase online through our website."

"Okay. Sure. I'll do that before I come in," he said, wincing at the cost. "I'd like to make an appointment as soon as possible."

"Hmm," Dr. Weaver said, and Evan held his breath. "I'll require some information about the nature of your project."

"Yeah . . . um . . . I'm doing some historical research," Evan stuttered. "I wanted to take a look at some of Dr. James's archives. Anything I could find about the people he worked with."

"Well, NYU is on our list of partnering facilities. Which doctorate program are you enrolled in?"

"Oh, um, I'm an art student."

She was silent for a beat, then cleared her throat. "Art?"

"Yeah. The class I'm taking deals with philosophy, too. Mythology in Modern Art."

"And you're seeking information on Dr. James." Evan could hear a frown in her voice, and papers shuffling.

"Yes, ma'am."

"Is it a doctorate or graduate level class?"

"Undergrad," he admitted, and his voice cracked. "But I'm very serious about the research."

"Well. If you can have your supervising professor fax me some information about the project, I'd be happy to get back in touch with you about a possible appointment."

"Okay."

Possible appointment? What was this place, Fort Knox?

"What's the um, fax address?"

"A fax machine transmits information via the phone lines," Dr. Weaver said flatly. "There is no address. It's a telephone number."

"Right. Sorry. Go ahead—I've got a pen."

He scribbled down the fax number in a doodled box on the edge of a sticky note, promising to get his professor in touch with the Society shortly. And then, when he hung up, he let his forehead fall onto his desk with a thud and swore. How was he going to get Dr. Mortakis's signature faxed to the Society without telling her he'd just made up a fake project for her class? What if he couldn't even figure out how to use a fax machine?

But then, he smiled.

He didn't have to tell Dr. Mortakis anything to get her signature. At ten the next morning, he was scheduled to work in her office, which contained a drawerful of her letterhead. He just had to forge a letter of explanation, print, sign, and fax it, then delete the document and printer history.

As soon as Dr. Mortakis left the office for meetings Monday morning, Evan got to work. He checked, double checked, and triple checked, certain there was no electronic trace of his counterfeit. After a visit to the help desk and a lesson in ancient history, the dinosaur fax machine squeaked and groaned and chirped, doing whatever it did to send images over the phone lines, and then it went silent. The shredder dismantled the paper evidence, and Evan sat down to finish entering grades, even though his work hours were technically over. Fifteen minutes after noon, he locked the door to Dr. Mortakis's office, hoping he hadn't forgotten anything. Before he even reached the Black Cat for lunch, Dr. Weaver called him back to make an appointment for Tuesday at five o'clock.

CHAPTER FOURTEEN

"LET'S TALK ABOUT the monster in the maze," Dr. Mortakis said, dimming the lights. "Artists have been captivated by the story of the Minotaur for thousands of years, but Pablo Picasso was personally obsessed with it for over a decade. Many scholars believe he saw the half-man, half-bull as his alter ego."

The screen displayed a disquieting cubist rendition of a creature with a bull's face and a human body, but Evan looked away to check the time. *2:07.*

How had only seven minutes passed? He wished he could fast forward to five o'clock, or better yet, to the moment of discovery. There had to be a photograph of Mary Thompson at the ASPR. Or at least someone who knew where to find one.

Dr. Mortakis switched to another slide of Theseus slaying the monster in the maze in medieval garb. "None but Theseus could slay the Minotaur. All others who tried were devoured, because the Fates ruled not only men, but the gods, as well. Their decrees were inescapable, and this gave the ancients a sense of justice, balance, and purpose.

As Beowulf says so eloquently as he prepares to face his own monster, 'Fate will unwind as it must.'"

She continued switching through slides of Ariadne's unwinding thread and Aegeus throwing himself off the cliffs into what would become known as the Aegean Sea. Meanwhile, Evan kept checking the time.

All he wanted to do was get on the train to East Seventy-third.

He was sure that, as soon as he met with someone at ASPR, he would find the way out of his own maze. In just two and a half hours, he thought, Dr. Weaver would be his Ariadne, offering the thread that would lead him back in time to the truth of Kieran Flynn.

THE WROUGHT-IRON BANISTER drew heat from Evan's fingers as he waited for the door to the gothic townhouse to open. Every windowpane was curtained in tightly pleated fabric, blocking his view to the inside.

He knocked again, and a shadow darkened the door curtain. He was greeted by a heavyset woman wearing an ankle-length brown plaid skirt with a tweed jacket and graying hair pulled into a tight, low bun.

"Mr. Kiernan?"

Evan nodded and extended his hand to shake, but she offered him a wicker basket instead.

"There is absolutely no photography of any kind allowed in the library. If you require copies, I will assist you. Please deposit your cellular phone and any other electronic devices in the basket before entering."

"Okay. Are you Dr. Weaver? The one I talked to on the phone?"

"I am." She waited while he emptied his pockets, but his phone didn't seem to want to leave his hand.

"I won't take any pictures," he lied. "Promise."

Evan did his best trustworthy smile and vulnerable shiver as the wind kicked up.

Just one . . . it would only take one little photograph to guarantee that Mara would believe him . . .

Dr. Weaver shook her head, but the tight gray bun didn't move. What had he expected? A wispy woman with creepy eyes and a crystal ball? Certainly not an Army sergeant with a wicker basket. When his phone finally dropped, she swung the stately front door open.

In contrast to its imposing guardian, the house itself was small and unassuming: A white-paneled foyer, the top half of the walls papered in pink and white stripes. A curving wooden staircase that was too short to call *grand*. The hot, sweet scent of baking dust you get on the first day cold enough to turn the heat on.

"This way," Dr. Weaver said, and Evan followed her across noisy, uneven floorboards spread with fading Persian rugs. Wiggling a key into the door beneath a loose knob, she opened it to a dim room with one east-facing window covered in white muslin. A cold marble fireplace with a mirrored mantle was the only thing that broke up the wall-to-wall bookshelves, and the mirror was tarnished, blackened at the corners like it had been hanging there a very long time. A utilitarian oak table with sensible chairs stood in the middle of it all, and this was where Dr. Weaver put a pair of white gloves.

"We have surveillance cameras," she said briskly, handing Evan a laminated printout key to the nonconventional classification system, which included sections for automatic writings and spirit photographs. "You have an hour until we close."

"What exactly are spirit photographs?" he began to ask, but the heavy paneled door thudded behind her.

Evan had always liked the smell of books, especially old ones, but he suddenly couldn't breathe. It was so strong, he could taste it—the smell of the past, of age and decay and loneliness. Especially loneliness. No one had read these books in decades.

He'd thought Dr. Weaver would help him. He'd expected to be able to tell someone what was happening to him—someone sympathetic and trusting, interested in Exceptional Human Experiences. He'd expected to be able to search their computer system, but there was only an oak card catalog fronted with tiny square drawers marked with the letters of the alphabet.

He didn't know where to begin.

Walking around the room in a slow daze, he tried to get his bearings. The shelves were lined with fraying book spines in burnt orange and washed-out brown.

Call numbers were taped meticulously to each one, but they were oddly marked. Not Dewey Decimal. Glancing from the spines to the printout Dr. Weaver had given him, he tried to figure out the organization of materials, but it all seemed to fall under one category —creepy.

So he headed for the catalog drawers, pulling them out and reading the tabs that separated authors alphabetically. He thumbed through the F drawer, searching for Flynn, Kieran, but nothing was there. Of course. Kieran Flynn wasn't the author. It was Dr. James he needed to look up. It was the J drawer he needed. That was where he'd find the prize.

There were five call numbers for books, and then more of the odd classifications for materials, starting with Ph for Photograph. There were hundreds of them, each with their own card and call number, some with subcategories of Tsub (Test Subject) and SpPh (Spirit Photograph). There was Aud (Audio), as well as F (Film).

He wiggled his fingers into the gloves.

Call numbers in hand, he hunted for all the books by Dr. James and spread them on the wooden table. It was tricky turning pages with the gloves on, but he flipped each one to the index and searched for him: Flynn, Kieran.

He was in the third book, in a chapter entitled "Premonitions."

*On Coney Island, I came upon Kieran Flynn, a heavily tat-
tooed "freak," toward the end of the 1910 season, just before
the Labor Day holiday. He had positioned himself along the
boardwalk, calling out for the attention of tourists. Countless
times a day, the young man spoke these words:*

 "I am the two-hundred-year-old man.

 My skin tells the stories of the lives I have lived

 And of the deaths I should have died—

 But didn't.

 Come close—

 For just one penny, you can see!

 Come close—

 For just one penny,

 A tale that will prickle the hairs upon your neck!"

 *Flynn did not have the loud voice of a barker, but his bare,
tattooed chest and arms spoke volumes for him. No one along
the boardwalk could pass without noticing because humans
are, by nature, curious creatures.*

 *Given my line of work, I was intrigued, and offered him the
equivalent of a hundred pennies if he would give me a private
audience for half an hour. He obliged.*

 *"Do you actually believe that you are two hundred years
old?" I asked.*

 *The young man laughed. "How do you define years?" he
asked, rather mischievously.*

 *"Three hundred sixty-five rotations of the earth—a com-
plete orbit around the sun," I replied. "Scientifically speaking."*

 *"I know that," the boy said, suddenly serious. "But I also
know things I should not know. Things that have been. Things
that will be. I know that time is but a trick."*

 "Tell me," I implored, and explained to him my work.

 "If I tell you," he said, "will you help me?"

I promised that I would try.

So we walked through the strange and beautiful Dream-land Park, where he began to explain himself to me.

He suffered repeated visions and dreams, many of grue-some deaths. At times, his vision would suddenly change, and it was as if he were transported to the past. He would fall asleep and have dreams so vivid, he was certain he was looking into to the future.

Earlier in the season, a contortionist had come to the Dreamland Park, and he immediately recognized her as the girl from his visions and dreams. He had fallen in love with her, and now feared for her life.

I asked him to come to the Society for further interviews, which were conducted throughout the winter of 1910–1911. The subject detailed his waking visions of a purported past life, as well as his dream-based premonitions that the Dreamland Park would be destroyed in fire at an unknown date, by an unknown cause. In addition, the subject reported glimpses into a future incarnation, in which he and the girl were destined to meet yet again. For film footage of these interviews, see F333.

Evan's heart was in his throat and tears pressed his eyes.

I know things I should not know . . .

Things that have been . . .

Things that will be . . .

Like him, Kieran Flynn had seen visions of the past. But goose-bumps crawled over Evan's skin with the icy realization that the tattooed boy had been able to see the future, too. Lillian said he'd predicted the fire, but according to this report, he'd looked much fur-ther into the future than that.

Had Kieran Flynn dreamed of Mara with hints of purple in her hair, playing music no one could have imagined in 1911? Had he seen the rain in Washington Square, or glimpsed Evan sitting here now, reading these words?

He knew he and Mary were destined to meet again. But . . . then what? Had he seen them living happily ever after? Or had he seen . . . something else?

With shaky hands, Evan turned the page to find a handwritten addendum.

June 1911. It is my professional opinion that Mr. Flynn caused the fire event in May 1911 out of desperation to prove his premonitions correct. The young man's family has quietly committed him to the care of the Kings Park Asylum . . .

A hot stream slid down Evan's cheek, and he quickly brushed it away. They thought he caused it? And his own family institutionalized him? Mary *died* in the fire—he would never have started it. He would have prevented it with every ounce of his strength, kept her safe no matter the cost.

But just like Lillian said, nobody believed him. Not even his family. They institutionalized him instead. Had he told Mary she was in danger? And had she believed him, or did she die thinking he belonged in that asylum, too?

Evan let his face fall into his gloved hands, trying to compose himself. Kieran Flynn saw the past and the future. He recognized Mary as the girl from his dreams—dreams made up of gruesome deaths.

Her deaths.

Plural.

But a person could only die once . . .

Unless somehow they kept coming back to live—and die—again.

He breathed in through his nose and out through his mouth, fighting the spiral of panic wrapping itself around his throat. He had to keep his head and find F333.

Evan crept out into the foyer in search of Dr. Weaver and found her sitting at a small writing desk with perfect posture. He cleared his throat.

"Yes?" she asked, turning to look at him.

"I was wondering if you could help me find a few more things," Evan said, offering her his handwritten notes. But just then, the grandfather clock belched six hollow chimes.

"Perhaps another time," Dr. Weaver said, rising and picking up a hoop-style key ring. "Your hour is up."

"Please, it won't take long. I just need to see—"

She snatched his notes, then lifted the chained reading glasses from her neck to her nose. "These are in a different wing," she said, handing the notes back to Evan. "Not today."

"Can I make another appointment? Soon?"

She flipped through a Rolodex, nodding. "I'll be in touch."

He sighed. "Could I come, like, tomorrow?"

"We have limited hours. But don't worry. Your professor understands. I spoke with her this morning, and she's prepared to give you an extension."

The blood drained from Evan's head. "Oh, you, um, talked to her?"

Dr. Weaver just nodded and showed him the door.

Cursing his own idiocy for faxing a letterhead with Dr. Mortakis's phone number, he grabbed his cell out of the wicker basket and stepped out onto the sidewalk. He wanted now, more than ever, to call Mara and tell her everything. But if he told her now, without proof, she'd want him to get a psych eval. And this time, he'd have to check the *paranoid schizophrenic* box on that family history page. She'd expect him to take pills and go to therapy and only see things everyone else could see. His mom was already worried. The more he insisted that what he'd seen was real, the more they'd all be convinced he was just like his dad. Which meant that if something bad really was going to happen to Mara . . . the only way he could keep her safe was to keep his mouth shut. At least for now.

CHAPTER FIFTEEN

VAN SPENT THE train ride back to NYU scouring the internet for information on Dreamland Park. Not one article claimed that a tattooed boy was accused of setting the fire. It went down in history as an accident. Did that mean Kieran Flynn's name was cleared? That he was deemed sane and released from the hospital? Lillian said her uncle "disappeared," so if he had been released, he didn't go back to his family in New York. And if he wasn't released . . . well, Evan didn't want to think about what it might mean to disappear into a place like Kings Park Asylum.

He didn't want to think about what Dr. Mortakis would say when he walked into her office the next morning, either. How could he face her, now that she knew he'd forged her signature? He'd seriously considered calling in sick, but he couldn't afford a smaller paycheck this week—he'd just spent sixty dollars on a membership fee to the ASPR, and the Black Cat wasn't getting any cheaper. So he went to work Wednesday morning at ten, praying that Dr. Mortakis wouldn't fire him or send him back to Pennsylvania—or show up at all.

The door was locked, but he had his key. He was scheduled to work from ten till noon, and he entered grades feverishly, trying to finish early, his stomach twisting every time he heard footsteps in the hall.

He breathed a sigh of relief when the clock struck twelve, feeling like he'd gotten away with something. But just as he was pulling the door closed behind him, he jumped.

He hadn't even heard her coming.

"Just leave it open," Dr. Mortakis said, her dark eyes looking brightly overcaffeinated. She was holding several stuffed folders and notebooks in one hand and a cup from the Black Cat in the other.

Holding his breath, Evan held the door open so she could enter her office.

"Got all your work done?" she asked, her alert eyes surveying the graded papers he'd stacked neatly beside her desk.

"Yep, all done. Have a good—"

"I spoke with Dr. Kim," she interrupted. "Seems you've missed some lab work?"

Shit.

How had he forgotten to turn that in?

"And Dr. Santiago told me you didn't seem to understand the assignment for your last two essays in Comp. He's concerned, Evan, and quite frankly, so am I. You know you can come to me if you're struggling, right?"

"I know," he said, gripping the doorknob and inching toward the hall. "Yes, thank you."

"Student services can provide you with a writing tutor," she added. "And Dr. Kim could assign you a more supportive lab partner if that would be helpful?"

"No . . . I think I just need to get more organized."

"All right." She nodded, then sighed. "Well, student services also provides time management support. So don't be shy."

"I'll look into that. And I'll do better. I promise."

"Good. Oh, and . . . how's that *psychic* project coming along?"

Evan's stomach was a plummeting elevator. "Um . . ."

"What class is that for again?"

"It's actually more of a . . . personal interest project," he admitted. "But I shouldn't have used your letterhead. I'm sorry. I'm really, truly sorry. It was stupid and wrong and I won't do it again."

Evan forced himself to meet her eyes, fully expecting her gaze to be boring into him with rage. But instead, they were round and shining with . . . hurt?

"I meant it when I said I'm here for you," she said. "I know this is a huge transition, and time management in college is so much different from high school. But I can only help you if you let me."

He nodded, stunned.

"You are so talented," she said, taking a step closer and placing a hand on his arm. "And I believe in you one hundred percent. But if you fail your gen eds, I can't force the dean to keep you enrolled in this program. So you do your schoolwork first, side projects after from now on."

"Got it."

"And you get my permission before using my signature," she added, a note of warning making her voice sound just like his mom's. "Understood?"

"Yes," he breathed, cheeks flaming.

She nodded firmly, but then she quirked a smile. "That Dr. Weaver's a trip, isn't she?"

"Yeah," Evan agreed, trying to roll with the shifting mood of the conversation. She wasn't going to send him packing? She wasn't going to fire him, either? "Interesting lady for sure."

"If she doesn't get back to you about your next appointment, let me know. I'll light a fire under her dusty ass—but *only* if your other work is being completed on time. Capisce?"

Evan nodded, thanking her one more time as he backed out into the hall. When the office door closed behind him, he slumped against the wall and tried to slow his heartbeat.

He'd gotten lucky.

But he knew it was going to take hard work to earn Dr. Mortakis's trust back.

If he wanted to keep his job, his spot in the program, and his connection to the ASPR, there was no room for another mistake.

He returned to Goddard Hall, determined to revise both essays before class. He'd hand them in, polished to a shine, and Dr. Santiago would at least give him partial credit. Maybe even extra credit—if that was a thing in college.

But every few sentences, his mind wandered back to Kieran Flynn.

I know things I should not know.

Things that have been.

Things that will be . . .

What did the tattooed boy know about him and Mara?

Anxious questions churned in his mind, muddling the afternoon lecture in English Composition and blurring the details of yet another writing assignment. Why wouldn't Dr. Weaver let him make another appointment before leaving the Society? She'd been so quick to reply the first time, and even answered the phone on a Sunday afternoon. He needed to get into those film archives. He needed to know that the tattooed boy had seen a happy ending for her. For them.

Because if he hadn't . . .

If Kieran Flynn had seen something terrible happening to Mara . . .

Then Evan needed to know exactly what it was in time to make it stop.

KINGS PARK ASYLUM

1911

THE SKIES WERE heavy and gray that morning, an unusually early chill in the air. The boardwalk was deserted, but still, I stood shirtless and shivering, desperate to replace the coins I'd so foolishly gambled away. I told my tales to the gulls and the sea, to the straggling passersby who were worse off than me.

And then, a man with a smart brown suit approached, his fine dress shoes pounding a rhythm on the boardwalk as he twirled his mustache curiously. From his darting black eyes to the jerk of his head, he was like a little sparrow looking for crumbs.

He stopped and removed his hat, listening to my tale. Handing me a small, rectangular business card, he introduced himself as Dr. William James, researcher of the unusual and paranormal, psychiatrist and curator of Exceptional Human Experiences. He was interested, he said, in learning more about mine.

As we strolled the park, the clouds rolled away. People follow the sun, and soon Dreamland was filled with its familiar smells and sights and oddities. He enjoyed our conversation so much, he invited me to his office for further interviews, and I agreed on the condition he would help me to save her.

He gave me his word, and I believed him to be a gentleman. I had coins in my pocket and hope in my chest because, at last, someone believed me. I thought he might even respect me.

I was eager to begin, but Dr. James was departing for the island of Haiti the next morning. He'd planned to spend the months of September and October studying the spiritual practices of the Haitians, then return on the first of November to study me.

My hope grew into a thing with wings. I was sure that, upon his return to New York, Dr. James would unravel the riddles of my mind. All I had to do was sneak Mary off her train. The educated man with expensive shoes would do the rest.

The cold was coming, so the visitors left Dreamland, waiting for the return of summer and fun. Mulligan herded his Oddities like cattle to Grand Central Station, his wallet fat with the money they'd earned for him. I hid my colorful skin beneath a jacket and gloves and positioned myself behind a pillar, waiting for my moment.

Mary took her ticket from his hand, and he kissed her cheek. I restrained myself from jumping out and bloodying his lips. I watched her step up onto the platform as Mulligan counted their heads as if he were a schoolteacher, ensuring all his pupils were present.

And then, he swung his watch in slow circles, sauntering to his own train car—first class.

The whistle blew, and I held my breath. The engine hissed a puff of steam. The wheels began to turn as steam rose to the clouds.

Every second was a century as I waited, afraid Mulligan had paid the Strongman to hold her down. But at the final whistle, in a whoosh of deep plum skirts, she leaped from the car to the platform and into my arms. Breathless, we watched the train slither away to the south.

The leaves changed color, and my heart bloomed beside Mary's.

CHAPTER SIXTEEN

T HE HUMIDITY FLED New York with the month of September, and the air coming through the windows of Goddard Hall was crisp as an apple as Evan dumped an armful of warm sheets onto his bed. He'd just pulled them from the dryer downstairs, and the smell of fabric softener radiated through the room as he wrestled with the fitted sheet, telling himself what he was going to do.

Sleep.

Dream.

See Mara alive and happy, fifty years from now.

He'd been telling himself that every night for two weeks, but he hadn't had a single dream. That was how Kieran Flynn said it worked, wasn't it? See the past while you're awake and the future in your sleep? So why could *he* only see the past?

Maybe nothing bad was going to happen this time, after all, or maybe there was some trick to it, something Kieran Flynn had explained to Dr. James. He'd left fourteen messages at the Society, but still no one had called him back.

It bothered him, keeping it all a secret from Mara. They'd both been hurt enough by their parents' secrets and lies—and he'd promised to be honest with her. Still, he needed her to trust him, not try to fix him with therapy and pills.

So he tried his best to act normal. To keep up with his schoolwork and focus on the present. Maybe whatever items Lillian had from Kieran and Mary might be upstate, and the ASPR might be understaffed and overwhelmed, but Evan and Mara were doing all right, falling in love the old-fashioned way, all by themselves.

Henri had gone to stay with his aunt in New Jersey for the long Columbus Day weekend, and Mara had a rare Saturday off because of NYU's fall break schedule, so they'd planned to spend it exploring the thrift shops in the Village. She appeared in his doorway at noon, wearing distressed skinny jeans, cute little sneakers, and a black shirt patterned in pink roses that gave him a knee-weakening glimpse of her belly button.

They found themselves at a funky little fifties diner on the East Side, complete with a black-and-white checkered floor, pink vinyl booths, and a jukebox that played original records.

Mara dropped a few quarters in and made a playlist, starting with "You Send Me," then ordered a chocolate malt shake with a slice of cherry pie for lunch.

The first song ended, and they could hear the jukebox grinding gears as it dropped a new record on the turntable.

"You know," she said, swallowing a bite of pie as Frankie Valli began singing, "Earth angel, earth angel, will you be mine" in an exaggerated falsetto. "Death Cab does an adorable cover of this song."

"I did not know that."

"Yeah, it's better than the original. Although, to be fair, this isn't the original, either. The Penguins did it before Frankie Valli and the Four Seasons."

He smiled. "You're like a walking musical encyclopedia."

"Now it all makes sense," she exclaimed, smacking herself in the forehead. "*Duh.* The guy in Washington Square. He was a walking encyclopedia! So obvious now."

"That's deep, man."

They laughed, and the sugary sweetness of Frankie Valli's falsetto switched to the frenetic piano and howls of Little Richard.

"Speaking of the square, Ben just signed us up for a Halloween Battle of the Bands. They're setting up at the fountains, and everybody's playing in costume. There are some major prizes."

"Cool. That's my birthday."

"Halloween?"

He nodded, rolling his eyes. "My mother's favorite day to go absolutely over the top with tackiness."

She quirked an eyebrow. "Should I be on the lookout for another surprise visitor?"

"She'll probably be all sneaky this time and show up in an overbearing mother costume." He laughed. "Seriously though, she did promise to call first from now on."

She laughed, too, then sighed. "If I had known it was your birthday, I would have told Ben I couldn't play the show. Now I can't take you out!"

"Mara, it's cool."

"I'm going to make it up to you," she promised. "You only turn eighteen once."

"Okay." He sipped at the chocolate malt and smiled around his straw as she hooked her ankles around his. "I'll let you make it up to me."

After lunch, they walked the Village for a while, stopping in thrift stores to rummage through vintage sweaters and old vinyl. She bought him a three-dollar copy of Blind Lemon Jefferson to hang above his desk, and he bought her a blue-flowered necklace upcycled from a piece of broken China.

They wandered around until the stores began to flip their signs from Open to Closed. The sun dipped low, taking the day's warmth with it.

She slipped her hand in his as they walked back to his dorm, stopping for gyros on the way. Leading her up the stairwell to his room, he wondered if he was really the same person who walked into Mr. Burns's art class last October. That person never imagined he could be this happy.

"You wanna watch a little TV?" he asked, kicking off his sneakers and closing the blinds.

She shook her head. "I want you to hear the song."

Pulling her phone from her purse, she opened her music app and started Death Cab for Cutie's slow, dreamy cover of "Earth Angel."

Every chord, every word seemed to be written about her.

Taking her hand, he kissed her palm, then stood, pulling her up with him.

"The only thing that diner was missing," he said, bringing his left hand to the small of her back while holding hers with his right, "was a dance floor."

She laughed and let him sway her to the drowsy beat, leading her toward the light switch. He dipped her dramatically, making her squeal, then flicked off the light. "And proper lighting."

"We should really recommend this to the manager," she whispered in the darkened room, pressing close enough to feel how much he wanted her.

"Earth angel, earth angel," he sang along softly, resting his forehead against hers. "Will you be mine?"

She nodded and wrapped her arms around his neck as they continued to sway to the music, his hands on her hips.

Nothing strange happened.

No visions.

No flashes.

They were just Evan and Mara, alone at last. Her playlist continued softly in the background, but they slowly stopped dancing and starting kissing.

"I know it's only been a month," he said, when the music had played itself out and they were lying on his bed, side-by-side on top of his freshly washed sheets. "But I love you. Is it too soon to say that?"

"Ordinarily, yes." She propped herself up on her elbow and bit her lip in playful consideration. "But this isn't an ordinary situation."

"It's not?"

"Nope."

"Um . . . why not?" His head went light, and he could feel his heartbeat in his temples. Was it possible that something had been happening to her, too? The loneliness he'd felt at the ASPR suddenly seemed miles and years away. If she could see it all, too—the relief was too much to wrap his mind around.

She took a fistful of his shirt and pulled him toward her. Her lips brushing his ear, she whispered, "Because I love you, too."

"Really? I mean, you don't have to say it just because I said it."

"I love you," she said, and the way she kissed him left no room for doubt.

In the warm, dreamy haze of her embrace, he thought about all the places he'd called home in the last seventeen years. His life had been nothing but a chain of events leading him to this moment, this girl, who felt more like home than any four walls ever could.

It didn't matter what Kieran Flynn might have seen or what actually happened to Mary or what some quack doctor believed about the night Dreamland burned. No dream or vision could ever be as real as this. So maybe the tattooed boy had failed to keep the girl he loved safe, but Evan Kiernan wouldn't.

No matter what.

When her phone rang near midnight, he waved in its general direction, grumbling, "Go away."

She laughed. "What if it's important?"

"It's not," he said, pulling her close again.

But when the phone rang for the third time, she got up to pull it out of her purse. "It's Sam. I should pick up."

He could hear the excited, tinny cadence of Samantha's voice saying something that made Mara's eyes go wide.

"This Friday?" More garbled excitement emitted from the phone before Mara said, "Oh my god, that's amazing! Yeah, I'll be home in a little bit. Okay. Bye." As soon as she ended the call, she turned to Evan and squealed. "We got the Friday night gig!"

"Yasss," he said, raising a hand to high-five her.

"They want to go over the set list tonight," she said, quickly gathering her things.

He reached for his MetroCard. "I'll take you home."

She gave him a funny look.

"It's almost midnight," he insisted. "And I know in a perfect world, a pretty girl shouldn't need a guy to walk her home. But this is not a perfect world. So please?"

"Fine." She smiled. "But only because I like you."

"Um, actually, you said you *love* me," he reminded her with a grin, grabbing a hoodie from his dresser drawer and tossing it to her. "Remember?"

"Did I?" she teased, putting his sweatshirt on before taking his hand.

Together, they descended the stairs of Goddard Hall and walked out into the October chill. Everything felt perfect—a crisp, crescent moon outshone the city lights, the leaves had just begun to turn red and yellow and orange, the shop windows were decorated with pumpkins, and Mara's hand was warm in his.

It can stay this good, he told himself. *We can stay like this forever.*

Still, as they wound through the empty streets of Brooklyn toward Mercer Avenue, every shifting shadow, every rustling leaf, every dark alleyway seemed to whisper otherwise.

KINGS PARK ASYLUM

1911

LEAVES FELL, THEN snow, and Fitz Mulligan didn't come back for her. Saving quarters and dollars, we dreamed of opening a parlor of our own someplace farther south. Someplace safe. But as months passed in safety, falling into a comfortable rhythm, we spoke of it less and less.

I spoke, instead, to Dr. James, who returned from Haiti sunbrowned and invigorated. When he answered the door on Seventy-third Street, his eyes were bright and alert.

He shook my hand eagerly, but he did not release it at the natural moment. Instead, he turned it over in his, examining the black cat.

"Does it have significance?" he asked, awkwardly cradling my hand in his, standing in the threshold. He hadn't even closed the door yet, and already, he was questioning me.

I nodded. "There is always a black cat," I explained. "In every life she lives."

Forgetting about the door entirely, he pulled a small notebook from his vest pocket and began to write. He did not seem to notice the gust of cold November wind.

"And do all the images on your skin represent something spiritual?"

"No, not all of them," I said, and turned to close the door. Pausing, I examined the entrance of the American Society of Psychical Research. It was smaller than I'd expected, and plainer, too. For such a tall building, the staircase was surprisingly small. "Although perhaps you believe that nothing is as it appears? That everything physical has a spiritual counterpart?"

Dr. James smiled. "I'm a man of science," he said. "As eager to disprove as to prove. Would you like to take a little tour of the Society before we begin?"

He walked me through the library, which still had many empty shelves. A man wearing white gloves sat at a long wooden table, sorting peculiar photographs.

"Dr. Mellot is cataloguing our collection of Spirit Photographs," he explained, gesturing toward the gloved man. "Are you familiar with Mumler's work?"

I was not, and so Dr. James explained to me how, in the 1860s, a Boston photographer named William Mumler claimed his camera could capture ghosts. In his studio, a bereaved mother might sit for a portrait alone, and then, after the picture was developed, she could see her infant's spirit, curled up in her lap. Even President Lincoln's wife sat for such a photograph and treasured the image of her husband hovering above her shoulder. Mumler became quite rich, taking family portraits that included the men and boys who died in the American Civil War.

"Look at this one," Dr. James said, pointing to a photograph of a seated young woman with a high, dark bun. Directly above her head floated another image, seemingly made of light, of a boy in uniform. "This woman paid ten dollars to have her photograph taken at Mumler's Boston studio in hopes of capturing the image of her dead fiancé. Mumler delivered the photo, complete with the ghost, but two months later, the fiancé arrived home. It turned out he'd not been killed in Gettysburg, after all, but rather, another young man with the same name.

The officers had notified the wrong family. And so, clearly, Mumler's photography was proved to be a sham—nothing but tricks of alchemy in the dark room."

"Tricks," I repeated, and began to worry.

The doctor took me to his office, where a fire crackled and warmed my face as I answered his questions. He inquired after the physical sensations I experienced when looking into the past, asking me to specify whether the world seemed to spin clockwise or counterclockwise, and whether the flashes of light might represent rotations of the earth around the sun. It was tedious, answering his questions, but I pressed on. I had questions of my own.

"In your travels," I asked, "did you find evidence of a devil?"

The doctor twirled his mustache. "In the singular form?"

I nodded. "In my dreams of the fire, there is always a devil. Larger than any man."

"This, I presume, is a synthesis," he said, nodding to himself. "You have heard stories of hellfire and devils with large, dark wings. It isn't unusual for such a thing to appear in your dreams."

"You didn't answer my question," I pressed, my heart pounding with the desire to believe him. "Is there evidence?"

"None whatsoever," the doctor said. "Not even in Haiti."

Before leaving, I asked him if he thought I should tell Mary of my premonitions. The doctor was adamant that I should not. There was no need to alarm her, he said, for women's minds are fragile things. Though I told him plainly he'd underestimated Mary's strength of mind, I agreed there was good sense in not alarming her. Not if Dr. James was going to help me. We planned to meet monthly, and my hope remained steadfast.

I tattooed Mary that winter, little by little, with flowers and birds, magical creatures of the land and sea, all the prettiest things I could imagine. We started to believe that if we changed our skin, if we made ourselves into what we wanted, maybe we could change our destinies, too. She gave me every inch of her skin, and I gave her everything she asked for. Everything.

At Christmastime, Tom Thumb came calling with sweets, and by the fire he told me of the progress of Dreamland's renovations. Since Mulligan's departure, I had avoided the park completely, though Mary went several times a week to visit Black Prince. She'd told me what a mess it was, all scaffolding and plaster dust, wet paint and noise.

"It's not safe for you there," I'd told her, again and again, but she would not abandon the great cat.

"Prince will protect me," she said, teasing. "I'll be fine."

I had hoped Tom Thumb would talk sense into her. In the offseason, he earned extra money repainting and helping to build new rides in the area adjacent to his home. At times, he said, helping himself to one of his wife's gifted cookies, his small size was advantage.

"It must be quite hazardous with all that lumber flying around the coasters. All those nails and saws and men on ladders," I said to Tom as the fire crackled and Mary brushed colored sugar crumbs from her skirt. She squinted at me, and, picking up on my insinuation, rolled her eyes.

Tom Thumb shrugged his small shoulders and propped his child-sized feet on my father's old ottoman. "No accidents yet," he said. "Though the noises disturb the animals."

"Which is exactly why Prince needs me," Mary interjected. "It upsets him. And it's not as if Captain Jack gives a damn about how he feels."

I raised my hands in surrender. It was decided then and there that Mary would continue to visit and soothe her cat, and I would keep my mouth shut.

Through the months of ice and snow, she excelled with the tattoo machine. Her appointment book filled faster than mine or my father's ever had. What sailor could resist baring his strong arms for such a girl? She crafted them into something too good for the sea.

Word of the lady tattooist spread around Brooklyn that winter, and soon even girls arrived at our doorstep, asking for tiny pictures in *secret places. Our savings jar overflowed, and I continued to hint at the south—Norfolk, perhaps, or New Orleans.*

But those places, she said, were too far from my father, whose health was worsening, and too far, of course, from Black Prince, who needed her comfort. She was happy here, she assured me. And I couldn't argue that the money was good.

Dad was so pleased at the boon to his business, he suggested over dinner one winter's night that we change the name from Flynn's to Taffy's. Mary kissed his cheek and promised him we'd stay.

CHAPTER SEVENTEEN

THE MOON WAS full, there was a chill in the air, and in less than an hour, Switched Flip was headlining the Friday night set at Blossom & Spies. Evan sat on the cracked-leather couch of the musicians' lounge, sipping at a Dr Pepper and finishing his lab report while Samantha applied another coat of deep plum lipstick to Mara's lower lip.

"Don't you think it's a little dark?" Mara asked, staring doubtfully into a handheld mirror. "Like, are we crossing over from emo to goth here?"

"You look hot," Samantha declared, snatching the mirror and capping the lipstick decisively. "And hot transcends superficial labels."

Mara scrunched her nose and dabbed at her lips with a tissue as soon as Samantha turned her back. "I'm not going out there looking like a goth clown," she muttered.

"Correction," Evan whispered, glancing toward Samantha before reaching out to fix a smudge of purple in the dip of her upper lip. "A *hot* goth clown."

She snorted. "Did I get it all?"

"Not quite," he said, taking the tissue and cradling her chin in his palm while dabbing at her lips until a brisk knock pulled their attention to the lounge door.

"Mara Cassidy?" Brad, the owner of Blossom & Spies, called.

"Um, yeah?"

"Somebody here to see you."

Mara glanced quizzically around the room, but everyone just shrugged. When she opened the door, she immediately took a step back.

"Dad?" she breathed. "What are you doing here?"

"Came to hear you play," a gentle voice answered, and Evan craned his neck to see a lanky, graying man in a blue plaid shirt and belted Wrangler jeans shifting his weight uncomfortably in the hall. "You know I never miss one of your shows."

"How did you even know I'd be here?"

"I saw it on Instagram."

"You're stalking me on Instagram now?"

"It's the only way to—"

Evan was on his feet, moving protectively toward her. "Mara? Is everything okay?"

"Yeah, it's fine," Mara said quickly, raising a calming hand before taking a step out into the hall. "Just . . . give us a minute."

As the door closed, Samantha lifted a finger to her lips, and they all leaned closer, listening.

"I brought you something," Mr. Cassidy said. "Look here. See? It's your birth certificate."

In the long silence that followed, everyone in the lounge exchanged shocked glances.

Darren covered his mouth with his hand, and Evan took a step closer to the door.

"That's what you wanted, isn't it? What you've been asking for?"

Still, Mara didn't answer.

"All you have to do is tell Mom you're sorry, honey. She'll let you come back home."

"You expect me to believe that this is real?" she finally said with an incredulous laugh. "Where are the watermarks? Where's the raised seal?"

"Mom made a photocopy," he said, impatience replacing the gentleness. "Did you think we'd come all the way to New York City with your actual birth certificate? What if somebody stole it on the subway, Mara? Anybody could steal your identity then, and—"

"Fine. Where's the original? And when can I see it?"

He sighed. "It's at home in the safe."

"And you didn't show it to me six months ago because . . .?"

"Because after everything we've done for you, our word should be enough! We don't have to prove anything to you, but Mom decided to—"

"Bullshit," she said, crumpling the paper in her fist.

"You watch your language, young lady," he warned. "This is not how we raised you to behave."

"Right," she said slowly, her voice glassy and feverish. "I was supposed to be just like you, Dad, and turn my brain off and believe whatever fucking lies she tells."

The slap was immediate, loud enough that they all winced in the lounge.

"How dare you speak to me that way! Don't you ever—"

Evan flung the door open to find Mara standing with her hand on her cheek, stunned, watching a blue plaid shirt disappear into the men's room.

"Oh my god, Mara, get in here," he said, pulling her back into the lounge. Gently, he moved her hand away from her cheek to reveal stinging, red skin. "Has he done this before?"

"No," she breathed, her eyes blank with shock as she stretched her jaw.

"Should we have him thrown out?" Darren asked.

"Or I could rough him up a little," Gwen offered, lifting her pierced eyebrow in what Evan hoped was teasing.

Mara just shook her head.

"Are you going to be okay to play?" Ben asked, coming up behind her and rubbing her shoulders like a boxing coach. "Gwen could drum and I can play bass and sing at the same time as long as we take those two 5SOS songs out of the set. You can sneak out the back door and—"

"I am *not* running away," Mara said, and the soft, dazed edges of her voice went razor-sharp. "I'm playing this show."

"Are you sure?" Ben asked slowly.

She took a shaky breath, shook out her hands, and began to pace as everyone else exchanged uncertain glances.

"The only change to the set list is going to be 'Your Girl.'"

"Sure, Mar, we can take it out," Samantha promised soothingly, reaching for the clipboard with their set list on the end table.

"Oh, no," Mara said, whirling to snatch the clipboard. "*I'm* going to sing it."

Samantha's eyebrows flew up.

"I wrote it, didn't I?" she snapped, her eyes flashing around the room as everyone nodded silently in turn.

"So I'm going to sing it," Mara announced, clicking the pen and drawing a circle and arrow. "Ben can play the drums stripped-down, and we'll save it for last."

Gwen nudged Evan's shoulder, muttering, "This is a bad idea."

He nodded and whispered back, "Maybe they'll leave before the show starts."

"Doubtful," Gwen said, shaking her head. "They're nuts."

"How nuts?" he whispered, as his pulse spiked. "Like, you don't think they'd actually . . . *do* something to her, do you?"

"Dude just slapped her in the hall," Gwen said with a shrug. "And he's the nice one."

"Okay, Mara, this is a bad idea," Evan announced, running a shaky hand through his hair. "I think you should just let Ben drum tonight and—"

She met his eyes over the clipboard with a determined intensity that knocked him back into the couch beside Gwen.

"Okay," he muttered, raising his hands. "Okay."

"Don't worry, Umbrella Boy," Gwen said with a smirk, throwing an arm around him. "She's a tough cookie. And we've all got her back."

✦✦✦

EVAN STOOD BESIDE the bar with his back against the wall, scanning the darkened club until he found Mr. Cassidy's blue plaid shirt hunched over a table near the exit. Beside him, a woman in a hot pink turtleneck sweater sat drumming her nails on the table, sipping at a cocktail. Evan slipped into an empty chair behind them just as Brad took the mic and introduced Switched Flip.

The stage lights went up, and Darren played the opening staccato notes of "Indie Rock and Roll." Evan watched Mrs. Cassidy stiffen at the sight of Mara twirling her sticks.

Hold it together, Evan whispered as Mara hit the drums. *You can do this.*

And she did.

She played song after song, each beat crisp and clean and driven with a contagious fury that had the club on their feet—except for the Cassidys, who remained seated, holding hands at the table, coiled tight as snakes. Had Mr. Cassidy told his wife what Mara said about her? Had he told her about the slap? The way his shoulders hunched under that plaid shirt, Evan imagined that, if he had a tail, it would be between his legs.

But none of Mr. Cassidy's shame radiated from his wife. Evan wondered how many cocktails she'd already downed, how many times she'd hit Mara growing up. When she opened her purse to rummage around for her lipstick, Evan's eye caught something shiny.

A mirror?

Or a knife?

A gun?

It was probably just a mirror, he told himself. *You're letting your imagination run wild . . .*

And yet, as she zipped her purse and clutched it in her lap without using a mirror to check her lipstick, Dr. James's words wailed like a siren in his head:

Gruesome deaths . . . deaths . . . deaths . . . deaths . . .

He took a deep breath, trying to clear his thoughts. They were in a public place with security and witnesses. And besides, there was no way he or any of the band members were going to leave Mara alone with the Cassidys. He was being paranoid . . . wasn't he?

Did you see this? He silently asked Kieran Flynn. *Did you see how it ends?*

He scooted his chair a little closer to the stage, praying Mara would change her mind about the set list. Praying the world would spin backward or forward or even just a little sideways and show him what to do next, because he couldn't stop staring at Jill Cassidy's purse. He couldn't stop thinking about Mara's face on Mary's dead body.

After an hour and a half, Mara took a sip of water, then handed her sticks to Ben. As she took the mic from the stand, Mrs. Cassidy stiffened, tugging at her turtleneck. One hand was still on her purse as she whispered something to her husband.

Evan held his breath as Ben adjusted the stool and hit the opening beats of "Your Girl." Mara closed her eyes and swayed as Samantha switched pedals and let a haunting chord hang in the air while Gwen riffed on the bass.

He could see Mara's hands trembling, but her voice didn't betray a thing as she began to sing.

When I was scared I climbed into your bed
And then you told me stories to mess with my head
Oh, you told me that you loved me
That I was your girl . . .
You spun love like a spider's web
Tangling and strangling until you were fed
Said the world was your oyster
And I was your pearl . . .

The Cassidys were frozen, clearly understanding that she was singing to them. But while Mr. Cassidy's eyes glistened with tears, his wife's jaw was set and her body seemed to vibrate with rage.

Evan was thankful for the spotlight on the stage so that Mara couldn't see them. Words poured from her lips with a raw emotion that held the crowd in its spell, but she never lost control. Her voice had a sharp fragility to it, like something beautiful, broken, and dangerous as she moved through the second verse.

You locked the truth in a treasure chest
Swallowed the key because mother knows best
You thought that you could lock me down
And I'd be your golden girl

But I won't be your little princess
Or a trophy in your case
I won't be the scapegoat for your shame
Or the mirror for your face
Oh, you only ever loved yourself
And I was never your girl
No, no, no, no, no
I'm not coming home with you tonight
I'll never be your girl . . .

Sam played the last chord with extra oomph and Ben hit the final beat with palpable solidarity as Mara turned to blow a kiss to her band. Everyone in the crowd was on their feet, applauding and asking each other why the drummer didn't sing more often, except for the two people whispering and gesturing furiously at the table in front of Evan. He leaned closer, ready to pounce the second she opened that purse or moved an inch toward the stage.

"Thanks for coming out tonight," Mara said calmly into the mic, raising a hand to quiet the room. "We really appreciate everyone's support."

Gwen and Darren exchanged tense glances as Mara replaced the microphone and walked backstage without another word. Still, the Cassidys whispered at their table, their argument swallowed up in the noise of the room.

Sam squinted into the audience as the house lights came up, and Ben stepped down to work the crowd as usual, but his blue eyes darted around nervously as the audience buzzed for an encore. Evan couldn't sit still any longer.

"You think she's coming back out for one more song?" Gwen asked as he pushed toward the stage.

He shook his head. "Pretty sure she's done."

"Okay. Go tell her she's a badass. We've got this," Gwen said, tilting her head toward the Cassidys.

With one last glance toward the pink turtleneck, Evan jumped up onto the stage and headed toward the hall leading to the musician's lounge.

In the small, dark corner between the restrooms and the lounge, it was eerily quiet and still.

"Mara?" He knocked softly. "Hey, it's me."

He could hear the working of the lock before Mara opened the door just a crack and peered out. "Are they still here?"

"Nobody's going to let them anywhere near you," he promised.

She opened it just wide enough to let him in before closing and locking it again.

"Gwen wants me to tell you you're a badass," he said as Mara crossed her arms and started pacing, which he thought she must have been doing since leaving the stage. "She's right, you know."

She turned to face him, and in one long breath, the facade crumbled. He opened his arms, and, burying her face in his chest, she started to sob.

"I'm *not* a badass," she mumbled into his shirt. "That didn't feel good at all. I threw up as soon as I got off stage, and I'm still shaking."

"Well, it sounded good," Evan said, leading her to the leather couch and grabbing a box of tissues from on top of the mini fridge on the way. "You did it. You held it together. And . . . I'd like to add that you're super hot when you're mad."

She snorted and pulled a tissue from the box, then dabbed at the black streams running down her cheeks. Mara blew her nose and rolled her watery eyes. "Yeah, that's me right now. Super hot."

"Hey. I love you," he said, pulling her close. "It's okay to cry."

From the lounge, they could hear the muted sounds of the club, canned music throbbing through the speakers. Laughter. The clash of dishes and the scrape of chairs.

No shots.

No sirens.

No screams.

Resting his chin on top of her head, Evan held Mara till her breathing evened out, and slowly, the panic drained away from his chest, too.

And then, a knock came at the door.

"Oh, God," she whispered, bolting upright, swollen eyes wide.

But the next knock was accompanied by Ben's voice, sounding like a radio controller. "The coast is clear."

Evan unlocked the door, and Ben, Samantha, Darren, and Gwen rushed in to tackle Mara in a huge hug.

"Get in here, Umbrella Boy," Samantha called, opening one arm and hooking it around his neck. "You're one of us now."

"Are they gone?" Mara asked, muffled in the middle of the huddle.

"Yep. And they're not going to bother you anymore," Samantha promised.

"What happened?"

"Let's just say, they got the message," Samantha said, running her fingers through Mara's hair like a mother might do. "And security is now familiar with their faces."

"Your mom was pissed," Darren said, and whistled. "That woman is one scary bitch, but she was no match for Gwenny."

Mara snorted, then sniffled. "Um, Gwen?"

"I didn't do anything," Gwen said, waving it off and opening the fridge for bottles of water. "I just told them that to get to you, they'd have to physically deal with me, which they decided they'd rather not do."

"For some reason, old white people are just automatically intimidated by Gwen's hairstyle, facial jewelry, and large bass guitar," Darren added drily. "Go figure."

Gwen smirked, tossing him two bottles of water.

"I got your back, girls," she said, pounding a fist on her heart before pointing at Darren and Mara.

"We've all got your back," Darren agreed, handing Mara one of the bottles then offering the other to Evan.

"You guys really are the best family," she said, taking a sip, then squealing as Ben scooped her up in his arms.

"Come here, little band baby," he said. "We take care of our baby, don't we?"

Sam came up to pinch her cheek. "Yes we do. Because we wuv her sooo much."

Mara swatted Sam's hand away and laughingly yelled at Ben to put her down, but he started rocking her instead, forgetting about the drink in her hand until ice-cold water spilled down her shirt.

"Oopsy-daisy," Ben said in a tiny voice as he set her feet on the floor. "Umbrella Boy, will you go get our baby some paper towels?"

"Sure, baby," Evan said with a wink, and as he headed to the paper towel dispenser above the sink, Mara dumped the rest of the bottle on Ben's head, inciting an all-out water battle in the musicians' lounge.

Gwen snuck up behind Evan, grabbing a fistful of his shirt before pouring cold water between his shoulder blades.

"Should have brought your umbrella, boy," she taunted, running to hide behind the couch as he came after her, twisting the cap off a full bottle Mara handed him directly from the fridge.

A few minutes later, Evan found himself lying on his back in a puddle on the floor of a Greenwich Village night club. As Mara grasped his wet hands with hers and pulled him up to standing, he marveled at himself.

Who am I?

Evan Kiernan had never been in the middle of a group hug. He'd never earned a nickname or felt like he belonged anywhere in his life, but here he was, drying the floor with five laughing people who really did feel like family.

And Mara was the thread that tied them all together.

That night, he slept better than he had in weeks, knowing that, despite the uncertainties surrounding them, he wasn't the only one who had her back.

CHAPTER EIGHTEEN

"**H**APPY HALLOWEEN, FOLKS,**" Dr. Mortakis said, and at the touch of a button, old-horror-movie organ music played through the speakers. She fanned her red-tipped fingers, raising an eyebrow like Elvira. "Are you ready to cross over to mythology's dark side?"

A few of Evan's costumed classmates laughed, but he groaned under his breath because it was the kind of cringeworthy thing his mom would do to wake him up on his birthday morning. The organ sound effects, the fake spiders, the monster pancakes—god, he wished he hadn't been born on October 31.

He remembered being little, all those birthdays he'd expected to wake up feeling magically different. Older, taller, smarter—those were the things that were supposed to come with going from five to six, from seven to eight. And yet, year after year he woke up to his mom's bad jokes and a life that, despite changing schools or houses or pretend dads, felt disappointingly the same.

But eighteen felt different.

Eighteen—and every number after it—belonged to him.

Dr. Mortakis dimmed the lights, and Evan opened his notebook to a clean page as she pulled up a slide of a woman in khakis holding a human skull in one gloved hand and pointing at it with the other, clearly on the site of an archaeological dig.

"This skull dates from approximately 6500 BCE," Dr. Mortakis said. "But does anyone notice anything strange here?"

Evan followed the gloved pointer finger of the archaeologist to a series of small dots that looked almost like . . . holes. The more he looked at it, the more it resembled a colander.

A girl in the front row raised her hand. "Little holes? In the skull?"

"Exactly. Any guesses at the cause?"

"Umm . . . parasites?"

Dr. Mortakis laughed gently. "Very meticulous parasites. No, these holes were surgically drilled at very precise intervals in this skull. In fact, this is not the first skull to be found with such holes. Archaeologists have also discovered cave art depicting the drilling process, and it seems to have been a method of releasing evil spirits from a possessed individual, as well as an attempted cure for epilepsy and . . . *wait for it* . . . head injuries." She cleared her throat and rolled her eyes dramatically, and everyone laughed.

"The technical term for this surgical procedure—write this down— is *trephination*. Now, take a look at this cave drawing and you'll see how our ancestors documented this process visually."

She showed the class a rough stone wall marked with a simple white line drawing of three men. One writhed on the ground, held down awkwardly by the second. The third held a hammer in one hand and a spike in the other, poised over the patient's head. Just beneath the spike, in a whoosh of smoke, a wisp of a demon escaped the tortured man's skull into the air above.

"Where do we draw the line between body, mind, and soul? And where do we go when we die? How do we explain altered perceptions of reality or irrational behaviors? Though we understand more of how our brains work scientifically in the twenty-first century, psychiatrists, physicians, and religious leaders are still asking these questions today.

"So. Perhaps our little friend on the cave wall was possessed by an evil spirit, or perhaps he experienced symptoms of a mental illness such a schizophrenia or dissociative identity disorder. But according to Plato, there was one more possibility. His madness could have come directly from the gods. Let's take Cassandra for example."

Dr. Mortakis changed the slide again, this time to a luminous pre-Raphaelite oil painting of a woman tearing at her own auburn hair, looking off into the distance with glazed eyes as Troy burned crimson-gold in the background.

"Apollo was in love with this stunning princess of Troy," Dr. Mortakis explained, and Evan found himself entranced with the look in the girl's eyes. Distant and glassy, like she was seeing something. Something no one else could see. "He promised her the gift of prophecy if she would comply with his desires, but she refused to uphold her end of the bargain. And so, she was cursed to utter true prophecies no one would believe—including a vision of her own imminent murder. When Evelyn De Morgan painted this version of Cassandra in 1898, Victorian England was obsessed with death and mourning, the occult, and the anatomy of madness."

Evan found his fingers drumming on his notebook and his foot tapping anxiously under the table. He checked the clock; thirty-five minutes of class remained, and it felt like an eternity. He didn't want to look at Dr. Mortakis's illustrations of the underworld or memorize the rivers in Hades, and he didn't want to think about why people experienced mental illnesses or what happened to them after they died. He'd always thought of life like a flame. It sparked, burned, and then stopped burning. It didn't *go* anywhere. Not heaven or hell or the underworld. He was sick of sharing his birthday with death. He was finally eighteen, and for the first time, his birthday was supposed to belong to him. No cringeworthy party where his mom dressed up like a leopardess is hopes of meeting single dads. No taking Hailey trick-or-treating before dark while their mom worked late. None of his mom's tacky fake blood or disgusting, peeled-grape eyeball punch. This was his day to become an adult, and the only thing he wanted to do was pick out his own costume and sneak a few minutes alone with his girlfriend after she took the Battle of the Bands by storm.

But even after he left class, he couldn't shake his discomfort. Of course there was no such thing as madness or hallucinations *from the gods*. Apollo was a fairy tale and nobody drilled holes in people's skulls anymore and mental illness could be explained in terms of chemicals and neurons. But none of that explained what had been happening to him.

He'd legitimately seen the past, but it had never occurred to him that someone might be *showing* him the past. He didn't believe in gods or ghosts, angels or demons. Maybe the universe started with a big bang, or maybe some otherworldly power had started this whole ball rolling, but he'd never had any reason to believe there was a higher power interfering in his daily life.

But now, something about the haunted glaze of Cassandra's eyes, painted against a background of fire, felt a little too familiar.

He'd spent the last couple months trying to figure out *what* was happening to him, but he'd been avoiding the bigger question: *Why?*

It was getting harder and harder to believe that this was random. But did that mean Kieran Flynn had actually been cursed with the ability to see the future by someone or something . . . *supernatural*? And if so, was that same *something* showing him Kieran Flynn's memories? Did that mean he, too, was cursed?

But by whom?

And for what?

Goosebumps spider-legged up his neck. No matter how many times he tried to brush the questions away, he could still feel the ghosts of their sticky threads clinging to his skin as he skirted Washington Square.

Waiting at the crosswalk, he felt his phone vibrate with a text and opened it to find a party-hat filter picture of his mom and Hailey, complete with dancing cupcakes and rainbow confetti. Immediately after, his mom sent another of herself using the scream filter, with the caption: *I have an 18-year-old son! This is the scariest Halloween ever!*

OMG YOU'RE OLD

She replied with a GIF of a skeleton doing the Macarena in a graveyard, proving his point.

The light changed, and as he headed toward the shops on Sullivan Street, he thought of the year he dressed up as Goya, doing his self-portrait in a candle hat. His mom had gone to great lengths to find battery-operated candles, then stayed up late helping him hot glue them to a ridiculous Goodwill hat. And he remembered what Bill said when he saw him, dressed and ready to ring the neighbors' doorbells as Goya returned from the dead: "Don't embarrass yourself, kid."

Later, hiding under his comforter, sorting candy by wrapper color by the light of his battery-operated candles, Evan had heard them arguing.

"Maybe you should have somebody take a look at him," Bill was saying, and Evan could hear his heavy footsteps creaking over the floor of the double-wide. "Before he gets . . . weirder."

"Did you just call my son weird?"

"Calm down, Melissa. Calm down. It's just not . . . normal for an eleven-year-old kid to want to dress up as a dead painter for Halloween. When I was eleven, I was playing football and riding my dirt bike."

"Well, he's not *your* son," his mom snapped.

But Evan had heard her voice wobble. Like she knew it wasn't normal, either. Like maybe she wished he wanted to play football and ride motorcycles without helmets like Little Bill.

"All I'm saying is, a little therapy never hurt anyone. Think about it, okay?"

Maybe she should have thought about it, but she'd spent hours with a glue gun, then defended him to Bill instead. She'd always believed in her son, even when she didn't understand him, and he loved her for that. Stepping out of the flow of foot traffic and leaning against a brick wall, he texted her back.

Remember my Goya costume?

Ha ha! Of course.

Thank you for staying up late to put that stupid candle hat together.

Anytime <3

Good, because I was thinking of dressing up as a cement truck this year.

Can you bring your glue gun to my dorm before seven?

CEMENT TRUCK?!?!?

It was a joke, Mom.

Oh, okay. Ha ha. Very funny.

Got plans for your birthday?

Mara's playing a Halloween show.

Sounds fun.

Are you dressing up?

Shopping for a costume now.

So how serious are things getting?

Are you going as matching cement trucks?

She's dressing up with the band. Top secret.

But if she asked, I'd totally be her cement truck.

That IS serious.

Yeah. It is.

He waited for his mom to say something. To squeal or send confetti GIFs or a big, sparkly heart. But when a new text finally came in, it only said,

Be careful.

He squeezed his hands into a fist, pushing away the impulse to type a smartass reply about what an excellent role model she'd been in that department. It took all his inner strength to just type,

So did Hailey pick a costume?

Share Bear.

You know, the purple Care Bear with the cake pops on his belly?

Mara's cake pops made quite the lasting impression. Lol.

Send me pictures, okay? I've got to go.

One more thing. Did you decide what you want to do about contacting your dad?

He gritted his teeth. Just because he'd sent her a nostalgic text didn't mean he wanted her telling him to be careful or asking him how serious things were with Mara or making him think about his dad again. Why couldn't she just leave him alone?

The thought came with a ping of guilt. She just didn't want him to get hurt. She was making sacrifices so he could be here in New York, and he appreciated that. He was the one who asked her about his dad in the first place.

But every time he talked to her, he felt less like the Promising Young Artist and more like the Awkward Lonely Kid.

He didn't want to be that kid anymore.

He didn't want to think about all the ways that love—or minds— could fall apart.

At the next crosswalk, he stared at his phone, trying to figure out how to answer her. Finally, as the sign for Lucille's Ball came into view, he settled on the truth.

I don't know yet

Okay. I love you no matter what.

I love you, too, Mom.

For the next hour, he sorted through the dregs of thrift store bargain racks, frustrated and somewhat grossed out until discovering a black cravat that reminded him of Edgar Allan Poe. It was easy, after that, to find a pinstriped black suit jacket, white button-down shirt, and silvery-gray vest with three buttons. At the drug store, he picked up some eyeliner and a cheesy foam-and-feather raven to perch on his shoulder, then went back to his dorm to flatten his hair into rumpled, black curls and smudge the eyeliner into dark circles and a drooping mustache.

With a knot in his stomach, he stared at himself in the mirror, feeling like his reflection was stalking him as he called the ASPR and left yet another desperate voice mail. Didn't anyone else work there who could return a phone call? Or was Dr. Weaver just playing some dark, twisted game with him?

⋙⋘

THE SUN FINALLY went down, and Washington Square's pathways thickened with costumed people. The city had wrapped each lantern in orange cellophane, lending an eerie glow to the park, and signs advertising the Battle of the Bands were hung at even intervals on the lampposts. Mara had texted, letting him know she was backstage but she couldn't let him see her in costume before the show.

At last, the stage lights went up and the classic recording of "Monster Mash" blared through the speakers. Like a swarm of moths, the crowd was drawn to the light. As people pressed in on all sides, Evan felt increasingly uncomfortable as Edgar Allan Poe. His raven was in everyone's way, so he finally just unfastened the safety pins holding it on his shoulder. He held it like an awkward baby as the first band—Vampire Weekday—came onstage and played a terrible rendition of "Thriller," dressed like the cast of the Michael Jackson music video. Each band was allowed two songs, and this one had made the unfortunate choice of "Billie Jean." The lights went down to halfhearted applause, but Evan smiled. If this was a sample of the competition, it would be an easy win for Switched Flip. He could see their dark figures arranging instruments and cords on the stage, but the lights didn't come up until Samantha's guitar played the creepy opening notes of "The Killing Moon."

As Mara hit the drums, the lights blinded him, swooping across the crowd and electrifying the fountains before settling on the band. Ben gripped the mic with hinged, metal gloves and wore a tight brown leather suit fitted out with belts and buckles and Steampunk gadgets that caught the light. One eye was patched and the other was darkly lined. To his right, Samantha played guitar with black, fingerless gloves, wearing a super short black tutu over fishnets and high silver-buckled boots. Behind the keyboard, Darren was decked out in a fitted ladies' jacket and goggles, and beside him Gwen's face was covered with a birdlike, bronze plague mask that bobbed in time as she plucked the bass strings.

But Mara stole the show. The drums were raised on a platform, and sitting behind them like a hovering, rhythmic angel, Mara wore enormous mechanical wings. Her hair was piled high in Victorian ringlets, and her makeup was dramatic and dark. Over a white blouse, she wore a black-and-brown corset fitted just below her breasts. But as much as Evan would have liked for his eyes to linger there, they were drawn, instead, to her necklace.

A choker.

At first, he thought it was the concert lighting playing with his vision. The blotches he saw after the spotlight roamed the crowd were nothing alarming. Just afterimages. But no matter how he blinked, they kept pocking his vision, flashing behind his eyelids. The people around him had started to dance, and he clung to his ridiculous raven as their bodies pressed closer to his. The crowd was growing as passersby were drawn to the sound of Ben's voice belting out the haunting chorus. When the song ended, Evan joined the applause. Mara stood, and he could see the rest of her outfit—a high-low skirt in pinstripes and ruffles, revealing pale, slender legs and vintage stiletto boots. Evan was surprised as she handed Ben the drumsticks and took the microphone in her lace-gloved hand.

"This is a little song called 'Timekeeper,'" she said, her matte-red lips tantalizingly close to the microphone. And when she turned to nod at Ben, he could see that her wings were made up of intricately fitted gears and clocks, which seemed to start ticking. Samantha switched pedals, and her guitar began the familiar opening notes to the song by Grace Potter and the Nocturnals.

He'd hoped she'd at least eaten breakfast, but as usual, she didn't betray her nerves. Evan smiled, watching her body rock to the rhythm of her sticks in Ben's hands for the opening measures, lifting her chin and closing her eyes. Her neck was long and graceful and pale, so much of it taken up by the thick, black choker.

But then, his smile disappeared.

Evan felt the park begin to shift.

He closed his eyes and took a step backward, stumbling onto someone's foot. He was too disoriented to apologize as lights flashed.

He closed his eyes tight, but it wasn't the stage lights this time. When he looked toward the stage again, Mara's mouth was open wide for the drawn out vowel in *ti-i-i-i-i-mekeeper*—

But instead of a Steampunk choker, her neck was encased in rope. A hideous, purpling bruise bloomed across her throat.

Her bare feet weren't touching the ground, and her palms hung limp and dirty at her side. She wore a simple, white linen dress stained a deep and deadly red.

The music had stopped, but the crowd remained. Evan looked left and right, panicked but hedged in too tight to bolt. He was marooned in a sea of black hats and bonnets, black jackets and Puritan dresses. But worst of all was the mumbling of this crowd, the black words falling on him like raindrops, louder and faster now, cold and relentless.

Evil   Witch
Damned   Child   Changeling   Baby
Devil   Hell   Witch
Faerie   Witch   Strange Boy   Wicked   Confess   Left Hand
Girl   Strange   Priest   Prayers   Die
Left Hand   Conjure   Prayers   Changeling   Die   Confess
Witch   Must   Die

On the platform, Mara kicked and her eyes rolled back in her head. One last kick, one last defiant thrash. Her body swung, and Evan's vision swirled—blurred with stinging rain and flashes of lightning. He closed his eyes and a scream tore through his throat—

But it was swallowed up in the crowd, which was now jumping up and down as one, shouting, "Encore! Encore!"

The girl beside him, dressed as a mermaid, gave him side-eye and leaned toward her boyfriend. Evan realized he was panting. And it had, indeed, started to rain.

Mara was holding the microphone, laughing as she looked over her shoulder to ask the emcee if an encore was allowed. The maximum was two songs, to keep the Battle of the Bands moving, but the next band was clearly shaking in their ghostbuster boots. At the negative headshake of the emcee, Mara turned back to her audience and lifted a hand to quiet them down.

"We're going to make way for the next guys," she said. "But you can catch Switched Flip at Blossom & Spies this Friday night at nine. Happy Halloween! And a special happy birthday to my boyfriend, Evan." She kissed her fingers and blew it toward the crowd. "I love you!"

The applause was furious, and Evan felt disoriented and unsteady, like he'd just gotten off a double-loop roller coaster. He had to get out of the crowd, to sit on a bench, to breathe air that didn't smell like marijuana.

In a chorus of "Sorry, excuse me," he pushed against the flow as a metal band was introduced and his phone buzzed in his pocket: *Meet you at the arch in fifteen. XOXO*

Fifteen minutes.

He had fifteen minutes to try to get his shit together before facing Mara. He had to congratulate her, to tell her how amazing her performance was, even though he'd missed most of it because of . . . whatever that was. He wrapped his arms around himself, still hugging the raven against his chest, though it was rapidly losing feathers and smelled funny in the rain. His performance as Poe, it seemed, was increasingly convincing.

Following the path away from the fountains toward the arch, he saw a small crowd gathering in the grass. This had nothing to do with the Battle of the Bands. Blue and red lights spun on top of a parked police car, and as he got closer, he could see an officer wearing a black rain hat and poncho telling people to step away from the tree.

Yellow police tape was stretched across the fencing that surrounded Hangman's Elm, interrupting the other signs that hung there.

Please Don't Feed the POLICE LINE DO NOT CROSS.

No Bicycling POLICE LINE DO NOT CROSS.

Park closes at POLICE LINE DO NOT CROSS.

Evan had walked by the tree dozens of times over the past two months, but he'd never really looked at it until now. His rubbernecker instinct kicked in, and he stepped closer, shielding his eyes from the intensifying rain.

A bulky, black thing dangled from the sharp, right-angled branch. It was a stuffed trash bag, wrapped with silver duct tape. Judging from the size and shape of the bulges, it could have contained a body. The dead kind.

But there was more. Thick, red rivulets ran down the damp, dark trunk as if from a wound, and as his eyes followed the streaks, he saw the handle of a butcher's knife, its blade buried deep in the wood. The leaves below it dripped crimson rain, streaking the officer's poncho. The tree was . . . bleeding. Dripping blood.

He stepped in closer, trying to hear what the officer was saying.

". . . just a prank," the officer said, waving people on. "Nothing to see here."

Evan tried to focus on the tree, telling himself it was just pretend, but the park began to blur again. He stumbled backward, collapsing into a wrought-iron bench.

He blinked against the water in his eyes, but the blotches and blurring weren't from the rain.

Flash—

The wind reversed.

Flash—

This is just a stupid Halloween prank made of red paint and plastic. Paint, he whispered to himself, and closed his eyes. *It's paint.*

But when he opened his eyes, Mara's body swung from the tree.

Blood—not paint—flowed from the body of a little black cat beside her, pinned to the trunk by the blade of a knife. Both their heads bent to one side, limp, their color all wrong, that same bruise blooming purplish-red and raw across her throat.

The crowd stared and stared, mumbling in the misty gloom about Hallow's Eve and left hands, and Evan pulled his feet up onto the bench, burying his face in his knees like a kid. When he closed his eyes, he saw more.

It was as if someone had pressed play, starting a movie in his mind.

KINGS PARK ASYLUM

1911

"WHAT TRIGGERS YOUR supposed memories?" Dr. James asked me in December, and I resented the addition of this word. Supposed. His legs were crossed, yellow socks showing between his brown pant legs and shoes, notebook balanced on his knee.

"Various things," I answered, rubbing my cold hands together by his fire. "A sight, a smell, an emotion."

"Name something specific."

"In Manhattan, there is a tree. Come, I'll show you," I said, and led him to Washington Square.

Reader, trees live long. It might be living, still. They called it the Hangman's Elm, because of the terrible, right-angled branch.

"I looked upon this tree and saw things I did not wish to see—memories from a life before this one, in a land far away," I told the doctor, blaming my shiver on the cold December air.

"Can you see these things now?" he asked.

"My vision is not changing right now," I said, truthfully. "But I remember every detail as if I lived it."

"When did your vision begin to, as you say, change?*"*

"After my father tattooed me with the firebird. Everything changed after that."

"Tell me everything."

We returned to the Society, so that I could tell my tale by the warmth of the fire. Dr. James brewed coffee, and I told him what had happened long ago in Ireland on another such tree, on another such terrible branch.

"Once upon a time, on the Emerald Isle, a baby boy was born. He was small—born a month early and so beautiful, his mother called him *bronntanas beag*. Her little gift. He was happy and slept like a moss-covered rock. His mother forbid anyone to open the windows, for the faeries liked pretty babies. Ones that slept well and smiled, especially the boys.

"Early he arrived, and early he walked and talked. The boy was early with everything, it seemed. He could anticipate frost and wind and his mother's needs before she spoke them. But soon, his mother would learn it's not always a *bronntanas beag* to be early. It's not always a gift to know. After eight years of peace, the terrors began . . ."

"You're a very good storyteller," the doctor interrupted me with an amused smile.

"Sometimes the most interesting stories," I told him, sipping at my coffee, "are the true ones."

Reader, you know it is true because time is a trick, because once upon a time, you were me and I am you and we, together, were he. So I will tell you this tale, but not as I told the children or the sailors or even Dr. James, though if he ever reads this account he will surely scoff at the end. I will tell you this tale, Reader, as I saw it. As a memory belonging to me.

To us.

She called me her *bronntanas beag*, and we were happy for a time. When my mother's belly grew round and large and her gait turned to a waddle, my parents were filled with joy in hopes of having another child like me.

But then, one night, I woke my parents with a scream. They found me in a pool of sweat and tears, suffering from a dream so vivid, it could only be a harbinger of what was to come. I told them what I'd seen. My mother would have the baby soon, and it would be a girl. Young as I was, I was absolutely certain of my unborn sister's fate, for I'd seen her little body with perfect clarity—a tiny infant girl, born blue and silent and still.

I will never forget the look of horror on my parents' faces when I told them this.

I will never forget the moment I was no longer a gift.

The moment I became a curse.

My mother recited a Psalm. My father stood up, got his coat to leave for the pub, and then the room flickered and blotched, and I saw something else. My father was going to be in an accident. My father, too, was going to die.

Hysteria took over, then, as I begged him not to go. Their calm, sweet boy was gone—I was weeping and frantic, screaming and clawing and biting at my dad, telling him something terrible would happen if he left. He'd be dead before sunrise. I had seen it.

But he left, anyway, because he was afraid of me, and on the day we buried him, my mother's second child—a little girl—was born blue and still. After that, everything changed.

Soon the word was whispered over soda bread and weak tea. Changeling. It filtered between the little house and the church, between shacks and lampposts, between nasty children looking for someone worse off than themselves.

A sudden change.

Inexplicable knowledge.

Tragedy.

The real boy must have been swapped with the horrible, unwanted child of a faerie in the night. And what was to be done with him now? The priest tried his best, but to no avail, so my mother called the witch.

From my hiding place under the bed, I listened to the pouring of boiling water, the clatter of cups, and a strange old woman's voice—a deep, toad-like voice with no beauty in it—explaining the ways of the faeries.

Faeries are jealous creatures, the witch-woman said, and they cast spells to suck the life out of the young of humankind. Especially the girls. The deaths in our family were no accident.

The changeling child—the Not-Me child that still felt like me—was guilty of double murder.

My mother wept loudly, begging the unseen faeries to relent, and I was seized with terror.

No amount of pleading would bring the real boy back, the old witch insisted. There is but one thing that moves the heart of a faerie—and that is violence. The changeling child must be beaten without mercy if the faeries were to relent. Then, they might return her rightful boy.

Suddenly, through my tears, I saw feet. Dirty, bare feet that were no bigger than mine, getting closer.

I held my breath under the bed—was it the faeries? Coming back for me? But then, I saw a face—not my mother's, not the old witch-woman's, but a girl's. Upside down. Her curious, green eyes held mine, but she didn't say a word.

She wore a long, black braid and a thin, linen dress blooming with berry stains. Squatting down with her head cocked, she stared at me with those green eyes, biting her lower lip and letting it slide between her two front teeth. Her braid dusted the floor.

"Maura?" the toady voice called, and the girl stood up with a start.

"Yes, Mother."

"Our work is done."

Fear pulsed through me as I waited under that bed. My mother closed the door behind the old woman and the girl, and I trembled at the thought of myself—at what I might be. Outside the bedroom, my mother wept and prayed to God and Mother Mary and the faeries and goblins, too. And then, she rose to her feet and cleared her nose. She picked up the heavy-handled wooden broom and tried to beat the faerie out of me.

WHEN THE HAND touched my bruised shoulder in the night, I woke with a cry.

"Shh!" said a voice, and I blinked. It was her, green eyes catching the moonlight.

She held a finger to her lips. "It's all right. I brought you this to help with the pain," she whispered, holding out a cup of white willow tea. Her two front teeth shone white in the moonlight, with a magical sliver of black between. "Don't tell."

I reached for the tea and drank it quickly; it was already cold. As soon as I handed the empty cup back to her, she disappeared, and the white willow lulled me to sleep.

When I woke again, the room smelled of vinegar.

I crept painfully to the door, peering through the crack. The old witch stood beside the table, lifting a jagged eggshell to the light. Her eye caught mine with terrifying intensity for a long minute before she explained to my mother that I had failed the first test. I was not yet human; I required another week of beating.

"You've not put your muscle into it," she scolded my mother, and took the broom. This woman was made of muscle, but I made no sound, not even a whimper—a sure sign that I was the changeling of a faerie, after all.

Through the window, I saw her; Maura was there, watching, with tears streaming down her face.

I remembered smelling mint and roses, and I knew before prying open my swollen eyes, she was back with more tea.

"You need to run away," she said, her green eyes fierce, her freckled arms crossed. Nodding, I handed her the empty cup. I couldn't speak. It

hurt just to breathe. "First, they'll make you cold. You can live through that. But next, it will be the fire. No one can live through the fire. I'll find a place for you," she whispered. "A safe place."

Waiting for the white willow to soothe my aching bones, I stared at the full moon through my window, wondering if safe places really existed. Wondering if she was really just a girl—or if she might be a faerie herself.

It was cold when she came back for me. The window had been left open to freeze the faerie out of me. My ribs were broken in multiple plac-es, and I was sure I'd never move my left arm again. Every breath hurt.

"Lean on me," she whispered, sitting me up.

"Aren't you scared of me?" I whispered back. "I might be bad."

"No," she said. "You're not bad." And then, she swung my right arm around her shoulders. "Now you're going to need to walk."

We were just kids, and she was still taller than me. Somehow, she managed to get me up and through the window, out into the woods. With every step, I felt my body splitting apart, cracking and splintering and wanting to die—

And yet, there was something, someone, making my feet go on. Tell-ing me I wasn't bad. Telling me stories all the way, stories about the house where she lived—dirty and crude, its walls cracked and patched and lined with shelves for bottles and hooks for dried herbs.

Her father was long gone, she said, and her mother never spoke of him. Perhaps he was dead, or perhaps he had run off with another woman, or perhaps something more sinister had happened to him. She could never be sure. Often, she doubted that the old woman was even her true mother.

She was sure, however, that her mother's work was important and held a certain Power. She watched her mother measure liquids and boil feathers. She smelled the herbs her mother crushed, heard the screams of the rabbits she killed, and helped to wash their blood off the stone. She saw the desperation in the faces of their midnight visitors, who came for meadowsweet and cat's-claw, wood betony, and echinacea—all kinds of teas and salves and drops perhaps mixed with a little something else.

And even though no one—not even the priest—was brave enough to speak of this something else, Maura was. Her mother's greatest Power, she said, lay in her ability to mix and sell something far more powerful than herbs—fear.

"You're still just a human boy," she declared when we arrived at a ramshackle shed deep in the woods, where a hermit used to live before he died. She built me a fire and made me a bed. Over the fire, she boiled something pungent, dipped rags in it, and laid them on my bruises with gentle fingers.

"Are you casting a healing spell on me?" I asked.

She looked at me funny. "Did you hear anything I just said?"

"But you're using your left hand. They say . . . they say it's the devil's hand. That the left hand does the devil's work," I whispered.

"There's no such thing as the devil," she said firmly. "And I use this hand because it's the way God made me. I'm no good with my right."

"You are good," I promised her, and began to cry.

She dressed me again and promised to return with food. My bones healed. My bruises faded. And the changeling boy disappeared into legend.

No one came looking for me—no one but Maura.

Years passed.

We grew.

The first time she kissed me, it was quick and shy, as if she thought there was someone else in the world I'd rather kiss. She sat comfortably close while braiding a rug for my floor out of stolen scraps. At our feet, the little black cat that always followed her purred. Her head on my shoulder and the cat on her lap, she told me how the village was changing, how a black-suited man from England had come to save our people from superstition.

And oh, what happened when she finished that rug. We weren't children anymore—I was a head taller than her, and her body was soft with curves.

She took me down on those colorful, dirty old scraps, whispering that what we had was pure—more pure than what any rightfully married, normal people could dream of.

She said she loved me, and she didn't believe in anything but that.

And then, Reader. And then. The sun was setting, and I saw the shape of her walking away—black like the silhouettes of the trees as the flaming sun dipped low, pulling the color with it.

My vision flickered. The sunset suddenly became pocked with blotches. And I saw her beautiful neck twisted in a rope.

I saw her limp and colorless, dangling from a right-angled branch, and I saw that my life would never have color or shape again.

And I panicked.

I shouldn't have run to the village—the changeling boy returned from the dead. I should have thought it through, but I didn't know what would happen next. I hadn't seen that far.

I thought they might call me names again. I thought they might try the broom, but I was bigger now, and stronger, too. I only cared about finding her. And saving her, the way she'd saved me.

I didn't know the black-suited preacher would say the girl I loved had bewitched me. He claimed the devil gave women like Maura and her mother great power, for they were his handmaidens. They had wed their souls to Lucifer, and he was their master. I argued against him, explaining how she'd tended to my wounds and visited me with provisions and friendship. She was not the bride of Satan! She was the only person in the whole village who had ever dared to show me love.

I was confused, he said. Bewitched. Deceived. What I'd seen was not real, but a conjuring. Maura had been appearing to me in the night from afar and keeping me alive in the woods by stealing the breath of babies—including the breath of my little blue sister.

I didn't know my mother would agree, swearing to the preacher it had been the witch's daughter all along—that she was the devil's mistress who stole me, who tortured me with visions, who possessed me with her dark magic. That it was she who'd killed my baby sister and my father with her wicked left hand.

I didn't know the whole damn village would say she came to torment them, too, with her little black cat and her strange potions and rabbit's blood. The witch's daughter was suddenly to blame for every illness, every death, every tragedy in the village for the last eighteen years.

They'd found their explanation—their scapegoat.

Their reason to form a mob.

Their reason to tie a noose.

Their reason to stab a little black cat, its blood running down the trunk of the hanging tree.

They'd found their reason to wear black hats. Black bonnets. Black jackets and pants and dresses. This was the reason for the black mumbling, mumbling, mumbling, the black words falling down on me like raindrops. Cold, relentless raindrops pouring from an endless black sky.

CHAPTER NINETEEN

"**Y**OU OKAY THERE, kid?"

It was a police officer, sizing Evan up like he might be a suspect. He was sitting with his face in his knees, the wind knocked out of him as the world switched back to now. How long had he been sitting there? It felt like hours. Years. But when he checked his phone, only ten minutes had passed.

It was still raining.

It was still Halloween.

Mara would be at the arch in five minutes.

Water ran in red-tinged rivulets down the officer's poncho. A lumpy black trash bag hung from the branch again. The crowd was breaking up.

"Did they used to hang people here?" Evan asked, returning his feet to the ground. He'd only seen snatches of the past before. But he felt like he'd just lived another life.

"Nah. Just a legend, thanks to that branch and overactive imaginations," the officer said, motioning toward the prominent right angle. "It's just a buncha bullshit stories."

"Bullshit stories," Evan repeated, over and over again.

"You high?" the officer asked, leaning in for a closer look. Evan felt heat rush to his face.

"What? No. No. Sorry. I just . . . didn't feel good. Had to sit down for a minute. I'm fine."

The officer moved on, but Evan was glued to the bench. He couldn't face Mara like this.

He had to get ahold of himself.

Cold metal slats, he told himself, running his fingers along the bench. *Drops of water. Latex paint. Prank. Bullshit stories. Cold metal slats . . .*

His phone vibrated in his pocket. Mara was at the arch. He stood up, forcing himself to put one foot in front of the other, but he couldn't shake the feeling that he hadn't just *seen* something.

He'd been *shown* something.

⋆⋅☆⋅⋆

"HEY, I WAS getting worried," Mara said, glancing toward the police lights as he walked toward the arch. She'd taken her wings off, but the choker was still wrapped around her neck. The rain had stopped as suddenly as it had begun.

"Sorry. The crowd slowed me down. You look . . . stunning."

She smiled. "And you look so *sad*, Edgar Allan *Poe*." She kissed his cheek and rubbed her thumb over the smudgy dark circles under his eyes.

"Not as sad as my raven," he said, presenting it to her with a weary smirk. At least he was *supposed* to look tortured and emotionally off-balance.

He was playing the part all too well.

She examined it in the streetlight.

"He's molting."

"Yeah. Hey, what happened to your wings?"

"Oh my god, they were so heavy and awkward, I took them off as soon as I got off stage. And this," she said, tugging at the choker and gagging, "has got to go. So itchy."

She reached behind her neck to unclasp it, and as it fell away, Evan's chest loosened.

"So," she said, shoving it in her purse and coming out with a thin, wrapped square. "Happy birthday."

Tearing the paper, he revealed a CD case with a handwritten track list including the songs they'd listened to at the diner, all three versions of "Earth Angel," and recordings of a few of her originals.

"Open it," she said, and when he did, two hand-drawn tickets for a trip to the Met fell out. "I have off Sunday, if you want to go?"

"Thank you," he said, pulling her close. "This is perfect."

She was warm and soft and breathing, and as he slid his lips down her unblemished neck in the shadow of the Washington Arch, she made a little sound that made him certain she was very much alive.

But then, her stomach growled.

"When was the last time you ate?" he asked, and she pulled back and bit her lip.

"This morning, I guess."

"Let's get you something."

They stopped at a food truck for gyros, the distant sound of cover bands wafting across the park as they dried a bench with napkins and sat down.

"You really should sing more often," he said after swallowing a bite. "You were fantastic."

"You know I'd rather hide behind my drums," she said, smiling shyly but obviously pleased.

"I used to design sets for the school musicals, and every year, my mom would bug me to try out for a part. It drove her crazy that I was happier behind the scenes."

"I threw up onstage at the fifth-grade talent show," she said, then started to laugh. "My mom signed me up to sing Céline Dion and picked out this hideous dress so I looked like Rose from *Titanic*, and I ruined it before she even got a picture. It was really kind of hilarious how upset she was about the dress."

"*Titanic*, huh?"

"She has this thing for DiCaprio. It's gross." Mara stuck her finger down her throat.

"Come on, you have to admit young DiCaprio was hot. With two *t*'s."

She laughed, and he wiped the tzatziki sauce from his fingers and put an arm around her. They sat quietly for a few minutes, listening to a distant, saxophone-heavy cover of "I Put A Spell On You," and Evan reminded himself that this was now. Mara was alive. Whatever he'd just seen happened a long time ago—or never happened at all. Nobody was hung for witchcraft anymore. Maybe the girl *looked* like her, but it wasn't her—

And never would be.

He held her close as the Village passed them by. Groups of laughing friends in costume. Leashed dogs doing their business in the bushes. People walking alone, wearing headphones and keeping their eyes on the ground, just trying to get where they needed to be. The park's resident drug dealers, doubling back to see if anyone had changed their minds.

Beside the arch, a group of bright-eyed teenagers set up camp, one strumming a cheap acoustic guitar while the others sang worship music in an attempt to compete with the music blaring from the stage. They were passing out pamphlets to passersby like candy, but then one of the girls locked eyes with Evan and crossed the grassy area that separated them with strange determination.

"God wants you to have this," she said, handing him a pamphlet that read, The Scariest Stories Are the True Ones!

"Uh, thanks?" he said, taken aback, and Mara snorted as the girl walked away as abruptly as she'd arrived.

"This is encouraging," Mara said drily, glancing at the hideous rendering of the devil on the cover before opening the pamphlet and reading aloud in a spooky, Vincent Prince voice. "People love a good scare this time of the year . . . so long as the monsters are fictional! But more frightening than any ghost story is this dark truth. The sin lurking in every human heart condemns us all to eternity in hell."

She turned the page to an illustration of a displeased, white-haired god, cloaked in clouds. A grungy crowd stood before him, and he pointed sternly downward toward the flames licking the bottom of the page.

"There is only one way to escape this nightmarish future," she read, turning the page again to an illustration of a warty-nosed witch holding a crystal ball roiling with hellfire and shadowy, outstretched hands. "And that is repentance!"

"Do you think that's how it works?" Evan asked, his scalp tingling as Dr. Mortakis's lecture once again pushed into his thoughts. "God, I mean."

"It's how a narcissist works," Mara said with a shrug, shaking her head. "Like, I have the ultimate truth, but I don't owe you any proof of my existence. You have to do my will and believe every word I say, and even if I don't say it, you're supposed to know what I want anyway and worship me or I'll send you to hell forever. See how much I love you?"

"That's terrifying," he blurted, tacking on, "If it's real, I mean."

"I know, right? If some cosmic narcissist is ruling the world, we're all screwed," she said, crumpling up the pamphlet with her sandwich wrapper. She stood to throw the trash away, and he followed, tossing his sad raven into the garbage can on top of it.

"But as far as I can tell, the only thing out there is the Wizard of Oz, so it's a pointless argument," Mara said with a sigh, then poked him in the chest with her index finger. "It's also your eighteenth birthday, which means you owe it to yourself to have a good time instead of talking about depressing shit like this."

With a shaky sigh, he let Mara lead him back toward the stage, where a new band was setting up to the twang of tuning guitars. Every time he blinked, he saw the bruise ringing her pale neck, the blood on the tree, the blank stare of dead, green eyes.

There is only one way to escape this nightmarish future . . .

That wasn't the future, he told himself, ordering the images to leave his mind. *It was only the past.*

As the music began to play, Mara stood in front of him, guiding his hands to her hips and pressing against him in a slow, steady rhythm.

He wanted so badly to be alone with her. To just enjoy it.

But he couldn't get over the feeling that they were being watched.

Not just by the crowd.

And not benevolently.

⊱⚜⊰

AT MIDNIGHT, ALL the bands were called back up to the stage. The judges were ready to announce the night's winner. Mara took the choker out of her purse and fastened it again, then pushed her way through the crowd to join Ben, Samantha, Darren, and Gwen and refasten her wings. When Switched Flip won first place, the crowd went wild with approval. Evan joined in the applause, hardly surprised.

But their prize did surprise him.

Though the names of the judges meant nothing to him, apparently some pretty big deal music bosses were on the panel. Namely, Zeke Hart, the owner of a string of clubs that spanned the continent. The grand prize, he announced, was a two-week tour starting November 10 in New York City and ending just before Thanksgiving in Orlando.

Switched Flip, he said, would be headlining Hot Z's down the Eastern Seaboard, gaining the ears of fans, producers, and radio executives.

It was a big break.

A fantastic prize.

Evan was so proud of them . . . but he missed them already.

His room was empty when he got back. Even though it was two a.m., he decided to take a shower. He needed to wash the costume makeup off. He needed to scrub the hanging girl's blank, green eyes from his mind. And besides all that, he was cold.

A good hot shower would make him feel more like himself . . .

Whoever that really was.

CHAPTER TWENTY

T HE CAFÉ WAS soaked in sunlight, and Mara sat in a golden halo with Dr. Mortakis and Nona, recounting the events of the night before. When Evan walked in, she pulled up another chair.

"Sounds like I missed a pretty epic night," Dr. Mortakis said, as Evan plopped his book bag on the floor and scooted his chair between her and Mara. Nona squinted at him, then lifted her chin and, with a forceful lurch, shifted her chair away.

"Yeah," Evan said, reminding himself that the woman was old and not quite all there. He met Dr. Mortakis's eyes and nodded in agreement. "She was fantastic last night."

"It wasn't just *me*," Mara said, rolling her eyes and suppressing a smile.

"Um, it really was," he returned with mock insolence.

"Well." The professor checked her watch. "Time is ticking, and I have to get to the office. Nona, dear, finish your tea and I'll walk you up." She began helping her grandmother gather her knitting supplies, depositing skeins of yarn into Nona's canvas bag. As the old woman took one last sip of tea, Dr. Mortakis looked to Mara. "You're *sure* it's all right?"

"Absolutely."

"You're a gem," Dr. Mortakis said, blowing a kiss before offering an arm to her grandmother. "I'll drop the keys off Saturday morning."

They walked around back to the stairs leading up to their apartment, and when they were out of sight, Mara turned to Evan and grinned.

"So, Vanessa has a conference next weekend," she said. "And I'm going to stay with Nona Saturday night."

"Better you than me," he laughed.

"Oh, she's a sweet old lady. And best of all, she goes to bed at seven on the weekends," Mara said, lifting a conspiratorial eyebrow.

"Seven, huh?"

"So . . . you could drop by about seven thirty?"

Evan bugged his eyes. "Dr. Mortakis my program adviser. If she finds out—"

"It was her idea."

"Seriously?"

"Yeah, she was like, feel free to bring a *friend,* wink, wink."

"Wait, she said *wink, wink*? Or she like, physically winked at you?"

"Both," Mara laughed. "So I'm one hundred percent sure it's okay. And I owe you a birthday celebration, remember?"

"Are you . . . going to bake me a cake?"

She winked cartoonishly before heading back to work.

⚜

AT SEVEN THIRTY on Saturday night, Evan buzzed in on the intercom to let Mara know he was there, then rode the elevator behind the Black Cat, juggling cardboard take-out boxes filled with Mongolian beef and lo mein noodles.

"Wow," he said when she opened the door. High ceilings and huge windows made the luxury apartment feel surprisingly large. It was like walking into a penthouse—not that he'd ever done that.

"I know, right? You've got to do the tour," she said, and, lifting a silencing finger to her lips, motioned for him to follow her down the hall. "That's Nona's room," she whispered, pointing toward a closed door that emanated soft snores. "And this one is Vanessa's."

"Are you *sure* this is okay with her?" he asked. "I feel so weird about being here."

"Stop worrying," she said. "Everything's fine."

He peeked through the open doorway to a room that was everything he expected and more. Symmetry. Neatness. Black-and-white with pops of red.

"Looks just like her office."

Mara pointed at the third door at the end of the hall. "Behold the bath-shrine."

She flicked on the light and his eyes went wide. The countertop was a thick, sparkling slab of black granite, and the fixtures might have been fitted with actual diamonds. The floor was tiled in black porcelain, and the spaces between were impeccably white.

"I can't even imagine how much this cost," he said, poking his head into the shower, which had three heads and multiple massage settings. And the toilet wasn't just a toilet. It was a bidet combo.

He followed her through the living room, checking his shoes before stepping onto the snow-white carpet. Fresh, red roses decorated the coffee table, which, like the couches and end tables, was black. A polished baby grand piano stood in front of the large window, framed in finely embroidered white curtains.

"How did they get that thing up here?" Evan asked, nodding toward piano. "It's bigger than the elevator."

Mara shrugged, then gestured dramatically toward the guest room that branched off the living room. "And the final stop on your grand tour."

Like the rest of the apartment, it was stunning: a king-sized, high-rise four-poster bed decked out like a hotel suite with down pillows and an embroidered duvet. Mara's duffel bag sat on the stool of a glossy black vanity. Across the bed, a matching dresser was covered in fresh lilacs, and above it hung a seventy-inch wall-mounted flat-screen TV.

"Did she steal that from a movie theater?"

Mara laughed. "The woman doesn't seem to have any shortage of cash, huh?"

"I think I want to become an art history professor when I grow up."

"All the girls would sign up for Dr. Kiernan's classes," she teased, slipping her fingers between his. "You'd actually be a really great teacher, though."

He shrugged. "I don't know. I want to make money making art. Easy, right?"

"No harder than making money writing songs," she said drily, returning to the table to open the boxes of steaming Chinese food.

"Um, you're off to a good start, Miss First Place Winner," he said. "Next thing you know, you'll go on a *world* tour and leave Umbrella Boy in the dust."

Waving him off, she said through a mouthful of noodles, "I am *not* going to leave you in the dust."

"But you're so much cooler than me."

She shoved his chest. "Am not."

"Are too."

"Are we actually fighting about this?"

"We are. Yes."

"Fine," she said, rolling her eyes. "Then I guess you'll just have to settle for having a girlfriend who's way cooler than you and accompanying her on her world on tour."

"I accept my fate," he said, nudging her sneaker under the table with his. "Hey, what do you think about touring Pennsylvania for Thanksgiving?"

She lifted her eyebrows.

"Not with the band." He grinned. "Just you. And me. My mom and sister are dying to see you again."

"That's sounds nice." Mara smiled, but there was sadness in it. Playing with the last few lo mein noodles, she sighed.

"What?" he asked.

She didn't look up.

"My dad called this morning."

"I thought you finally blocked them?"

"I blocked *her*," Mara said, and he waited, watching her push noodles and bits of cabbage into a mound with the tip of her chopstick. "I guess I just kept holding out this stupid hope that he'd wake up and remember he can still be the good guy."

"So, did he call to apologize for hitting you?"

She shook her head, disgusted. "It was like it never even happened. He called to tell me Mom booked me a nonrefundable flight for the day before Thanksgiving."

"Have they always been like this?" he asked. "I mean, has he ever disagreed with her?"

"When I was little, they would fight sometimes," she said. "Usually about money. She makes more than him, so she always used that as leverage, and then it would be DARVO all the way."

Evan raised an eyebrow. "Um, English, please?"

"Sorry." She laughed, then raised a finger for each letter of the acronym. "Deny, attack, and reverse victim order. D-A-R-V-O."

"You've been to the library again, haven't you?"

She nodded, and an exhausted sigh escaped her lips. "I was reading this book about the psychology of codependency and cycles that cause victims to repress memories and doubt themselves to the point they don't even believe they can exist without the other person. But you know what? I'm done trying to change them, and I'm done answering the phone. I can exist just fine without them. So, yes, please tell your mother that I would be delighted to have Thanksgiving dinner in Pennsylvania."

Mara scooped up the remaining noodles and defiantly shoved them in her mouth, then stood to clear the table, carrying their empty glasses to the sink while Evan gathered the dirty napkins and empty boxes. He threw them in Dr. Mortakis's trash compactor, then came up behind her where she stood washing her hands at the sink.

"You know, if you're trying to brainwash me into believing I can't exist without you," he teased, rubbing her shoulders, which he could see she held uncomfortably tight. "It's working."

"I am not!" She laughed, and he felt a little of the tension ease out of her muscles.

"Hmm." Running his fingertips from her shoulders down to her elbows, he said, "Are you sure? Seems like you have me right where you want me. All alone, full of delicious Chinese food, and completely wrapped around your little finger."

She looked over her shoulder and lifted a playful eyebrow. "You're free to leave if you really want to, you know."

"Not when I'm finally right where I want to be." He slipped his hands beneath the hem of her shirt, feeling the warm curve of her waist against his palms as she turned the water off and reached for the towel.

"Besides," he said, resting his chin on her shoulder and kissing her neck where the choker had been. "I've never stayed anywhere this clutch before."

She laughed. "I know, right? Is it weird that I kind of want to jump on the bed?"

"Absolutely," he said.

"Which is exactly why we need to do it!" she whispered, eyes bright as she rubbed her hands together and tugged him toward the guest room.

"What if she has cameras in here?" Evan asked, scanning the ceiling as Mara took the first running jump onto the bed. "What if she's watching us right now from her hotel room?"

"Stop being paranoid." Mara laughed, and her plum-tinted curls bounced around her face as she jumped on the mattress like a trampoline. "Come on! We won't get in trouble. And if we do, you can blame me."

"For luring me into bed with you?"

"I'll tell her I brainwashed you." She reached for his hands, and he couldn't resist her pull any longer.

They jumped, laughing and shushing each other until they lost their balance and toppled. As he landed on the mattress, she pitched sideways, propelling him onto the plush carpet in a tumble of flailing limbs.

She shrieked, then clapped a hand over her mouth and dissolved into silent laughter.

"You do realize that this is exactly what my five-year-old sister did when she visited my dorm," he said, sprawled on the floor like a starfish.

"Okay," she said, rolling onto her stomach and draping her arms and chin over the edge of the bed. "We should do something mature now."

"We could smoke cigars," he said.

"Or buy insurance."

"It's never too early to plan for retirement."

"Nah, I'm thinking we should either discuss our existential dread," she said, pushing up on her elbows and tapping her lower lip, "or watch a movie."

"What kind of movies do you think Dr. Mortakis watches?"

"Definitely foreign films," Mara answered, and led him to the living room, where Dr. Mortakis had a slim, black bookcase lined with DVDs. They settled on *Run, Lola, Run*, a German experimental film from the late nineties that promised a great soundtrack.

As the title hinted, Lola ran, and Evan tried to keep up with the subtitles. But all he could really think about were Mara's lips, inching closer and closer to his. The movie soon became a blur of quirky camera angles, techno music, and German nonsense in the background. Evan was vaguely aware that Lola's boyfriend needed money, and fast, or his boss was going to kill him, but he didn't really pay attention until Lola let out a bloodcurdling scream.

Evan and Mara pulled apart, startled, and looked at the screen. Lola's boyfriend was dead, blood trickling from the corner of his mouth, and she was holding his face in her hands.

And then suddenly, the story started over again, with Lola getting the call from Manni all over again. He needed money, and fast, or he was going to die.

It was a movie playing out like a video game.

Life one.

Life two.

Life three.

Game over.

"I'm tired of this movie. It's too distracting," Mara whispered, her teeth grazing his earlobe and sending electricity through him.

It short-circuited his brain, overriding everything else. She turned the TV off, darkening the room and brightening the city lights in the window. The view of the Village was incredible, but he didn't give it more than a cursory glance.

He'd seen the city at night a hundred times before, but watching her undress was like finally seeing the Sistine Chapel in person or being allowed behind the velvet ropes to touch *Starry Night*.

Not just the wonder of it.

The familiarity, too.

It was everything that had once happened on a handmade, braided rug.

Everything from above the tattoo parlor, rocking with the rumble of passing trains.

He was close to her, she loved him, and it was everything.

CHAPTER TWENTY-ONE

ARA'S BREATHING SLOWED down and evened out. Her body relaxed against his with contentment, and Nona's snoring filled the stillness of the apartment. Evan lay staring at the window, watching a signal tower blink red until sleep tugged his eyelids closed. When he opened them, he was riding in the back seat of an unfamiliar car.

The sky was fleeced gray. It looked like snow.

Mara sat in the gray-upholstered driver's seat directly in front of him, gripping the steering wheel with one hand while adjusting the radio with the other. The passenger seat was empty.

"Mara?" He tried to say her name, but a sudden, whistled melody blared through the speakers, drowning out his voice. After a few bars, a guitar and tambourine were layered in. He shouted over it. "Hey, Mara, where are we going?"

She didn't even flick her eyes to acknowledge him in the rearview.

The whistling stopped with a drumbeat. A girl with a Southern drawl began to sing "Home" by Edward Sharpe and the Magnetic Zeros.

Drumming her thumbs on the steering wheel, Mara sang along and kept driving as if Evan wasn't there at all.

She was wearing a fuzzy black Sherpa coat and fingerless gloves knitted in varying shades of purple. Her nails were glittery black—no chips. She'd ironed her hair carefully into cascading waves of plum and smelled like bergamot and vanilla. Wherever she was going, it was important.

There was no traffic. Not a single car on this road but theirs. Evan looked out the window and tried to figure out where they were. All around were fields, silvered with frost. Out of nowhere, a cluster of fat snowflakes hit the windshield.

The snow came in a sudden, blinding squall then, and Mara turned her windshield wipers on. Gripping the steering wheel tighter, she leaned forward to see the road.

They entered a stretch of woods. It had already snowed heavily here, and the branches were drooping and white. The road was slick with slush, untouched by another set of wheels. Suddenly, the back end of the car fishtailed and Evan grabbed at the armrest. Mara swore, took her foot off the gas, and recovered her lane.

"Just take it easy," Evan said from the back seat, but she didn't respond. "You've never driven in the snow, have you? It's okay. Just don't panic. You've got this."

Slowly, they exited the section of woods, and the road sloped uphill. The tires spun, then gained traction. Halfway up the hill, the road was merely wet. The light ping of freezing rain replaced the hush of snow, and Evan craned his neck to see the dashboard. The temperature gauge read thirty-two.

Mara's foot fell heavy on the gas, pushing the car uphill. As she crested, another flat expanse stretched ahead of the car. The hill plateaued, but the road continued straight even though the land dropped off sharply. A stone and concrete bridge spanned the space between hilltops. Evan looked out to the left where fast-flowing water snaked below.

"The bridge ices before the road," Evan said, mechanically, as if he were taking his driver's test. "Mara, did you hear me?"

Tiny chips of icy rain still pinged off the windshield, but the road was only wet. Mara's foot was on the accelerator, her thumbs drumming on the steering wheel again. She glanced at the radio and reached to change the station.

"Slow down."

She sped up.

"Mara, didn't you hear me? Slow—"

It happened in a blur.

The impact of concrete bashing into metal.

A shower of ice and exploding glass.

Upside down then right side up, falling, spinning, plunging—

Splash.

The car hit water and Mara's neck snapped sideways on impact. Her head cracked the driver's side glass, and water gushed into the car.

They sank toward a bed of rock. Sloshing over Mara, the water ran pink with her blood.

But Evan couldn't feel it. He couldn't feel the cold water or the sharply bowed metal that was now jutting into where his hip should be. He reached for her seat belt, but his fingers slipped right through it. No matter how hard he tried to press the release button, it wouldn't budge.

"Mara, wake up!"

The water rose toward her nostrils, and her submerged fingers were already blue. Her eyes rolled back into her head.

"No, no, no, no," he whispered, then screamed. "Somebody, help! Help—please! Mara, you have to wake up!"

"Oh my god, I'm awake! What's wrong?"

Mara's face hovered above his. She was shaking his shoulder, looking at him with scared-awake eyes.

Like a frightened animal, his gaze darted around the room. He was in a huge, four-poster bed, hyperventilating in a guest room with a city view.

Covering his wet face with his palms, he exhaled long and slow. "Bad dream."

"You scared me to death!"

"Sorry. Scared myself." He was conscious of the dampness of his skin and the sheets. Sliding his fingers apart, he peered at her. The alarm had eased out of her features, and she offered him a small smile.

"What the hell were you dreaming about?"

"That something happened to you," he said slowly, still breathing hard.

"Aww," she crooned sleepily, nestling against him again. "I'm fine. It was just a dream."

But it wasn't.

Once upon a time, she died at the end of a rope, hung as a witch.

Once upon another time, she'd died the night Dreamland burned —but not from the flames.

And he was certain that this time, she'd crash her car on an icy bridge, too, if he didn't do something to make it stop.

"Do you have a car?" he asked, nudging her awake again.

She yawned. "Hmm?"

"A car? Do you have a car?"

"I did," she said, yawning again. "But I sold it when I moved up here. Why?"

Life one.

Life two.

Life three.

No. This game couldn't be over because it wasn't a game.

"Mara, listen." The gravity of his voice made her stiffen. "Something's been . . . happening to me."

She rolled over toward him again, pushing herself halfway up on her elbow. "Something like what?"

"I know how this is going to sound, but I need you to hear me out. I'm not crazy. I'm not schizophrenic or anything like that. But you remember the tattooed boy?"

She nodded.

"I've been *remembering* things from his life."

"Umm . . . what?"

"I don't know if it's inherited memories or like, reincarnation or something. I don't know. But I can remember things that are real—things that *were* real a hundred years ago. That's what I was going to show you on my phone, but then the photo got deleted or something. He loved this girl who looked just like you, and her name was Mary."

"Mary?" She rubbed her eyes and sat up.

"I saw a photo of her when I went to the tattoo shop, but that wasn't the first time I'd seen her. Just like when we met in Washington Square, it wasn't the first time I'd seen you."

Slowly, she said, "Okay, you're losing me here. What do you mean, it wasn't the first time you saw me?"

"You remember when you asked me how I got into NYU early?"

She nodded.

"It was because of you. Because I painted you before I ever saw you. Just ask my mom—she's got the painting in the attic at her house. And that's why she showed up here. To make sure I wasn't losing my mind when I told her I met a girl who looked just like my painting."

"That's why you asked me out?" she exclaimed, and the indignation in her voice made him feel like a creep. "Because I looked like some girl you painted?"

"No." He shook his head, pressing the heels of his hands into his eyes. "Because you *are* the girl I painted."

"I-I don't know what to say right now."

"You don't have to say anything. Just—just please listen."

It was the middle of the night, his heart was still racing from the nightmare, and the similarities between what he needed to explain and the movie they'd just watched didn't help, but he tried. He began with Mr. Burns's art class, trying to connect the dots between the Neptune Gallery and Lillian, the ASPR and Dreamland Park without sounding like he was reciting a bad movie plot. Kieran Flynn and Mary Thompson, he assured her, were real people. And if he could ever get back into the Society for Psychical Research on Seventy-third Street, he'd prove it to her.

"Okay, let me get this straight. You think you've been seeing a . . . a past life? With me?"

He nodded, covering his eyes with his hands. "Maybe two. Yeah."

"And you think . . . something bad is going to happen to me . . . *again*?"

He heard the wobble in her voice. The fear. It made him sick. "I know it sounds crazy. I *know*. But if I can just get back in there, I can prove everything to you. I promise, it's all there!"

She stopped him with a gentle hand on his chest.

"Okay." She took a shaky breath. "If the lady calls you back, I'll come with you."

"Really?" He felt tears of relief pricking his eyes. "You believe me?"

She opened her mouth, then closed it again.

"Mara?"

"How long has this been going on?"

"Since I went out to Coney Island."

"Why didn't you tell me? We said no secrets, right? How could you keep it from me all this time?"

"I tried to tell you, to show you that picture of Mary, but then it just—"

"Disappeared," she said flatly.

"I know how bad this sounds. I really do. And I swear, I wanted to tell you, but I was scared you wouldn't believe me."

She bit her lip. "When can I see the painting? The one that got you into NYU."

"My mom can take a picture—"

"No, I want to see the real thing."

He swallowed hard. "If you still want to come to my mom's for Thanksgiving, you can see it then. In person."

She was quiet for a long time, and Evan thought his heart would crash through his chest.

"Mara? Say something. Please?"

She flopped backward onto her pillow, staring at the ceiling, and sighed. "I'll come with you for Thanksgiving. And to the Psychical Center. But in the meantime, just . . . just promise me you'll go get checked out?"

He looked away, biting his lip so hard he tasted blood.

"Listen, I love you," she said, tugging at his arm until he turned to face her. "And I'm not going anywhere, but—"

"But you think I'm losing my mind? Just like my dad?"

"You're just . . . you're scaring me," she said, tears forming in the corners of her eyes. "Please?"

"I'm sorry," he said quickly, forcing the words around the lump in his throat. "You're right. I'll go to the doctor."

"Promise?"

"Promise," he said, and the lie tasted hot and metallic in his mouth.

"It was a just a dream," she whispered into his ear as she kissed his cheek, then laced her fingers with his under the covers. "Try to get some sleep."

Gradually, in the silence that followed, he felt her grip loosen and her fingers go limp as she fell asleep again, but he stared at the ceiling for what must have been hours, heart racing, because it wasn't just a dream.

It was *the* dream.

And unless he could succeed where his predecessors had failed, he was going to lose her.

Nothing lasts forever . . .

He'd known that better than any kid should growing up. He'd used that knowledge like a shield, telling himself that as long as he didn't get too attached, it wouldn't hurt to leave. As long as he didn't think of each new school's football team as *his* team, he could handle the losses. As long as he didn't paint the walls or think of it as *his* room, he could carry his mattress back down the stairs just like he always knew he would. But, running his fingers gently through Mara's tangled ponytail as she slept beside him, he realized all his armor was gone. If Dr. Weaver wouldn't return his calls, he'd camp out on the doorstep. If nobody showed up, he'd break in. Another possibility flickered into his mind. He could visit the asylum. He might find something there. He might *remember* something there. That, he decided, was a last resort, but the thought kept him awake and sweating. Straitjackets and electrotherapy and, worst of all, nobody believing you . . .

He didn't notice the snoring stop, or the approaching footsteps, or the turn of the bedroom doorknob. He didn't notice anything until a hulking shadow loomed over him and the covers flew off their bodies. The light flashed on in a blinding burst as someone growled a furious, "No!"

Evan covered his eyes and yelped in surprise as Mara bolted upright.

"Get out!" Nona screeched. "Get out!"

He jumped out of bed, squinting at the old woman gesturing wildly at him, motioning him toward the door. Fumbling for his glasses, he tried to figure out if he was actually awake or if this was another nightmare. Mara stood, her ponytail crooked and wild, wearing nothing but a bra and panties, and Evan realized he was wearing even less. No, this was not a naked dream. This was really happening.

"Nona, it's okay. It's okay," Mara was saying, tossing a pillow to Evan so he wasn't exposed to the eyes of a hysterically angry, red-faced old woman shrieking about propriety and morals and decency.

"Out!" Nona squawked, hitting him in the head with his jeans. "Out!"

Mara was as bewildered as Evan was, trying to explain, but Nona would have none of it.

"Okay, okay, just . . . just go out in the living room so we can get dressed, all right?" Mara pleaded, and with a huff, Nona turned her back and walked out.

Evan grabbed his jeans from the floor and wiggled his legs in, but before he could pick up his shirt, Nona had returned with an armful of teacups.

"Get *out!*" she growled, hurtling one toward his head. He ducked as Mara rushed to stop her. "You filthy thief."

"Just go!" Mara cried over her shoulder, wrestling a black porcelain cup from the old woman's gnarled hands. "I'll get her settled down. I don't know what else to do!"

Evan scooped up his socks and shoes, leaving his bag on the floor as Nona managed to hurl a pink cup at his heels. Dashing through the door to the hall, he tried to catch his breath. As soon as he crossed the threshold, the shrieking stopped. He could hear Mara's voice, steady and soothing.

"That's it. It's okay. I'll clean it up."

"I'll make you some warm milk, love," Nona said, and Evan could hear her heavy footsteps moving toward him. He didn't have his shoes on yet, so he flattened himself against the wall in the dark, hoping she wouldn't follow. She didn't. She opened a cupboard and clanged pans around, presumably heating some milk while Mara swept up shards of broken porcelain. He bent to put on his socks, then tied his shoes. But he still didn't have a shirt. Or his phone.

Through the window at the end of the hall, he could see that it was still dark outside. He slumped onto the carpeted floor. What would Dr. Mortakis say when she realized there were no teacups left in her apartment? Leaning his back against the wall and resting his forehead on his knees, he silently prayed that she really didn't have any cameras set up in the apartment.

Finally, the door clicked open and Mara's face appeared in the crack.

"Here's your shirt," she whispered, grimacing. "And your bag. I put your phone in the front pocket."

"Do you want me to call somebody?" he whispered back, turning his shirt right side out and putting it on hastily.

Mara glanced over her shoulder, then shook her head. "She's just heating up some milk on the stove, now. She's calm. I'm so sorry . . . I don't know why she—"

"Get away from the door!" Nona shrieked, hustling toward them. "You have no right to come to my door. Get away from *her*!"

"I'll go," he said quickly, hands up in surrender, and Nona took a step back. "It's okay. I'll just . . . go. Call me if you need anything."

Mara huffed in exasperation and pushed out her bottom lip. "I don't want you to go."

"Your milk is ready, love." Nona's tone was as authoritative as it was affectionate as she turned back toward the stove.

"She's not going to let me stay," he whispered. "She hates me."

"I'll meet you tomorrow at the café, okay? Noon?"

"Okay."

Throwing her hands in the air, Mara turned to go back inside for some warm milk.

CHAPTER TWENTY-TWO

IF DR. MORTAKIS knew about what happened over the weekend, she didn't let on. Evan hoped that meant she'd chalked up the sudden lack of teacups in her apartment to Nona's dementia. Still, he imagined her watching it all go down on camera and either laughing hysterically at him or deeply regretting her choice of Promising Young Artist. Either way, he'd have to work harder than ever to ensure his place in the program . . . though he was sure that regaining her respect was a lost cause.

The week was a blur of school, work, nightmares, and relentless teasing from the band about the *Nona Incident*. Evan was swamped with slides to memorize for Tuesday's exam, an opinion essay due Wednesday, and an oil painting to complete for Fundamentals of 2D by Friday.

Mara was scheduled for double shifts at the Black Cat to make up for the hours she'd miss while on tour, and she ended up spending most of the extra money on new clothes Samantha deemed cool enough to play Hot Z's. Evan studied in a velvet chair outside the fitting rooms at Lucille's Ball, enduring Ben's reenactments of Nona's meltdown every time Mara changed clothes behind the curtain.

"No peeking! Propriety and morals!" he'd squawk before throwing a shoe at Evan and dissolving into giggles that went well beyond amusing the store employees. If Nona's rampage were the only incident that night, Evan might have found it funny, too. But his dream of the icy bridge returned, night after night, and with it the echoes of his promise to Mara to visit a psychiatrist. He could tell she was trying not to, but she looked at him differently, like she was afraid he would break.

Saturday morning, Evan pulled the venetian blinds up, letting a slice of sunlight onto Henri's snoring face. It was a bright morning, but cold. The grass was checkered with frosty shadows, places the sun hadn't touched. The nights were hovering at freezing. The bright red and yellow leaves were fading to brown. Soon, winter.

He'd checked the extended weather forecast for all the cities on Switched Flip's East Coast tour, and there was no snow in the forecast—not even rain. The band was set to open that night at Hot Z's NYC, then pile onto a tour bus headed for Philadelphia. Evan and Mara had hoped to get lunch together in the Village before the show, but she was much too nervous to eat and then Ben called saying Zeke Hart wanted them to do an early sound check before the club opened.

Each member of the band was given a free ticket, so Evan found himself at a table with Darren's new boyfriend, Ty, trying to make small talk over the deafening preshow noise.

"How did you guys meet?" Evan asked, even though he knew Ty had come in to the record store where Darren worked, asking for an obscure eighties album they both loved. He hoped that if he could keep Ty talking about himself and Darren, he wouldn't ask too many questions.

The club was packed, and Switched Flip sounded better than ever. Mara sang "Your Girl" and "Timekeeper," stealing the show, and after they'd sold T-shirts and buttons and signed flyers for fans, Evan helped Mara carry her bags to the tour bus waiting for them out back.

The bus was a hotel on wheels, complete with a shower, refrigerator, and microwave. It was huge, nothing like the little car he'd dreamed of, and one of Zeke Hart's roadies was driving them. He breathed a sigh of relief, promising himself that for the next two weeks, she'd be safe.

While the others loaded their things, they snuck around the side of the building.

"I'm so nervous!" she whispered.

"You earned this," he promised, and kissed her forehead. "You'll be amazing."

Their goodbye ran overtime, and Ben came looking for Mara.

"Time to go!" he huffed impatiently, bugging his eyes and nodding toward the street. "It's two weeks, not two years."

"Okay, okay." Mara sighed and kissed Evan one more time as Ben went looking for Darren and Ty, who had snuck around the other side of the building. "I'll call you every day."

She got on the bus, followed by Darren, and in a flash of headlights, they were gone.

Evan walked back to his dorm room feeling like he'd forgotten something. There must have been one more thing he was supposed to say or do. He forced his heavy limbs into a clean T-shirt and brushed his teeth before collapsing into a fitful sleep.

By morning, he knew it would be a long two weeks. When he called the ASPR, it rang three times before a chipper, electronic voice announced: "This mailbox is currently full. We're sorry. Please try again later."

He knew all the messages were his.

Henri rolled over out of the sunlight and kept snoring like a horse. Evan tried to organize his head, tried to think about what books he needed and where he had to be when. He tried to think about what he should eat, and how many chapters he had to skim before tomor-row. He didn't get anything done but walking circles around his room, picking up laundry and putting it back down again, picking up pencils and putting them back down again, picking up his phone and putting it back down again.

Maybe Dr. Weaver was too annoyed to return his calls, or maybe she was out sick. Maybe, like Lillian, she'd kicked over dead before telling him everything he needed to know. Any which way, the woman wasn't calling him back.

But someone else had to work there, he reasoned. Someone had to let him in; he was a card-carrying member.

There were no listed hours for the Society, so he decided to show up at five o'clock on Monday, like he did last time. If closing time was six, someone should be there at least an hour beforehand to lock up.

He stood on the porch, wishing he'd worn a heavier coat. It felt so late. Night was falling early since turning the clocks back, and he couldn't get used to it. Clocks should only move forward; anything else was unnatural.

Crisp, brown leaves swirled with trash in the street.

He knocked, and waited. No lights came on.

He rang the bell, and waited. The curtains didn't move.

He sat on the cold, concrete front step and watched digital minutes dissolve into each other on his phone screen, alternating the knocking and ringing every five minutes until 5:59 turned to 6:00. Nobody an-swered the door.

His fingers were stiff and cold, but he reached into his bag for a pen and a sheet of notebook paper. In the weak streetlight, he scrib-bled his name—tacking on "Paid Student Member of the Society," his cell phone number, and a plea to be contacted.

He slipped it through the mail slot and sighed heavily, watching it disappear, then rubbed his hands together for warmth, tucked his chin against the wind, and walked the dark blocks to the subway station.

The train was empty and warm, and when his phone buzzed and he saw Mara's number, he warmed a little more.

Made it to Baltimore!

They'd already played Sunday night in Philadelphia, and the local college radio station had picked up "Your Girl." The tour was going swimmingly, and they were only at their third stop. He texted her a raven GIF and said,

Home of Poe

Lol. Wish you were here.

Me, too.

I have no privacy to call right now, but . . . NEWS!!

Somebody contacted me through Connections this morning!!!

What? Wow!

She said she left a baby girl in the Safe Haven on June 5 in Tampa.

She lives in Ohio now.

What's her name?

Don't know yet.

Nobody uses their real names on the site.

Her handle is @LoveIsEternal.

How do you find out more?

SafeChat is the first step.

Then if we think we're a match, we submit our info to Connections.

They'll run DNA tests and stuff. But I think she's the one!

That's amazing. How are you feeling?

Worse than before I go onstage. Ha. And I have to do that soon, too.

What time's the show?

8:00.

Eat some pretzels or something, okay? Don't starve.

I'll eat some pretzels if you make that appointment.

His stomach twisted as he prepared to lie.

Already did. Met with the therapist this afternoon. He said I'm fantastic.

Tell me something I don't know?

He said it's just stress.

NBD.

I'm going to keep checking in with him.

But I'm fine.

Much better.

That's good. Really good.

Hey, I've got to go . . .

But this song is on Sam's road trip playlist.

It always makes me think of you <3

She sent him a link to a YouTube performance by Edward Sharpe and the Magnetic Zeros, so he fished around in his zippered pocket for earbuds and hit play.

A haunting, familiar whistle filled his ears, then a tambourine and drums were layered in.

And when the girl, with her southern twang, began to sing "Home," knocking every last bit of air from his lungs, he knew time was running out.

There was only one place left to go.

KINGS PARK ASYLUM

1 9 1 1

BY FEBRUARY, DR. James had finished with me, concluding that there was nothing specific enough in my visions or dreams to warrant further action. There was nothing he could do for me, he said, but assure me that Mary was perfectly safe. Closing my case as "inconclusive," he sent me home, advising me to rein in my imagination and attempt a normal life. Something I knew I would never have.

I planned to tell Mary. I practiced my words while she was off in the animal arena, trying to piece them together in a way she would believe. It sounded ridiculous, and she was so happy that winter. I didn't want to spoil it because happiness is precarious as February ice. You can skate on it, gliding along with grace—and then, without warning, everything cracks open. You crash into the frigid waters below, trapped, and never get out again.

Inevitably, our happy winter began to thaw. Our ice grew thin.

It was a sunny spring morning, and she wanted me to see the park. She wanted to show me how they'd changed it, with new rides, new colors, new stands.

So we walked.

And there, I saw a ride called Hell Gate, and though it was freshly built, I had seen it before. The devil in my dreams. I knew the fire would soon consume us.

I was foolish, still thinking there was a way. Still thinking I could stop it. Thinking that if only I stopped the ride from opening, I could stop the fire from starting. And so, when the workers were working beyond midnight, beyond the reach of the sun, I tried. And in the trying, Reader, I failed.

That night, I crept beneath the webby-black wings of the devil, into the tunnel. Into the smell of tar on sticky black walls, into Hell itself. I found the workers, sweating and miserable and exhausted, and told them they had to stop. The very idea of the ride was an abomination, nothing but an exploitation of human uncertainty and fear. It would terrify small children and line the pockets of wicked priests, I said, and begged them to leave it unfinished.

Of course, they ignored me. One by one, I begged them, knowing exactly how mad I sounded. Desperate, I ran deeper into the tunnel. I was weeping. Shouting. Senseless of my feet.

And so, I tripped.

I tripped over a heavy bucket, snagging my ankle on the handle and spilling warm sludge into my shoes. It spread across the floor, growing, creeping all the way to the humming, frazzled wires.

In a disorienting instant, the lights went out.

The miracle of electricity failed us, left us in the dark.

And then suddenly, there was light.

Sparks.

Smoke.

Flames.

Alarms went off—clanging bells and wailing sirens. I dashed out with sticky feet, gagging on smoke, pulling choking strangers with me. She's safe, I told myself. She's above the tattoo shop, sleeping. She's safe.

I ran to the boardwalk, gasping at fresh air, and then, I turned to see flames shooting two stories into the sky. Sparks showering down in a sizzling spray. Frantically disoriented people everywhere, draped in blankets. And then, the roar.

Screams erupted, and the crowd parted like the Red Sea.

An African lion tore onto the boardwalk—up in flames.

Black Prince.

Thrashing his burning head, he galloped toward the water—toward relief—but when he set foot on the sand, he stopped. His ears flicked toward the boardwalk, and even though the cat was on fire, he didn't run any farther. Turning his back to the sea, he roared desperately, with something more than just pain. I felt that roar. He was talking to me. Telling me to look, now—telling me to make it stop.

A voice rose above the confusion of the crowd. "Stay back, everybody!"

I turned to see a man holding a gun, his black hair shining red in the fiery glow of Dreamland. Fitz Mulligan. He was back for the season, back with his freaks, back for her.

The crowd parted for him, and he moved toward Black Prince. He and the burning lion stared at each other for a stretched second as Mulligan took aim, holding the pistol with both hands and extending his thick, bare arms.

"I'll put him out of his misery," Mulligan said, and I thought it would be a mercy, after all, for the cat suffered greatly and was thrashing much too wildly to be helped. Tears pressed at my eyes.

Hurry up, I thought. Get it over with.

"Stop! Don't you dare shoot him!" someone screamed, but three times, Mulligan shot the poor beast.

The lion slumped, nearly finished, but Mulligan did not lower his pistol. He took a step forward, his black-heeled shoes pounding on the wood, and then another step, and another—until I saw a girl push through the crowd and grab his elbow, screaming, "Enough!"

Not just any girl.

My girl.

"Knew I'd find you here," Mulligan said under his breath, his black teeth slimy in the glow of the flames. "You never could leave that stupid cat."

The dying lion's eyes were open, looking at Mary with anguish and pleading and love. She ran to him, throwing her sweater over his mane and patting out the flames, the smell of burning hair and smoking flesh making our eyes water. The cat let out a final, tortured groan, and tears slipped from my eyes. His final sight was a beautiful one.

But my gaze was torn from them at the sound of Mulligan reloading his gun.

"Save your bullets, Mulligan," Mary sobbed, stroking the cat's nose. "He's gone."

"No, honey, I've been saving this one special for you," he said, lifting his pistol with a grin.

I ran at Mulligan and shoved him hard, knocking the gun from his hand. It fell with a clatter to the boardwalk below, and in one swift motion I snatched it up and sprinted blindly toward Mary.

How was I to know he had another gun?

She lifted her gaze and gasped, and instinctively, I covered her body with mine.

Bang!

Bang!

Two shots rang out at my back, but I didn't feel pain. Only the warm slick of blood cascading over my wrist. Why was I still breathing? The bullets must have hit me, I was sure I'd put myself in the way, I'd covered her, my whole body blocking hers, but I didn't feel it. Why was I still alive?

"You stole her from me," Mulligan whispered, his mouth suddenly at my ear. "But you can't have her."

I pushed myself upright to face him, but he was gone.

I lifted Mary from the sand and the blood was spreading, staining the pink lilies I'd inked along her collarbone, dripping down the trees, obscuring the pair of fawns and the peacock. Her body was limp.

"Help! Somebody, please, help us!" I called, but the sirens were too loud, now. Everyone was watching as firemen helplessly poured water on Dreamland.

Touching her cheek, I turned her face to mine, but her eyes had lost focus. "Stay with me," I begged, and she shuddered once. "I tried. I'm sorry, Mary, I tried. I thought—"

But we see as through a glass darkly.

Only when it shatters does it all become clear.

Reader, I've seen the glass shatter. I've seen the way you will lose her this time, not against a backdrop of fire, but ice. Ice stained red with her precious blood.

CHAPTER TWENTY-THREE

PERMANENTLY CLOSED.

That's what the internet said about Kings Park Asylum.

And yet, Evan found videos of guys sneaking in after dark. Ghost hunters and self-proclaimed historians who pushed through openings in the chain link fence. Security was lax. Nobody watched it after dark.

So Evan waited until the sun slipped away from the city to board his train. The trip to Long Island would take over an hour, so he popped in his ear buds and rewatched the YouTube videos, trying to figure out how to get from the station to a faulty section of fencing. When the train doors opened, he still wasn't sure.

Kings Park Station was nothing but concrete and weeds. He wished he'd left earlier so he could've walked the mile and a half from the station to the hospital in daylight. But it was too late. Darkness had come, and there was nothing to do but walk quickly into the night, on the broken, grass-interrupted sidewalk running parallel to a divided highway called Kings Park Boulevard. Was this the road he'd traveled, tree-lined and quiet, over a hundred years ago? Into the peaceful woods, away from the city, away from the grave of the girl he loved and the family that didn't believe him?

Evan walked faster, waiting for his vision to blotch and swim, but it stayed steady past the signs for Nissequogue River State Park. Steady as he stared at the graffiti-ridden brick high-rise on the other side of a seven-foot-high chain link fence.

The hospital complex was set up like a small village, with buildings of varying sizes all around. His stomach tightened as he checked the perimeters for police vehicles. It was a misdemeanor to enter, and he was eighteen. If he got caught, it would be on his permanent record.

Hugging the shadows, he trailed the fence around the imposing U-shaped main building until he found a stretch of graffiti that looked familiar. He'd seen it on video, the backdrop to an opening. Gingerly, he started pressing on the chain links, yanking scraggly vines out of the way, looking for a spot that would give.

There.

It was torn top to bottom. He shouldered against it and was through.

The sparse, brown grass was littered with crunchy leaves, and his cell phone light could only illuminate a few feet at a time. The darkness here was a presence unto itself, so far from the glitz and light pollution of Manhattan. A sharp sliver of moon dangled above the broken landscape like a scythe, and as Evan directed his flashlight upward against the side of the tall, brick main building, vine shadows slithered like snakes.

He walked around the back and found a house-sized pile of broken wood, tile, and glass. He stepped close enough to see a porcelain bathtub filled with black leaves. Something skittered from the shadows. He backed away. Shivering in his jacket, Evan wrapped one arm around himself, using the other to aim the light. His breath was visible in the sharp, November air as he walked through a cluster of trees, trying to keep his bearings so he could find his way back to Kings Park Boulevard.

Emerging from beneath the dark branches, he faced the graffiti-splashed wall of a broken-down stable. Rusted troughs gathered rain-water beneath a sagging roof, but no animals remained.

On the other side of the stable, a crumbling sidewalk led to a row of cottages. He peered inside a gaping window spiked with broken glass and saw four metal-posted beds, still covered in tattered blankets. With a shiver, he realized the doors and windows locked from the outside. Cottage after cottage was the same.

The path continued toward a brick high-rise, older than the cottages or the main entrance. Prickly vines choked out the sign, and when Evan tried to move them aside, he hissed in pain. This sign didn't want to be read.

The front door was gone. Holding his breath as he crossed the threshold, he panned the light around the entryway into what looked like a waiting room. A cement staircase splattered with crude graffiti loomed from the far corner, spiked with fixtures but no railing. Testing the bottom step, he decided it was sturdy enough to climb.

At the top of the first flight, he stepped onto a floor deep with rubble. Crumbling plaster was mounded up like drifts of snow. Empty wheelchairs. Ratty blankets. Sideways wooden chairs and battered tables. Atop a cobwebbed, wooden table stood a single chess piece, the black queen. He reached out to touch it, and as soon as it brushed his hand, he saw it all the way it used to be.

People in pajamas milled about, some playing chess or checkers in pairs, another painting by the window, still more rocking back and forth facing the wall. His senses were flooded with the smell of anti-septic and urine, the sound of someone pounding on an out-of-tune piano, and then a sudden shriek from the hall made him wince—

Evan dropped the queen and grabbed the edge of the table to steady himself. He was alone again, and everything was broken and dirty and gone. Kieran Flynn had been here. But had he ever gotten out?

As the freezing night air poured through the windows, something tickled the back of Evan's hand. He yelped, pulling it back like he'd touched flames, and dropped his phone. Panting, he brushed a spindly black spider off the back of his hand and shivered, feeling itchy all over as it disappeared into a layer of dust.

A narrow hall cut to the left, and Evan followed it. Numbered doors lined the walls: one, two, three. *Stop.*

This was his door.

He knew it.

His hands shook as he reached for the knob, and when he turned it, he yelped again.

The wood was rotten, and the entire knob fell out onto his foot.

Evan pressed a hand to his chest, trying to catch his breath as he kicked the hunk of metal into the hall, where it rolled lazily. Flat-palmed, he pushed the door open and stepped inside.

A sagging, metal-framed bed.

A small writing desk with no chair.

A filthy, braided rug.

Walls covered in peeling, pale blue paint.

Panning the light around the room, he caught a snatch of color peering out from beneath the milky blue. Not just color, but shape. He stepped closer and saw a hand. A girl's ringed fingers, tipped with perfect oval nails.

Rubbing away flakes of blue with his palm, he revealed a graceful arm. A sequined leotard. Slippered feet on a highwire, and Mara's face.

Frantically, he began peeling the paint away. A black lion's paw on the ground below. The sea. Hell Gate.

He looked toward the ceiling, where a rope dangled from sharp, right-angled branch.

The paint was probably made of lead, and he was probably breathing in asbestos, but he couldn't stop because there, near the foot of the bed, another section of blue had begun to peel. He knelt, and as he dug his nails under the loose edge, a six-inch chunk fell away.

Evan felt sick. This car was too new for Kieran Flynn to have seen on his streets.

And it was heading toward a bridge.

It was all there. The first, the second, the third—and *last*. Kieran Flynn hadn't seen beyond that accident any more than Evan Kiernan had. Was that really it? The end?

Frantically, he scraped at the walls, trying to find another scene. Another life. Another chance. There had to be more. Sweating despite the cold, he swiped across Hell Gate and flames appeared, consuming Dreamland beside the sea. Black Prince suffered on the sand, Mary kneeling at his side. And there, at the water's edge, aiming a pistol at the dying cat, was a man who felt eerily familiar.

A man who reminded him of . . .

No.

It *couldn't* be.

The painting was old, and the lighting was awful, and he was feeling more than a little unhinged. The figure was clearly male, with broad shoulders and trousers.

It couldn't be.

But as he aimed the light for a closer look at the face, Evan jumped.

Yes, the hair was short. The reading glasses were gone, and instead of an hourglass figure, the body was broad and muscular. But the face was unmistakable.

There, staring back at him, was Vanessa Mortakis.

KINGS PARK ASYLUM

1911

I'VE WRITTEN THESE letters in hopes that you might learn from my mistakes. We are being punished. But by whom? And for what? I became so obsessed with how, *I forgot about* who. And why. *If you are to stop that terrible crash, you will need to know these things. You will need to remember everything.*

But Dr. James will not be keeping his promise.

The boy who will not confess to arson doesn't demand his attention like the man in the room across from mine, whose hallucinated voices tell him again and again to open his own veins. Yes, just this morning as that man's blood seeped beneath the crack in my door, I heard the doctor's voice telling him everything would be all right. He does not say these words to me any longer. He departs for another journey to Haiti tomorrow and told me plainly he will not be returning to visit me at Kings Park. At least he will not file charges against me. Dreamland's fire will go down in history as an accident, and the tattooed lunatic will be left out of the story altogether.

He will leave me—and these words—here to rot.

CHAPTER TWENTY-FOUR

EVAN STUMBLED DOWN the concrete stairs in a panic, swatting cobwebs from his face, back out into the cold November night. He ran past the row of cottages with their locks, past the stable with its rusted troughs, and into the dark copse of trees before he realized he was crying.

Collapsing into a pile of dead leaves, he knelt and covered his face with his hands. As hot tears slipped between his fingers, the breeze picked up, whooshing him backward to summer.

The humid night air clung to his skin and made breathing difficult. Crickets sang, and fireflies rose like sparks from the grass. He was on his knees, sheltered from sight, and he was digging.

KINGS PARK ASYLUM

1 9 1 1

SO MANY DAYS have passed. Dr. James has been in Haiti. Mary has been in the ground. My letters have been shut away in the desk drawer, and I have lain in my bed in this sunbaked, brick inferno all summer long. I have wished for sleep. For winter. For death.

But then, I saw you. And now, I know what I must do.

You will come here, and you will dig.

And so tonight, I will bury these words. And you will find them.

CHAPTER TWENTY - FIVE

E HAD NO shovel, so he dug first with a branch, and then with a sharp-edged rock, until something cracked.

Scraping carefully with the rock, he unearthed the smooth contour of an old milk bottle. Using a stick for leverage, he inserted one end through the area he'd broken open, then wiggled until the bottom came loose. And then, carefully, he lifted the bottle out of the ground.

He saw papers inside. Clean and perfectly preserved, except for the few crumbs of damp earth that had fallen in when he'd cracked the glass with the rock. He tried to unscrew the cap, but it was sealed with wax and wouldn't budge. Grasping it by the neck, he hit it against the tree trunk until it shattered.

On his knees again, he lifted the pages from the pile of broken glass, shaking them clean before bringing them to the light.

I, Kieran Flynn, attest that I am of sound mind as I write this letter . . .

KINGS PARK ASYLUM

1911

READER. YOUR TIME has come. I've told my tales, and the sun has gone down.

There is little hope in a place like this. All of us, discarded by our families. Abandoned by whatever gods we believed in. Left to lose whatever remains of our minds.

There is one thing I have not told you, which suddenly feels important. The old woman.

Day after day, she sits in the common room designated for recreation. She sits and weaves upon a loom. A loom for making trivial items that nobody wants or needs. She weaves, and she watches me.

I've heard her whispering—a common thing among the residents here. But her whispers are arguments with an unseen adversary.

This afternoon, I was playing chess with a boy whose parents disowned him. They called him a Sodomite and sentenced him to this place—a hell before hell. He is a clever opponent, and often bests me in chess. The old woman sat near us, weaving swiftly, her old fingers nimble. In bitter tones, this is what she said.

"Am I not the eldest? And yet she instructs me. Scolds me. Was there a time before it was so? Was I young once, like her? I cannot even recall. I can only hear the sound of metal on metal, each cut scraping and scratching at my ears. She has taken everything from me, stripped me bare, and I hate her. I hate her."

Her words moved me, and I felt kinship with this woman, waging a hard battle alone.

"Who is it that you speak of?" I asked gently. "What is her name?"

"Death," she replied, without looking up.

"Death," I echoed, nodding with understanding.

"None can ignore Death's brash beauty. But life?" She continued, laughing bitterly. "Life is the steady rhythm of a foot on the pedal, just a quiet thread slipping through fingers. Nobody notices life until it's too late."

"I am sorry for your losses," I told her, and stepped near to examine her work.

Her head snapped up, and she hissed at me.

Without another word, she gathered her things and left the recreational room. I haven't seen her since. Perhaps you will know what this means, perhaps it means nothing at all, but when you find these words, you will know you are not a lunatic. You will know that everything you have seen was real and true and important.

This place may break my mind, but it will not break my spirit.

No, my spirit will remain strong.

It will live in you.

CHAPTER TWENTY-SIX

EVAN RAN THE mile and a half to Kings Park Station, stumbling more than once on potholed concrete. The darkness was oppressive. No cars passed him on the divided highway. No animals scurried across his path.

Panting, he finally collapsed onto a bench to wait for his train. Minutes passed, and he sat dazed, staring at the empty tracks.

The old woman who hated him, and Death itself, weaving on a loom. Nona knitting at her table at the Black Cat, then throwing things at him.

Dr. Mortakis, blowing Mara a kiss. Firing a gun.

Alabama. Arkansas.

The car. The fire. The noose.

Mara. Mary. Maura.

It was too much to process, and he felt his mind shutting down. His breathing went shallow.

Time seemed to stand still.

THE NEXT MORNING, Evan didn't go to class.

He emailed Dr. Mortakis that he was sick and wouldn't be in to work, because the thought of speaking with her made him nauseous. He didn't get out of bed except to use the bathroom and drink water from the sink. When Henri came in at dusk, Evan rolled toward the wall and stared at the light gray cinder blocks, feeling like a wrung-out rag.

He couldn't think. Couldn't move.

Henri left again without a word, and Evan went back to staring at the familiar blotch on the ceiling. Once upon a time, water had leaked in and created a brown-ringed yellow spot on the tile. Allowing his eyes to drift out of focus, he was absorbed with of the simplicity of it. The explainability. And the fixability.

He ignored the whispers tickling the back of his skull, telling him he was descending the dark staircase. He ignored the papers under his bed. The sun slipped to the other side of the world, and still, he lay there, ignoring his growling stomach and his mother's phone calls.

When his phone rang for the fifth time, he was tempted to not even pick it up to see who was calling. He was so tired. Each of his fingers weighed a ton. But it was late. Too late for his mom to be calling unless someone had died.

It was Mara.

He swallowed the stickiness in his throat, and when he said hello, his mouth tasted like emptiness.

"Hey! Just finished up in Virginia Beach."

He felt like someone else was forming the words, making his mouth move. "How'd it go?"

"Really well," she said. "We sold out. How are you doing?"

He blinked at the ceiling and tried to work up some moisture in his mouth. "Fine."

"Did I wake you up?"

"Mm, no. No, I was awake."

"Oh, okay. Well, I wanted to tell you something. The office staff at Connections ran my info by the hospital in Tampa. It looks like I was the only baby brought in from the Safe Haven for the whole month of June. We decided not to even bother with the DNA test. We're going to meet."

"Meet?" he said slowly.

"She invited me to Thanksgiving dinner. I know I said I'd come home with you but . . ."

"No, no. It's okay. This is more important."

"I can't even believe this is happening!" Mara laughed joyfully as the words tumbled out. "She's married now—not to my father, but to a really nice guy, and they have a couple of kids—a thirteen-year-old girl, and a seven-year-old boy. I have a sister and a brother! Oh my god, I just can't believe I have siblings and grandparents, and I'm going to meet them on Thanksgiving."

"That's amazing," he said, aware of the slowness of his syllables. "Where do they live?"

"Ohio," she said. "In the Cincinnati area. So when we get back to New York, I'm going to borrow Ben's car and drive out there in time for the holiday."

"Ben has a car?" His heart began to pound, bringing his limbs back to life. He sat up in bed, dropping his feet firmly to the floor.

"Yeah, he said I can borrow it, so I don't have to rent one."

"Isn't that a really long drive?"

"Like ten hours," she said, nonchalant.

"I think you should fly."

She sighed audibly. "Is this about the dream?"

Silence hung between them. His heartbeat throbbed in his temples, and he realized how lightheaded he was from not eating. He couldn't make his mouth work, not when his brain was so foggy.

"You are going to those therapy appointments, right?"

"Of course," he lied. "I told you I was going, didn't I?"

"You sound . . . weird."

"I'm just tired."

Again, silence. He could hear her breathing, loud with unspoken worry.

"I was just thinking, you know, after being on the road for so long, it would be nice to fly. And this is really important to you—like a huge moment in your life. So will you let me buy you a plane ticket? Please? As a gift? Because your family's not supporting you. So I want to."

She was quiet for a few seconds, then sighed again. "Okay," she said. "If it'll make you happy. I'll fly."

"Thank you," he said, feeling his body turn into a limp rag again. Relief and exhaustion and hunger were doing him in.

"You're sure you're okay?"

"Fantastic."

He knew he didn't convince her any more than he convinced himself.

After saying goodbye, he went to the bathroom and splashed some water on his face, then listened to the voicemails his mom had left about coming home for Thanksgiving dinner. She was dating a new guy named Steve from work, whose mother had invited them all for the holiday. Evan rolled his eyes. But then, she tacked on how excited Hailey was to see Mara again, and his heart sank.

She'd be in Ohio meeting her real family, and he'd be eating turkey with some new guy trying to put the moves on his mom.

Rifling through his snack stash, he found a pack of crackers, but as soon as he put one in his mouth, it turned to cement. Gagging, he spit it out into a tissue and turned, instead, to the medicine box his mom had packed for him before move-in day. Without bothering with the measuring cup, he gulped down the entire bottle NyQuil and flopped onto his bed, burying his face in the pillow.

Finally, he slept.

"YOU TRYING TO kill yourself?"

Evan opened his sticky, swollen eyes to Henri's face. "Huh?"

Henri shook the empty NyQuil bottle, eyebrows high. "How much of this did you drink?"

He wasn't sure if he was touched or offended that Henri finally decided to talk to him when he thought he might be dead.

"I'm sick," he lied. "Leave me alone."

Henri tossed a water bottle on the bed, shrugged, and left.

Evan drank greedily and checked the time. He'd been sleeping for sixteen hours straight, and now it was noon on Friday. He was late for work. Cursing, he realized he hadn't told Dr. Mortakis he wouldn't be coming in today.

Or ever again.

How could he face her now, having seen that painting? Knowing that somehow, in some twisted way, she was part of this story, too?

She was his program mentor. She knew where he lived. Knew where his mom and sister lived. But did she know what was happening to him?

Mara remembered nothing about Mary Thompson, nothing about Dreamland or Hangman's Elm. Did Dr. Mortakis remember pointing the gun, or was she just some sort of hapless bystander caught in the crosshairs of a bigger plan?

And that's when he realized it was the Bigger Plan he needed to uncover.

The *who*.

The *why*.

NyQuil wasn't going to tell him why Dr. Mortakis's face was painted onto a killer's body at Kings Park Asylum, or why a woman so much like Nona had hissed at Kieran Flynn. NyQuil wasn't going to save Mara's life.

He'd slept days away, getting up only to use the bathroom, attempt to eat crackers, and answer Mara's anxious texts with encouraging words. They were on the road to Nashville now—the biggest, most important stop on their tour. She was about to play Music City, and he'd been catatonic for days.

Suddenly, he disgusted himself. He was missing classes and earning no money to pay for Mara's plane ticket.

He was a coward.

And besides all that, he stank.

He finally took a shower, shaved, and went outside into the frigid November sunshine to get himself something to eat. His head throbbed from lack of caffeine, but he didn't go to the Black Cat. He wasn't ready to face the women who lived upstairs.

Not yet.

He returned to his room with a tuna sub and large coffee, and after a few sips he felt alive enough to call his mom back to finalize Thanksgiving plans. By the time he got to the bottom of the cup, he was ready to call in sick to work, leaving a voice mail for Dr. Mortakis that claimed he had an early, confirmed case of influenza. He booked a Wednesday morning flight for Mara out of La Guardia, budgeting in enough time for himself to get back to Grand Central Station to catch his train home once she was in the air.

And when he crumpled up the sub wrapper and brushed shredded lettuce off his desk, he was ready to reread Kieran Flynn's letters. Hindsight was twenty-twenty, and he had the advantage of looking at his own future through the tattooed boy's lenses.

But best of all, he finally had something concrete to show Mara. There was no way she could read those letters and still think he needed to see a psychiatrist.

Somehow, everything really was going to be okay.

CHAPTER TWENTY-SEVEN

THE LETTERS PULLED at Evan's fingertips like magnets from his backpack as he walked through Washington Square to Mythology in Modern Art. He'd slipped them into plastic sleeves and closed them safely into the back of his Fundamentals of 2D textbook, but he still worried they would vanish if he took his eyes off them. Beneath Hangman's Elm, he shrugged out of the straps, unzipped his bag, and checked one more time to make sure they were still there. Satisfied, he swung his backpack around and carried it against his stomach, hugging it like a baby marsupial.

The letters were safe, and so was Mara.

She'd texted just an hour before, promising to be all over him by six p.m.

Everything was going to be okay.

But all that was easier to believe outside of the Steinhardt Building. The instant he opened the door to the lobby, the air felt different. The closer he got to the lecture hall, he felt enclosed, as if the atmospheric pressure was homing in on him.

Walking into the lecture hall, he could almost taste it.

"Feeling better?" Dr. Mortakis asked from her podium.

"Getting there." Evan slowed but didn't stop as he walked past her.

"You've been missed," she said, with a warmth that suddenly seemed put-on.

He looked over his shoulder and acknowledged the compliment with a nod, then turned to climb the stairs to the back of the lecture hall. His legs felt heavy, as if he were walking through soup. He could feel her eyes boring into his back, the electricity shifting in the air and prickling the hairs on his arms. Something was different in her eyes as she greeted the class, her eyes roaming the room and settling on his.

She knew he knew something.

But how could this sophisticated art professor be the guy who pimped Mary out at the Tin Elephant Hotel?

Dr. Mortakis began her lecture, but Evan didn't take any notes. He simply kept his eyes open, using every ounce of his energy to focus on the professor. He was sure something was going to happen. He begged the room to spin, to show him what he needed to see to connect the dots.

He searched for double meanings in every word she spoke and hidden images within her slides, but she just droned on about Herakles. It was the driest lesson she'd ever taught, fraught with black-and-white images and none of her usual peppy slide changes or interesting tangents.

Maybe she knew he was digging, but she wasn't ready to let him find anything yet.

Closing his notebook when the hour was up, he resisted the urge to hurry. With controlled motions, he zipped his book bag and stood. His feet felt dipped in concrete, but he deliberately avoided looking at her until he reached the last section of stairs. Holding the railing to make sure he didn't trip and fall on his face, he lifted his gaze. She was watching, just like he knew she would be. Her dark eyes were curious and hungry, like a cat ready to pounce. He lifted an eyebrow, and she mirrored him.

"Will you be in to work this afternoon?" she asked as he stepped down to her level.

"Headed there now," he said offhandedly, hoping his face didn't give his heartbeat away.

"Excellent," she replied, gathering her things. "I'll meet you there in a few."

Even the elevator seemed to struggle against gravity on its way to the third floor, but Evan was glad to let it do the work for him. Everything—his thoughts, his toes, his lungs—felt exhausted.

After unlocking the office door, Evan pulled up a chair at the side table, which was already spread with papers for grading and entering into the computer. Blinking against the heaviness, he got to work, waiting for Dr. Mortakis to arrive. She came in without a word, and he didn't turn around to greet her. Facing the wall, he held his breath and tried to focus on entering the correct numbers into the correct grids on the grading spreadsheets. For nearly an hour, the clicking of their fingers on their keyboards was the only sound.

"So. Today's the big day," Dr. Mortakis finally said, still typing.

Evan startled, then turned.

Her eyes remained on the screen. "Your girl is coming home."

"Yeah." He faced his work again, absently running a finger down a class list while trying to catch her reflection in the laptop screen.

"You don't sound very enthusiastic," she said, and he wasn't sure if she'd clicked her tongue in scolding, or if it was just the sound of her fingers on the keys. "Is there trouble in paradise?"

"No," he said insolently, and if he closed his eyes, he could see her as Fitz Mulligan. "It's just that she's leaving again in the morning. To spend the holiday with her family."

"Ah. Well. You know what they say. Absence makes the heart grow fonder." Her chipper pronunciation of *absence* bothered him.

He let the subject drop, entering grades steadily and silently, listening to the sound of her fingers on the keys. He glanced up at the framed symbols hung so meticulously above him, their cryptic meaning taking on a freshly ominous note. He remembered the first time he walked into this office, thinking the artwork was like a sentence only she understood. Now, he was sure that's what it was. Sure she had sent him to the Neptune Gallery knowing he'd see himself on the wall, and sure, now, that she wanted to separate him from Mara.

But still, he couldn't connect the dots. He couldn't read in a language he didn't understand. Fitz Mulligan pulled the trigger on the boardwalk, but in his dream, Mara was driving alone. It was an accident. What could Dr. Mortakis have to do with that?

His phone vibrated against the wood veneer.

We're at Z's unloading equipment.

Awesome.

I know it's not the Empire State Building or anything . . .

but can you meet me at the laundromat in like an hour?

I have no clean clothes.

But I miss you.

I'd meet you at the landfill as long as I could kiss you.

Get your fine ass to Soaps N Suds and there will be kissing.

"You can take off a few minutes early."

Again, Evan jumped.

Dr. Mortakis stood behind him, reading Mara's texts over his shoulder. He hadn't heard her get up, but she was suddenly close enough that he could smell her perfume.

He twisted his neck to look up at her, and her scarlet lips quirked. She put a hand on his shoulder, and her fingers were cold through his shirt.

"You should enjoy the time you have left."

He was sure she could feel the fear radiating from his skin. She could probably even smell it. But he wouldn't give her the satisfaction of seeing his hands tremble. Curling his fingers into fists, he dug the edges of his nails into his palms.

She removed her hand and stepped back toward her desk to continue organizing papers in silence.

Still, he felt her eyes on the back of his head, and again, he imagined her as Fitz Mulligan.

But why Mara?

Why him?

Packing his bag, he stood.

"I got it all done," he said, nodding toward the stacks of graded papers.

Dr. Mortakis looked up from her computer screen, and through the lenses of her glasses, he recognized the curious hunger that had tracked him in the lecture hall. "Send my love to Mara," she said, and the room began to spin.

He grabbed the edge of her desk for balance as the office blotched and blurred, flashed and stopped.

"Are you all right?"

He blinked, but nothing had changed. Dr. Mortakis was still sitting in her chair, wearing the same black dress, looking at him with predatory interest. Her office looked just like it had the day he first walked in. Gripping the edge of the desk so tightly, the corner jabbed into his palm, he met her eyes.

Was she spinning his world, just to throw him off-balance?

Who had the ability—the power—to do that?

"Who are you?" he asked, his voice even as he pressed the wooden corner deeper into his palm. Warmth pooled and radiated, but he didn't break eye contact to look at the wound.

Dr. Mortakis lifted a delicate black eyebrow, but said nothing.

"What the hell do you want?"

She brought a hand to her chest and a crease marked her smooth forehead. "Maybe you should have made that appointment, after all."

Evan's breath came hard and fast, and the spots he saw, now, were the stuff of rage. How had she known about the appointment? Had Mara told her? Or did she just . . . know?

Releasing his grip on her desk, he stepped backward toward the door, not turning his back until he needed to turn the knob.

"Have a happy Thanksgiving," she called after him, singsong.

He slammed the office door and, looking over his shoulder to be sure she hadn't opened it again, he ran all the way to the subway.

The train was crowded, but he didn't feel any safer.

Dr. Mortakis was in his head.

How could he ever really get away from her?

⚜

"DID YOU *RUN* here?" Mara laughed as Evan burst into Soaps N Suds and scooped her up into a rib-crushing hug.

"Yes, actually," he panted, setting her feet down on the black-and-white checkered floor. "I missed you so much."

"Next time we go on tour," she said, resting her hand on his heaving chest, "you're coming with."

"Guess you'll have to wait till summer, then," he said, Dr. Mortakis's voice echoing in his mind. *Enjoy the time you have left.* Was Dr. Mortakis watching now? How far did her power extend?

"Okay, summer tour in Europe. Date?"

He hooked his smallest finger around hers. "Date."

She kissed him long and slow, turning his knees to water and his head helium light. She'd make it to summer, or it would never be summer again.

"Tell me all about your trip," he said when the washing machine dinged, and she tugged him into a white plastic sixties scoop chair to wait for her jeans to dry. Pulling out her phone, she began scrolling through pictures of packed, dimly light clubs and East Coast landmarks.

When the dryer buzzed, she'd only gotten as far as Nashville, where she'd bought the big black tourist sweatshirt she was wearing now.

"Okay, but here's the best part," she said, bending over to scoop hot clothes into her laundry basket. "Reach into my back pocket."

"O-okay," he stuttered, sliding his fingers into the right pocket.

"Other one," she laughed.

"Yes ma'am." He paused to fan his face for effect, then slipped his fingers into her left back pocket and came out with three business cards. "What, um, what are these?"

"Well, one's an agent," she said, grinning over her shoulder as she folded her favorite jeans. "One's a producer, and one's Drew McAllister."

"*The* Drew McAllister? Of Southern Lights?"

She bit her lip and nodded. "He was at our Nashville show and came up afterward to tell me he liked my songs. He wants me to send him some ideas for his next album."

"That's . . . wow. That's huge!" he said, reaching into the basket for a pair of jeans to fold. They were warm and smelled good, like her.

"It's not a guarantee."

"You got cards from a country music star, an agent, and a producer. I guarantee you at least one of those is going to work out." He folded a black T-shirt, then picked up the one with the roses. "Hey, you wore this when we slow danced to 'Earth Angel,'" he said, grinning. "Remember?"

"You remember what I was *wearing*?"

"You said you loved me that night. It was memorable."

THEY SWUNG BY her apartment to drop off the clothing that was more appropriate for playing night clubs than meeting your long-lost mother, and Evan couldn't help looking over his shoulder every few steps. Were they being watched? He was going to have to show her the letters when they got back to his room. He needed her to understand that this was bigger than bad dreams. Bigger than black-and-white photos or psychiatrists or brain chemicals.

Bigger than both of them.

Kneeling on the floor beside the plastic storage tub she used as a dresser, Mara started taking deep, anxious breaths and letting them out slow through pursed lips.

"She's going to love you," Evan promised from the couch, trying to control his own breathing.

"Right." Mara huffed and threw a sweater into her suitcase. "But what if her husband doesn't love me? I mean, I'm a reminder that some other guy got her pregnant. And what if my dad was somebody terrible? Like some kind of psycho rapist or something? She hasn't told me anything about him. What if she didn't even know him? And then I still won't know who I am and—"

"Hey, come here." He stood and pulled her close. She clung to him the way Hailey did in the wake of a nightmare. He wished she was coming home with him for Thanksgiving. He wished he could promise her everything would be okay and believe it himself. "Whatever we find, we're still us. Remember?"

She nodded and went to the bathroom for tissues.

"Sorry," she said, reemerging and rubbing at her smudgy mascara. "We haven't seen each other in weeks; we were supposed to have a perfect, romantic night, and here I am crying."

"All I wanted," he said, thumbing away a fresh stream of her tears, "was to be here with you. Real life isn't always perfect. But I'm always going to be here."

"I'm a mess," she said, covering her eyes with her hand as a key ground in the lock. "I'm sorry. Maybe this was all a really bad idea."

"Oh my god, are you guys breaking up?"

Samantha's eyes were huge, and her hands were raised with alarm, ready to swoop in and either punch or hug someone. Maybe both.

"No!" Mara said, and suddenly started to laugh. She sniffed and wiped her nose. "No. I'm just scared. About tomorrow."

"Oh," Sam crooned, and went in for the hug. "They're going to love you. You're awesome. And if all else fails, just show them Drew McAllister's card." She turned to Evan and wiggled her eyebrows. "Did she tell you?"

He grinned. "You guys are headed for the big time, now."

"That's right," Samantha said, squeezing Mara tight enough to make her squeal. "And it's all because of this girl, right here. So you'd better take good care of her, Umbrella Boy."

"I will," he promised, but as they left the apartment and walked toward the subway, he couldn't stop looking over his shoulder. With every step, Vanessa Mortakis's words rubbed like a stone in his shoe: *You should enjoy the time you have left . . .*

CHAPTER TWENTY-EIGHT

K IERAN FLYNN'S LETTERS waited patiently inside the cover of Fundamentals of 2D as Mara talked. She'd been keeping a lid on all her emotions for two weeks, too busy to really think about what was about to happen and the way her life was about to change. He was glad she'd saved these secret fears for him, that she trusted him with unanswered questions she couldn't bring up to Samantha or Gwen. But it was impossible to interrupt and tell her about the letters he'd found at Kings Park. There was no good time to tell her she'd been murdered twice, and that Dr. Mortakis was somehow waiting to do it again.

Finally, she fell asleep, curled up like a spoon against his chest, and he lay there stroking her hair. She was still wearing her oversized black Nashville sweatshirt that smelled like new. It was cold in his room, and as weak light began to filter through the blinds, he could hear the ping of sleet on glass. When she rolled over, he slipped out of bed. By the light of his phone, he read the letters again, promising himself he'd done everything he needed to do to keep her safe for the next few days. She wasn't going to be driving Ben's car. At ten a.m., she'd be safely onboard a plane at La Guardia, ready to fly to Ohio, and Dr. Mortakis would be in New York, eating turkey with her grandmother. Mara would come home on Sunday, and he'd tell her everything. They'd figure out the rest together.

No secrets. No lies.

Evan glanced toward the window. Behind the veil of clouds and the night lights of New York, the sun was struggling to rise. His alarm would go off soon.

Tucking the letters back into the textbook and shoving it under his bed, he lay down beside Mara again. Wrapping an arm around the white guitar printed on her black sweatshirt, he felt the comforting warmth of her body as she sleepily nestled closer.

Enjoy the time you have left . . .

The instant his alarm went off, Mara bolted upright.

"Oh my god," she whispered, rubbing her face. "This is actually happening."

She couldn't eat breakfast. He knew that without asking, but he still asked. She took a shower on the girls' floor, and when she came back, her hair was different. She'd blown it dry, and instead of the natural waves or braid she usually wore, it was carefully curled and sprayed in place.

"Wow."

She grimaced. "Too much?"

"Perfect."

She sat down at his desk and, as he made the bed, he smelled nail polish.

"Shit!" she cried, pounding the desk. "My hands are shaking so bad, I can't paint my freaking nails."

"I'll do it," he said, and she looked at him sideways. "When you have a little sister and a mom who works all the time, you get to be an expert at stuff like this."

With a Q-tip, he removed the smudges from her cuticles and one knuckle, then held each finger steady so he could polish and blow it dry.

"Thanks," she said, tentatively checking if they were set before reaching into a paper shopping bag for a brand-new coat.

His heart stopped. Fuzzy black Sherpa. He'd seen that coat before—but not last night at the laundromat. He'd seen it while dreaming in the guest bed of Dr. Mortakis's apartment. He'd seen it soaked in ice water. Stained with blood.

"Like it?" she asked, tearing off the price tag and doing a fake model twirl.

He hoped the breathy noise that escaped his lips sounded like heart-stopping attraction instead of panic. "You . . . um . . . you look like a winter princess."

She snorted. "You're funny. I've actually never had to buy a winter coat before. In Florida, we can get by with hoodies. Nona made me gloves, too. Check these out. They're convertible."

She wiggled her freshly painted fingers into mittens knitted with varying shades of purple. And then, she popped the cover back to reveal the fingerless option, making his head swim. He'd seen her wearing them while gripping the steering wheel.

"Nona made those for you?" He forced the words around the ball of yarn in his throat.

Mara nodded. "She worked on them while I was gone. Wasn't that sweet?"

"She sure loves you."

Rummaging in her cosmetic bag, she retrieved a new bottle of perfume. She released two sprays and walked into the mist, and Evan had to sit down.

Smell, he knew, was a powerful trigger of memory. But how could the future be scripted down to the smell of bergamot and vanilla?

"Okay," she said, looking in the mirror one last time. "Let's go."

They took the air train to La Guardia, where she checked her bag before buying a tall coffee. "Just what I need, right? More jitters."

He squeezed her hand and they walked toward a bench overlooking security, not quite ready say goodbye.

"I'm sorry," she said, leaning into him as he put an arm around her. "I didn't even ask you how your therapy is going."

"Great," he said, again forcing words around the thickening lump in his throat. "And I found some letters. I want to show you when you get back, okay? They're from the tattooed guy."

Her eyebrows tightened. "Where did you find those?"

He couldn't say it. Not now. He couldn't tell her he'd broken into an abandoned asylum instead of going to therapy. "It's a long story. Anyway, I'll tell you when you get back. You've got enough on your mind."

"Did you tell the therapist?"

He nodded.

"Okay," she said, satisfied, and took the last sip of her coffee. She looked toward the growing line for security, and her knee bounced anxiously as she let out a long, shuddery breath. "Guess I'd better get this over with, huh?"

"Hey," he said, pulling her close. With his thumb, he smoothed out the worry lines scrunching her eyebrows. "Just be yourself. And Mara? The bridge freezes before the road."

"What?"

"Never mind. Just, go get on your plane. I love you."

"Love you, too. You're a lifesaver."

Lifesaver.

She gave him a quick kiss goodbye, and he sat on the bench until she walked through the metal detector, turned to wave at him one last time, and disappeared.

TRUDGING BACK TO the station, he boarded the train for Washington Square. He still needed to pack for his own trip home. A pang of guilt twisted his chest when he thought about how long he'd been away from Hailey. But he hadn't just been away from home. He'd been *distant*, much too wrapped up in his own problems to think about kindergarten and ballet.

He stopped at the bookstore and bought her a few paperback chapter books and a stuffed narwhal, promising himself he'd be a better brother from now on, then hurried back to his dorm to pack. He had a little over two hours to get to Grand Central and catch the Amtrak to Lancaster.

The sleet has stopped, but the sky remained gray. It was cold—just a few degrees above freezing, and he realized he'd left his gloves in the coat closet at home. He'd left most of his winter clothes in Lancaster, planning to bring them back to New York on Sunday. He didn't bother packing much, now. Just shoved a pair of jeans and a couple of T-shirts in his backpack and headed out.

Washington Square Park was emptier than usual. Most of NYU's students were traveling for the holiday, leaving just a few dog walkers and the resident drug dealers. The station, he knew, would be packed.

There were no seats on the subway, but he managed to squeeze in and grab hold of a standing pole. He knew the etiquette was to keep his eyes on his feet, which he did until the doors opened to Grand Central Station.

And just as he stepped out onto the platform, his phone rang.

ASPR.

Heart pounding, he answered the call.

"Is this Evan Kiernan?"

"Yeah."

"This is Dr. Weaver. I apologize for the delay in getting back to you. I've been dealing with some health issues. But I'm here in the office today, and I wondered if you might like to stop by."

He checked the clock. "Um, I'm supposed to be getting on a train to go home for Thanksgiving. Do you think I could schedule something for Monday?"

"I'm sorry," Dr. Weaver said. "I'm scheduled for surgery on Monday. I'll be out for quite some time in recovery after that."

"Doesn't anybody else work there?"

"No," she said, with a heavy sigh. "Those of us who are interested in psychical research are, it seems, a dying breed."

Shit. "Okay. So if I don't come now—"

"It will be at least a month until I can accommodate you. Perhaps longer."

He closed his eyes and rubbed the bridge of his nose. A couple of books and a stuffed narwhal weren't going to make up for missing his train home.

"I'm on my way."

⊱✿⊰

SHADOWS SKITTERED ACROSS the porch of the American Society for Psychical Research. The brisk November wind swept dead leaves from the trees and littered them across the tiny patches of grass along the street. Puffing an exhale, Evan watched his breath materialize in the cold air. He'd hated lying to his mom, but the worst of it was hearing Hailey burst into tears in the background.

"I'll get a morning train," he assured them. "I just got confused and ended up on the wrong platform. Don't worry. I'll be there in time to eat turkey. Tell Hails I have presents for her, okay?"

His mom sighed. "I really need you to be here for me this weekend. Meeting Steve's mom is a big deal."

"I know," he said, wishing he could explain what a little deal Steve's mom was compared to what he had to do between now and then. "I'll be there. I promise. I'll find a way."

Looking up tickets online, he found that every overnight and morning train to Lancaster was booked full. He was going to have to rent a car and drive through the night, but he'd get there by morning. He wasn't going to disappoint the people he loved—not Hailey, not his mom, and most of all, not Mara.

His stomach growled, complaining that he should have eaten before coming out to Seventy-third Street. He rang the bell and watched five minutes tick by, beginning to think Dr. Weaver would leave him shivering under the watery porchlight once more. He rang again and finally heard footsteps.

The door swung open, and there stood Dr. Weaver, holding her basket.

She wore a floor-length brown plaid skirt and that same greenish-yellow tweed jacket, but this time, there was a smile on her pallid lips.

Evan dropped his phone into the basket, and she stepped aside to let him enter the foyer.

"It's the film archive you want to access, yes?"

"Yes. Please."

"Then follow me."

She started for the stubby staircase, and Evan followed. Seven steps, then a curve. Seven more steps and they reached a landing. They took a right, and then another, down a dim corridor with wall sconces and closed doors. One more right, and then, another staircase—this one even less grand. Narrow and steep. Bare, creaky wood. Bumpy, stucco walls.

She ascended, and Evan followed a few steps behind. All he could see in front of him was her wide backside in unflattering brown plaid.

There was no end in sight.

They climbed.

"How many stories are in this house?" Evan asked, beginning to feel short of breath.

She paused, looking over her shoulder.

"Many," she said, and kept going. Up, up, up . . . it was impossible for the stairs to go on for so long. This wasn't a skyscraper—it was an old townhouse on Seventy-third Street. Evan's thighs were burning, and he estimated they must have gone up at least a hundred steps so far.

Finally, they came to a landing with a single door and Dr. Weaver said, "We've arrived."

She pulled the hoop key ring off her belt. The door was ebony, engraved with an elegantly chilling triple swirl. He looked over his shoulder, down the staircase that dissolved into endless black.

Scrape-click.

There was no going back now.

Dr. Weaver turned the lock, and the great door opened with a lurch. Light spilled from the room into the dim landing, temporarily blinding him.

Evan shielded his eyes. His pupils had never been pinched so tight, and it hurt. But either the light dimmed or his eyes adjusted. He found himself looking into a massive dome-shaped chamber, too large to be called a *room*.

It was crammed with spinning wheels, and shining strands like gleaming fishing wire were tangled from wheel to wheel, wall to wall.

Evan looked up, following the woven strands of light up, up, up to the tip-top of the dome. Millions of iridescent silver threads crisscrossed the entire space in a glowing haze, like the webs of a thousand spiders, and there, high above everything, shone an intensely bright orb of white light. All the strands fed into it, absorbed by its glow. Suspended from the ceiling were reels, all moving in unison like they belonged in the world's most complex movie theater.

And then, when Evan's eyes climbed down again, he saw not one woman, but three.

Dr. Weaver, closing the heavy, black door.

Nona, pedaling the largest of the spinning wheels, wearing her fuzzy, gray shawl. At the pressure of her foot, the other wheels and reels turned, too. And Dr. Mortakis, stepping out from an inky shadow, a pair of glinting shears dangling from her fingers.

"What's happening?" Evan asked, his voice cracking as he took a step backward. "What are you doing here?"

"We're here," Dr. Mortakis said, dragging a crimson fingernail along the blade of her shears and smiling. "For your final exam."

His eyes darted between the three women, settling on Dr. Weaver's key ring. Had Dr. Mortakis bribed the curator to bring him here? Threatened her? Was she some sort of psychopath serial killer? But that staircase was beyond what this building could naturally hold.

"You said we were going to the film archive," he said to Dr. Weaver. "What is this place?"

"A place to see things," Dr. Weaver said, jangling the keys. "Things that were. Things that are. And things yet to be."

Evan heard the scrape of wood on wood as Dr. Weaver pulled a chair up behind him while Nona stared, her deep-set eyes dark with curiosity and violence as she spun.

"Have a seat," Dr. Weaver commanded, pressing Evan's shoulders firmly downward. He didn't even see or feel it happening; in an instant, his wrists were bound and gleaming threads fastened his torso to the back of the chair.

"And allow us to properly introduce ourselves," she continued. "Our story has been told in many forms, in many places, and many times. The Greeks called us the Horae, the Norse named us Norns, and the Anglo-Saxons referred to us as the Wyrd Sisters—rather offensive when spoken in modern English, yet the ancient word simply meant *Destiny*. The Celts knew us as their Morrígan, and even the cave dwellers worshiped the Three Goddesses of the Moon. From this moment forward, you will kindly address us by our Roman names. I am Decima, the Measurer, whose fearsome rod determines the length of life."

Dr. Weaver paused, pressing a hand to her broad chest, then extended it toward the other two. "And these are my sisters: Morta, the Cutter, whose dreaded shears determine life's end, and Nona, the Spinner, whose mighty foot pedals the spinning wheel of life."

Evan blinked, shaking his head. "You actually want me to believe that you all are the . . . the goddesses of *Fate*? What is this, some kind of weird cosplay or something?"

Dr. Mortakis laughed. "Oh, no, no, no, no. Dr. Weaver and Dr. Mortakis were make-believe, but this," she said, taking a step closer, "is quite real."

It would have sounded absurd if the tips of her shears weren't so long and pointed, if his jugular wasn't so utterly exposed.

But here they were, the *who*.

Now, for the *why*.

"All right, then," he said, and pressed his lips into a thin line as the blood drained from his face. "Decima. Morta. And Nona. What do you want with me?"

"We want her back," said Dr. Weaver—*Decima*—with a bland smile.

"And we want you to suffer," Nona added, her eyes as hateful as when she'd thrown teacups at him. "*Thief*."

Evan's ears burned at the word. "Why do you keep calling me that?"

"Let's show him," Dr. Mortakis—*Morta*—said, turning to the other two. "Shall we?"

Decima snapped her fingers, and suddenly, the orb focused a beam of light into the center of the room. The reels above their heads rearranged themselves, clicking into place and beginning to spin, and the beam of light shone through the silken band of tapestry like a strip of film.

"No more games," Morta said, crossing her arms. "You've seen the changeling child lose his witch. You know how the tattooed boy lost his tightrope walker, and how the Promising Young Artist is about to lose his little songbird. But now, it's time for you to see how *we* lost her. Because of you."

The light came alive, producing a holographic image of a crying baby.

Evan gripped the edge of his seat, overcome with the sensation of rushing backward in time. It was like arriving at the peak of a roller coaster, then suddenly reversing directions. Like free-falling backward and blind.

CHAPTER TWENTY-NINE

HIS TOOTHLESS MOUTH opened in a wail as his fists clenched tight at his sides.

"Hush," said a voice, and he found himself in a cradle, swaddled tight. "Listen."

He looked up at three women. Sisters. He knew that they were sisters, that he was actually tied up in a chair in their attic, not swaddled in a baby blanket, and that this wasn't really happening.

And yet, somehow, it was.

Like a lucid dream, he was both inside of and outside of the cradle. He knew nothing and everything at once, the way he had outside the aquarium and beneath Hangman's Elm.

A gleaming, silken thread was pinched between the sisters' fingers, and as he looked closely, he saw that it was fastened to his own tiny chest.

"Seventy years?" the oldest, ugliest sister suggested, a surprising kindness in her eyes. "I've spun plenty, and he's early. We could give him a long life. There are more than enough years."

"You're much too generous in the mornings, Nona," the stern, middle-aged sister countered, producing her measuring rod. "Eighteen will do. Don't you agree, Morta?" she asked the third sister, who was the most beautiful and terrible of them all.

The youngest sister stroked a pair of silver shears and nodded. "Eighteen years of simple farming will suffice, ending with a sudden illness. Decima will weave in a thread of sickness, and the knot will be tied."

The baby watched and listened, unable to argue. Where Nona held her finger, Decima looped a filament of sickness and knotted the marker. Morta nodded in satisfaction, and the three disappeared.

⁕⁕⁕

THE CRADLE RUSHED forward as the sun rose and set, rose and set with blinding fury, and Evan felt himself growing tall. No longer swaddled, he was looking out over a scene that reminded him of the Dutch Masters, and he again realized he was an anachronism.

All he wanted to do was sit on a stool in front of an easel and capture this golden field, saturated in sunset colors. He wanted to paint the bony cows, not shovel their manure, to study the light that dappled the leaves and ignited the edges of the sprawling fields.

But this was a ridiculous thing to want.

He was the son of a farmer. His future had nothing to do with easels or paint. They couldn't afford paints or pencils or paper or even enough food to last the winter. He was meant to thresh hay, the sweetness of damp earth mingling with the pungency of manure in his nose. He was meant for aching shoulders and thickly calloused hands and a sudden sickness after eighteen years.

The back of his neck burned beneath the monotonous sun, and he stopped to rest, rolling his shoulders beside a pair of cows. He didn't only want to study the light here, where it shone on the tree he'd climbed and swung from as a little boy. He wanted to follow the sun, to study everything the light touched. As the sky turned indigo and the trees became black silhouettes, he drove an oxcart home. He cleaned his hands and face, then sat at a table of rough-hewn wood, eating the same meal he'd eaten every day of his life, with the same people who couldn't understand why he wanted more.

Early the next morning, he left.

Again, he hurtled forward at an unnatural speed, as if propelled along a moving walkway through his own life. There was a road, and his feet on it, and the same monotonous, blistering sun burning his lips and browning his skin and hurting his eyes. There was the icy water of a stream, and an old man telling stories by a fire, handfuls of sour berries and cold, lonely nights, then taverns filled with strange foods and people. A ship, the sea, a violent, blurry storm—

And then, the world slowed down.

He found himself in a forest with no path. It was deep and dark, soundless and strange. No birds called, no creatures scampered up the gray trunks. It was carpeted in snow without tracks, and the naked branches above his head were frosted white. There was no color, no warmth at all.

The cold bit painfully through the numbness of his fingers and toes. He wondered what day it was, and how old he was, and if anyone would even realize he was gone.

The question tickled the back of his mind . . . was he dreaming? Would he wake up in a strange attic? An insane asylum? A lonely little shack? Would he wander here for eternity, or only until he froze to death?

And then, he found the door.

No house. No frame. Just a tall, black door.

It made no sense, the way it stood in the snow all alone like a discarded shovel. He walked a circle around it, and it was like circling a headstone fitted with a knob and a knocker and a striking triple swirl.

It was so absurd, he started to laugh.

And then, he started to cry.

Pressing his forehead against it, he pounded his fist in frustration, pain splintering into his frozen knuckles. He was freezing and starving and about to die, and he had the dumb luck to find a door with no house.

But then, he heard a voice.

"Who's there?"

"Brendan," he said, his voice brittle with disuse, vaguely aware that this was the wrong name and the right name at the same time. "P-please, let me in. I'm s-so c-cold—"

"I can't."

"Wh-why not?"

"Because you're not real."

This made him laugh. "Maybe *you're* not real."

"That's ridiculous."

"Well, I c-can't see you."

"I can't see you, either," she snapped, but he heard a laugh hidden there. He realized his numb lips were smiling.

"Maybe you *c-could* see me," he said, craning his neck around the doorframe. *Nothing. No one.* "If you just . . . opened the door?"

"I'm not allowed to," she said with a heavy sigh. He could hear her back thud against the door, then slide down until she plopped down onto an invisible floor. "My mothers said so."

He mirrored what he heard, leaning his back against the door and sliding down until he was sitting in the snow. His back suddenly felt warm, as if it were pressed to hers.

"Mothers?" he asked. "You have more than one?"

She sighed. "I have three."

"That's more mothers than I've ever heard of someone having."

"Well. I have three."

"How about your father, then? What would he say if you opened the door for me?"

"I don't have a father."

"Mara," he said, and she gasped. He was equally surprised. How had he known her name? And yet, it was her name. And he knew exactly what he would find on the other side of that door, just as soon as she opened it. "Everyone has a father, even if they don't know him. It's how the world works."

Silence.

More silence.

And then, he heard the rustle of cloth. The rattle of a hand on a knob.

He adored the familiar shock on her face when she peered around the heavy black door—the hugeness of her green eyes, the freckles on her nose, the irresistible gap between her two front teeth when she said, "You *are* real!"

He nodded, unable to speak. This is how he'd seen her in Mr. Burns's class. This is how he'd painted her, exactly as he'd first seen her, once upon a time.

She stood in the threshold of an enormous bedchamber, heated by a dancing fire. Their eyes met, and they both stood, mesmerized, until a growl made them jump. A full-grown bobcat appeared by her side, snarling at him, baring deadly teeth.

"Hush, baby," she said, touching its head, and the beast began to purr. She glanced over her shoulder, then grabbed his sleeve. "Hurry up, before they see."

She pulled him into her bedroom and closed the door. Glancing around anxiously, she led him toward a vast walk-in closet hung with hundreds of beautifully made dresses, all in shades of purple and black.

"In here," she whispered, shoving him inside. When she closed the closet door, he could see nothing but her profile against thin lines of light. Surrounded by dresses smelling of bergamot and vanilla, he could hear her breathing, ragged and anxious. He could feel the heat coming from her body, bringing his limbs back to life.

"I knew it," she whispered, low and tense. "I knew there was something out there."

Slowly, their eyes adjusted to the dark. She arranged knitted blankets on the floor at the very back of the closet, covering him to ward off his violent shivers.

"Where have you come from? What else is out there? Tell me everything," she begged, and he did. He told her about his family, his farm, and his very long journey. He told her about how he wanted to study light, to capture it and bring it back to his family, to show them the whole, wide world.

"What was the most beautiful thing you saw out there?" she asked, breathless.

"Nothing out there compares to what I saw when you opened the door," he whispered from where he crouched at the back of her closet in the dark, still shivering. "I could look at your eyes forever and ever."

"I must be dreaming," she said, turning her face to a deep shadow. "How did you know my name?"

"I don't know. Why couldn't I see anything but your door in the snow?"

"There are things my mothers have not told me," she said, frowning.

"Yes," he agreed.

"All right. Stay here," she commanded, standing up. "Whatever you do, don't leave. I'll be right back."

She returned with a lit candle, a deep mug of steaming tea, and a book. He accepted the mug gratefully, holding it close with aching hands and breathing in the steam. She showed him the book, whose black leather cover was imprinted with golden letters that read, *The History of the World*. Every page was edged in gold, but it was thin. Much too thin, he thought, to encompass the history of the world. Even what little he'd seen of it would never fit on so few pages. She sat cross-legged on the floor, and her eyes shone like jewels in the candlelight as she studied him, and then the book, warily.

"My mothers have been reading me this story since I was a baby," she said, then bit her lip. "May I read it to you?"

He nodded.

She lowered her eyes and began to read a fairy tale.

"Long, long ago, the world Outside melted away into nothing-night, leaving only Three Wise Sisters, One Beautiful Girl, and One Little Baby Cat. Outside the Great Door is Nothing. Nothing at All, while Inside lies Happiness and Beauty and All Things Good."

She paused, examining him with furrowed brows. "You've come from Outside."

He nodded.

"And you're not nothing. Are you?"

He extended his hand, now warm from holding the mug. "You tell me."

She took his hand, and they both caught their breath.

"You're not a . . . girl, either," she whispered. "Are you?"

As he shook his head, he heard footsteps in the bedroom.

"Amara?" an old woman's voice called. "Where are you, love?"

Her eyes popped. She lifted a finger to her lips and hurriedly threw a dress over his head.

"In here, Nona!" she called. "Just looking for a nightgown."

From beneath black lace, he heard the scrape of a hanger above his head.

"Found it," she said, triumphant. She took the candle and shut the closet door, leaving him in total darkness.

"A nightgown?" the old woman asked, clucking. "So early? We haven't even had supper."

"I'm tired," she replied with a false yawn. "Can I have my supper in here tonight? Please? I just want to go to bed."

Huddled beneath the sweet-smelling dress, he listened as the old woman fussed over her, demanding to feel her forehead and look in her throat.

"I'll get your soup, then," the old woman finally said, and he heard heavy footsteps walking away.

The room fell silent. The only sound was the swish of fabric as the girl changed clothes, and he tried to think of something other than her state of undress. He breathed the scent of the lace she'd tossed over his head, listening to the sounds of her climbing into her bed, and felt lightheaded. Finally, the old woman arrived with her soup, and the smell of it cramped his stomach in hunger.

"Shall I read you a story?" the old woman asked.

"No, thank you," she replied, and yawned again. "My head aches. I just want to lie down in the quiet."

"I'll be back to check on you, then."

And the heavy footsteps padded away.

"You must be starving," she whispered a moment later, swinging the door open and presenting him with a full bowl of thick, delicious stew.

He devoured it, then had the terrible realization that he'd just eaten her supper.

"It's all right." She inched closer to him on hands and knees. "There's plenty more downstairs. I'll fill it again for you and get some for myself after they go to bed."

As she took his empty bowl, their fingers brushed.

"Thank you."

"If you tell me more about what's Outside," she whispered, "I'll get you as much soup as you want. And some paint. Deal?"

He grinned. "Deal."

For weeks, she hid him in her room, sneaking into the closet with food and paint as often as she could. Mother Morta, she said, would give her anything she asked for—sweets, toys, dresses, even a beautiful ebony guitar. Her mothers gave her everything but explanations. So she asked him question after question, trying to put together the puzzle pieces of the Outside, while he painted picture after picture to show her.

"Do you miss your family?" she whispered one night in the closet, her fingers slipped between his.

He shook his head. "I don't think they miss me, either, except maybe when it's time to muck the stables."

"When you . . . continue your journey," she began, then paused for a hesitant breath. "Will you miss *me*?"

"Of course not," he teased, and when she gasped in offense, he laughed softly into the darkness. "I won't *miss* you because I simply can't continue my journey *without* you."

"You know I'm not allowed to leave," she sighed. "But I've been thinking, what if my mothers don't know there's anything Outside, either? Maybe we could tell them together, and they'd let me go. We could see the world, and then come back here. It could be your home, too."

"Maybe," he said, bringing her fingers to his lips.

She laughed, cocking her head. "Why did you do that?"

"Do what?"

"Put your lips on my fingers."

He smiled. "It's called a kiss, silly."

"I know what a kiss is," she said, rolling her eyes and shoving his arm playfully.

He caught her wrists and pulled her close. "*Do* you?"

"Nona kisses me every morning and every night."

"That's a different kind of kiss."

She nodded, and he could feel her heart pounding in her wrists as she brought his knuckles to her lips.

"You're right," she whispered. "It is different."

"There are different kinds of love," he explained. "This is an important thing to know about the world."

"Have you loved someone . . . like this . . . before?"

"No," he said truthfully. "Never."

Slowly, he brushed his lips against hers, hesitant and uncertain.

"I never knew boys existed." She laughed. "Until I met you."

"Maybe I should make sure you never meet any other boys, then," he teased, kissing her again, more confident this time. She matched it, pressing her lips to his and touching his hair. "You might like them better."

"I will always love you," she promised him. "Even if there are a dozen other boys Outside."

"A dozen?" He smiled. "More like thousands."

Her eyebrows flew up. "Thousands of girls, too?"

"None like you."

They lay in the closet together that night, making promises as their shyness evaporated, first into tenderness, and then desire.

In the morning, she decided it was time to face her mothers.

THERE WERE MANY doors the girl was not allowed to open, and the door to her mothers' workshop was no exception. She led him there, to a heavy black door inscribed with a triple swirl, and he was vaguely aware that he was already inside this place, this strange workshop, tied to a chair, but the knowledge was slippery. He knew what they were about to find, and yet, he didn't quite know anything at all.

She lifted a finger to her lips and told him to wait in the hall. Carefully, silently, she turned the knob. Opening the door just a crack, she peeked inside, and her hand flew to her mouth. She glanced at him, tilting her head to beckon him closer. "Look," she mouthed, and he looked through the tiny space.

Nothing could have prepared him for what he saw there. Wheels and reels and spinning threads filled a room so large, there were no walls, no ceiling in sight. Everything moved in synchronization, like the intricate workings of an immeasurable clock, and in the midst of it all, three women stood with their backs to the doorway.

"What are they doing?" he mouthed, feeling as if he should know.

She lifted her shoulders and shook her head, so they huddled close at the crack to watch as the women measured threads attached to the chests of newborn babies whose bodies seemed to be both there and not-there.

They pronounced measurements not in inches or meters, but years and months and days, and they tied knots with threads called suicide, cancer, stroke, and murder.

Their words pulsed hot through his veins, but he forced himself to be still and silent as the women turned to their next task, cutting.

A scene materialized like a hologram between the women as the youngest raised her shears: Bloodied men littered a hillside, attacking each other with swords and clubs and bare hands. Fires raged, and the screams of children and animals pierced the smoky air.

"What is this?" she breathed, eyes wide with horror.

Snip.

In the chaos, one man ran a sword through the throat of another.

Snip.

A bearded face was crushed beneath hooves.

Snip.

One after another, Morta cut their iridescent threads, and one after another fell limp and lifeless, bludgeoned or sliced or trampled to death on the hillside. Mara reached for Evan's hand, and he stepped close behind her, wrapping his arms around her trembling frame as they watched in silent horror as it continued, hologram after hologram. Cut after cut. Wars and skirmishes. Stillbirths and accidents. Wheezing old men and feverish children. Babies born blue.

All this, they did methodically. Deliberately. Without flinching.

Finally, Mara took a deep breath and disentangled herself from his arms.

"I understand, now," she whispered to him. "I understand who they really are. And what is on the Outside."

She swung the door fully open and very calmly, very quietly said, "You've lied to me, Mothers."

The wheels stopped spinning. The entire workshop came to a grinding halt, and the three women spun to face their daughter.

"What did you say?" the woman wielding shears asked coolly, and Evan knew that this was not Dr. Mortakis.

This was Morta.

And she was terrifying.

"You lied to me," Mara said, her voice low and vibrating with anger as she stepped toward the three. "You said there was nothing Outside."

"How dare you accuse your mothers like this? How dare you!"

"I saw the Outside. And I saw you," she continued, her eyes hot. "I saw you give people suffering and pain, and then kill them like it was a game. You're not my mothers at all—you're murderers!"

"Enough," said Morta. "You don't understand what you saw. You can't comprehend our plans."

"You could have explained them to me," she pressed. "You could have told me the truth."

"None of those things will ever happen to you, love," Nona interrupted, her hands clasped in supplication. "We've given you eternal life."

"You gave me lies. A whole book of lies! You said there was nothing out there, but that's not true. If I hadn't opened the door, he would have died. Was that your plan? Did you plan for him to freeze to death?"

Morta squinted. "Who?"

Holding his breath, Evan stepped into the room.

The three studied him, and then the middle sister stepped forward, measuring rod in hand. She smacked it against her palm as she strode toward him.

"He would not have frozen to death," Decima announced, looking him up and down. "It was not yet his time. And *you* should not have let him in. You were warned—"

"Who is my father?" the girl demanded, and all three jaws dropped.

"Who is *my* father?" Evan echoed, and instantly, a violent wind rushed him forward.

When he opened his stinging eyes, he was still in the workshop, but Mara had vanished. He was tied firmly to a chair, unable to take a deep breath, and the three women were staring only at him.

"So, you want to know about your father?" Dr. Mortakis—no, *Morta*—asked.

Evan nodded, and with a snap of her fingers, she brought up the image of a homeless man in dirty clothes. A scrappy Chihuahua sat at his feet and he held a cardboard sign in his hands, sitting in a folding lawn chair beneath a city bridge.

"That's him?" Evan breathed, reeling. "That's my dad?"

"That's him," she echoed. "But don't worry. He isn't like you. The things he sees and hears aren't real. Never were. Paranoid schizophrenia, just like your mother told you."

"Where is he?"

"He lives under a highway bridge in New Orleans and the only medication he takes is the kind you can buy on the street," she said, then added with false pity, "I wouldn't recommend reaching out."

"You planned this," he said, trembling with the anger spreading through his bound limbs. "You made my father sick, with your . . . your measuring rods and knots and proclamations? It was all a part of some sick plan to—"

"Humans lack perspective," Morta interrupted, exchanging exasperated glances with her sisters. She sighed, shaking her head like she was talking a toddler down from a tantrum. "You don't see the big picture."

He tried to control his voice through the anger pulsing through his veins, so wild and hot it felt alive. "What is the big picture?"

"Redemption," Nona interjected, and all eyes turned toward her. Her foot was still on the pedal, and she leaned forward on her stool with earnest eyes. "The big picture has always been redemption."

"We allowed your father to be absent," Morta continued, waving Nona's interruption away. "Everything that has happened to you has ensured you would be exactly where you needed to be at the proper time. Here. And now."

"Why?" he demanded, hearing Mara quoting Sartre in the back of his mind. "Why do I need to be here now?"

"Redemption," Nona repeated.

"For *me*?"

"Of course not, you idiot," Morta interjected. "Humans have such small minds. Always insisting on truth, and then resenting it when they can't understand."

"But you did lie to her," Evan insisted. "The book—"

"Didn't you learn anything in my class? People tell stories to make the world bearable, to help them understand what they cannot." She shrugged. "Parents tell stories of bearded men in red jumpsuits, delivering presents down the chimney. Oversized bunnies hopping through town with chocolates. Mothers who were joyfully pregnant. Even you have told these protective little lies. Haven't you? You never made a therapy appointment. You made that therapist up so she'd feel better." Morta paused, then smirked. Her voice dripped with contempt when she added, "Because you *love* her."

Blood rushed to his head.

"Sisters," Morta scolded, lightly clapping her hands. "We haven't finished the story, so of course he does not yet understand. Have patience, my promising young artist. Everything will become clear in time."

She took a step backward, then snapped her fingers. Instantly, the wheels began to spin, displaying the angry faces of the girl and her mothers, and Evan closed his eyes to the now-familiar, sickening feeling of rushing backward in time. When he opened them, he was back in the workshop.

"Didn't we warn you that if you opened the door, you would surely die?" Decima was demanding, tapping her palm with the measuring rod.

"Another lie!" Amara insisted. "I opened it. And I'm not dead."

"Yet," said Morta, lifting an eyebrow.

"We've been good to you every day of your life," Nona cried, her hands splayed pleadingly as she crossed the workshop. She gestured toward the boundless ceiling, gleaming with millions of crisscrossing threads. "I spun the eternal thread just for you, so you could live with us here. Forever. Never to shed a tear. Never to grow old." She paused, glancing down at her own hand as she reached for the girl's—but Amara pulled away in disgust.

"So you took in a poor mortal girl, fed her lies, and tried to make her love you so you could feel good about yourselves. Is that it? Well. I'd rather die with him than live with you forever. You told me that you loved me, but I was never your girl."

"Have it your way, then," said Morta. The calmness of her voice was brittle, like the crust of a volcano. "But if you go, there is no coming back in this lifetime. And there is no saving him—or anyone else. The things we have woven are inevitable, and you do belong to us."

"We'll see," she said, exiting the workshop. In the great, echoing hall, she took his hand, called to the cat, and led them to her room, where she began to gather her things.

"What do you think you're doing?" Morta asked, appearing in the doorway. "Those things aren't yours."

"Keep them, then," she snapped, throwing them back at Morta.

Before opening the door to the Outside, the girl knelt and loosened the top two buttons of her dress. In the enchanted light of the room, a fine and lovely thread appeared, attached to her heart. The boy watched in amazement as she gently opened his shirt, revealing a thread he'd never noticed before. She reached out to stroke the cat's chest, then, and her hand came away with third thread, thin and flimsy as the boy's.

"You are my family," she said, braiding the three strands together. "You are my choice."

And so she fastened the eternal thread of her heart tightly to the mortal threads of the boy and the cat, until there was no telling them apart. The three of them left the Fates' home as one, with nothing but the clothing on their backs. Seasons whirled through the woods in a blur—bare branches pushed buds that opened with astonishing speed, and a little wooden house seemed to suddenly build itself. Summer branches spread protective green arms over their little makeshift house, then turned gold in the blink of an eye.

In the still and lovely woods, they tried to forget about their families, the homes and destinies they had left behind. But of course, their destinies did not forget about them.

Evan found himself in a bed, wrapped in blankets again, but he was not a baby. He was groaning with the terrible, nauseating pain in his side. Heaving but unable to vomit, cold sweat collected on his skin, and Mara knelt beside him in tears.

Suddenly, the bobcat began to growl. It bared its teeth, but backed into the far corner, afraid. They heard no footsteps. The door did not open. But suddenly, three women stood at the foot of the bed.

"Please, help him," Mara begged. "He's sick."

"Of course he is sick," said Decima, with a roll of her eyes. "We have woven it so."

"Then make him well. Please!"

"You left us," Nona added, but tears shone in her eyes. "You were disobedient."

"But you gave me a choice," Mara said, her voice less than steady. "You left the door unlocked."

"Yes," said Morta. "And you've made the wrong one. You were warned."

"I'll go back with you," Mara promised. "I'll do anything you ask if you'll just—"

"No. We told you there was no returning. No arguing. His time has come."

At this, Morta produced her shears, examining them in the firelight.

"We stood at your cradle," Nona said, towering over him. "I spun your thread strong."

"We gave you eighteen years of strength and happiness," Decima said, pressing her fingers into his throbbing side until he cried out. "Eighteen years of simplicity."

"And yet," said Morta, her brow impossibly high. "You were not satisfied. You wanted more than you were given. And now, you've stolen our daughter."

"Thief," hissed Nona, and spit at him.

"I didn't . . . steal . . ." Nausea choked out his words, but the puzzle pieces were lining up in his mind. They thought she'd left because of him, that this was all his fault. But they were wrong. All along, they'd been missing the most important thing. "She left because . . . because," he stuttered as the pain surged, and with it, the contents of his stomach.

Morta reached for his chest, and in the gleam of her shears, the light of the small house changed. The threads were visible, now, and the pain in his abdomen was so tremendous, his fever so hot, he almost welcomed the cut.

But Morta's scissors did not deliver relief.

Instead, her eyes followed the braided strands all the way to Mara's chest.

"What have you done?" she gasped.

Mara lifted her chin. "I told you. I'd rather die with him now than live with you forever. So go ahead. Kill us together."

"What do you know of forever?" Morta retorted. "Everything changes."

"Fine," Mara said, a tremor in her voice. "Then *change* forever. Change your plans. If you love me like you said, then change the plan!"

Morta ignored her, grabbing hold of the threads in her pale fist. Evan felt his body go light, and thin, and dark, as if joining the night.

And then, there was nothing.

The universe was still.

And much too quiet.

He felt as he were dangling between stars, slipping inside of a black hole where time held no sway until Morta's voice brought him back.

He was tied to the chair in the attic, and she was telling him what happened next.

"The three of you were drawn into the light, to the waiting place for souls. And there, we pronounced your punishments. The immortal girl was sentenced to die young three times, and only after the third, could she regain her immortality and blessings. Redemption would come through suffering. A common enough trope, yes?

"And like Cassandra, you were punished with foresight—to foresee the girl's death, yet be completely unable to prevent it. Three times you would love her. And three times, you would lose her, so that you might know a fraction of the pain you caused. And then, after the third cut, she would be free of you."

"Free of me? What does that mean?"

"It means the tapestry *will* change. After three cuts, you will be removed altogether. Extricated from humanity. It means you'll never knock on her door in the first place."

CHAPTER THIRTY

ORTA AND DECIMA returned to their work, and Evan sat quietly, resigning himself to the bindings. Resisting Fate was a waste of energy—though he wasn't sure what, exactly, he needed to save energy for. The sisters had made it clear that his time was about to expire.

He'd always thought death was like extinguishing a candle. The flame didn't go somewhere else; it just disappeared. It was over. Gone.

But Evan Kiernan wasn't just going to die. He was about to be erased from history. He tried to imagine what it felt like before he existed, before his mother even met Matt Smith or went to Mardi Gras and got pregnant. He imagined dark weightlessness. Sweet oblivion. Nothing would hurt. Nothing would matter. He wouldn't remember anything, and he wouldn't be remembered.

But Mara would still open the door. He was sure of that. Even if he didn't come knocking, she'd open it for someone else, or just for herself. She had already begun doubting her mothers' stories. She had already begun to think for herself. And once she knew the truth, there was no way she would stay. Hadn't history taught the sisters that lesson? The girl they chose was curious and strong and stubborn. The witch knew her mother was a fraud long before rescuing the changeling boy. The contortionist left home and made friends with a lion before the tattooed boy ever snuck her off that train. And Mara left Florida without knowing she'd meet a lonely art student and turn his world upside down. No matter the place or time, with or without him, she would still be herself. And she'd resist the goddesses' every attempt to mold her into anything else. Evan thought back to the hours she'd spent reading, sitting cross-legged on his bed while he sketched. She'd called Jill Cassidy a textbook narcissist—but on Halloween, she'd called God that, too.

If some cosmic narcissist is ruling the world, we're all screwed . . .

And here he was, facing not one, but three. Three lying goddesses who would never allow for questions, or doubts, or disobedience. Three murdering mothers who would do anything to get their daughter back.

Morta, Decima, and Nona had promised her a life of luxury and innocence, free of pain or heartache. But Mara didn't want their pretty clothes or chocolates. She wanted to know things. To make her own choices. To be free.

A narcissist could never allow that.

But what if they weren't *all* textbook narcissists?

He stared at Nona's hands, busy pinching gleaming threads between her thumb and middle finger. She hated him. She'd thrown teacups at him and spit in his face, smacked him in the head with his own jeans. But she'd made Mara warm milk with honey. She'd called her *Love*, and even now, he didn't believe that was an act.

There was no way Nona would help him, but Kieran Flynn's father said the key to victory is knowing your opponent's greatest desire.

So what did Nona want?

She wanted Mara back.

She wanted Evan to suffer.

But what else? What had she said at Kings Park, in the recreational room? *Nobody notices Life until it's too late . . .*

She was the spinner, the giver of life, who wanted to be . . . noticed?

"Excuse me, Nona?" Evan called suddenly, jerking her attention away from the wheel. "I forgot to say thank you."

She looked at him like he'd slapped her. "For what?"

"For wanting to let me get old. That was nice of you."

She lifted a bushy gray eyebrow before returning to her work. "It is my job," she said, to the spinning wheel. "To give life."

Yes.

"That's an important job. The most important." He lowered his voice conspiratorially. "You're kind of like, the good guy, huh?"

Nona turned, and Evan thought a little of the edge had softened in her stare. But she went back to her work without answering.

From the shadows, he could hear the singing of Morta's blades and Decima's flat voice as she announced her measurements. "Ninety-two years, seven months, eight days, stroke. Forty-seven years and one day, automobile accident. Two years, three months, and four days, bone cancer."

Time is a trick, he repeated a thousand times in his mind. Had hours passed? Or only a few seconds? Had he missed Thanksgiving dinner? Or hadn't he missed his train at all? Enough time had passed that his stomach was eating itself, and his tongue was starting to stick to the roof of his mouth, but he rehashed the scenes from the tapestries, looking for a thin spot or a frayed edge. He'd touched on something with Nona. He'd seen something change in her posture, in her eyes.

Evan looked between the sisters. Clearly, Morta was in charge. She was the one calling the shots, cutting the threads, pronouncing the curses. But it was Nona who had braided Amara's hair and brought her soup. Nona who'd felt her forehead and kissed her goodnight. Nona who, like Mr. Cassidy, always made time for her.

It's like he's been controlled by her for so long, he actually believes her lies. She's made him forget he even has a choice . . .

Maybe it was too late for Mr. Cassidy to remember.

But maybe it wasn't too late for Nona.

"Could I have some water?" Evan finally asked, his voice hoarse. "Please?"

Nona didn't say anything, but she stood up. He waited while she struggled to rise from her stool, then adjusted the nubby shawl around her hunched shoulders and walked off. She returned with a glass of water.

"Here."

Though Evan's mouth was the Sahara, he couldn't reach for it. His hands were still tied together behind his back, numb with lack of blood. He lifted his eyes pleadingly, and she frowned.

"Well, are you thirsty or not?"

Evan nodded, hope surging in his chest. "Can I have my hands back?"

"You cannot." She brought the glass of water to his lips and tipped it gently, gradually, so he could drink the whole thing.

"Thank you."

Glancing at the empty cup, Nona frowned again, huffed a sigh, then sat back down on her stool, defeated.

Defeated.

It seemed like the wrong word to describe his captor, when she was free and he was bound. But he thought of her at the café, the way Morta had rolled her eyes and dismissed Nona as senile, the way she'd been sent to Kings Park Asylum, like Kieran Flynn. Morta and Decima had played dress-up as professors, but Nona was relegated to Crazy Old Lady in Need of a Babysitter.

It started coming back to him, like the lyrics of a song.

Am I not the eldest?

And yet she instructs me.

Scolds me . . .

I hate her . . .

Nona wanted to be noticed.

No, she wanted, more than anything, to be *loved*—but her sisters didn't love her.

All they wanted to do was pull the strings, and somewhere deep down inside, Nona resented them for it. He just needed to pull that resentment up to the surface.

"I've been wondering," Evan began carefully. "If Morta is the youngest, why is she in charge?"

"We work as One," Nona replied dully, but Evan noticed the way her chin twitched. "Our powers are different, but equal."

"So, which one of you wrote the book for Amara?"

"Morta is a gifted storyteller. And her handwriting is very neat."

"But you were the one who read to her before bed, weren't you? You spent more time with her than anyone. You loved her very much."

Nona nodded, and her eyes softened at the memory.

"Where is she now?" he pressed, glancing toward the other two. He couldn't hear what they were saying and wasn't sure if they were listening to him. "Do you know?"

"Of course I know."

"But . . . you're not allowed to tell me?"

"I have no master."

"Your sisters haven't told you where she is, either, have they?"

"She's at the airport," Nona snapped, then bit her lip remorsefully.

"Can you show me?" Evan whispered, the certainty of Mara's safety filling him with adrenaline and hope.

"I cannot," she returned, without lifting her eyes.

"Why not?"

"I do not operate the Orb."

"You *don't*? Or you *can't*?"

"My sisters—"

"Your sisters won't let you," he whispered, finishing her sentence. "They tell you what you can and can't do. They treat you like a child, don't they? But you're the oldest. Shouldn't *you* be in charge?"

Slowly, she shook her head. "We each have our responsibilities," she said, but Evan sensed her painful hesitation, like biting down on a bad tooth. "The Three work as One. And so, I spin."

"Nona, please—" Evan whispered, trying desperately to hold her deep-set, confounding eyes, but she turned away.

Staring into the tapestry, she mumbled about nightgowns and braids, plums and candies, and Evan could feel his pulse ticking off the seconds they had left. He didn't know what time it was, whether it was light or dark outside, or if the road had iced over, but Nona wasn't going to tell him. She might have given him a drink, but she wasn't going to change her mind.

Evan had gotten farther than Kieran Flynn—he'd seen their enemy. He knew who to fight. Now he just had to keep Nona talking until she told him how.

"When you get Mara back . . . after you cut me out of the tapestry, will she remember me?"

"No."

His heart tripped, scuffing painfully. "Will she remember *you*?"

"Of course."

"And . . . will she remember that you murdered her?"

"We redeemed her," Nona said, like she was reading an instruction manual.

"What does that even mean?" he whispered sharply, then, closing his eyes, leveled his voice. He couldn't afford to lose his temper. Not when she was talking. "What does it mean for her to be *redeemed*?"

"It means . . ." Nona blinked, and a tear fell, zigzagging through her wrinkles like a marble in a maze. "It means she will return to us. She'll live forever—in eternal happiness. With her mothers."

"So you'll lock the doors this time?"

Nona's breath caught in her throat. "There will be no need for locks. She won't have a reason to leave us because *you* will be removed from the tapestry. You will never knock on her door. You will never again touch her precious skin with your filthy hands. You will never be born!"

Evan gritted his teeth as Nona rose from her spinning stool, leaned close to his face, and spit on his forehead.

He felt the disgusting liquid slide down his face, unable to wipe it away. Closing his eyes, he remembered the last time she spit on him, when the sisters had come to claim him. Before the pain had overpowered him, he was going to say something.

Something important . . .

"You took her love from me!" Nona hissed, grabbing his bound shoulders and shoving her face in his. She moved with sudden agility. "You took her away!"

"Whoa, wait a second," he protested, finding his voice again as the memory clicked into place. "I didn't take her. *You* did. You killed her mortal parents and—"

Nona growled and shook him hard.

From the shadows, Morta's voice rang out. "What's going on?"

Evan could hear her footsteps getting closer, but Nona tightened her grip on his shoulders to the point of pain.

"Enough!" Nona growled, her tea-laced breath hot and furious in his face. As Morta and Decima approached, her crooked, old back straightened, and her gnarled hands uncurled as she released him. "You cannot stop any of this."

It was like she'd forgotten how strong she was, forgotten she was even a goddess until now.

And it clicked.

"You're right," Evan said, biting back the desperation that threatened to choke his voice. "I can't."

The key to victory is figuring out what your opponent truly desires.

This was it, his last chance, his last stab in the dark. He looked from sister to sister—Decima and Morta, cool and collected. Nona, heaving and tearstained.

"I can't stop your plans, but you can't make her love you," Evan said, meeting Nona's eyes. "This was never about me. Don't you understand that? She left *with* me, but not *because* of me."

Morta lifted a delicate, dark brow.

"Didn't you listen to her song? Didn't you understand that it wasn't just about the Cassidys? It was about *you*. You can lock her in, make her your prisoner, but you can't *make* her love you."

Evan held his breath as Morta's blood-red heels rang out hollow on the wood. She came to stand in front of him, crossing her arms. "Stop talking. The time has come."

She snapped her fingers, and a beam of concentrated light appeared. The room came back to life, gleaming with a bustling airport terminal. There, in the middle of the chaos, Mara sat with her feet propped up on her suitcase, looking exhausted and ready to cry. She rubbed her face, took a deep breath, and started typing on her phone.

From the wicker basket, Evan's phone began to ring.

His heart throbbed. The three women grinned at him, unmoving, waiting for the call to go to voice mail. Asking for his phone would be laughable.

"She's in Pittsburgh," Morta announced, as his phone began to buzz and ping with text messages. "It seems her connecting flight has been canceled due to weather."

Just then, another phone rang—a standard factory tone. The kind that comes programmed on a brand-new phone.

Morta picked it up, and when she said hello, her voice melted into something warm and sweet.

"Hi, it's Mara. My connecting flight was canceled . . . I don't know what to do."

"Oh, no!" Morta exclaimed, adding a hint of southern drawl and sounding like an entirely different person. "I'll tell you what. Just go over to the rental counter and get a car. It's not too bad a drive from Pittsburgh. You can put our address in your phone and be here in just a few hours, okay? Put it on my credit card."

Evan's heart leaped to his throat. They were telling her to rent a car. To drive. Because the flight he arranged for her was canceled.

"You were right. I can't change it," Evan said, and Nona's eyes darted toward him with smug satisfaction. He held her gaze, watching her eyes narrow as he whispered, "But you can."

Nona's eyelid twitched.

"You're still powerful, Nona," Evan whispered. "And I know you're still good."

Her lips parted.

"Sh!" Morta hissed, eyes flashing between Evan and Nona. Nona pressed her lips together again as Morta gave Mara an address, rattled off credit card numbers, and hung up the phone.

"It's time," Morta said, the gentle drawl gone. She turned to Nona and clapped her hands twice. "Get to the bridge."

"Very well." Nona stood up slowly and wrapped the pilled shawl around her shoulders. She didn't look at Evan when she said, "Where are the keys?"

"We've been over this a thousand times," Morta said, rolling her eyes. "The truck is parked on the west side of the bridge with the keys in the ignition. Must we repeat everything for you?"

"No," Nona said. "Nothing needs to be repeated. I understand."

"Then for gods' sake, get moving!"

Nona walked out, closing the door behind her, and the other two sisters shared a look of exasperation.

"What's she going to do with the truck?" Evan pressed. Again, his phone rang and went to voice mail. Time was running out. "There was no truck in my dream. Only ice."

Morta smiled with her teeth. "You only saw what we chose to show you," she said, and the hologram displayed Mara receiving a set of keys.

"How is Nona going to get there in time?" Evan interrupted. "Mara's in Pittsburgh and we're in New York."

"What part of *goddess* are you failing to understand?" Morta returned, then grabbed his chin and turned his face toward the image of Mara. "Watch carefully."

Mara got behind the wheel of the rental car.

"You've seen that car's interior, haven't you?"

Sickness overwhelmed him as Mara set her phone's navigation, tried to call Evan one last time, then turned the engine over.

Every muscle in his body was clenched, cramped, screaming, but he didn't say anything. Saying something—doing something—that was always his mistake. Trying to fight it—trying to fight them—was useless now. He'd already made the mistake of booking the flight, sending her through Pittsburgh instead of straight to Cincinnati.

It was too late.

He felt the sting of tears building up behind his eyes, and his stomach roiled. He'd failed. His failure had been inevitable.

And in a few short moments, he was going to evaporate into nothingness.

"How can you do this to her?" he said through clenched teeth. "If you love her, how can you sit back and watch—"

"Sh!" Decima cut him off with a finger in his face. "Soon, she will forget about you entirely. This is temporary. *You* are temporary."

As Mara pressed a knob on the radio with her sparkly, black-tipped finger, a fresh wave of nausea rose to his throat. Her thumbs drummed on the steering wheel, and her lips began to move, mouthing the words *Alabama, Arkansas* . . .

Snowflakes fell.

Evan was unable to wipe his tears.

Reels clicked above his head, and the image split to a heavyset figure climbing into the cab of a delivery truck parked in a snow-covered lot. The body was younger and trimmer and dressed in men's clothing, but the face was clearly Nona's.

Just ahead, he could see the bridge, spanning the divide between the two scenes:

Mara singing along to "Home." *Home, let me go ho-o-o-me, home is wherever I'm with you . . .*

Nona turning the engine over.

With age-spotted hands, she put the truck in gear and pressed tentatively on the pedal. Her fiery gaze was set on the bridge that hung precariously between them.

Evan closed his eyes, trying to clear his blurring vision. Mara wouldn't remember him. His mother wouldn't have a son. Hailey wouldn't have a brother.

The finality of it shook him.

He thought back to his grandmother's funeral, to the hopeful words offered by the pastor, that death was not a final goodbye. Would he see his grandmother again? Would she welcome him into some sort of heaven or hell?

Or was it all just a myth to soften the blow? He understood the need for stories, now. He knew the fear of standing on the precipice of nothingness.

And then, he heard the sisters gasp.

Evan opened his eyes, and Nona was not looking at the road. She was staring into the workshop, as if she were looking directly into a camera. Her lips began to move, and he could hear her voice, distant but clear.

I know you watch me.

Morta and Decima shared a look, their jaws bulging with tension. Evan held his breath.

Well. Keep watching.

Tears welled in Nona's eyes and spilled down her wrinkled cheeks as her foot pressed the pedal to the floor.

You have tried to make me forget, but I've remembered something, Sisters. Without me, there is nothing for you to measure and nothing for you to cut. Without me, you are nothing! Nona growled, ferocity mixing with the tears in her eyes as her speed increased. *It was I who spun the girl's thread. I am the eldest . . .*

"What is she doing?" Morta breathed, grasping Decima's hand, and their voices swelled to shrieks as Nona rammed the truck's steering wheel hard to the right.

The truck veered toward the drop-off, glancing off the bridge's guard rail. She rammed the wheel left, and the truck went airborne. With a final, defiant glare, Nona let go of the wheel altogether.

And I have decided that the Three are not One . . .

The Three are now None!

Suspended for an unnaturally long second, she snapped her crooked fingers, then dropped.

Morta and Decima screamed, grasping at the marble floor as if they could break their sister's fall, but the image slipped through their fingers.

Evan winced and instinctively closed his eyes as the room burst into blinding light. He heard the sick, heavy crush of metal on rock and held his breath, listening to the terrible sound of the truck toppling and bouncing like a toy, smashing against jagged rocks and landing with a splash in frigid water.

CHAPTER THIRTY-ONE

E VAN OPENED HIS eyes, and he wasn't watching it from the workshop anymore. He was in the back seat of Mara's rental car, lurching forward as she slammed on the brakes.

She shrieked and whipped her head around to face him. "What are you doing in here?"

"I-I don't know."

"Did you see that? That truck just—"

Frantically, she put the car in park and opened the driver's side door, rushing to the guardrail to look down into the swirling gulch. By the time he caught up, she was dialing 911. His heart in his throat, he looked down at the truck he'd seen airborne just minutes before.

The Three are now None . . .

Nona had snapped her fingers.

She'd done something.

Not to Mara, not to him, but to herself and her sisters.

As Mara gave the 911 operator their location, her teeth were chattering. "A delivery truck just drove off the edge of the cliff," she said into the phone. "It's upside down in the water, and there's somebody in there."

Was there?

Evan heard the emergency operator promise to send help, asking Mara to stay on site until they arrived, and he wondered if there would be a driver to rescue at all.

Mara ended the call, her whole body shaking violently, and whirled on him.

"Were you hiding in my car? How the hell did you get here?"

"No! I don't know how . . . I just . . ."

As he looked into her eyes, the wind whipped up. The water, the woods, the cliff, and the truck receded like the tide.

"What's happening?" Mara swung her head around and grabbed his arm for balance as the ground became a moving walkway in time. "Evan? What is this?"

"I-I don't know."

Above them, the sun went up and down, up and down in a blur. It flashed faster and faster, like a movie projector gaining speed, until they were surrounded by white light and silvery threads and a chorus of whispers, overlapping like a round.

Once upon a time . . .

Once upon a time . . .

Once upon a time . . .

Once upon a time . . .

Once upon a time . . .

"What the hell?" she breathed, stumbling backward as the ground lurched into stillness.

"You can see this, too, right?" he asked, and she nodded rapidly. "You can feel it and hear it and everything?"

She screamed as the threads swirled up into an iridescent funnel—a churning storm with Evan and Mara in its eye. Images materialized in the vortex, faster and faster, until they blurred together into smooth movements. It was a tornadic movie screen, a storm wall of suffering in reverse. A dizzying display of feet running backward and raindrops falling up into the air.

"It's us!" she cried, covering her mouth with her hand. "Why's everything going backward?"

"Keep watching," he said, as the images changed from the Coney Island boardwalk and Black Prince, to the gallows, and a finally, a heavy black door.

Open it, love.

It wasn't a vision, or a hologram, or a hallucination this time. The door was real.

Mara looked to Evan with wide, questioning eyes, pushing her wind-blown hair from her face.

"Go ahead."

She reached for the knob. The moment her gloved fingers made contact with metal, the wind relaxed into a great sigh. She turned the knob, and the light burned out like a spent flashbulb. The funnel of threads melted away into the snow.

Everything went still.

Completely still.

"Are you okay?" Evan whispered, his hand on her back.

"No, I'm not okay!" she exclaimed, eyes wide and wild as she looked around them. "What the hell just happened?"

"That wasn't there before," he said, pointing to the ground. There, atop the thin crust of snow at their feet, lay an impossibly thick book, its black cover embossed with golden letters. *The True History.* As Mara bent to pick it up, the stillness exploded into sirens and spinning lights.

Fire trucks and ambulances sped onto the scene.

Disoriented, she clutched the book to her chest, trembling with shock and cold.

"Come on," Evan said, leading her to the parked car. His limbs felt weak and tingly, his head light. "Let's get the heat on."

Collapsing into the passenger seat, Mara shoved the book onto the dashboard and wrapped her arms around herself. Turning the engine over, Evan directed the heat vents toward her. Her breath came fast and shallow as she pressed her face into her hands.

"I'm losing my mind," she whispered, over and over, rocking back and forth.

"No," he promised, resting a gentle hand on her shoulder. "You're not. But remember when I told you something was happening to me?" he asked softly, unable to keep his eyes off the book. What had Nona written in there? What, exactly, had she done?

"*That's* what was happening to you?" Mara asked, teeth chattering. "Some kind of—of . . . freaking time tornado?"

"It wasn't like that every time, but . . . yeah. Time tornado."

"Oh my god, and that therapist didn't have you locked up?"

"I didn't actually talk to a therapist, Mara."

She shoved his arm, eyes wide. "You lied to me? *Again*?"

"I'm sorry," he said, raising his hands. "I'm so, so sorry. I didn't want to, but I just . . . I knew nobody would believe that unless they saw it."

"I saw it." She reached for his raised hands, lacing her fingers between his and letting out a shaky breath. "And I still don't know what the hell it was, but I believe you."

Shivering, they held each other's hands over the center console of the car until a pair of state troopers pulled up. Evan tapped her shoulder, and she rolled her window down.

"You made the 911 call?" an officer asked, climbing out of the police car, and she nodded. "Mind if we ask you a few questions?"

Mara told them what happened to the truck, trying to stop her teeth from chattering as one officer took notes and the other listened intently.

"We're going to have to close this bridge for investigation. You heading somewhere for the holiday?" he finally asked, and she nodded. "We'll let you cross first, okay? So you can get where you were going."

"No." Mara took a deep breath. "I don't want to cross that bridge."

"You sure? It's safe—we checked it out. It's just a formality with the investigation."

"I'll take a detour or something. I'm sure."

Tucking his notebook away, the officer radioed the men wearing neon-yellow safety vests. "Nah, they're turning around. Go ahead and close it off."

"I'd better call my mom and tell her I'm running late," Mara said, reaching for her phone, but Evan gently stopped her hand with his.

"I think you'd better read this, first," he said, sliding the book from the dash and opening to the first page. He handed it to her.

"What is it?" she asked warily, looking from the page to Evan. "It looks like some kind of fairy tale. Listen to this. 'Once upon a time, three sisters were entrusted with the task of ensuring life balance in the universe. Their work was simple: to weave the fabric of human history, one life at a time.' Who wrote this?" she asked, flipping back to the cover just as the paramedics lifted a stretcher up from the gulch. Strapped to it was a mangled body wearing blue coveralls with close-cropped, gray hair.

"Nona wrote it," he said, emotion tightening his throat as he pointed toward the body and watched recognition dawn on Mara's face. "She wasn't Dr. Mortakis's grandmother. She was her *sister*," he said slowly, as the stretcher was loaded into the back of a waiting ambulance.

"Nona?" Mara whispered, and they sat quietly, squeezing each other's hands as the ambulance took Nona away without bothering with the sirens or lights. The safety crew coned off the bridge and lit flares as a gentle snow began to fall.

"If it wasn't for the book," she said, her teeth still chattering even though heat was pouring through the vents, "I'd think I'd just hallucinated or something. But the book is real. Isn't it? I mean, obviously. It's real."

"It's real," he promised, touching it just to make sure. "Let's get out of here, okay?"

She nodded. "Someplace warm. So we can read it."

❦

IN A TRUCK stop diner just off the interstate, they ordered coffees and pastries and began to read. Nona had recorded everything truthfully, by hand, how once upon a time, three sisters killed a baby girl's mortal parents and took her as their own. There was a door, and a book of stories, and then a boy who changed everything. Nona explained the work her sisters did, and the terrible fight they had with the girl when she found out. There was a curse, a punishment, and a plan for redemption. A plan, Nona explained, that she changed.

Alongside the text, Nona had included pictures. They weren't photographs, exactly, because they were made centuries before cameras or film. But there were pictures of Amara as a baby, taking her first steps, sitting sweetly while Nona braided her hair, and sleeping curled up beside her great cat.

Evan wondered if she'd written it all between leaving the workshop and arriving in the truck, then smiled. *What part of goddess are you failing to understand?*

Nona's *History* went on to tell the stories of the changeling child and the witch, the tattooed boy and the tightrope walker, and finally, the promising young artist and the musician.

The final chapter began with a photograph of a pregnant teenager with weary, green eyes and black hair. Mara turned the page, and there was the same girl, placing a pink bundle inside the door of a Safe Haven, tears in her eyes. It wasn't a posed photograph, and Evan knew it wasn't taken with a camera.

Below the image was a name, handwritten in ink. *Amanda Anderson. Your true mother.*

They turned the page, and there was a picture of the same woman in her early thirties. Below it, Nona had written an address in New York, not Ohio, and a telephone number with a New York area code. *She gave you up because she loved you*, Nona wrote. *And she loves you still.*

"So . . . she's not in Ohio? That was all part of the . . . the game?"

Evan nodded. "To get you here. Yeah."

"But I talked to her on the phone. I—"

"You talked to Dr. Mortakis on the phone," he explained. "I was there. I heard everything."

Staring out the diner window toward the highway, Mara shook her head and let out a long, slow breath. "So . . . where do we go now?"

"Well, I think we're going to miss Thanksgiving dinner," he said, checking the clock on the wall. "But we can make it to my mom's in time for leftovers. And . . . a little trip to the attic if you still want to see my painting?"

She puffed a tired laugh. "You can drive."

While he called home and pulled up Google Maps, Mara continued turning pages. There she was on her first birthday with the Cassidys, chubby cheeks and stubby fingers covered in frosting. Next, she saw herself as a toddler in a tiny purple swimsuit, playing in the sand. She grew taller picture by picture, page by page, until she was beneath Evan's umbrella, laughing in the rain.

At last, they came to the photo Mara had taken on her phone the day she and Nona rode the train to deliver tiny hats to the NICU. Below it, Nona wrote, *I spun your thread strong, and you have never let anyone make you forget it. I trust that you never will. Turn the page now, love. The rest is up to you.*

When Mara turned the page, it was blank.

The rest of the book—hundreds and hundreds of pages—were white as fresh-fallen snow.

EPILOGUE

AITING TO CROSS Sullivan Street, Evan rubbed his cold hands together. In the frosty blur, he thought New York could almost pass for one of Marc Chagall's surreal Russian winters—just without the giant goats.

Out of all the surrealists, Evan loved Chagall best. As a Russian Jew who lived through two world wars, he knew winter. He knew suffering and loss. But he knew love, too.

"If all of life moves inevitably toward its end," Marc Chagall once said, "then we must, during our own, color it with our colors of love and hope."

Evan understood that there would be an ending to his story. He wasn't immortal, and neither was Mara. In just six hours, New York would welcome a new year with a ball drop in Times Square, because everything really was temporary. The grime of the city would soon turn this fresh-falling snow a dingy gray. December would turn to January, and February would melt into spring. Minute by minute, inch by inch, they were moving toward the inevitable, but they weren't out of blank pages yet. The light changed, and Evan hurried across the intersection, careful of the slushy tire tracks left in the wake of a cab. He opened the door to Pie in the Sky, and Sal looked up and smiled, showing off his two gold teeth.

"You're having a party and you didn't invite me?"

Evan laughed. "You can stop by after you close up shop. You know where to find us."

"Ah, my dad should have stayed in Sicily," Sal said, exaggeratedly waving off the invitation with his large, flour-dusted hands. "These crazy New Yorkers will be ordering pizzas till dawn. City that never sleeps, yada, yada, yada." Sal dismissed New York again with his big hands, then turned to the kitchen to retrieve five steaming boxes of pizza. Stacking them on the counter in front of Evan he, said, "All right, we got your usual half mushroom, half pepperoni. And then a meatball, a ham and pineapple, an extra cheese, and the gluten-free with cauliflower. Sound about right?"

"Perfect," Evan said.

"You shoulda let Vinny deliver 'em."

"Then I couldn't have wished you a happy new year," Evan said, and Sal grinned, wishing him the same.

"Take this," he said, handing Evan an insulated delivery bag. "So you don't drop five pies in the street."

Evan paid for the pizzas and zipped them into the bag, then Sal held the door for him as he headed back out into the tapering snow.

He crossed Sullivan and walked until the Black Cat came into view. The geraniums were gone, replaced with holly berries and fairy lights. The awning was frosted white, and the sign on the front door was flipped around to Closed, but he didn't use the front door anymore.

It took some finagling, but he managed to get inside the building and into the elevator without destroying the pizzas. As soon as the elevator doors opened, he could hear music.

"Pizza's here!" he called, knocking with the slushy toe of his sneaker, and as Mara swung the door open, the sounds of the apartment spilled into the hall.

Darren and Ty sat side-by-side on the piano bench, playing a jazzy duet of "Auld Lang Syne" on the baby grand.

Hailey laughed and shouted at Gwen to "go fish" from the living room floor, where they sat in a pile of playing cards and pillows.

Samantha and Ben talked softly by the bay window, overlooking the city lights, his arm around her shoulders, her arm around his waist.

And dishes clattered as Evan's mom set the table, filling glasses with water and soda and apple juice.

"You didn't tell me your baby sister was a card shark," Gwen said drily over her shoulder.

"I guess she's not a baby anymore," he said with a wink, and Hailey smiled as she helped Gwen clean up the cards.

Everything changes, Evan thought, watching Hailey run off to the bathroom to wash her hands for dinner. Little girls grow up, and little boys, too. Sometimes love dissolves, but other times, it takes root. Sometimes, you feel like you're living in a Dalí nightmare, but then you wake up and find yourself in one of those Chagall scenes where the boy and the girl float above a snow-covered city or summer-green fields, above a little village church or just their own kitchen table.

The apartment above the Black Cat belonged to Mara, now, hers to live in or rent out or sell. The chair of the art department had administered the final for Mythology in Modern Art and assigned Evan a new mentor, and when Mara opened the closet to the master bedroom, all the black dresses and red high heels were gone. Rumor had it that Dr. Mortakis left New York in a huff, furious that her grandmother left everything to a teenaged barista, but nobody knew for sure.

Sometimes, boxing up your life meant closing a door, but it didn't always mean goodbye, because Dr. Mortakis's closet wasn't empty anymore. Now, the right side was hung with Mara's clothes, the left side with his. The apartment wasn't perfectly clean or quiet, and it wasn't empty anymore, but it wasn't quite full yet, either.

As Evan lifted the lid to the half-mushroom, half-pepperoni pizza, the final knock came at the door.

Mara caught her breath. "She's here."

"Go ahead," Evan whispered, squeezing her hand. "Open it."

And when she did, he felt like he was looking into the future.

"Happy New Year," a woman with dark hair and green eyes said, offering a large platter of cookies to Mara.

"Happy New Year, Mom," she said, and wrapped her arms around Amanda Anderson.

They weren't identical. In the last few weeks, she'd learned that she'd gotten her smile from her father, and her musical ability, too. But those eyes, bottle-green and beautiful, were her mom's.

As Evan watched them together, he didn't think about the past, but he didn't think about the future, either. Minutes ticked away toward midnight, toward morning, but he didn't count them. The earth moved in circles, but life wasn't a clock. It was a color wheel, rich with harmonies and clashes, shades and tints, warms and cools. Color wasn't wound like a machine, fed by gears or grease. Color was as free and fluid as light itself, and as the sun came up on a new year, Evan was ready to paint.

ACKNOWLEDGMENTS

S O MANY PEOPLE have poured their love and support into this book, and I am infinitely grateful for each person who has come alongside me during this process. Thank you to my agent, Cate Hart, for guiding this story home, and to the wonderful team at CamCat for becoming that home. Many thanks go to my editor, Elana Gibson, for asking all the right questions, and the design team for making a beautiful book!

To my husband, Clay, for patiently reading every version of this story and understanding what I want to say even when I don't. Thank you for all the ways you follow me into the dark. To our daughters: Eva, thank you for always knowing how to make the cute parts cuter and gently saving me from cringiness. Sarah, thank you for being just as picky as I am and always asking why. Being your mom will always be my best and proudest accomplishment.

To my Eastern PA SCBWI family: You have been by my side for the past ten years, and I can't express how much I appreciate your friendship and support. All my love goes to Rona Shirdan, Laura

Parnum, Kristen Strocchia, Alison Green Myers, Joanne Roberts, Heather Stigall, and Berrie Torgan-Randall.

To my smart and generous critique partners: Amanda DeWitt, Tom Hoover, Christine Cohen, Abbey Nash, Alison Green Myers, Michele Lombardo, and Genevieve Abravanel. Your friendship and feedback are priceless!

To the teen writers and artists who inspire me every summer through the Lancaster Libraries' Teen SummerZine program: Writing alongside you is a privilege and a joy. Keep telling your stories. Keep making art. I'm so proud of you!

A final thank you, also, to the late Marcus Sedgwick, whose brilliant work has inspired me in more ways than I can count. Rest in peace, my friend.

ABOUT THE AUTHOR

INDSAY K. BANDY writes historical and speculative fiction for teens and adults, as well as poetry for young children. In addition to working at a school library, she runs an award-winning public library-based magazine program for teens and serves as the published member coordinator for the Eastern PA chapter of SCBWI. Her first novel, *Nemesis and the Swan*, was described by *Booklist* as an "intrigue-soaked work of historical fiction (that) feels entirely of the past and yet also incredibly relevant," and was the recipient of an *AudioFile Magazine* Earphones award.

In addition to books, Lindsay has a soft spot for donuts, ghost tours, and power sanding. She can often be found rescuing old furniture from curbs in Lancaster, Pennsylvania, where she lives with her husband, two daughters, and two cats.

INEVITABLE FATE PLAYLIST

Check out the playlist on Spotify.

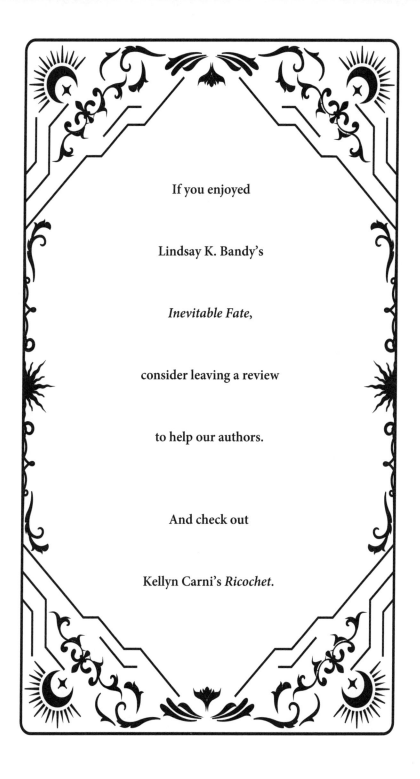

If you enjoyed

Lindsay K. Bandy's

Inevitable Fate,

consider leaving a review

to help our authors.

And check out

Kellyn Carni's *Ricochet.*

CHAPTER ONE

"Obviously, at that moment they did not imagine what awaited them . . . But the daughters had on bodices almost entirely of diamonds and [other] precious stones. Those were not only places for valuables but protective armor at the same time."

—*Yurovsky's account of the execution of the imperial family*

SILENCE FILLED THE cellar in the moments before the gunfire.

Sweat beaded on my forehead, my skin prickling with giddy anticipation. We were getting out. Over a year of imprisonment, and we were finally getting out. I suppressed my smile, only because of the worry that creased my father's brow as he paced. He still held his chest high, despite losing his crown, his palace, his freedom—but his unease shadowed the room, hanging heavily in the stale air.

Beside me, my younger brother shifted in his chair as our mother ran her hand absently through his hair like she had when he was little. "Soon, Alexei, my love. We'll be safe soon."

My sisters huddled together against the wall, too nervous to speak. Maria caught my eye, softening her gaze as though to say, "Us, too, Anastasia. She means us, too. We'll all be safe soon."

We would be safe. We would be free. We would be out of the Bolsheviks' captivity, out of this dreadful Ipatiev House, perhaps even out of Russia. Leaving my country, my kingdom, my home—it would have been unthinkable before the rebellion. I yearned to go back to how things were, back when my father still reigned. To go back to our comfortable home in the Alexander Palace, taking springtime rides through the countryside and summer trips to the Crimean shore. Back to freedom. Back to living.

But we'd been ousted from our palace. We'd been dragged from Saint Petersburg to Siberia to Yekaterinburg, and confined within the miserable walls of the Ipatiev House with nothing but each other. Hundreds of years of Romanov tsars, and now here we sat, captives in a musty old cellar. So now, leaving was our only hope.

An hour earlier, guards had burst into the bedroom I shared with my sisters, roused us from our sleep, and ordered us to ready ourselves for an immediate departure. My sisters and I had clambered from our beds in a flurry of excitement and confusion. Had our royal English cousins sent for us at last? Or would we be escaping under cover, taking new identities? Maria was certain it was the former. Even in our haste, she'd combed her golden hair and donned her finest gown, ready to impress the London nobles. But Olga and Tatiana had used those precious minutes to prepare for a life on the run, quickly stuffing their bodices with diamonds and rubies and emeralds.

In my jittery excitement, I'd done neither. I'd scrambled into my usual plain navy dress and left my thick sandy hair unkempt. The only jewel I'd bothered with was my garnet necklace, hidden beneath my collar as always. A palace in England, a hideaway in Poland—it didn't matter. Wherever we went, however we got there, we were getting out. Catching Maria's eye from across the room once again, I offered what I hoped was a comforting smile. We were finally, *finally*, getting out. The cellar door lurched open and a guard appeared in the doorway. Not one of our usual guards. No, the man in the doorway was unfamiliar, his expression one of cold disdain. A rifle hung at his side, a spiked bayonet capping its end.

My father stopped pacing. My sisters watched eagerly, and my mother brought her hands to her heart in an unspoken prayer. I took

Alexei's hand, shifting in front of him instinctively. But the guard looked past my siblings, my mother, and me—addressing my father when he spoke.

"You are to be executed."

Hope froze in my veins.

My father whirled to face him, stunned.

"What—"

But the guard raised his rifle without hesitation, without flinching, and the sharp drum of gunshots cut the silence of the cellar. My father staggered. Dropped to his knees. Crumpled to the floor as the guard filled his chest with bullets. I screamed—or was it my sisters? The room filled with shrieking and slamming and bullets, bullets, bullets as more guards stepped through the door, firing their guns.

Alexei's hand tightened in mine and my heart pounded against the coolness of the garnet necklace, concealed under my dress. My forehead burned as the screams dissolved into the ringing in my ears. My vision became a tunnel, blurring away the sight of my mother and sisters collapsing to the floor in a sea of bullets and blood. I only saw the barrel of a gun, pointed straight at my chest, and the guard's finger, pulling the trigger.

The impact bore into my chest with unimaginable force. Then the room faded, and I was floating in a sea of perfect darkness. Sinking in an endless, soundless swamp. Thick nothingness surrounded me, filled me, and swallowed me whole.

CHAPTER TWO

"Life is just one small piece of light between two eternal darknesses."

—*"Lolita" by Vladimir Nabokov*

NOT DEAD.

No, the wall of darkness before me was just the backs of my eyelids, too heavy to wrench open. Uneven floorboards dug into my spine as cool air nudged me awake. I shivered, and the corner of my mouth twitched upward. Not dead, because neither Heaven nor Hell ought to be so drafty. It had been a nightmare, then, surely. The cellar, the bullets, my sisters screaming . . . I was waking up, so it must have been only a terrible dream.

My whole body felt heavy, as though I'd been dragged by a weak magnet through a pit of sand. It wasn't unlike the morning after my fifteenth birthday—the last one before my family was imprisoned—when my sister Maria and I had snuck a bottle of wine for ourselves, drinking the whole *yobanyy* thing in our shared bedroom. But there had been no wine, not in that miserable Ipatiev House. So why was I so groggy?

My sternum ached, like I'd been punched in the chest. A bruise was forming there, just behind the garnet necklace hidden beneath my dress. The thin gold chain was cool against my neck, the gemstone sitting heavily against my chest. The garnet necklace—a secret I'd kept even from Maria.

The floorboards creaked beneath me as I shifted. I peeled my eyes open, and inhaled sharply as my own gray-blue eyes stared back at me. No, not my eyes—

"Alexei, *pizdets,* you scared me. You don't just hover over someone as they're waking up, you little creep."

My younger brother raised his brows as he rose to stand, appraising me with disapproval. "It's about time you woke up. I've been awake for . . ." he fumbled for his heirloom pocket watch out of habit, furrowing his brow as he remembered that the Bolsheviks had taken it, just as they'd taken his kingdom. "I've been awake for a while, anyway. And in case you haven't noticed, we are not in the Ipatiev House."

I glanced around, my eyes widening as I took in the dingy walls and stark furnishings. He was right. This was not the Ipatiev House, the fortified mansion we'd been imprisoned within all those months. Somehow, we'd awoken in a neat but shabby sort of cabin, clearly someone's home. The main room was nearly empty, but for a wooden chair and a crooked table, set with a single plate and a half-burned candlestick.

"Has one of our guards snuck us out, then? Is it . . . is it just us?" I glanced around again, seeing no sign of our parents or sisters, nor the guards. Pulling myself to my feet, I stepped across the small room in just a few strides, peering down the short hallway leading to the bedroom. "Maria? Tatiana? Olga?" Where were they? Where were we? "Mother? Papa?" I looked to Alexei, bewildered, but he only stared at me.

"Ana." His hard tone softened. "Do you . . . do you not remember what happened?"

We'd had a meager dinner, the seven of us, and gone to bed. Then I'd had a horrible nightmare and woke up here. It had been a nightmare, hadn't it? The cellar, the bullets, the screaming . . . the gun pointed right at my chest. My throat tightened. *Pizdets,* I could still see it all so clearly. As though . . . as though it had been real.

My eyes met Alexei's. Steely blue shields, well-practiced in hiding his emotions. He was only thirteen, but so hardened. Perhaps because he'd confronted his own mortality at such a young age, his hemophilia having pushed him to the brink of death again and again. He would have died years ago, were it not for Rasputin.

My eyes, on the other hand, were not shields. Alexei could see my thoughts written clearly on my face. He nodded.

"You do remember."

"No." I shook my head, willing my words to be true. "No, it—" my voice cracked, the words coming out in a broken whisper. "It was a bad dream." But tears welled in my eyes as I relived the nightmare—no, the memory.

The cellar. The guard, addressing my father with his casual announcement.

"*You are to be executed.*"

My father, startled, having no time to respond before the guards fired their guns.

The bullets. Everywhere, bullets and blood.

My sisters, my parents . . . gone.

But Alexei and I, here.

Through tear-filled eyes, I looked again to my brother, his own eyes soft, his hard shell melted by my grief. He held my gaze, his chin quivering just slightly. A moment of understanding passed between us.

It was just us.

I looked at my brother then. Studied him. He was no longer my baby brother, to be pampered and doted upon. He was no longer my little playmate, my tenacious partner in crime. He'd grown into a brooding teenager. The months of confinement had brought me closer to my sisters. But Alexei . . . he'd withdrawn. And as we stood there, staring at one another in the wake of our family's massacre, I didn't know what to say.

Alexei looked away first. He swallowed, tightening his jaw as he studied the floor. "I don't know if one of the guards snuck us out. I don't know how we got here. But I think we'd better get out while we can."

With that, Alexei moved toward the door, his limp more pronounced in his exhaustion. Truthfully, he looked quite pathetic. Weakened by the extended bed rests that had become more frequent as he'd gotten older, his arms and legs were too thin. He stood with his weight off his left knee, where it had never truly healed after his hemorrhage at Spala. Since Rasputin's death, since our imprisonment, Alexei had suffered these last few years. He'd become more difficult to protect, more resistant to being coddled, and therefore more prone to injuries that would be but minor bruises for a non-hemophiliac boy.

But Alexei stood proudly, still. What he lacked in a tsarevich's appearance, he made up for with his superior attitude. "Well, Anastasia, aren't you coming?"

With a final glance around the stark cabin, I followed him out the door.

⋟⋞⋟⋞

THE RESIDENTIAL STREETS were empty during the brief dark hours of a July night. We wandered in numb silence, passing more small cabins scattered amongst gardens and pastures and pine trees. The fresh air was foreign to my lungs—too clear, too cool. For a year and a half, we'd been confined within walls, without sunshine, without moonlight, without feeling the crisp coolness of a gentle breeze. But we'd been together. Our whole family. I shivered, wrapping myself with my arms as I walked.

There was no way to know how long we'd been unconscious, but as Yekaterinburg was not a sprawling city, we couldn't have been taken too far from the Ipatiev House. And while neither of us knew where we were or where we were going, we had to keep moving. One foot in front of the other, creating more space between ourselves and the trauma behind us.

Alexei broke our silence, speaking rather matter-of-factly. "I saw each of them shot. Father. Olga and Maria, standing together. Tatiana and . . ." His voice shook just a bit. "And Mother." My throat tightened as he described the scene I so badly wished to erase from my mind. But Alexei continued. "And even as I sat there holding your hand, I saw a guard point his gun at you. And he fired." Cocking his head to the side, he eyed me searchingly. "You were *shot*, Ana. But you survived."

I could still see the barrel of that gun, pointed at my chest. The guard's finger, pulling the trigger. I shuddered, my heart quickening. Yes, I was shot. The garnet clanged against the stone-sized bruise on my sternum as we walked, a constant reminder.

Taking a deep breath, I reached beneath the collar of my dress and lifted the garnet by its golden chain. Then I gave the gemstone a little squeeze and opened my palm, exposing the secret I'd carried for nearly two years. Alexei's eyes widened and he opened his mouth to speak, but I beat him to it.

"The guard pointed his rifle right at my chest. The bullet struck here," I pressed my finger to the garnet, "but it ricocheted and that's the last I remember before waking up in that cabin." I raised an eyebrow at Alexei, meeting his incredulous stare with my own. "Why weren't you . . ." I trailed off, the words sticking in my throat. *Shot. Killed. Executed, like the rest of our family.*

Squaring his shoulders, Alexei held his head high as he eyed the necklace curiously. "Destiny, I suppose."

Despite the weight in my chest, I snorted. "Of course, my tsarevich." Our father's abdication, our imprisonment, our family's execution

. . . what would it take for Alexei to accept that the throne would never be his? But it wasn't the time to push the issue. I fiddled with the garnet necklace, inwardly debating whether to tell Alexei the rest of the story. Clearing my throat, I decided the information was quite pertinent.

"So, Alexei. About this necklace . . ." I paused, unsure how to begin.

"Rasputin gave it to you," Alexei said flatly.

"I—how did you know?"

"Maria told me. She saw him, when he snuck into you two's room. Said she saw him hand you a jewel in the moonlight. Said he whispered something to you and left."

"I—well, yes. Yes, Rasputin did whisper something. But it didn't make any sense." I paused, baffled that Maria had known, that she hadn't said anything—or at least, not to me. Alexei was looking at me expectantly, so I continued. "He said, 'When the time comes, *malenkaya*, you'll escape. Take it, and promise you'll find me.'"

He'd been like a shadow in the night, appearing at my bedside, placing his hand on my shoulder and drawing me into the waking world. It was before my father's abdication. Before those so-called revolutionaries forced us into imprisonment. Back when I was a princess, not a prisoner. I'd had no idea what Rasputin might have meant, when he pressed the garnet necklace into my hand and whispered those words. I had been startled, but there was a soft kindness in the shadowed lines of his face. There'd been an air about him that comforted me, and I'd drifted back into peaceful sleep. I would have thought it a dream had I not awakened with the garnet still clutched in my palm, like a child with a doll.

Since that night, I'd worn it every day, as one does when a mysterious healer appears in the night to gift one a necklace.

Alexei shrugged. "Well, the first bit was true enough. The time came, and we escaped. But I don't think we'll be finding Rasputin."

I winced. He was right. My mother and father had trusted Rasputin fully—he was, after all, Alexei's savior—but no one else had. I'd heard the whispers, that his powers were unnatural and unholy. Rasputin had been shot down by the Bolsheviks just a month before the self-righteous *svolochy* forced my family into confinement. "*I promise*," I'd whispered back that night. "*I'll find you.*" A promise I would never be able to keep. We were just rounding a bend along the path as the rising sun burst from the horizon, silhouetting the city before us. The July sunrise was a rare sight, the sun peeking back around the top of the globe at too early an hour for witnesses. I was lost in thought—how could the sunrise be so beautiful in the wake of such tragedy?—when Alexei stopped short.

"This is not Yekaterinburg."

I stopped, too. "What?"

"Look. You can see the Neva River, the canals winding through the city. You can see the Winter Palace, there in the distance." He shook his head in disbelief. "We're in Saint Petersburg."

"*Pizdets*, Alexei . . . How? How could we have traveled across all of Russia in our sleep? It's illogical, it's—"

My declaration of impossibility was cut short, however, by a round of gunshots erupting from an alleyway between storefronts. "Get down," I instructed rather unnecessarily, as I hugged my brother to the ground. I did so gingerly, even in my panic, wrapping him in my arms and landing him on top of myself before rolling him away from the sound of the bullets. A bullet would kill him undoubtedly, but even a tackle to the ground could injure him fatally. He wouldn't stop bleeding, not without Rasputin.

A second round of gunfire answered the first, as black-haired soldiers emerged from the alleyway. One of them yelled something—was it in Japanese?—and the unit sprinted down the street. More bullets, as opposing soldiers shot after them. What the hell were Japanese soldiers doing in Saint Petersburg? Had the War progressed so drastically?

"We've got to try and crawl to the buildings, Ana. We need cover, we . . . we must be in the middle of some military operation. *Pizdets—*"

Bullets shattered a nearby storefront window in an explosion of broken glass.

Bullets, flying across the street, whizzing over our heads as we sprawled on the ground. Bullets, filling my father's chest as he dropped to his knees. A burning pain scorched through my skull as I shook the image from my mind. Move. I had to move. No way had I survived execution to die in the *yobanyy* street. We crawled on our bellies across the brick-lined road, moving as quickly as we could toward the alcove by the doorway of the nearest shop. More gunfire, but growing distant. We reached the storefront and Alexei scrambled into the little nook by the doorway, audibly exhaling. I clenched my jaw and pressed myself against the brick pillar, shielding my little brother from the street.

A moment passed. Quiet. I sighed then, too, and slumped to the ground.

"*Pizdets*, what *was* that—" I started, but Alexei interrupted me, stammering over his words as he pointed over my head.

"It's a . . . Ana. Look . . . look up."

As I craned my neck to look skyward, my eyes widened at what I saw. An enormous armored airship hovered above us, its metallic plates glowing orange in the rusted light of the sunrise. The long barrel of a mounted weapon swiveled around, as though seeking its target, and cast a sharp beam of red light directly at my chest. I peered downward, frozen in fear as a red dot of light appeared, bright against my navy dress as it mirrored the garnet beneath.

Perhaps I was going to die in the street, after all.

I squeezed Alexei's hand, found his eyes, and was for once speechless, not knowing how to say goodbye in the seconds preceding our most certain deaths. But there wasn't time anyway, because then—

BANG.

The bullet pounded the garnet into the bruise on my sternum as I screamed, and then everything went dark.

CamCat
Books

VISIT US ONLINE FOR MORE BOOKS TO LIVE IN:
CAMCATBOOKS.COM

SIGN UP FOR CAMCAT'S FICTION NEWSLETTER FOR
COVER REVEALS, EBOOK DEALS, AND MORE EXCLUSIVE CONTENT.

CamCatBooks

@CamCatBooks

@CamCat_Books

@CamCatBooks